It was like looking at an ex[...] In the semidarkness it app[...] dark blue naval uniform h[...] curtain. As had most of t[...] corpse was slumped sligh[...] elderly person might fall asleep in [...] tipped back, mouth agape. In the skull, eyeless sockets gazed blankly at the ceiling. The open jaws revealed teeth set in a rictus. Strips of what looked like grey parchment clung to the ridges along the cheek bones and the front of the skull. It was as if the skeleton had developed some kind of creeping fungus.

One thin and withered arm lay across the knees. The other arm, the right one, hung down by the side of the chair. The remains of a hand protruded from the mucus-coloured sleeve. Caught in the bright beam from my flashlight, a slender finger of grey-white bone reached down towards the pistol that lay on the deck plates. A Luger automatic . . .

By the same author

Trigger Men
Crow's War

2

It was evening and they were loading the submarine.

The rain had eased to a thin drizzle. In the wan glow of the lights along the dock, the wet quaystones gleamed like polished leather.

Prohl wondered how quickly the lights could be doused in the event of incoming aircraft. He didn't relish finding himself in the middle of a night-time bombing run. The cities along the coast had suffered massive air-raid damage; the Blohm and Vos yards in Hamburg in particular. Being slap in the middle of a designated target area didn't do anything for a person's nerves. And the enemy was very close.

The immediate area around the U-boat had been cordoned off. A contingent of the Schutzstaffel patrolled the quay. Prohl had watched their arrival with quiet loathing. He had no time for the SS, especially after his conversation with Kruger regarding the threat they posed to Doenitz.

The main part of the consignment had arrived in two canvas-covered Henschel trucks, complete with armed escort. The containers turned out to be wooden crates; two dozen of them. They were about half the size of ammunition boxes, each one weighing in at fifty kilos – all except two, which were nearly twice as large although, strangely, they were approximately the same weight as the others. To Prohl's relief, it hadn't been too difficult to manoeuvre them into the boat via the fore and aft torpedo-loading hatches. They had all the boxes stowed by the time the last part of the shipment arrived, in a smaller vehicle, a Steyr six-wheeler. In the rear of this truck was another crate. It was slightly longer than the other two large boxes. What also set it apart was the fact that it was accompanied by Kruger and a civilian.

Prohl was on the bridge supervising the operation when he recognized Doenitz's aide. He descended to the grating and went up the catwalk on to the wharf.

Kruger stepped forward to meet him. By this time Prohl had changed back into his wet-weather gear. Kruger was wearing a greatcoat and cap. The civilian was also wrapped up against the weather, in black leather topcoat and dark fedora. Kruger made the introductions.

'This is Herr Moessinger,' Kruger said. 'From Berlin,' he added, as if the appendix was particularly relevant. And was it Prohl's imagination, or did Kruger's tone indicate more than a slight trace of disaffection? Prohl nodded anyway. Moessinger returned his subdued greeting with what appeared to be taciturn indifference. The man was quite young, perhaps thirty or thereabouts, certainly no older than Prohl. He was thin, and what could be seen of his face below the brim of his hat seemed pale, almost translucent. A pair of hooded eyes only served to enhance his sinister appearance, not made any more pleasant by a scrawny neck and a pronounced Adam's apple. He wore a party badge in the lapel of his coat. Moessinger carried with him the stench of the Reich security apparatus, the RSHA. Which made him one of Ernst Kaltenbrunner's acolytes. Prohl's bid to conceal his immediate sense of dislike and distrust was not entirely successful.

Especially when Kruger dropped his bombshell.

'Herr Moessinger will be accompanying you,' he said. 'Once you have been made aware of your final destination you are to take your orders directly from him . . .' – a

26

pause – '. . . no matter what you may hear to the contrary.' Ignoring Prohl's slack jaw, he added, 'That is on the direct order of Reichspresident Doenitz.' Kruger's voice was like the rasp of a file. 'Is that understood?'

Prohl clenched his fists. 'No,' he said. 'Actually it isn't, not entirely.'

Kruger's head jerked up. 'Nevertheless, Captain,' he snapped, 'you will obey orders. Need I remind you of the penalty for insubordination?'

'No,' Prohl said stonily, conscious of Moessinger's cold, almost reptilian stare. 'You have no need to remind me. However, I request that my objection to this situation be officially noted.'

Kruger visibly relented. It was with something close to regret that he said, 'Your objection will be duly entered in your record, Captain.'

'Thank you,' Prohl said brusquely. He turned to Moessinger. 'I suggest we get that last crate on board without delay.' He returned his attention to Kruger. 'Will that be all?'

Kruger nodded. 'Except to give you these,' he said. He handed Prohl the watertight package. 'Your orders.'

Prohl took the packet. 'In that case, you will allow me to return to my vessel.' He saluted and turned abruptly.

Kruger watched the angry U-boat skipper regain the deck of the submarine. Inwardly he knew how Prohl felt. He didn't like Moessinger or his type either. But the man was here not only on Doenitz's orders but also Bormann's, and the former Reichsleiter, now Party Minister, was a very dangerous man to antagonize. Kruger envied Prohl neither his mission nor the constrictions he would have to function under. Prohl wasn't the only one forced to obey orders he didn't agree with.

The empty trucks and their escort had been driven

away. The cargo had been stowed, the hatches battened down. The U-boat was ready to slip her berth.

Prohl had culled his crew down to the required eighteen men. Moessinger made the nineteenth. He had left himself with Schepke as his first officer; Bauer, his chief engineer; Meyer, the chief navigator; four seamen, one wireless operator, two mechanics, two electricians, two engine room artificers, two stokers and one cook. As he had expected, it hadn't been easy. It was ironic that the men he had been forced to leave behind would at least reap the benefit of gaining a period of well-earned rest before they were reassigned. Those personnel who remained with Prohl hadn't even had the chance to wash the salt out of their eyelids before they were faced with weighing anchor once more. It was a mark of the esteem in which they held their commander that Prohl didn't have a mutiny on his hands. What he did have, though, was a tired crew.

But at least it had given them room to breathe, even allowing for the size of the cargo.

U-boats were built for action, not comfort. On a routine patrol, with a full complement and ordnance, the living and working conditions on board were positively fetid. Food was generally stacked along the passageways and suspended from the overhead rails, with the freshest provisions being made the most readily accessible, for obvious reasons. Spare clothing was stashed out of sight behind pipes and in every other nook and cranny that could be found. There was no spare room for the crew to gather between watches either, except in their bunks or hammocks, which were usually squeezed into the fore and aft compartments between the unarmed torpedoes.

Despite the consignment having taken up the space in the sub normally reserved for the torpedoes, and allowing for the restocking of provisions, Prohl's men were still able to take some comfort from the depletion in their number. Compared to what they had been used to, the result was something close to luxury.

At least, everybody except Moessinger thought so.

'The bastard only wanted to know where his bloody cabin was!' Schepke exclaimed hotly as he joined Prohl on the bridge. They were preparing to get the boat underway.

'What did you tell him?'

'I told him he was lucky not to be sleeping in one of the bow tubes. I put him in the PO's quarters.'

Prohl grunted.

'What the hell's he doing here?' Schepke asked.

Prohl told him.

Schepke stared at his captain, shocked. 'Can they do that?'

'They just did,' Prohl said. 'We're stuck with him for the duration. How long that's likely to be, I've yet to find out.'

'In that case, I hope the creep gets seasick.'

'I hope he doesn't,' Prohl said. 'The smell down there's bad enough as it is.'

Schepke took a call on the voice pipe and relayed information.

'Crew at stations, sir. All secured. Main engines, motors and steering gear set.'

'Very good,' Prohl acknowledged. He yelled down to the rating on the bow casing, 'Let go forrard!'

A line snaked up the side of the quay.

'Let go aft!'

There was a rumble and vibration beneath their feet as the electric motors fired up.

The U-boat pulled away from the wharf. Slowly her bow turned towards the harbour entrance. The water boiled around her as air was forced into the ballast tanks.

'Slow ahead both,' Prohl directed.

The dimly illuminated dockside began to merge into the darkness behind them. The submarine picked up speed as it headed towards the mouth of the estuary.

They ran on the surface until they hit the open channel. Somewhere in the Stygian blackness astern, Prohl thought he could detect the *crump* of heavy guns. He peered out to shore but couldn't see anything.

The moon came out from behind the clouds and they rode along on a ribbon of phosphorescence.

'Diving stations!' Prohl ordered.

Spray began to splatter the conning tower.

The U-boat sank below the waves leaving no trace of its passing.

Beneath the moon-flecked waters of the North Sea, Prohl opened his sealed orders. They contained charts and coordinates. Prohl studied them behind the drawn curtain of his tiny compartment. He rechecked the grid references, ran through the charts once again, then sat back and tried to glean some sense from it all. Finally, lips compressed into a tight line, he gathered the papers together, walked into the control room and summoned Schepke and Moessinger to the chart table.

Incredibly, Moessinger was still wearing his dark suit. Tiny beads of sweat lay along his forehead and top lip. Already he was displaying signs of claustrophobia. Most people did on their first voyage in a sub. The creaks and groans caused by outside pressure on the hull were enough to deter the stoutest heart. And they'd only been at sea an hour. Herr Moessinger was out of his element. He knew it and so did everyone else on board.

'Did you know?' Prohl asked, waving the orders under the civilian's nose.

Moessinger nodded. 'Of course,' he replied stiffly.

Prohl spread the chart on the table. Schepke stared down at it. It showed the Atlantic coastline of South America, covering the stretch from Montevideo south to the Falkland Islands. He looked up. 'Where the hell are they sending us, skipper?'

Prohl stabbed the chart. 'There,' he said.

Schepke followed the end of Prohl's finger from the mouth of the River Plate and the port of Buenos Aires, moving south.

Prohl said, 'On the coast of Bahía Samborombón, north of Punta Norte. A town called San Clemente del Tuyu.'

Schepke swallowed drily.

Their destination was Argentina.

It was 1514 hours on the third day when the signal was received. They were two hundred and thirty miles south of the Faeroes, running on the surface, conserving battery power. The sky was the colour of tempered steel.

Only a fool would have attempted to negotiate the busy shipping lanes of the English Channel. So Prohl had taken them around the northern reaches of the British Isles. He had shaved some time by slipping through the sound between Fair Isle and Sumburgh Head rather than sailing the longer way around the Shetlands. It had been a calculated risk but one that had paid off. He had banked on the inclement weather dampening the likelihood of British air cover. On this occasion the elements had been on their side.

The face of Heller, the radio operator, was pale as he left the radio shack and climbed up the ladder to the bridge to pass Prohl the message.

ALL U-BOATS, ATTENTION ALL U-BOATS. CEASE FIRE IMMEDIATELY. STOP ALL HOSTILE ACTION AGAINST ALLIED SHIPPING. DOENITZ.

'What do you think?' Schepke asked, wiping a gobbet of spray from his eyes.

Prohl told him he didn't know.

But he could guess. Most probably it meant that the Russians had finally taken Berlin, the Allies had pushed their troops towards the coast and the Danish border, and the northern defences had been breached. And, maybe, after six years, the madness had finally come to an end.

'Get his lordship up here.' Prohl ordered.

'Yes, sir,' The radio operator disappeared down through the hatch. Minutes later Moessinger appeared. The boat was cleaving the water like a porpoise, at something approaching sixteen knots. There was a fair degree of deck motion involved, and Moessinger was looking decidedly green around the gills. But at least he was dressed more in keeping with his environment by this time. Prohl had eventually taken pity on him and the slop chest had been raided. Moessinger was now wearing an old white sweater and a pair of blue navy fatigues. Three days of shaving in cold water had also left their mark in the crimson rash along the line of his jaw. Aptly, he still looked like a fish out of water.

Prohl showed him the signal. 'Does this alter our orders?'

Moessinger shook his head. His Adam's apple bobbed jerkily as he answered. 'Maintain your course, Captain.'

Behind Moessinger's back, Schepke watched the expression on Prohl's face. It was one of resignation. By virtue of the orders he had received from Kruger, Prohl's hands were tied. Moessinger was in command. When Moessinger left the bridge and returned to his bunk, Prohl slammed his fist against the wall of the conning tower as a measure of his anger and frustration. The U-boat continued to plough its way into the Atlantic swell.

MY U-BOAT MEN. SIX YEARS OF WAR LIE BEHIND US. YOU HAVE FOUGHT LIKE LIONS. A CRUSHING MATERIAL SUPERIORITY HAS FORCED US INTO THIS TIGHT CORNER FROM WHICH IT IS NO LONGER POSS-IBLE TO CONTINUE THE WAR. UNBEATEN AND UNBLEMISHED AFTER A HEROIC BATTLE WITHOUT EQUAL, LAY DOWN YOUR ARMS. WE REMEMBER WITH RESPECT OUR FALLEN COMRADES WHO GAVE THEIR LIVES FOR FUEHRER AND FATHERLAND. COMRADES, PRESERVE THE SPIRIT IN WHICH YOU HAVE FOUGHT SO LONG AND SO GALLANTLY FOR THE FUTURE OF THE FATHERLAND. LONG LIVE GERMANY. YOUR GRAND ADMIRAL.

The message came through twenty-four hours after the first one. Prohl's immediate reaction was one of relief. He had survived.

So had his crew. Below decks the men were jubilant. All except one.

Prohl was making his way through the boat, enjoying the embraces and handshakes as much as everybody else. Someone had broached the 'victory bottle', usually reserved for celebrating a successful torpedo attack or a birthday. A pack of American Lucky Strikes had appeared as if by magic. An impromptu singsong began.

Moessinger laid a talon on Prohl's arm. 'A word in your quarters, Commander.'

The small compartment hadn't been designed to accommodate visitors. It was a tight fit.

'What is it?' Prohl was beyond trying to hide his contempt. In the four days that Moessinger had been on board, up until the receipt of the last signal, the mood on the boat had been one of suspicion and resentment. Prohl was a popular and much admired skipper. His men were not happy with the fact that he was having to dance to another man's tune. And Moessinger had done little to ally himself with the boat's complement. Despite finding his sea legs, he'd remained aloof and unapproachable. Which, in a vessel the size of a U-boat, was something of a marvel. Not that the men had made any overt attempt to break the ice. Moessinger wasn't a seaman. He wasn't one of them. He was, they all suspected, a fully indoctrinated servant of the state. The secret state. In other words, a party hack.

Not that the U-boat service did not contain ardent supporters of the Nazi party. Wolfgang Lueth of the U-181 was a vociferous advocate of national socialism. Vogelsang of the U-132 was another. But they were the exception rather than the rule, at least at this late stage in the war. Generally speaking, the U-boat arm had little time for political intrigue. Most skippers were preoccupied with expending their energy on what they considered more worthwhile endeavours – like sinking enemy shipping and trying to keep themselves and their crews alive.

Moessinger said, 'I would remind you, Commander, that this news in no way alters your prime directive.'

Prohl frowned. 'But, damn it, you read the signal. The war's over, or as good as. We suspected as much when the first message came through. Surely this confirms it?'

Moessinger's eyes were like flints. 'The fighting may well be over, Commander. This mission is not. We have a delivery to make. And a rendezvous to keep: the refuelling ship. You have not forgotten?'

They were supposed to meet with the milch cow at a point due west of the Cape Verde islands. The milch cows were the supply boats, the 1700-ton Type XIV submarines that Doenitz had commissioned to restock U-boats at sea, thus enabling his vessels to extend their range of activities.

'But, don't you see, if it's true that the war is over there's no guarantee that the damned supply ship will even wait for us!'

34

'It will wait,' Moessinger said confidently. 'Its captain has his orders also.'

'Good God, man!' Prohl felt his exasperation beginning to rise. 'Don't you want to go home?'

'Not until we have fulfilled our obligation.'

Prohl could see that it was useless to argue. 'All I can say, Moessinger, is that this cargo must be something really special. It's another seven thousand miles to San Clemente. I hope to Christ it's worth all the effort.'

On the sixth day, their half-realized hopes were confirmed. Doenitz transmitted word to all U-boats to surface and report their positions. This was followed by a list of designated ports into which the submarines were to proceed with all haste.

Prohl's boat was three hundred miles west of Cape Ortegal. The sea was running high. They had recently surfaced, after Prohl had taken them down to avoid a confrontation with an eastbound convoy. Twelve fat merchant ships, heavy in the water, and a couple of tenacious destroyers as escorts. A tempting target, if the sub had been armed. Prohl had cursed inwardly and ordered the scope to be lowered, in a sharp tone that had not been missed by those in the control room. Schepke had noted the taut jaw muscles and the angry glint in his captain's eye as Prohl clenched his fists in frustration. Then they had all fallen silent and listened to the sound of the ships passing over them, the thud of the screws receding gradually into the distance like a fading heartbeat.

When word got out about the surrender, chatter and speculation filled the passageways. The question on every man's lips was, What port were they going to head for? Brest was the first suggestion. That finally gave way to the possibility of returning to Germany. Some opted for the neutrality of Lisbon. They looked to Prohl for guidance.

35

Prohl decided it was time to approach Moessinger again.

Moessinger's voice was as brittle as broken glass. 'Now listen to me, Captain. Get this into your skull. For the last time, you will not report your position. You will ignore the summons to surrender your vessel. You will sail her to wherever I direct you. There will be no deviation. None. Do I make myself clear?'

By this time Moessinger's voice had risen several octaves. His words ran through the hull. Men paused in their chores and exchanged startled glances. Eyes were hastily averted as Prohl stormed through the control room and took himself up the ladder on to the conning tower.

The waves crashed over the deck, foamed along the casing and cascaded over the bridge. Prohl shut his eyes and let the cold Atlantic douse his face, as if, somehow, the drenching would wash away the rage within him.

'Skipper?' Schepke was behind him, planted against the compass housing. The wind sucked at his oilskins. Undeterred by Prohl's lack of immediate response, Schepke took a deep breath. He had to raise his voice above the crash and roar of the ocean. 'The men are wondering how long this is going to go on for. They want to know what's happening. Are we going home?' Schepke's hands gripped the rail for balance. His knuckles gleamed white.

'I've been asking myself the same question,' Prohl replied, spray streaking his face. 'It would appear that the answer is no. Our passenger has other plans.'

'But can't you do something?' Schepke begged.

Prohl shrugged resignedly. 'I am doing something. I'm obeying orders. As an officer and a gentleman, that's what I'm supposed to do. It says so in the rule book. You remember the rule book, Lieutenant? Thou shalt obey the orders of your senior officers. Well, it seems I'm stuck

JAMES McGEE

Wolf's Lair

GraftonBooks
A Division of HarperCollinsPublishers

GraftonBooks
A Division of HarperCollins*Publishers*
77–85 Fulham Palace Road,
Hammersmith, London W6 8JB

A Grafton Paperback Original 1990
9 8 7 6 5 4 3 2

ISBN 0-586-20739-2

Printed and bound in Great Britain by
Collins, Glasgow

Set in Times

01 MAY 1945: 0740 HRS

To Grand Admiral Doenitz . . .

Testament in force.

. . . BORMANN

Part One

1

Weser Estuary – May 1945

The U-boat moved under a leaden sky, its razor-sharp bow slicing through the swell like a knife. Waves broke across the pitching hull, sluicing the deck, driving freezing spray into the faces of the men grouped on the bridge. They were dressed in oilskins, eyes narrowed against the aquatic onslaught.

Through the haze, land was visible but indistinct: a low dark smudge on the horizon, over which menacing black clouds hung and roiled like cannon smoke on a distant battlefield. The wind carried ice in its jagged teeth. Born in the Baltic, it had come of age over the north German plain, driving the rain before it like a stampede, flattening the coastal marshlands, whipping the surface of the estuary into a maelstrom of dirty whitecaps.

Lieutenant Commander Dieter Prohl placed both hands firmly on the rail and stared out rigidly from the salt-encrusted conning tower towards the encircling coastline. He was a slim, gaunt man. The rigours of five years in the U-boat arm of the Kriegsmarine had left their legacy in the deep lines of tension that were etched into his pale, unshaven face, making him appear at least a decade older than his thirty-two years. He was something of a veteran; most of his crew were in their early twenties.

'Bloody weather!' The observation came from over his left shoulder as Rudi Schepke, his first officer, burrowed in beside him, head down under the collar of his slicker, cheek turned against the deluge.

Prohl didn't answer. He raised the binoculars to his face and scanned the shore. Behind him the other two lookouts watched the skies. Prohl thought it was unlikely that anything would be flying in that murk. But you couldn't be too careful, even this close to home.

Home. This wasn't home. Home lay elsewhere, beyond the horizon, much further south: Laufen, down in the Ober Bayern, a stone's throw from the Austrian border. An area of verdant meadow, forest, lake and river. Picture-postcard scenery. Probably already churned into a muddy wasteland by the tracks of American tanks. He dragged his thoughts back to the present. Through the glasses the shores of the estuary began to take on substance.

Schepke raised his own glasses, rested his elbows on the rim of the tower and peered into the dimness. He cursed as the U-boat shuddered down into a trough.

Schepke was twenty-four, short and stocky. He, too, was unshaven and looked tired. Like a prisoner newly released from a long stretch in solitary, he was pasty-faced, his eyes unaccustomed to natural light; the inhabitant of an artificial world, the parameters of which were as constricting as a rabbit hutch. Despite his youth, Schepke was an experienced officer. His partnership with Prohl had lasted for almost the duration of the war. After they had served together on a previous boat, Prohl was given his own command, and he'd asked for Schepke to be assigned to his vessel. Schepke had accepted the honour gladly. Together the two men made an effective chain of command that drew well-merited respect and trust from the U-boat's complement.

The rigours and demands of the service and the confined working conditions on board left no room for personal differences to fester and disrupt the coordination required from all members of the crew. These men had served together from the Mediterranean to the convoy routes of the North Atlantic, called by many the worst battleground in the world. The long years at sea had forged them into a formidable fighting unit.

Schepke had the distinct impression that he was looking at an alien landscape. In the bomb-damaged wilderness, isolated towers and derricks stood like stranded herons on the foreshore, their delicate legs implanted among the shells of burnt and ruined buildings. British and American airborne raids had left few landmarks unscathed. The scene captured an awesome sense of desolation and foreboding.

'It looks pretty bad,' Schepke muttered. 'The Allies must be very close. What do you think? Maybe they're waiting for us.'

Prohl thought about that. He and his crew had been out for almost ten weeks, patrolling the convoy routes south of Iceland. In that time they had received little news from the home front. Most of what they knew had been gleaned by listening in to Allied merchant ship chatter. Prohl was aware that over the past couple of months the British and Americans had made remarkable advances. Montgomery and Bradley had crossed the Rhine in March. The Russians were closing in from the east. Opposition was faltering. It could only be a matter of time before the two flanks converged. In an effort to consolidate his forces, Doenitz had long since ordered his U-boat fleet to their northern bases at Bergen and Trondheim. Which was where Prohl and his crew had been heading when they received the signal to proceed to Bremerhaven instead, at flank speed. No reason for the diversion had been given.

The dockside was now in full view. Prohl could detect movement. Men and vehicles. Concerted industry, however, was not readily apparent or even audible. No throb of generator, no whine of heavy drill or clang of hammer on steel plate. The only preparations being made, it seemed, were those required for a rapid exodus.

Prohl ordered the ensign raised and watched critically as the red and black emblem fluttered soggily from its staff on the rear gun platform. Might as well keep up appearances, he thought.

The submarine drew closer to the wharf and the big concrete pens. The snouts of submarines were just discernible in the shadows; wolves about to slip from their lair.

The arrival of Prohl and his crew did not appear to have caused any special interest. As Schepke observed wryly, there obviously weren't going to be any flowers on this visit. He was referring to the abandoned custom of greeting a returning crew with champagne and garlands. A thing of the past, along with the brass bands that had at one time been used to send the boats off on patrol. That had been during the happy times, *die glueckliche Zeit*; the months between the summer of 1940 and the spring of 1941, when the U-boats had achieved their most consistent tally of enemy shipping. An average of eight ships per sub per month: a phenomenal success rate.

'Shall I assemble the men on deck?' Schepke asked.

Prohl shook his head. 'There's no one here to salute them,' he said quietly. 'Prepare for docking.'

'Aye aye, sir.' Schepke rapped out orders to the watchmen. The submarine nudged the side of the quay. Lines were secured.

As the U-boat was brought to rest, a car drove on to the dock, tyres splashing through the puddles. A black Mercedes. It pulled up and a door opened. The uniformed driver emerged and ran forward. He called hesitantly up to the bridge. 'Commander Prohl?'

'Guilty,' Prohl acknowledged laconically, staring down.

12

Following a brief moment of indecision the driver saluted. 'I have orders to deliver you to the flotilla commander, sir.'

'Two minutes,' Prohl called. 'Get back in the car. You'll catch your death.'

The message bearer gave another flustered salute and sprinted back under cover.

'Maybe it's a promotion,' Schepke said with mock cheer.

'That'll be the day,' Prohl grunted. 'See to the men. I'm going to change. Might as well try and look presentable, though, just in case you're right.'

Schepke grinned and Prohl left the bridge. He dropped down into the control room and walked through into his cramped compartment. After the brief hour or so he had spent topsides, he was instantly aware of the smell below: cabbage, wet rubber, diesel fumes, bilge water and sweat. The boat reeked. But then so did the crew; bodies crammed together like sardines for months at a time. You soon got used to it. Of all the qualities required of a submariner, tolerance of the foibles of his fellow men was high on the list.

Prohl shucked off his slicker and his top clothes. Beneath the oilskins he was wearing a British Army battledress. Purloined from captured personnel, it was an item of clothing much favoured by crews. His own uniform was damp and creased. He dressed quickly, slipping the medal ribbon over his neck. The Knight's Cross with Oak Leaves, Swords and Diamonds, awarded to skippers with two hundred thousand tons of enemy shipping to their credit. The U-boat arm's highest honour. Prohl picked up his cap and returned to the deck.

Schepke eyed him critically. 'And very smart too, sir,' he said, one eyebrow raised. He snapped his feet together and threw up his right hand in a crisp naval salute.

13

'Don't push it, Lieutenant. One day, all this could be yours.'

'I was afraid you might say that,' Schepke replied, feigning glumness. He looked at the car. 'Your chariot awaits.'

Prohl nodded. 'Tell the men to remain on board until I return. I don't want them straying.'

Schepke glanced around at their dismal surroundings. 'I don't think there's much chance of that,' he said to himself as Prohl made his way up the catwalk on to the dockside.

Once on solid ground, Prohl immediately felt rubber-kneed, the penalty for too long a spell at sea, at the mercy of the waves and the idiosyncrasies of his particular vessel. He managed to make it to the car without losing his balance completely.

But he got wet through in the process. The rain had increased in force and was slanting across the harbour, striking the widening puddles like machine-gun bullets. Prohl sank into the rear seat of the Mercedes with relief.

The car moved off.

Staring out of the windows, Prohl found himself hemmed in on all sides by frantic activity. This was mirrored in the expressions and attitudes of the men in the workforce. The desperation and fear was all too evident in their faces. With the Allied lines so near, they were living on borrowed time. The car sped past a dozen trucks in convoy carrying men and equipment towards the area of dockyard that contained the submarine pens. He saw U-boat hull sections lying under rusting steel girders like racks of partially gutted fish. In the dry docks, rain-slicked metal cylinders lay stranded like beached sharks as labourers moved around them like scavenging crabs. An impending feeling of doom hung over the whole place. And it wasn't due entirely to the weather.

14

Prohl leaned forward in his seat. 'What's the news from the front?'

'All bad,' came the grim reply. 'The British have taken Bremen.'

'Christ!' Prohl breathed. 'They're that close!' Bremen lay less than forty miles to the south. He added quickly, 'And Berlin?'

'Surrounded.'

'Americans?'

The driver gave a swift shake of his head. 'Worse.'

Prohl fell back into the leather seat. That could only mean one thing: the Russians.

The news wasn't bad. It was catastrophic.

The car slowed, aquaplaning briefly as the tyres lost their grip in the wetness. Then it came to a halt. The driver was about to get out and open the door but Prohl motioned for him to remain where he was. He let himself out and sprinted up the steps into the building.

The high-ceilinged lobby was crawling with personnel, most of them in a state of rapid transit. Trolleys laden with boxes and files were being trundled around like baggage carts. The place resembled a disturbed ant hill. A huge desk was positioned directly opposite the main doors. Behind it, a hard-pressed, anxious-looking aide was fending off enquiries and rapping out orders to scurrying minions. Prohl thought it would take him a week to push his way through.

Until a hand fell on his arm.

'Commander Prohl?' The question was posed nervously by a prim individual in the uniform of the Kriegsmarine. A lieutenant.

'Who're you?'

'Lieutenant Becker, sir. I'm with Staff Operations. We've been expecting you. Please follow me.'

15

'What about my report to the flotilla commander?' Prohl asked.

To his surprise he was told that could wait. Before he had a chance to respond, Becker turned abruptly and headed off through the scrum in the lobby. Prohl found himself hurrying to catch up. They entered a long corridor where there was at least some semblance of order. Nevertheless, everyone who passed them seemed to be in a rush. It was as if they expected the Allies to come bursting through the front door at any second. Which, given their proximity, probably wasn't so far from the truth, Prohl reasoned.

After a long walk Becker halted and opened a door. He ushered Prohl into the room.

The office was in total disarray. The desk was overflowing with paper. Cabinet drawers lay open with files protruding. Bulging packing cases were stacked against the walls. It looked like a general and hasty clear-out. Becker picked his way through the debris and opened another inner door. He beckoned Prohl quickly.

'Lieutenant Commander Prohl, sir,' Becker announced, and withdrew into his untidy den.

Prohl removed his cap and walked forward.

He hadn't been sure what to expect. Certainly it wasn't this.

The room was very large, with long narrow windows facing out on to the sleet-ridden dockside. To counteract the afternoon gloom, all the lights in the room were on. Three walls were covered with charts and maps – Northern Europe, the Baltic, the North Atlantic and the English Channel. Coloured tapes, secured by tiny flags, radiated from grid references like spokes on a wheel. Adolf Hitler gazed out sternly from a photograph on the fourth wall behind the desk. Two men were in the room; both in naval uniform.

They looked up sharply at Prohl's entrance. Prohl's breath caught in his throat.

One of the uniformed officers stepped forward, a middle-aged man of medium build, his high brow bisected by a severe widow's peak. He waved away Prohl's hasty salute. 'Welcome, Captain. I am Lieutenant Commander Kruger. You made excellent time. Come in, please.'

Prohl tucked his cap under his arm and automatically ran a hand through his tousled and greasy hair. He stared at the second man. Introductions were hardly necessary.

Grand Admiral Karl Doenitz, Commander in Chief of the German Navy.

The admiral regarded Prohl's confusion with a tight smile. He was a slim man, with close-cropped hair, a thin mouth and a pointed nose. But it was the eyes that drew Prohl's attention like a magnet; bright blue and very clear, like those of a bird.

'We meet again, Captain,' Doenitz said. 'It is an honour.'

'Thank you, sir,' Prohl responded hoarsely. Conscious of the unpressed state of his attire and as if seeking reassurance, he touched the ribbon at his throat. The last time he'd met Doenitz had been on the dockside at Kiel when the admiral had presided over the medal award ceremony.

To Prohl and his fellow submariners, Doenitz was a living legend. A submarine commander in the First World War, he had been captured and interned by the British. On his release he had resumed his career and risen through the ranks, eventually to command the battle cruiser *Emden*. Grand Admiral Raeder had been the man instrumental in appointing Doenitz to take over the new U-boat arm of the German Navy. The former watch officer had virtually rebuilt the submarine service from scratch. Little wonder that his men referred to him as the Lion.

'At ease, Captain,' Kruger said. 'Tell us, how was your patrol? It went well?'

Prohl hesitated. He wasn't sure whether to give them the truth or something they wanted to hear. He decided to suffer the consequences and chose the former.

Kruger and Doenitz listened in silence as Prohl told them he had lost four boats, all taken out by convoy escorts; three by depth charges, one by ramming. It was yet another indication that the U-boats had lost the initiative in the war at sea. The close-convoy system, increased and improved air cover, the development of short-wave radar and the German cryptographers' inability to break the new Royal Navy code signals all spelled disaster for the wolf packs. Time was running out. The German High Command knew it.

Kruger pursed his lips and exchanged glances with Doenitz. 'It is much as we suspected,' he said. 'It cannot be long now.'

Doenitz nodded thoughtfully.

'Shall I tell him?' Kruger continued.

Another nod, this time more severe. Prohl wondered what was to come.

Kruger said, 'Adolf Hitler is dead.'

The shock hit Prohl like a hammer blow. His heart began to beat faster as the ramifications of the news struck home. He felt their eyes on him. What should his response be? A rampant display of grief or stoic acceptance of the fact and calm anticipation of new orders?

Fortunately, he wasn't permitted the time to choose an option. Doenitz said, 'The Fuehrer died a hero's death in the capital. He gave his life for the Fatherland. It was the supreme sacrifice of a man dedicated to stemming the flood of Bolshevism. Not only Germany but the entire world is in his debt.'

Then Kruger stiffened perceptibly as he added, 'Before his death, the Fuehrer appointed Grand Admiral Doenitz as Head of State and Commander in Chief of the armed forces.'

Prohl stared. Doenitz was Hitler's successor? The new Reichspresident? Had he heard correctly?

A light flared in Doenitz's blue eyes as he said, 'The fight will continue. I have assumed command of all arms of the services with the intention of taking up the battle against the Bolsheviks. Our people in the east must be delivered from the threat of slavery and destruction. I will also maintain the struggle against the British and Americans for as long as they attempt to hinder me in that resolve.'

The man sounded as though he was rehearsing a speech. The words had the ring of oratory but lacked the late Fuehrer's cant.

Prohl fought to bring his emotions under control. He gritted his teeth and said firmly, 'I would be honoured to serve you in any capacity, sir.'

Kruger said, 'Excellent, Captain. I felt sure we could count on your loyalty. In fact, that is precisely why you have been summoned here. I must advise you that you have been selected to undertake an important mission on behalf of the Reich.'

Prohl waited.

Kruger said, 'Three hours from now, a special consignment will be delivered and secured aboard your vessel. You will also receive a set of sealed orders containing destination coordinates. You will set sail immediately upon their receipt. Is that clear?'

Dazed, Prohl could only nod. He glanced at Doenitz

19

and was disconcerted to find the admiral watching him like a hawk.

'Yes, Commander,' he said. It wasn't, of course. He didn't understand any of it. How could he?

'Good,' Kruger said. 'Admiral, is there anything you wish to add?'

Doenitz turned to Prohl. 'Only to stress the importance of this mission. Be assured, Captain, that the task to which you have been assigned is of paramount importance to the future of the Reich. Do not fail us, I beg of you.'

At that, Doenitz stepped forward and gripped Prohl's arm like a vice. 'Remember this: if we do what is in our power, God will not abandon us after so much suffering and strife.' Relinquishing his hold, Doenitz stepped away and saluted. Prohl put on his cap and returned the salute.

Doenitz looked at his watch and said, 'I have stayed too long. My plane is waiting. I must get back to head-quarters. Rear Admiral Godt is expecting my speedy return. There is work to be done.'

As if on cue, the door opened and Lieutenant Becker materialized. 'Your car and escort are ready, Admiral,' he said. He carried Doenitz's cap and coat in his hand.

Doenitz made for the door. He turned.

'I will leave it to Lieutenant Commander Kruger to finalize the details,' he said. 'Until we meet again, gentlemen.'

And then he was gone.

Prohl stared at the closed door and tried to collect his thoughts. 'My God! He's going back to Berlin? I thought the Russians . . .'

Kruger shook his head. 'Much has changed since you've been away. The capital is in ruins. The admiral has moved his headquarters north, to Ploen.' Kruger then added, 'As you may have been aware before you left, the Fuehrer had already placed him in command of the northern regions; Kesselring was given the south. Thankless tasks for both of them. I envy neither. Needless to say, the grand admiral has had to face opposition to his appointment. Himmler, for one, is not pleased. It is clear he saw himself as the Fuehrer's natural successor. There could be complications. I managed to persuade the admiral that he should employ an armed escort. They are all Kriegsmarine. Ali Cremer's in command. You know him?'

Prohl nodded. Cremer was a much decorated U-boat skipper. 'We were at Kiel together. He's a good man.'

'He'll need to be,' Kruger said. 'Himmler's personal guards are all SS, Das Reich Division. They're battle-hardened veterans.'

'My God! You seriously think Himmler will try something?'

'If he does, we're fully prepared,' Kruger replied grimly.

Prohl was appalled. So, he thought, that's what it had come down to: a squabble for power. Wild dogs scrapping over a carcass, fighting amongst themselves while the greater enemy was sniffing and scratching at the door. How long before the Russians took the city? How many would survive the final assault?

'Where's everyone else?' Prohl asked. 'What about Schnee? I thought he was with Staff Ops.'

'He's testing the new boat,' Kruger said. 'We needed someone to take her out for sea trials.'

'The XXIs? They're ready?'

Twice as large as Prohl's vessel, the new sub had a streamlined hull and spacious living quarters more in keeping with a surface vessel than an underwater craft. It made the old Type VIIC look like a relic. With automatic torpedo loading, sophisticated hydrophones that could pick up the beat of a ship's prop at a range of fifty miles, it could dive to nearly seven hundred feet and reach an underwater speed of seventeen knots – twice that of its predecessors. It outmatched anything the Allies had. It would be invincible, and regain command of the seas.

Kruger sighed. 'A little too late, I fear.' He gestured Prohl to a seat. 'But now we had better discuss your orders. There are a few points you will have to consider.'

Kruger walked to his desk. He picked up a silver cigarette case and helped himself. He offered the contents to Prohl, who declined. Kruger tapped the cigarette on his wrist, placed it in his mouth and lit up. He picked a shred of leaf from his lower lip and inhaled deeply. Exhaling, he narrowed his eyes as the fumes drifted before his face.

Prohl said, 'I'd like to ask a question.'

'Of course.'

'What is it that I'm transporting?'

Kruger sighed. 'I can't tell you.'

The look on Prohl's face spoke volumes, prompting Kruger to add quickly, 'That is because I do not know. The grand admiral did not seek to confide in me. Besides, the contents are of no concern; only their safe passage.'

'All right, I'll try again. How big is it?'

'Ah, now there I can help.' Kruger opened a manilla file in front of him and scanned the contents. He took a long pull on his cigarette before replying. 'It will consist of a number of containers. Total weight approximately thirteen hundred kilos.'

Prohl's eyes disappeared towards his hairline. 'God Almighty! You cannot be serious?'

'Never more so, Captain.'

'But this is ludicrous! How the hell am I going to find room for them? You know how important space is on one of those tin cans. Every available square inch is utilized, mostly for food, as you are well aware. There's no room to swing a cat, never mind stack extra cargo. I've got forty men under my command. How do you suggest I fit everyone in?'

Kruger paused a while before he replied.

'The nature of the cargo is such that you will be required to reduce your complement considerably. Give yourself only enough men to cover the minimum watch rotation. I would estimate that will leave you with a total of eighteen crew including yourself. Also – '

'Eighteen!' Prohl couldn't believe his ears.

'—for the duration of this assignment your vessel will not be armed.'

'What?' Prohl gasped.

'I repeat. In order to facilitate room for the cargo, you will carry only a skeleton crew and no torpedoes. The consignment will thus occupy the space in the forward and aft torpedo compartments.'

Prohl could contain himself no longer. His fist slammed down on to the desk top. 'This is lunacy! No means of defence? What if I should run into the enemy?'

'It is up to you to make sure the situation does not arise,' Kruger answered smoothly.

Prohl shook his head in exasperation as Kruger went on. 'The safe delivery of the consignment is the all-important factor here, Commander. Nothing else matters.'

Prohl forced his voice to remain calm. 'And what happens to the men I leave behind?'

'They will be split among the remaining boats in the flotilla.'

Prohl fell silent, absorbing the full impact of Kruger's words. He stood up and moved to the window. By now it was dusk. The sky was the colour of slate. Rain continued to lash the building.

'What about provisioning?' he asked.

'It is already being taken care of. At this moment your boat is being restocked and refuelled.'

Prohl pursed his lips. 'In that case I'd better be getting back. I'll have to talk to the men. Pick who is to go, who is to stay.' He added heavily, 'It's not something I'm going to enjoy. We've been together for a long time. We've become a family.'

'No one ever said command was easy, my friend,' Kruger murmured.

The door opened.

'Lieutenant Becker will escort you back to your car, Captain,' Kruger said. He held out his hand. 'I will be there to see you off. Unless there is anything else you wish to discuss?'

What would be the point? Prohl smiled sadly, shook his head and followed Becker out of the room.

with that, seeing as they don't come any more senior than the Reichspresident.'

Schepke cursed under his breath. He drew closer. 'Skipper, you know those men will follow you anywhere. To the gates of hell if need be. Moessinger's nothing but a jumped-up penpusher; a cut-price Gauleiter. He's not fit to lick your boots.' Incensed, Schepke took hold of Prohl's arm. 'Dammit,' he said, desperation creeping into his voice, 'you don't have to put up with this shit!'

Prohl whirled, nearly losing his footing in the process. 'That's enough, Lieutenant!'

But Schepke hadn't finished. His eyes blazed. 'No, you listen! I was wrong when I said that these men would follow you to the gates of hell. They've already been there! They've sweated their guts out in this stinking coffin. Six bloody years! They've had it up to here. We all have. You owe it to them, for Christ's sake!'

Prohl recoiled as if he had been struck. Then he realized they had an audience. He and Schepke had been standing close together but the lieutenant's heated words had been overheard. The three seamen lookouts positioned around the bridge flicked anxious glances at one another, their observation duties momentarily neglected. But with their captain's gaze suddenly upon them they turned away quickly.

My God, Prohl thought. What's happening to us? With the war over, we have everything to be thankful for. We should be cracking open the champagne. Instead we're at each other's throats. Bloody Moessinger. The man was eating away at the boat's morale like a cancer. And they still had over six thousand miles to go. Prohl knew that something would have to be done, otherwise the cancer could prove to be terminal.

* * *

37

Night.

The boat was running in a calm sea, under a full moon. The lookouts were two hours into their watch. Below decks it was quiet, save for the thrum of the engines. Lights had been dimmed. Bodies reclined groggily in bunks and hammocks.

Prohl left his compartment and moved aft.

A weak glow came from the lamp in the radio shack. Heller, the wireless operator, was hunched over his table, reading a magazine. He didn't look up.

There were two men in the control room: Schepke, who was the watch officer, and Werner, the control room hand.

Prohl passed through the compartment towards the mate's room and the galley. The cook was peeling potatoes. Prohl carried on, ducking under a couple of occupied hammocks. No one paid him any attention. Beyond the galley lay the diesels, the electric motor and the emergency steering position. Further on was the aft torpedo compartment.

The crates were stacked as far aft as they could be, adjacent to the trim tank. Twelve small, one large. Prohl eased his way down the narrow passageway. There wasn't a great deal of room.

The crates were constructed of stout wood. The lids were nailed down and bounded by flat metal strips to provide extra security and strength. On each crate were stencilled the words: *Geheime Reichssache*. Top secret.

Prohl looked forward towards the galley area. The cook was out of sight. In the diesel compartment a couple of the crew were moving about. This far back, Prohl was virtually invisible. He listened to the sounds of the boat for several seconds. He was unlikely to be disturbed.

There was a tool kit in the stowage locker. Prohl rooted

round and selected the largest screwdriver he could find and a pair of bolt cutters. Then he went to work.

He selected the large container first, using the bolt cutters to snap the metal retaining strap and the screwdriver to lever the lid off the crate. A layer of burlap hid the contents. On it was written *Reichsbank Hauptkasse*. Prohl held his breath and peeled it away.

Paper. Wads of it.

Prohl leant forward and picked out one of the bundles. It hit him immediately.

Not just paper. Currency. Foreign currency. All types – French, English, Italian. Notes of all denominations. Hundreds of them. No, not hundreds. Thousands.

A fortune.

Prohl put the notes back and replaced the lid. Then he attacked one of the smaller crates.

God in heaven. His throat went dry.

There were four gold ingots in the case. Prohl lifted one out. It was so heavy he had to use two hands. The gold was stamped with the Reich insignia: an eagle, wings outspread, talons clutching the laurels and swastika. The letters *RB* were etched into the metal as were the figures *1938* and *10,455*. He presumed the numerical inscriptions referred to the smelting date and the weight in kilos. There was another number: *41192*, most likely the serial number of the ingot. This was confirmed when he replaced the bar and took out the next one. The serial number was sequential.

Prohl returned the ingot and secured the lid. He removed the two severed metal bands completely, compressed them as much as he could and dropped them in the torpedo stowage container beneath his feet.

Then he sat back against the hull and thought about what he was going to do next. And what it all meant.

Who was the gold intended for? Prohl considered the

possibilities. If, as he suspected, Moessinger was with the RSHA, then the man he was answerable to was Ernst Kaltenbrunner. And Kaltenbrunner was SS, the second most powerful leader of the organization after Reichsfuehrer Himmler. And yet, according to Kruger, Moessinger was acting under Doenitz's orders. What did it all mean?

With the Russians encircling the capital and Adolf Hitler dead, his cabinet would likely have been in total disarray, with Himmler, Bormann and the others scrambling for power with the voracity of foxes in a chicken coop. In those final hours, Prohl imagined, it must have been like Dante's interpretation of hell.

But maybe they hadn't been scrambling for power. Perhaps, he theorized, they had been running for cover. For, once the Americans and British had crossed the Rhine and the Russians had crossed the Elbe, there would have been nothing to stand in their way. The noose around Berlin would have been drawing inexorably tighter. In which case, it would have been every man for himself. It wasn't outside the realms of possibility to suppose that the SS chief and the rest of them had escape routes and destinations already planned. And if they were looking for a bolt hole, they'd need funds to sustain them when they got there. And why not South America as a logical sanctuary?

Prohl was aware that there were substantial numbers of German expatriates in the neutralities of Argentina and its neighbour Uruguay. He'd come into contact with seamen, U-boat crews among them, who'd sailed in and out of Buenos Aires and Montevideo. Men who'd entertained Prohl with stories of the generosity of the German communities towards their fellow countrymen, giving parties and dinners in their honour. Many of their hosts had been businessmen, wealthy landowners who ran

40

factories and lived on vast estates and ranches up in the cattle country. They'd be sure to welcome men like Himmler and Martin Bormann with open arms. Especially if they took with them enough funds to ensure that they would live like kings. It all seemed so plausible.

Prohl wondered if there were other consignments like the one he was carrying. Perhaps other U-boats, instead of transporting the riches, were carrying the men. When he'd asked about Doenitz's former aide, Adalbert Schnee, Kruger had told him that Schnee was out testing the new boat, the XXI. Suppose that was a ruse. Suppose, instead, that Schnee was carrying Himmler and Bormann and the rest of them out of Germany to safety on the other side of the world, leaving Doenitz and Kesselring to hold back the Allies in order to give them time to escape and sacrificing their armies in order to effect their own salvation.

If that was true then he was helping them!

He felt the anger building again; like a dam about to burst under pressure. His fists balled. And then, in a moment of startling clarity, the solution came to him. The more he thought about it the more he was certain that it was the obvious thing to do. With a grim smile on his lips he got to his feet and made his way back along the passageway.

Schepke looked up from the chart table as Prohl entered the control room. He was startled to see the almost feral grin on the captain's face.

'Give me our present position,' Prohl ordered.

Schepke checked his calculations. 'Forty-one-seventeen-north, fourteen-twenty-three-west. We've just passed Finisterre.' He tapped the point with the dividers.

Prohl nodded. 'Steer one-four-zero,' he said, after a pause.

Schepke frowned. That would bring them in closer to the Portuguese coast. 'Sir?'

'Do it,' Prohl said. His tone brooked no argument.

'Aye aye, sir.' Schepke relayed the instructions to the helmsman.

'Lieutenant Schepke, to the bridge, if you please,' Prohl said. He was already heading up the ladder by the time his order had been absorbed.

With a grimace to the control room hand, Schepke followed him up.

When Schepke had joined him, Prohl ordered the upper watch to go below. He and Schepke were left alone. The sea was the colour of jet, flecked with silver. It seemed to stretch into infinity as it merged with the midnight sky.

'Sir?' Schepke couldn't conceal his curiosity any longer.

'There's been a change of plan,' Prohl said.

Then he told Schepke what the change was.

Schepke listened in awe, his brain reeling. 'My God!' His voice was hoarse. 'Can we do it?'

'Who is to stop us?' Prohl replied. 'Answer me that.'

Schepke considered for a moment. 'No one,' he said at last. 'No one at all.'

3

Schepke thought that they might have to restrain Moessinger physically. The man looked as if he was on the verge of having a seizure. He was almost incoherent when he discovered that Prohl had ordered a change of course.

'How dare you disobey my orders!' Moessinger screamed, his face contorted with fury. He was positively spitting venom. 'I command you to resume your correct heading immediately! Do you hear me, Captain?'

'Perfectly,' Prohl said. 'So does everyone else on board, for that matter. However, on this boat you command no one, my friend.' He paused for emphasis. 'I, on the other hand, do.'

'This is treason!'

Prohl shook his head. 'No it's not,' he replied deftly. 'It's common sense. It's over, Moessinger.'

'Over? What do you mean, over?' Moessinger seemed to falter.

'Everything. The war, this escapade . . .'

'Escapade?' A definite uncertainty had appeared in Moessinger's eyes.

Prohl said, 'I know what the consignment is, Herr Moessinger. I know what we're doing here.'

It had suddenly gone very quiet.

'You opened the boxes?' Moessinger whispered disbelievingly.

'Not all of them. Just a couple. Enough to get the picture.'

'You had no right . . . !'

'Wrong. As commander of this vessel, I had every right.'

'You were given explicit instructions . . .'

'I know what my instructions were. But I'm telling you here and now that all bets are off. Tell me, Moessinger, where are the rest of the rats? With Schnee or one of the others? Lueth, perhaps? Or maybe they're carrying someone's nest egg too. You bastards! You thought you'd got away with it, didn't you? Leaving Uncle Karl to carry the can while you sneaked out by the back door. What was your job, Moessinger? Going out there to grease a few palms? Off to smooth the way for poor old Heinrich, were we? I suppose the rest of them are in on it as well – Bormann, Fat Hermann, that weasel Goebbels, your boss.'

'My boss?'

'Kaltenbrunner. He's got his tongue so far up Himmler's backside he can't see straight.'

Moessinger reacted as if he'd been shot. Schepke thought the man was going to hurl himself down Prohl's throat. He braced himself to come between them.

It didn't come to that. Moessinger appeared to compose himself. He swallowed, glanced at Schepke and said, 'I would like a word with you alone, Captain.'

'I don't think so,' Prohl said. 'Anything you have to say can be said in front of my lieutenant.'

Moessinger considered the offer. 'Very well,' he said. 'Captain, you have stated that you are aware of the nature of the cargo. You will appreciate, therefore, that I could make it worth your while to resume our original course. I am not without influence in certain quarters. It is most likely that the Reichsminister would show a substantial appreciation of your loyalty.'

Prohl pursed his lips. 'Would he now.' He looked at Schepke. 'What do you think, Lieutenant?'

Schepke said, 'I think we should tell the Reichminister what he can do with his appreciation, sir.'

'You mean he can put it in the same place as Kaltenbrunner's nose, right?'

'Precisely, sir.' Schepke gave Moessinger a benign smile. 'If it'll fit, that is.'

'Ah, well, Herr Moessinger,' Prohl sighed regretfully. 'It would seem that you can't win them all.'

Despite the smile on Prohl's face there was iron in his voice.

'What do you intend to do with me?' Moessinger asked. His bluster had evaporated. He knew he was at Prohl's mercy. There wasn't a man on board who would lift a finger to help him. His future was dependent upon the captain's whim.

Prohl said, 'I haven't decided yet. I can't very well clap you in irons. So you're free to move around the boat for the time being. I know there's not enough room to spit, but I'd advise you to keep out of my way. And don't try to subvert my crew either. It won't work. They don't like you any more than I do. Right now I'm not sure how long this good mood of mine is likely to last. Which means that the slightest hiccup on your part could result in my turning very unpleasant. You wouldn't want that, Moessinger. Believe me.' Prohl turned to Schepke. 'When he's back at his bunk join me in the control room.'

Schepke nodded. 'Very good, sir.'

When Schepke reported back Prohl said, 'I don't want our friend given access to our charts. For the time being I want him kept in the dark as regards our destination. Tell the other watch officers.'

'You've decided where we're going to head for, then?'

Prohl nodded. 'Yes,' he said. 'I've decided.' And he told Schepke the rest of his plan.

* * *

The U-boat entered the strait at periscope depth on the evening of the tenth day. Ahead lay the Pillars of Hercules, ten miles apart. The Rock of Gibraltar was to port, Jebel Musa and the Moroccan mainland on the starboard beam. One very heavily patrolled bottleneck.

Prohl had confined Moessinger to his bunk in the PO's mess. He wanted a clear head, no distractions. With Schepke at his shoulder he pored over the hydrographic chart.

'We'll go in on the surface,' Prohl said. 'We can take advantage of the eastern current.'

Schepke bit his lip.

'I know,' Prohl said, 'but it's the quickest way. We'll stick close to the southern coastline. Could be that the Brits have let themselves grow lax about the news from their European fronts. With a bit of luck they'll be too busy celebrating to notice us sneaking past.'

'Aye aye, sir.' Despite the acknowledgment Schepke didn't look too convinced.

Prohl didn't give his lieutenant time to dwell on his apprehension. After squinting through the 'scope, he gave the orders.

'Stand by to surface! Blow all main ballast!'

A low rumble sounded as the water was forced out of the tanks. The submarine rose like a breaching whale.

'Equalize pressure!'

The fans came on, sucking the sea air into the boat.

'With me,' Prohl said, beckoning to Schepke. Water rained down from the hatch as the two men climbed up the ladder.

The night was cool and all the better for it. Down below it had been warm and clammy.

There was a slight haze but through it they could see the blue-black outline of the Spanish coast and the running lights of a slow-moving vessel. Probably a trawler

46

heading back to Algeciras, Prohl decided. No immediate threat there. He completed a full sweep with his night glasses. Much closer, on the opposite quarter, Africa slumbered, wrapped in darkness save for a few glimmering pinpricks of light that twinkled like fireflies. It all looked very quiet.

'So far so good,' Prohl said. He didn't want anyone else topsides in case they had to submerge quickly. The U-boat trembled and slunk forward. Moonlight shimmered in its wake.

As they drew closer to the looming mass of the Rock and its southernmost tip, Europa Point, the number of surface craft began to increase. It looked as if the British naval defences were still in a state of vigilance. However, the U-boat had the advantage of travelling in darkness. On the ships around it, navigation lights were aglow. The difficulty was keeping tabs on all of them at once.

And in that Prohl and Schepke failed.

The first inkling that Schepke had of the danger was when he heard Prohl bellow, 'Enemy to port!' followed by the clamour of the alarm bell. Then he was moving fast.

'Clear the bridge!' Prohl slammed Schepke between the shoulder blades. 'Dive! Dive! Dive!'

Schepke had only time to see the sudden bloom of the searchlight before his knee grazed the side of the hatchway and he was falling into the control room. Stunned by the pain, he was vaguely conscious of Prohl tumbling after him.

'Open all main vents!' Prohl was yelling again as he swung the hatch closed above his head.

The control room hands were slamming the vent levers open. Water surged into the tanks. The U-boat's snout plunged sharply and everyone hung on as the trim shifted.

'Take her down!' Prohl gasped. 'Fifty metres!' He glanced at the depth-gauge needle, then at Schepke. The look communicated what every man was thinking: Too damned close for comfort. It was probably already too late.

'Jesus!' Prohl cursed. 'The bastard came from nowhere!'

'What the hell was it?' Schepke panted, massaging his kneecap.

'Bloody destroyer!'

As the U-boat headed down, a massive booming noise could be heard, approaching fast, like the roar of a speeding express train. Everyone stared at the ceiling as if expecting it to be rent asunder by the warship's keel.

The U-boat began to level out.

The barrage of sound seemed to enclose them; then, just as quickly, it began to recede astern as the warship passed over their heads.

'Slow ahead both,' Prohl directed cautiously.

Schepke spotted Moessinger's pale face staring at him from the control room hatchway. I bet you're crapping bricks, he thought.

A voice said, 'Propellers bearing two-four-zero, closing.' The hydrophone operator.

'Shit,' someone muttered.

'Stop engines!' Prohl hissed immediately.

The boat lurched. Everybody fell silent, knowing what was to come.

Moessinger said, 'What . . . ?'

'Shut the fuck up!' Schepke snapped brutally.

The pounding of the props echoed through the hull like the tread of giant footsteps. The interior of the U-boat was flooded with sound. Once more the vibrations began to dissipate. The crew held its collective breath.

Then came the signal. A faint succession of clicks, as if a child was pulling the trigger of a toy gun.

In the deathly silence that followed, time stood still.

The explosions, when they finally came, seemed massive. Struck by a giant hammer, the U-boat reeled. Deck plates rattled. Lights went out. Glass shattered. Someone cried out in pain as a bone cracked against metal. The lights flickered and came back on.

'Propellers bearing one-zero-seven, closing.' The hydrophone operator's warning was followed by a steady chorus of pinging sounds and every man knew with sickening finality that not all the darkness in the world could make them invisible from the destroyer's Asdic.

'Hold on!' The warning was given needlessly.

The hull was rocked by a further series of detonations as yet more depth charges were activated.

Somewhere up there, Prohl knew, a British commander would be wondering why an enemy submarine had chosen to disobey Doenitz's instructions to surrender. He'd be calling in support, if he hadn't already done so. The strait would be sealed tight. The cork would be back in the bottle. They wouldn't want this one to get away. They'd want blood and they wouldn't be satisfied until they had it.

The next fifteen minutes were a prolonged nightmare, the time stretching into an infinity of sensations, all of them terrifying, as the boat was subjected to a further two attacks. It was increasingly evident to all those trapped that there was now more than one surface ship in the hunt. Which meant that it could only be a matter of time before the submarine was finally destroyed through sheer weight of numbers.

Prohl made an urgent call for damage reports.

Inevitably the U-boat had not emerged unscathed from the poundings. A number of seals had ruptured in the forward compartment. Water had entered the hull. Smoke had begun to seep from the steering position, indicating a short circuit of some kind. This was smothered immediately by the chief engineer; fire below was a horror that every crewman feared. Some of the cargo had shifted. But so far, miraculously, the pressure hull was holding out. Nevertheless, Prohl knew that he would have to do something quickly if he was to save them.

So he sold his soul to the Devil.

The ruse was spawned out of a will to survive, but above all by anger and a burning sense of betrayal.

'Prepare bow tubes!' Prohl cried suddenly. 'Lieutenant Schepke, I want spare clothing, blankets, food containers, magazines – anything that will float – taken to the forward compartment at the double. Chief, I want you to stand by to jettison oil on my command.' Prohl weaved his way to the hatch. 'Right. Move it!'

Galvanized into action and fuelled by desperation, they loaded the bow tubes with the items that Prohl had demanded.

'My God!' Schepke whispered breathlessly as he stuffed a mess of blankets into the tube. 'Do you really think they'll fall for it?'

As he spoke, another series of rapid explosions bracketed the submarine. A hollow sound like the striking of a thousand anvils reverberated through the. hull. The U-boat was shaken as if by a giant hand. Men lost their footing and scrabbled for a grip as the bow lifted violently. From the galley there followed the cymbal clash of plates and crockery. The lights went out once more, strobed briefly, and came back to life with the eerie blue glow of a dying candle.

'If they don't,' Prohl replied grimly, 'we're dead. All of us.'

In the grotto-like gloom his face had assumed the proportions of a skull. His eyes were dark sockets. 'All we need now,' he said, 'is a body.'

Schepke felt a chill run down his spine. He stared at Prohl, hearing and understanding for the first time the full and awful significance of his commander's plan.

'They'd have to believe it then,' Prohl said. 'Wouldn't they?'

For the merest second it seemed to Schepke that his heart had ceased to beat.

Prohl said, 'Bring that bastard up here! Now!'

It took four men to drag Moessinger along the narrow passageway. Some sixth sense must have warned him of Prohl's cold-blooded intention. He was kicking frantically and screaming into the hand that was clamped over his mouth; his fingers clawed for something to hold on to, anything to prevent his progress towards the fate that awaited him.

They lifted him through the final hatchway, oblivious of his hysterical, garbled pleas for mercy.

Prohl swung open the door of the torpedo tube. Moessinger's shriek was cut off by an arm around his throat.

'Get him inside!' Prohl ordered.

Moessinger struggled wildly, like a man possessed. His eyes bulged with terror. His muted cries intensified as they held his arms by his sides and fed him head first into the opening. Moessinger's fingernails scratched impotently along the bore of the tube as he fought for a purchase. The effect was like chalk grating down a blackboard. Blood welled from the abrasions along his knuckles. He let out one final, dreadful bay of despair as the door of the torpedo tube slammed closed behind him. His faint mewlings could still be heard as Prohl and his crew prepared for the final assault.

Back in the control room Prohl gave the order. 'Stand by!'

The rumble of turning screws could be heard as he spoke.

'Ready all hands!'

This time the depth charges came very close. The boat shuddered as if racked in a death spasm.

In the aftermath Prohl yelled suddenly, 'Foreplanes hard-a-rise! Take her up! Twenty-five metres! Stand by to flood tubes! Chief, prepare to jettison oil!'

The planesmen responded like automatons. The bow began to lift slowly.

'Now, Chief!'

'Pumping, sir!'

'Compensating! Flood tubes one and three!'

'Flooded!'

'Fire one! Fire three!'

With a whoosh of compressed air, the debris packed into the bow tubes was ejected into the sea.

'Flood two and four!'

'Flooded!'

'Fire!'

Schepke thought of Moessinger trapped in the darkness, the bow doors opening, the water rushing in, cutting off his screams like the blade of an axe descending on a victim's head.

'Foreplanes hard-a-dive!'

The planesmen spun their wheels. Sluggishly at first, the U-boat began to respond. Then the bow dropped sharply and they began to descend. The needle on the depth gauge began to creep clockwise. Twenty metres, fifty; seventy. They were sinking.

'Hold at seventy metres! All quiet!'

Far below the surface of the strait the U-boat floated in a vacuum-like silence.

Over the next twenty minutes, the tension in the submarine was almost unbearable. Not daring to make the slightest noise, the crew focused their attention on the sounds around them: the heavy drip of condensation from the pipes, the groaning of the hull, the trickle of water from buckled seams.

The twenty minutes grew into twenty-five and then into thirty. There had been no further explosions.

Schepke found he was grinning inanely. 'It worked! It worked!'

'Silence!' Prohl cut his lieutenant off.

Despite their commander's reprimand the men began to relax. But they knew he was right; they weren't out of danger yet.

Prohl ordered an update on the damage situation. The men moved to their positions quietly. An inspection was carried out, then the officers reported back.

The chief engineer was the first. 'All major leaks secured, sir. Motors are serviceable. Steering not affected by the short. Not bad at all. I think we've been bloody lucky.'

The other reports were consistent with the first. All departments declared they were fully functional.

The boat had survived. They'd come through.

Prohl kept them in position for another hour until he was satisfied it was safe for them to restart the motors.

Slowly, hesitantly, maintaining depth, the sub inched its way forward.

Two and a half hours after the first depth-charge attack, the U-boat entered the Mediterranean.

In the control room, Prohl consulted his charts. Schepke was with him. Both of them breathed a sigh of relief.

They were on their way. They could resume their journey. True, they still had a long way to go, but with skill and some luck they would make it. The attempt to make a surface passage through the strait had been an error of judgement that had almost cost them dear. But they wouldn't make the same mistake again. From now on they would be very careful. But at least they would be aided by one considerable factor in their favour. This would be the last place anyone would think to look for them.

Because, in a sense, they were going home.

Part Two

4

The Sea of Crete – summer 1990

Demetrius believed they had been very lucky to have survived the storm. The gods, he said, had protected them. His son Andreas, on the other hand, laughed good-naturedly and said the gods had had nothing to do with it. It was good seamanship that had seen them through. Wasn't that right, Georgiou?

Georgiou saw the knowing look on his grandfather's seamed face, and smiled at his father and said, 'Perhaps.' Georgiou was just thankful that they were still alive.

The storm had been ferocious; the rain torrential, the waves frighteningly huge. The caique had been tossed around like a cork and at times Georgiou had seriously doubted that he would ever see his sixteenth year. But the caique had been soundly constructed. His grandfather had built it in the traditional way, with his own strong hands, in the way his father had taught him and his father before him. He had fashioned the timbers, hammered the nails, laid the deck and caulked the seams. The eyes he had painted on the curved and weathered prow had watched over them and guided them to safety.

But they had lost their nets and most of their haul. For everything, it seemed, there was a price to pay. But nets could be replaced and their catch replenished. To the old man the loss had been a small price to pay for their salvation.

Now, with the sea calm and the morning sun low on the horizon, they were heading home.

It was Georgiou who spotted it. At first glance he thought it was nothing more than a large piece of flotsam. But as they drew closer he saw that it was in fact a small boat, a wooden dinghy, very low in the water, drifting. Georgiou called his father's attention and pointed excitedly.

The caique altered course. Quickly, Andreas handed over the tiller to his father then joined his son at the bow.

'There's a man!' Georgiou exclaimed suddenly.

It was true. In the bottom of the boat a figure lay face down.

Steadily the caique drew alongside. Andreas leaned out and grabbed hold of the dinghy's gunnel. The dinghy rocked violently. The prone man did not stir.

It was Georgiou who made the first move. He went over the side of the caique and dropped into the tiny boat.

'Careful!' Andreas cried. 'You'll tip it over!'

Georgiou swallowed nervously. There was water in the bottom of the dinghy and the man's face was half submerged. One arm lay underneath the body, the other was outstretched, the hand clenched.

Gingerly maintaining his balance, Georgiou turned the body over. As the face came into view he shrank back. For a brief second he looked like an old man. Andreas could see why.

The dead man's face must have been submerged for a very long time. It was wrinkled like a shrunken leather mask. The eyes were open but they were opaque and bulging as if the corpse had suffered some terrible shock or perhaps seen a vision that his tortured mind could not fully comprehend. The hair was so grey it was almost white.

Andreas jolted his son into action. 'Get your arms

under his shoulders. I'll pull him in. We can't leave him where he is, the boat will sink.'

Trying not to let his gaze dwell on the ghastly face, Georgiou did as he father bade. With difficulty he managed to ease the body around. Grabbing the arms, Andreas heaved the stiffened torso into the caique.

As he assisted his father, Georgiou's attention was arrested by a piece of sacking that had been previously hidden by the body. It lay under one of the dinghy's thwarts. He reached down and picked it up.

At least, he tried to. He was unprepared for the weight of the bag, so much so that he overbalanced. As he stumbled, the bottom of the sack, rotted and weakened by its immersion in the water, gave way. Georgiou had only a fleeting moment to catch sight of what the sack contained before it struck the side of the dinghy and splashed into the water between the boats. Openmouthed, he watched the heavy brick-shaped object sink into the depths beneath his feet. It was gone so fast that he thought at first he might have imagined it. But he knew what he had seen. The unmistakable gleam of gold!

The wheel abandoned, Demetrius hurried forward. Andreas was helping Georgiou back over the side of the caique. Georgiou was still clutching the remains of the sack.

'What's that you've got there?' his grandfather asked.

Georgiou was staring over the side. 'It was gold,' he said in awe. 'It was gold.'

Andreas and his father looked at each other.

'What was?' Demetrius asked, confused.

'The thing in the sack,' Georgiou replied. 'It was gold.'

'Don't be foolish,' Andreas said. 'You must have imagined it. Now, I wonder who he is?'

Demetrius looked at the dead man. 'I do not know.'

59

He frowned suddenly. 'There is something in his hand.' He pointed to the clenched fist.

Andreas followed his gaze. Curious, he knelt down and caught hold of the fingers and thumb. He prised them apart.

There was indeed something in the corpse's hand.

There in the palm, attached to what had once been a piece of red, black and silver ribbon, lay what looked like a piece of jewellery. A black metal cross edged in silver. Above it, also in silver, were two small crossed swords surmounted by the carving of an oak leaf. On the lowest arm of the cross was a date.

1939.

5

The Turkish coast – late summer 1990

Poor Mehmed was crying in his sleep again. He had assumed his usual foetal position, huddled against the opposite wall of the cell, half hidden under the grimy folds of his lice-ridden blanket. Now and then a long whimpering moan escaped his lips, the thin sound rising and falling like the keening whine of a small animal in pain. Out of the corner of my eye I spotted something tiny under a shiny carapace scuttle beneath his exposed, scabby thigh, heading on minuscule feet for the edge of the straw-filled palliasse that supported his scrawny body.

Small wonder he wasn't sleeping so well. In four days' time they were going to hang him.

I shuddered, clamped my hands behind my head and stared up at the cracked and pitted plaster above me. *Homes and Gardens* it was not. Not by the most fevered stretch of anyone's imagination. The cell was cramped, dirty and dismal, with illumination courtesy of a narrow three-barred opening set high in the wall facing the door. The place was hardly big enough for one occupant. With two of us it was downright claustrophobic, although it hadn't taken the weeks that I'd endured its less than cosy hospitality to convince me that two to a cell was pretty nigh civilized compared to the indignities inflicted on some of the other inmates.

They call the place the Citadel. It's built on an island, and legend has it that back in the sixteenth century it was the stronghold of the pirate admiral Barbarossa, who used it as a base from which to launch raiding parties along the coasts and islands of the Mediterranean. I don't know if that's in the history books – let's face it, they say every legend has a grain of truth – but whatever the facts were, its reputation as hell on earth is justly deserved. Nowadays the Turks use it as a penal colony for serious offenders.

A pale orange light had begun to infiltrate the cell. Dawn coming up. Force of habit made me look to my wrist. A waste of time – no pun intended – as my Seiko had been confiscated, along with my other meagre possessions, when they jumped on me that dark and sultry night three months previously

Correction: they hadn't confiscated the watch, I'd exchanged it. For food. In the end, of course, it had amounted to the same thing. Looking back, one small bar of carbolic soap, three oranges and an over-ripe melon hadn't seemed much of a bargain, even then. And the oranges had been sour. Bastards.

I lay back, thought about the new day and listened to my companion bleat and snuffle. If I listened very carefully I could also hear the roaches foraging.

The prison was beginning to come awake. From the corridor outside came the sound of tramping boots; the guard detail announcing reveille, hammering on the doors with their correction staves. A chorus of hawking and spitting greeted the arousal. The guards were yelling back in a futile attempt to restore discipline. I heard the rattle of a key in the lock and the door swung open, hinges rasping.

The standard of room service left a lot to be desired. Kasim gave me his usual twisted leer and a hefty thwack across the soles of my feet with his truncheon.

One day, I promised myself, come the revolution, I was going to ram that stave up Kasim's arse. Savouring the thought, I gritted my teeth and tried to ignore the pain that was shooting up my legs.

'Up! up!' Kasim yelled, and bounced his staff gleefully along Mehmed's thigh.

My cellmate came fully awake in a second and shrieked like a spanked infant. The blanket fell away from his body, revealing a rake-thin torso and shaven head. Mehmed screwed up his eyes and wailed in distress. Kasim snarled and struck him again for good measure, before retreating into the corridor in search of fresh victims.

I saw Mehmed's back then. The scars still hadn't healed. They ran from his shoulders down to his kidneys. Crisscrossed many times, they were raw and suppurating. They looked like the scratch marks of a huge claw. The pain must have been excruciating.

I recalled the day, seven weeks before, when Mehmed had first arrived. He had been full of bravado then. As the door slammed behind him he had made a very obscene gesture and followed it up with a fluent stream of invective that had cast various aspersions on the guards' ancestry, much of which, as far as I had been able to determine, had been to do with beasts of burden and syphilitic ladies of ill repute. Not that my command of Turkish is that hot, but the gesture he'd used to illustrate his point was pretty much universal. I remember he was grinning at the time. Sad to say, his good humour hadn't lasted.

'*Gunaydin,*' he'd said, shaking my hand. '*Nasilsiniz?*'

Roughly translated that meant, 'Hello, how's it going?' So I told him I'd known better.

'Ah, you are *Ingilizce*?'

'Spot on, Abdul.' Thinking this was where he'd start showing me pictures of his sister, I prepared to repel boarders.

'My name Mehmed.'

63

One mystery cleared up. I'd sleep easier nights, knowing that. (At least, that's what I'd thought until I discovered later what it was he was in for – stabbing his male lover with a knife after a domestic tiff. Nothing trivial. If I dropped anything, I reminded myself to make sure my back was to the wall when I picked it up.)

'Logan,' I told him. 'Michael Logan.'

'*Memnun oldum*, Michael,' he announced solemnly. And that was it. Formalities over.

He squatted against the wall then and scratched gamely at his armpit. In that state he resembled a dirty, lecherous imp. Not so far from the truth, I suppose.

'You have cigarette?' he asked cheerfully.

Being a nonsmoker, I shook my head.

He shrugged then and seemed to lose interest. I watched him as he took stock of his surroundings. I think that was the moment when the full realization of where he was finally hit him, for, suddenly, he appeared to shrink. Some of the animation left his face and the light in his brown eyes dimmed as though a candle flame had been snuffed out.

And his deterioration into a kind of madness began almost immediately. That night, at any rate.

They had come for him a little after dark. Two guards, Kasim, slim and effeminate, and an obese, bald-headed lout called Baraq.

Mehmed was a young lad, not much out of his teens. He had that smooth, rather sloe-eyed look, which meant that as far as those inmates with homosexual tendencies were concerned, and given his own proclivities, he was considered fair game. With some of the guards, too, as it happened.

I don't know where Kasim and Baraq took him that night, but they were away for a couple of hours. When they finally returned and threw Mehmed back in the cell he was damned near in a state of catatonic shock. Which was how it had been on nearly every evening since. Within a couple of days they had started to subcontract his favours, no doubt havng been duly rewarded for their procuring services. And they whipped him into submission if he resisted their advances.

There were times when Mehmed told me how he looked forward to the day of his execution.

And there were moments when I got to considering that, given the squalor of our surroundings and the sentence hanging over my own head, perhaps Mehmed had a point. To some of the inmates of the Citadel, death would probably be welcomed as some kind of a release. As the sand in my cellmate's hourglass continued to run out, the more I became convinced of it.

The Turks never have shown much leniency towards drug traffickers, as Timothy Davey and Billy Hayes would no doubt testify. With two decades in the Citadel stretching ahead of me like a dark tunnel, perhaps it would have been a blessing if I'd been put in front of a firing-squad. As I said, maybe Mehmed had a point.

About the only way to make life bearable was to bribe the guards to bring in luxuries, like food and toiletries. My Seiko, however, had been my last item of currency. It now adorned Kasim's bony wrist, a fact of which he never failed to remind me every time we met, which, as he happened to be in charge of my block, was every bloody day. He didn't have to say anything, he just had to roll up his sleeve nonchalantly as if he had an appointment to keep, and that was enough. Even after all this time it still rankled. And he knew it.

Going by the position of the shadows on the cell wall it was somewhere around six A.M. It was likely to be another hot day. We'd had something of a heatwave over the past couple of weeks, which meant that the noonday temperature tended to be somewhere around the hundred mark. The nights weren't much better. The only things that took your mind off the heat were the bugs and the smell. It was worse in the morning because all the slop buckets were full. They were removed from the cells at two-day intervals. Today was the second day, so the accumulative stench had to be experienced to be believed. In the end it was probably something you got used to. I hadn't been there long enough for that, however, and it still got to me. But today it wouldn't be so bad because I was detailed for an outside working party. There was a new jetty they wanted built. It would be back-breaking work, but I'd be outside and the smell of the sea was always welcome.

Kasim came back for me at seven. He was grinning, as usual.

'Your time come, *Ingilizce*. You go work now.'

And then he tapped that bloody watch.

I hadn't got a uniform as such. I was still wearing my own clothes, what there were of them: the remains of a sleeveless grey tee shirt, a pair of dirty blue jeans which consisted of more holes than denim, a pair of well-worn leather thongs. My only other possessions were a woollen blanket, a stub of candle wax and a stick of charcoal. God knows why I kept the last item. I was no artist and I didn't have anyone to write to. Wishful thinking, I suppose. I'd seen Sudanese refugees with greater assets.

Kasim escorted me and the rest of the detail through the yard. There were a dozen of us plus two guards. I was the only European. The rest of the group were a motley bunch, mostly Turkish nationals, but there were a couple who looked like Arabs. No one I knew, anyway. I hadn't made any particular buddies inside as yet. Mostly I'd kept to myself. There were a couple of other Europeans in the place, or so I'd heard through the grapevine. A Spaniard, and a Belgian mercenary. I think they'd been in solitary for most of my stay. In the cages.

We passed those on our way to the main gate. They consisted of a line of holes in the ground, topped by metal gratings. During the heat of the day they became ovens. I saw some poor devil removed from one once. He looked as if he'd been turned on a spit for a week. The cages were used as a means of punishment. To qualify you had to have committed some heinous crime, like telling one of the guards to fuck off. Something pretty bloody serious, anyway. That's why I kept my mouth shut, just in case Kasim happened to be listening. I didn't want to give him an excuse. Sometimes, though, I'd come very close. Like this morning.

God, but it was good to get out into the open away from the smell of confinement; the foul and claustrophobic odour of unwashed bodies, piss and shit. I stood still for a moment and let the sea breeze wash over me like a healing balm. The sea was a beautiful turquoise, dark and calm. Across it I could make out the mainland, eight miles distant, low and wooded. We were on the western shore. If I looked south I could gaze on freedom. Kerkis, the highest mountain on the Greek island of Samos, seemed to rise out of the sea like a high wave. Twelve miles separated us. It might as well have been a thousand. No one in his right mind would have thought of making a break for it. Even if they'd been able to scale the walls and make it down to the shore, they wouldn't have been able to outswim the patrol launch.

It was there now, motoring slowly, one hundred yards offshore, deck gun trained on the ramparts behind me. It was like a shark circling a life raft, waiting to pick off survivors.

I felt a stunning blow between my shoulder blades.

Kasim had lashed me with his stave. I reeled and fell to my knees, grazing my elbow on the stones.

'You work, *Ingilizce*! You no work, you go in cage!' Kasim yelled, revelling in his authority.

The rest of the work party and the second guard looked on without pity.

I got to my feet and followed them down to the water's edge. There wasn't a beach as such, just a jumble of rocks leading out in a narrow promontory. It was at this point that they wanted to erect the jetty as a replacement for the older one that was beginning to rot away. The timber was ferried over from the mainland. The foundations were easily obtainable. They came from the remains of the stone that had been used to construct the original keep. It littered the shore like the debris in a quarry. All we had to do was carry it from one end of the shore to the other. The stuff that was too big to carry we had to break down with picks.

Perversely, I was beginning to enjoy the exercise. It was damned hot but the sea air kept the temperature down to a low simmer. Nevertheless, all of us had broken sweat under Kasim's watchful eye and the liberal use of his correction stave. And, apart from the sound of our work tools, it was almost soporific.

Or it was until the patrol launch blew up.

I'd noticed the speedboat some time ago. It was a long way off, perhaps a mile or so. Probably just on the edge of the prohibited zone that the Turks had placed around the island. The launch was patrolling a course parallel to the shore, maintaining distance and vigilance with equal resolution. I had no doubt that the chief officer had had the speedboat under observation for a while, but as it hadn't posed any obvious threat he'd evidently been content to ignore it.

We were on what the guards euphemistically called a

meal break. One of the trustees had delivered a pail of water, some rolls and a tureen of foul-smelling gunk which, one of the Turkish prisoners assured me, was *kadin budu*, meatballs with rice to you and me. We ate with our hands.

And that was when it happened.

I remember the patrol launch was lying motionless at the time, floating on the millpond sea like a child's toy. Somewhere beyond it I could just detect the far-off whine of the speedboat, sounding like a distant buzz-saw. Some rich brat taking advantage of a new plaything, I guessed with minor envy. Most likely with a girl on board whom he was trying to impress.

The explosion tore the launch apart in a balloon of flame. I saw a couple of bodies cascade into the air like raggedy dolls, uniforms on fire, then another massive boom as the ammunition went up. The noise echoed around the shore like a clap of thunder. We all jumped to our feet, mouths open, staring seaward.

So, when the figure emerged out of the sea twenty paces offshore, we all saw it at the same time. When I first saw the shiny black head I thought it was a porpoise – they sometimes swim in close to the shallows – but as soon as the rest of the body came into view I knew I'd been mistaken. What I had thought of as being a black and shiny skin was, in fact, a wet suit.

The swimmer was carrying something in what looked like plastic wrapping. In a move that was incredibly swift, the wrapping was ripped away. Despite the shock of seeing this apparition rising from the surf like an alien in a sci-fi movie, sundry facts registered. The sub-machine gun was very compact, probably the extra-short version of the H & K MP5. Nine mil, thirty-round magazine. A weapon favoured by antiterrorist squads because it's easily concealable.

Kasim recognized the threat first. He had tossed his

stave aside and was reaching over his shoulder for his rifle when the first bullets took him in the chest. They were fired at such close range that they punched their way through his breastbone and erupted from his shoulder blades in a spume of blood and bone. His spine must have literally shattered under the impact. He was punched backwards, the rifle spinning from his hands, an expression of shock on his shrew-like face. His companion wasn't any quicker. The second burst stitched him from crotch to chin. He was dead before his body had ceased to twitch.

The echoes of the shooting died and everyone else began to scatter. Including me.

'LOGAN!'

It didn't register at first. He had to call again. 'LOGAN! THIS WAY, YOU STUPID BASTARD!'

I spun round.

The swimmer was beckoning frantically. I stared.

'DON'T JUST STAND THERE, MAN. SHIFT YOUR ARSE!'

Then I became aware of another noise, the sound of a motor approaching fast. I focused in time to see the speedboat coming in like a bat out of hell. It had swooped through the space vacated by the demolished launch and was starting to swing in towards the shore.

'GET A FUCKING MOVE ON!'

So I did.

In sandals, over those rocks, it wasn't exactly easy but I didn't have far to go. The swimmer was sweeping the shore with the muzzle of his gun. Behind me I could hear cries of alarm, both from the fleeing work detail and the guards up on the ramparts. Some bright spark was beginning to shoot back, but we were some distance from the walls and the guards were in a state of shock, and they weren't exactly sharpshooters.

I'd reached the water by this time. I still hadn't a clue who it was who was calling me. Whoever it was must have thought I was demented, because no sooner had I reached him than I stopped and ran back. I heard a muttered oath as I bent over Kasim. He was in an awful mess. I could see the silvery gleam of bone in his chest cavity. Blood was soaking into the pebbles beneath him. His eyes were wide open and staring at me, but they were glazed like marble. He looked like a sick beetle skewered on a pin.

'Serves you bloody well right,' I muttered. I grabbed his wrist and retrieved my watch. Then I really did start to motor.

I hit the water at a stumbling run, fell base over apex, and surfaced spluttering as I was grabbed under the armpits and dragged towards the speedboat. Strong arms bundled me over the side and I lay there winded as the throttles opened and the boat surged forward towards open water.

I heard someone yelling, 'GO! GO!' and I saw another wet-suited rump settle into the helmsman's seat before I fell back and cracked my head on the side gunnel.

Somewhere in the middle of all this activity, I heard a voice which I found vaguely familiar demanding, in strident tones, just what the hell I thought I had been playing at back there.

'W-watch,' I mumbled, coughing. 'The bastard nicked my watch.'

'Jesus!' the voice said. 'I'd have bought you another bloody watch, you daft bugger!'

I started to focus again. A figure was bending over me. The swimmer. By now he had pushed the hood of his wet suit off his forehead and I could determine features. He had a rugged, weatherbeaten face, salt and pepper hair and the beginnings of a dark beard. He had grey eyes, and there was the hint of a smile on his lips.

I peered at him. 'Christ!' I said. 'Harry Donovan? Is that you?'

A grin split his gritty features. His face came alive. 'Hello, Michael. Welcome aboard.'

I stared up at him.

'It friggin' took you long enough,' I said.

6

It might have been yesterday.

Only it wasn't. It was longer ago than that. A lot longer. Before the Gulf War, before the *Stark* and the *Bridgeton*. Before they laid the mines in the Strait of Hormuz. Before all that.

I'd had a call from the Persian. There was another run on.

They used to call it the Venice of the East. God knows why. They both straddle busy waterways. Venice has its canals and Dubai has a meandering tributary known as the Creek, a six-mile stretch of jade-green effluent that bisects the state and winds into the southern end of the Persian Gulf. But that's where the similarity ends.

Dubai is one of the tiny United Arab Emirates. It's also been called the clearing house of the Gulf, which is probably a sight more apt. Not a particularly prepossessing metropolis as far as its dockside is concerned, although it does remain free of the big tankers, which is a blessing. It's too shallow for them so they take on and off-load at the oilfields themselves, some sixty miles from the mainland.

I threaded my way cautiously through the crowds waiting impatiently on the quay for the water taxis to take them over to the opposite bank. There's always a steady stream of traffic from one side to the other. The *abras* plough their way between the dhows like squat water beetles, always full, always busy.

I skirted Sheikh Rashid's palace, the old customs house,

and wound my way through the souk towards the Persian quarter.

It was late afternoon, well past the heat of midday, but still oppressively warm due to the dry winds sweeping in off the desert. Away from the waterfront, the closeness of the bazaar was stifling. A thousand different smells bombarded my senses. As did the noise. Vendors flogging their wares, donkeys complaining about their loads, camels breaking wind, motorcycles clattering like lawn mowers.

The place has changed a lot over the years and not for the better, sad to say. Ironically, the new-found oil wealth has had a lot to do with it. They only discovered the stuff here in the mid-sixties. So, whereas everyone else's regeneration took aeons, Dubai made the quantum leap from feudal womb to the twentieth century in less than two decades. Too much, too soon, quite frankly. It's still suffering from postnatal shock.

I made my way down one of the hip-wide alleyways that formed a maze of passages that would have done justice to a termite's nest. The Persian's office was sited off one of the small courtyards. It's not easy to find. Which was the general idea.

When I arrived, Idrisi was pacing the floor under a creaking fan. Despite his considerable wealth, Idrisi's appearance tends to give the visitor the impression that he's for ever on his beam-ends. A deception enhanced by the fact that he is a dead ringer for Akim Tamiroff, albeit with a tan and a djellaba. His so-called office doesn't do a whole lot to dissuade people from that belief either. A few threadbare astrakhans on the floor, cushions scattered around. At least it was cool, thanks to an ancient yet ingenious device on the roof known as a wind tower. It's the world's earliest form of air conditioning. Breezes are trapped in the tower and funnelled to the rooms below. Life becomes almost bearable at times.

Idrisi stopped pacing. 'Ah, Michael!' He shook my hand and beamed, as he always does. 'How good to see you! Will you take some sherbet?'

It was traditional to precede business with refreshment, so I nodded. Idrisi clapped his hands and a servant appeared with a tray and glasses. Hassan, Idrisi's bodyguard, wasn't in the immediate vicinity but I knew he'd be around somewhere. He was never very far away. I was quite flattered, for it showed the measure of trust that the Persian had in me, but then we'd been doing business together for a couple of years by this time. Our partnership was based on both respect and friendship.

I took a seat on one of the rugs, my back propped against a large cushion. The sherbet was rather too sweet for my taste. I took a couple of sips and set the glass aside. And waited for Idrisi to open the proceedings.

'I have another shipment, Michael,' he said. 'It is to go tonight. Is your boat ready?'

'Raring to go. You'll deliver the stuff to the quay?'

'Yes. And packed as usual. I will see to it.'

'How much this time?'

'One thousand bars.'

I whistled. 'Christ! That much!'

'It is for a valued customer. And there hasn't been a run for several months. The Indians have been remarkably vigilant of late.'

'Okay,' I said. 'I'll get things organized. Will you be there to see us off?'

I knew he liked to check the cargo stowage himself.

'Possibly. I have some other business to take care of. If not, I will send Malik.'

'We'll be waiting.'

I didn't stay long after that. Just enough time for me to

finish my drink. Once agreement had been reached the meetings were never prolonged. And we never discussed fees either. I had never had any complaints. He paid us very well. I suppose you could call it danger money.

Because the cargo we would be carrying was gold.

They imported the stuff into Dubai from Europe quite legally from bullion dealers in the UK and Switzerland. We formed the next link in the chain. We delivered the gold from Dubai to India.

India probably values gold more than any other country on earth. Over there it has an almost holy significance. They even used to sprinkle it on food at one time, before the government banned the practice. The smuggling racket dates back to the forties, when India put a block on legal gold imports because in purchasing the stuff it was delving too deeply into its foreign reserves. But there was still a large demand for it. The way I looked at it, we were actually doing them a favour.

The trade had declined a lot, of course, over the years. Due mainly to the massive increase in the gold price, profits dropped and a lot of the smugglers went out of business. In fact, as far as I was aware, Idrisi was the only trafficker still in the trade, mainly because he dealt in such large amounts. He was overseeing perhaps four trips a year. In the past, though, they'd run perhaps three times that number; until the risks became too great. The standard of the Indian customs patrols had improved and intensified, with the use of better boats and more sophisticated tracking equipment, which, in turn, meant that we had to transport the cargo a lot further south than before. Sometimes as far down as Ratnagir.

The trips normally took twelve days. We used a vessel known as a *boum*. She was powered by three three-hundred-horsepower Rolls-Royce engines removed from a trio of Centurion tanks left behind in Sharjah by the

British. We could outrun just about anything, including Indian customs launches. The usual plan called for us to rendezvous with Indian craft and transfer the goods fifteen miles out from the Indian coast. Sometimes we'd trade the gold for silver. Well, it had always seemed a pity to me to make the return trip empty-handed.

It was unusual for Idrisi to employ Europeans. In the past his crews had been mostly Indians and a couple of Pakistanis, although I did know of another Englishman who'd been in the business – a mercenary by the name of Keel – but he was long gone. He'd made his packet and moved on to pastures new.

Donovan and I had been making the occasional deliveries, on and off, for eighteen months. I suspect that the total value of the gold we had carried in that time ran into many millions of dollars. There had been times when we'd considered hijacking a consignment, but we knew, deep down, that it simply wasn't worth it. Idrisi had more contacts than a hedgehog had fleas. We would never have lived to spend the stuff. A few others had tried over the years. And failed. They'd ended up as shark bait. Not for me, thanks all the same. Besides, as I said, we were handsomely rewarded.

I'd known Donovan for close on three years. I'd been working as a military advisor to the Muscat navy. Donovan had been employed by one of the local sheikhs as a bodyguard and our paths had crossed a few times in the course of both our duties. At the end of my contract I'd decided I quite liked the place and, on Donovan's recommendation, I had been appointed to the sheikh's staff, as a cross between Donovan's right-hand man and training officer to his highness's private army.

A year of that and then we heard about the gold runs. We'd got an introduction to the Persian from a mutual contact and, after running a check on us, Idrisi had

77

offered us a trial run. We'd pulled that off without a hitch and that's how it began.

We had done all right so far, too. So much so that after the next trip we had decided to call it a day. Ironic, as it turned out.

Donovan was asleep when I returned to the boat. He was stretched out on one of the seats in the saloon.

I kicked his foot and his eyes opened. He was immediately alert. 'We in business?'

'One thousand bars. We leave tonight.'

'One thousand!' He sat up. 'Aye, well, that'll be a good one to go out on. Did you tell Idrisi, by the way?'

I shook my head. 'Thought I'd wait until we got back.'

He shrugged. 'Fair enough.' He stood and ran a hand through his hair. 'Better check the old girl over, then.'

He was older than me by about five years, although the odd grey streak in his hair added another five to his appearance. He was forty-three at the time. He was a rugged man, about my height – just under six feet – but of sturdier frame. He had a quiet self-assuredness about him, which gave those meeting him for the first time an easy feeling of wellbeing. Under that imperturbable façade, however, lay an acute capacity for self-preservation. I knew without a shadow of a doubt that, if I was ever in a tight corner, I'd want him on my side.

He had never wholly filled me in on his background, just as I hadn't let him in on all of mine. There are some things best kept concealed from the light of day. Regarding Donovan, and given our chosen professions, I suspected there was every chance we could have been on opposing sides at some time in our past. Mostly to do with the situation in a far-off place called Ulster.

Over the years he'd let slip odd names and places with which I was familiar, and there had been hints of ties broken and allegiances compromised. Once, in a moment of quiet reflection, I had discovered there had been a wife and child, both now dead. I never found out the circumstances. I knew he was good with weapons and explosives and I was also aware that for a long time he never laid down his head to sleep without there being a gun under his pillow. I couldn't ever see him being in awe or afraid of any man, but there was something about his past which was not for general consumption. I honoured his privacy. I knew that if he felt it necessary to tell me he would.

'What time will the stuff be here?' he asked.

'As soon as it's dark.'

He nodded acceptance of the fact. 'Okay, Yanni and I'll give the engines a quick check. They should be okay, seeing as we only had them serviced a month back.'

'Fair enough.'

Yanni was our mechanic-cum-cook and general bottle-washer. He was a local lad, coal-black, proud of his West African roots that could be traced back via a great-grandfather who had arrived in the Gulf as part of a slave caravan back in the eighteen-nineties.

We normally made the run with a crew of five, the other two men being provided by Idrisi as both insurance and protection.

With telepathic instinct Yanni appeared through the forward hatchway, his ebony face split by a cheerful grin. 'Mistah Mike! How are you? We have sailing soon, yes?'

He was wiping his hands on a piece of rag. I knew Donovan wouldn't need to check the engines. Yanni treated them as gently as the girls he boasted of having in every port along the Gulf. He was the best mechanic on the waterfront.

I left them to sort things out between them and wandered back on deck. There was a haze lying over the Creek. Through it the sun hung and shimmered like a round orange kite. The quayside was still full of people. I walked up the plank on to the wharf. I had a few hours to kill before Idrisi brought the gold on board; time enough to sort out the provisioning we would need for the round trip. Food and fuel, that sort of thing.

In the end it wasn't Idrisi who turned up; it was his lieutenant, Malik. Malik was a Baluchi. Back in the early seventies, as part of a mercenary army, he'd fought alongside British officers employed by the ageing Sultan of Oman in his war against Marxist rebels in Dhofar. Frankly, I'd never really taken to the man. He had something of a shifty look to him, which I'd always found rather unsettling. Although, I suppose, given the range of Idrisi's nefarious activities, there wasn't much point in employing choirboys. Donovan and I were proof of that.

It was dark when he turned up. Our boat was moored at the end of the quay, so we were afforded some privacy when we transferred the cargo from Malik's Mercedes.

The gold was in the form of ten-tola bars, each weighing three and three-quarter ounces. They were contained in pockets in specially made waistcoats; fifteen in all. When the gold reached India, the couriers wore the waistcoats to smuggle the stuff to the dispersal points. Which meant that the waistcoats weighed something in the region of twenty pounds apiece. Pretty heavy, and bloody damned valuable too. At current rates we were talking well over a million dollars for the total value of the cargo. This was not chicken feed.

I wasn't that impressed with the hired help. They weren't the men Idrisi usually employed. I asked Malik why that was and he told me that the regulars were away with Idrisi on company business, whatever the heck that meant. So, we had been provided with Yusef and Murad. They were both young, about Yanni's age, but whereas Yanni was black these men were of a more sallow complexion. They didn't smile much either. They looked about as friendly as a recruiting poster for the PLO.

We stowed the cargo in the hold. I supervised the casting-off of the lines. We chugged away from the mooring and headed down the channel. From the stern I could see Malik watching us like a hawk.

It took us six incident-free days to reach the rendezvous point. We were right on schedule. We'd travelled on one engine for most of the way, keeping the remaining two in reserve in case we were jumped on by the Indian coast-guards. It helped, knowing we had hidden reserves of power.

It was late afternoon and dead calm. We were ten miles offshore. Yanni was at the wheel, keeping an eye out for patrol boats and our contact. The rest of us were lifting the waistcoats out of the hola and laying them on the deck in preparation for transferring them to our Indian couriers. We also brought them on deck for another reason. If an Indian customs boat did appear, our instructions were to heave the stuff overboard. This had always seemed a rather drastic solution to me, but it was standard practice. It hadn't happened very often but I'd known other crews who'd admitted dropping as much as a couple of hundred pounds of gold into the sea to avoid getting caught. And it was no use going back to look for it either. The sea-bed roundabouts was very soft and the gold would have sunk under the silt. Added to which the water was pretty murky and the sharks were always hungry.

We'd got all the waistcoats on deck and were sitting around waiting for contact when it all went horribly wrong.

Donovan was smoking a cigarette at the time. He was gazing shoreward, taking it easy, when Yusef sauntered up beside him and stuck a gun in his ear. It was a

Browning automatic and Yusef was holding it as if he knew how to use it.

Donovan said something profound, like, 'Oh, shit,' and turned slowly. 'Michael, I think we have a problem.'

'What?' I said, and found myself looking down the business end of Murad's gun at about the same time. Only his wasn't a pistol. It was an Ingram-10, a mini sub-machine gun, thirty-round mag with a rate of fire that was capable of cutting a man in half; or so Hollywood would have us believe. Right there and then I was quite prepared to take the dream factory's word for it. They must have brought the guns aboard in the holdalls they had been carrying.

'You will sit,' Yusef said, and gestured for us to put our backs against the gunnel.

He could afford to be polite, seeing as he was the one holding the ordnance. We did what he wanted, though. It would have been foolish not to.

While he was keeping us covered, Murad was walking casually towards the wheelhouse. I hoped to God that Yanni wasn't about to do something stupid.

Unfortunately, Yanni's telepathy didn't extend that far.

Murad was halfway there when Yanni stepped out on to the deck. As he left the wheel he must have seen Murad's gun, for he immediately tried to duck back. We kept a pistol in a compartment under the chart table. He must have been trying for that. Murad shot Yanni in the chest. It was a brief, vicious burst of fire, perhaps a second's duration. The gun's reputation was fully justi-fied. The bullets shredded Yanni's chest like grapeshot. His corpse was punched back along the deck like a discarded rag doll. As Murad fired, Yusef's gun hand wavered slightly and I felt Donovan tense.

'No!' Yusef spat, swinging the pistol into line.

The Irishman relaxed.

It was obvious Yanni was dead. I wondered how long Donovan and I had left.

'I take it,' I said, 'that you aren't working for Idrisi.'

'No chance,' Donovan cut in. 'They're working for Malik. Isn't that right, fellas? Methinks Idrisi's boy is pulling a sly one.'

'You're out of your tiny minds,' I exclaimed. 'How far d'you think you're going to get? As soon as Idrisi finds out, your lives won't be worth a fart.'

Yusef laughed. 'We do not intend for him to find out that it was us.'

'Oh, oh.' Donovan grimaced. 'Something tells me I'm not going to like the next bit.'

Murad had restarted the engine. The boat was swinging round.

'We are going a few miles further south, to Kuguri,' Yusef explained. 'We are to be met by our own contacts. We will transfer ourselves and the gold to another vessel. When the boat that you were to have met reaches the rendezvous point it will wait for a while. That will give us a little more time. Eventually this boat will be found, along with your crewman's body, but the gold and you will have disappeared. It will be assumed that you have taken the cargo for yourselves.'

'You've got admit,' Donovan said, with the merest hint of admiration, 'it's pretty bloody devious.'

I found I was developing cramp in my right leg. I eased myself cautiously into another position. Yusef followed the movement with the Browning.

My mind was racing. Were they going to kill us and dump our bodies before or after they transferred the gold? Did it really matter? Well, yes, actually. The longer they waited, I realized, the more chance we had of finding some way to get ourselves out of the mess.

Which made me either a born optimist or some kind of idiot.

Up until now, Donovan had remained remarkably calm. Even now, he was reaching slowly for another cigarette. He had flicked the butt of the first one over the side. He lit up and expelled smoke.

We had travelled about twenty miles or so when the boat shuddered suddenly as Murad cut the engine. We had evidently arrived at the point where the cargo was going to be transferred. Donovan and I didn't have much time left. The boat that was to collect the gold, along with Murad and Yusef, could arrive at any moment.

Beside me, Donovan shifted his weight, drawing his leg up in front of him. He was sitting on my right, his right arm resting casually over his right knee, his left hand holding the half-smoked cigarette.

Murad yelled and pointed out towards the land. Coming in fast was a launch. It appeared our time was up. Then I did a double take.

'Wrong boat, Yusef,' I said.

The oncoming vessel had altered course slightly. The high prow, bridge and electrical equipment were unmistakable. Indian customs.

The cavalry. Sort of.

Yusef swung around quickly, his jaw dropping in shock. He screamed a warning at his partner.

Donovan attacked.

I didn't think anyone could move that fast. He seemed to flow off the deck, his right hand snaking down to the side of his right boot like a gunslinger going for his peacemaker. Instead of a six-shooter, however, the Irishman came up holding a knife. The blade was scything fast towards Yusef's belly. His left hand was going for Yusef's gun hand. Yusef's mouth opened in a silent scream as the knife took him under the ribcage. I actually heard the

84

sickening thump as Donovan's fist followed through with the blow. Such was the force of the attack that Yusef dropped his gun. I was reaching for it as Murad sprang forward from the wheel.

My fingers curled round the Browning's grip, and as Donovan and I flung ourselves towards the deck, I fired. The bullet missed Murad by a mile and buried itself in the mast. Murad fired, the Ingram bucking in his hands as it spewed out bullets. I felt exquisite pain in my left bicep as the slug ploughed into me. I jerked and dropped the Browning, and, out of the corner of my eye, saw Donovan scramble for it as Murad fired again. The ratchet sound of the Ingram hammered into my senses.

Through a mist of pain I saw Murad's face disintegrate and the back of his head explode as Donovan's bullet found its mark. As Murad died, I went over backwards. My last recollection was of Donovan's body tumbling awkwardly over the side of the boat, then the rear of my skull bounced on the deck with a resounding crack that brought instant, blissful oblivion.

I had no idea how long I was out for. I came to with the inside of my mouth as dry as a sand dune and my head pounding in time to the heavy diesels throbbing below decks. My eyes focused slowly on the bearded face of an Indian customs officer, a stern-looking Sikh.

I lifted my head from the narrow bunk and groaned as my brain fell out and rolled along the floor. At least, that's what it felt like. Through hastily narrowed eyes I saw that my arm had been roughly bandaged. It, too, was throbbing painfully. The bullet was still in there.

The Sikh peered into my eyes. 'You do not look very well at all,' he remarked with devastating accuracy. Which didn't reassure me a whole lot either.

'You should see the other guy,' I said. Hardly original

and not a particularly wise utterance under the circumstances.

'I have,' he replied seriously. 'The others are dead.'

I creaked my eyes open a bit wider. 'Donovan as well?'

'I am sorry?' he asked, puzzled.

I blinked. 'Donovan. The other European.'

He shook his head. 'I do not understand. There was no other European. No Donovan, as you call him.'

I tried to sit up again. And failed.

The Sikh said, 'I think you had better rest. There are many questions you will have to answer.'

I reached up and grabbed his arm. 'Did you search the area?'

He frowned. 'For what?'

'For Donovan, for Chris'sakes!'

He unhooked my hand and said woodenly, 'There was no other man.'

'Dammit . . . !'

'Apart from yourself,' he interrupted, 'we found the bodies of three men. Two had been shot, the third died from a knife wound. Also on board we found a number of waistcoats, the contents of which we are only too familiar with. Gold-smuggling is a serious offence, my young friend.'

So was murder, I thought drowsily, and wondered why he hadn't said so.

'How did you know about the shipment?' I asked. At least I think that's what I said. I was pretty close to passing out by then and to my own ears the question had come out more than a trifle garbled.

'We have our sources of information,' he replied mysteriously.

If he volunteered anything else I didn't catch it. I went under for the second time. When I opened my eyes again, my chaperon had disappeared. I was obviously still on

86

board the customs launch; but with a bullet in the arm and a king-sized hangover, I wasn't about to try and jump ship. All I could do was lie there and ponder on my future.

Donovan was dead, that much was certain. I'd seen him hit, I'd seen him go over the side into the sea. I tried rerunning the events in my mind but that didn't work too well. I got as far as the part where Murad shot me and I saw his face shatter again as the bullet entered his cheek, but I had no lasting image of Donovan at all. I remembered all the shark stories and thought about the Irishman's corpse leaking blood, drawing the predators in, the dark fins circling, the flash of grey-white belly as the scavengers twisted to attack and tear and wrench flesh from bone. I hoped to God that he hadn't been conscious for long. I tried to erase the terrible vision from my mind but it was impossible. The more I tried to pin down my random thoughts into some kind of sane and credible image the more confused I became. And my head was still pounding like a jack hammer. I was also feeling pretty sick. Relief came only when they gave me another shot of morphine. I welcomed the next bout of darkness with open arms.

The customs launch towed our boat to Bombay, where I was granted the privilege of having a police escort take me ashore. They had an ambulance waiting. Three shrouded bundles accompanied me. The bodes of Yanni, Murad and Yusef.

I was kept under observation for a couple of days, both police and medical. In that time statements were taken, with the result that two weeks later I was brought to trial.

Two things I had already decided. I was not going to compromise Idrisi. With Donovan gone I was on my own.

At least, the court appointed a lawyer to defend me. And I'll give Mr Mukerjee his due; he tried his best. I think he was a bit put out when I pleaded guilty. To gold-trafficking, that is. As far as the three dead bodies were concerned, I pleaded something else entirely.

Self-defence.

I told the court that Yanni and I had been partners. We had been on a run and had taken Yusef and Murad on board after we'd chanced upon their own vessel in distress off the Gulf of Kutch. When Yusef and Murad discovered the identity of our cargo they had attempted to seize it for themselves. They had murdered Yanni and would have killed me had I not acted to defend myself. I used my own injuries to support my story. Well, it was close enough to the truth, and there certainly wasn't anyone around who was going to contradict me. I didn't even mention Donovan. Funnily enough, neither did the Sikh customs officer when he gave evidence. I think he was of the opinion that I had been delirious after they'd picked me up. Or maybe I was correct in my surmise that my words had been garbled. Whichever it was, Donovan was dead, he could rest in peace.

The verdict? I got three years. I suppose they were quite lenient, really.

In the end I served a little over twenty-three months. I never did find out why they had reduced my sentence. Maybe it was because I had been a model prisoner. I don't know. All I do know is that two years after they brought me ashore with a bullet in my arm, I was sitting on the dock of the bay trying to hitch a berth back to the Gulf, several pounds lighter and a lot wiser.

I never got to see the Persian and explain. By the time I got back to Dubai, Idrisi was dead. The story was that he had been killed by a Khomeini death squad for allegedly smuggling supporters of the old Shah out of Iran.

I didn't hang around. I cleaned out my safety deposit

box at the British Bank of the Middle East and bought a one-way ticket to Athens. It took me a month to find the right kind of boat. A month after that the *Kallisti* and I were in business as a one-man charter operation.

Donovan was nothing more than a memory.

7

It was a helter-skelter, bone-shaking ride.

I rubbed the bruise on the back of my head and winced as the boat bounced across a wave and came down hard. We were travelling at some velocity. Samos was looming close, the Turkish coast was falling behind. The man in the driving seat had his eyes glued to the sea in front of us. Intent on his task, he hadn't acknowledged my existence so far. Donovan was still crouching over me. He looked quite paternal. And older than I would have expected. Maybe it was the beard.

By this time we had already passed over into Greek territorial waters. My hurried departure had undoubtedly caught the Turks on the hop. There had been no opportunity for them to mobilize another patrol boat in the time it had taken us to cross the narrow gulf. Nevertheless, somewhere, wires would be humming. You don't just invade Turkish territory, take out a patrol launch and a brace of prison personnel, and engineer the escape of one major felon, and expect to get away with it.

A ticklish situation, I would have thought, given that relations between Greece and Turkey were still somewhat strained. The memory of Cyprus still lingered. I fancied that the Turks would definitely be asking for my extradition, though. They'd have to go through the motions, at least. To save face, if nothing else. Frankly, I wasn't entirely optimistic about the Greeks viewing Donovan's act of international piracy with much sympathy. If anything, I suspected they'd be rather embarrassed by the whole incident. They might even want to hush it up.

Which could entail handing me back, unless Donovan had made onward travel arrangements for me, that is.

'You okay?' Donovan had to shout over the roar of the inboard.

I managed to sit up. It wasn't easy with the boat bounding along like a gazelle. I nodded weakly, grabbed hold of the side gunnel and hung on, closing my eyes against the inrush of spray.

Donovan grimaced. 'You look like shit!'

I managed to give him a ho-ho-very-droll kind of grimace. He responded by laying a gentle hand on my shoulder.

He laughed suddenly. 'By God!' he cried. 'It's good to see you, Michael!'

I looked up at him. 'I'm glad to see you too,' I murmured, adding, half to myself, 'I think.'

I was aware then that we were slowing. The crossing had been remarkably swift. The boat was gradually settling back into the water.

'Right, we're here,' Donovan observed. 'All ashore who're going ashore. Lively now.' He sounded as if he was really enjoying himself, as if he'd just completed a quick trip around the harbour in the *Saucy Sue*. So far, his companion still hadn't said a word.

We were coasting towards a point on Samos's north coast, a mile or two west of the main town, I guessed. It was a beach of sorts. Not very attractive. Not that I cared where we'd ended up. Any damned where would have done. There weren't many people around either. It was too hot for the tourists and the locals didn't need to sunbathe anyway.

We grounded and Donovan helped me over the side. As I climbed out on to the sand I got my first good look at his accomplice.

91

Donovan said, 'I suppose I'd better introduce you. Michael Logan, meet Martin Ritter.'

He was younger than Donovan, clean-cut, with short fair hair. Good-looking, I suppose, in a Germanic, square-jawed sort of way. He favoured me with cool, slightly quizzical look.

I held out my hand. 'Thanks,' I said, which seemed pretty bloody inadequate under the circumstances.

His grip was firm, the nod almost curt in its acknowledgement. Not particularly illuminating.

Donovan interrupted the touching moment. 'Come on, people. Let's move.' He led the way across the sand. A Fiat was parked under the trees. Donovan unlocked the boot and the two of them began to slip off their wet suits. Donovan still looked fit. He was close to fifty, but there wasn't an ounce of fat on him. It was all muscle. Ritter had an athlete's frame; slim but powerful. They had taken their clothes from another holdall, jeans and tee shirts.

Donovan threw me a bag. Inside were a pair of trousers and a short-sleeved cotton shirt. I changed into them and bundled my soiled effects into the bag. I looked cleaner although I didn't feel it.

'Don't worry,' Donovan assured me. 'We'll soon have you spruced up. It's just that we don't want you getting on the plane looking as if you've just spent a couple of months on Devil's Island.'

'A bit difficult,' I said, 'seeing as I just have.' I rubbed a hand through the stubble on my chin. Then I thought, plane?

'Well, you know what I mean,' he said.

'What now?' I asked, as we finished dressing.

'Athens first,' Donovan said, 'to overnight. It'll give us a chance to relax. We fly to Santorini tomorrow morning.' He threw his wet suit into the boot and slammed the lid.

I stared at him. 'Hold it,' I said. 'Santorini? You want to tell me what this is all about?'

Donovan looked at his watch. 'Later. We've got a flight to catch.'

Ritter sat in the back, Donovan took the wheel. The airport was on the south side of the island, west of the old capital of Pythagorio. A thousand questions were teeming around inside my mind. Presumably, somewhere in the not too distant future, I might even get to ask some of them. For the time being, though, all I could do was sit back and enjoy the ride. I closed my eyes again and tried to relax.

Donovan already had the tickets. We made the flight with thirty minutes to spare. It seemed to me that my rescue and subsequent flight to the mainland had been timed right down to the last second. I was impressed.

We were seven thousand feet above the Aegean, with Ritter a couple of rows behind, when I said, 'Now, would you care to elaborate just a little bit?'

Donovan chuckled and patted my knee. 'You always were an impatient bugger, Michael.'

'Come on, Harry,' I said. 'Stop pissing round. Talk to me. How did you know where I was?'

He grinned again. 'You made the headlines, old son.'

Yes, I thought. And I'm about to make them again. Then I asked him about the patrol launch. Its demise had been swift and sudden and uncompromising.

'Magnetic mine. Remote-controlled. I fixed it to the hull on my way in. Martin detonated it from the speedboat.'

I recalled the small rectangular object that Donovan had thrown over the side of the launch during our rapid transit of the gulf. Obviously a transmitter of some sort. He'd dumped the H & K into the sea at the same time. One way to remove the evidence.

'And how did you know I'd be in the open?'

'Come again?'

'How did you know I'd pulled work detail?'

'Jesus!' Donovan snorted, as if I was some slow student asking an inane question of a tutor. 'Bribery and corruption, of course! What else? You didn't seriously think we were going to spend the entire term of your sentence tooling up and down the bloody beach in case you just happened to wander along for a swim, did you? Come on, Logan!'

'Well,' I said, 'I did wonder.'

He leaned close and said, 'It's a job, Michael. I need you.'

I stared at him.

'First things first, though, old son.' His face mirrored concern. 'About the bust. You want to tell me about it?'

I turned away. I had the window seat. Below us lay a long thin island, Ikaria, floating lazily in a turquoise sea.

I said, 'I was set up.'

'Christ!' he hissed vehemently. 'You think I don't know that! Come on, Logan. Talk to me!'

I took a deep breath. 'A few months ago I was hired to go in and pick up a cargo from the mainland. A small bay up on the Asim Korfezi. A straightforward job. In and out. Nothing to it.'

'Hmn,' he grunted knowingly. 'They always say that. What did you think it was?'

I shrugged. 'Antiques.'

'Ah ha,' Donovan murmured.

'All right, I know. It's not exactly legal. But a fellow has to make a living.'

'I never said a word.' Donovan held up his hands. 'Besides, who am I to throw stones?'

I looked at him to see if he was being facetious. To my surprise it didn't look as though he was.

'Anyway,' I said, 'it went wrong. I was jumped by a squad of the local police and the Gumruk.'

'Gumruk?'

'Turkish customs. They decided to open up the boxes.'

'And no antiques?'

'Correct. More like twenty pounds of prime horse.'

'Ouch!' Donovan winced.

'Quite. By the looks on their faces, you'd have thought it was Christmas. They threw the book at me. Twenty years in the slammer.'

'Yeah,' Donovan said. 'The press said you'd copped a fair stretch. I take it you know who set you up?'

I sighed. 'Oh, yes. I know, all right.'

He frowned. 'What are you going to do about it?'

'Deal with him,' I said.

'Don't do anything rash, old son. I didn't get you out of the Château d'If just so's you could get busted again.'

'*Moi?*' I said, clasping my chest in innocence.

'Don't get smart, Logan. This is Donovan, remember?'

I took a deep breath, nodded slowly and let it out.

We lapsed into silence then, occupied with our own thoughts. Mine were concerned mostly with the shock of Donovan's reappearance, on top of which I was quite exhausted. In fact, I closed my eyes for what I thought would be only a few seconds and opened them again to discover that we were coming in to land. I vacated my seat with some regret. Luckily we didn't have any baggage. The scuba gear had been hired, along with the car and the launch, and we'd dumped my prison gear into a wayside drainage channel on Samos. So we went through the arrivals formalities in fifteen minutes. In twenty-five we were in a taxi heading for the hotel.

The Caravel, no less. Up near the Hilton. I wondered who was footing the bill. In fact, there were a lot more questions I had to ask Donovan. Like who the heck was Martin Ritter, for instance. Sooner or later, I supposed, someone might decide to let me in on the big picture and I'd find out.

I don't think I've ever stayed so long under a shower, before or since. I must have spent a good thirty minutes beneath the jet, eyes closed, letting the water sluice away the grime and sweat and memories of the prison from my pores. At one point there was so much steam around me the room looked like the inside of a sauna. I followed the hot shower with a cold one and finally emerged from the cubicle like Lazarus arisen from the grave.

We had arrived too late for me to withdraw funds from my bank so I'd had to rely further on Donovan's charity. He'd provided me with toiletries as well as another clean shirt, underwear and a pair of shoes. All the right size, too. After three months encased in prison grime I was like a kid in a toyshop.

Even though I still hadn't a clue as to what was going on.

I was shaving. There was a knock on the door. I froze, the razor buzzing impotently in my hand.

Another knock. 'Michael? You okay?'

Donovan.

I breathed a sigh of relief, switched off the razor and padded barefoot to let him in.

'You look better,' he said, giving me a critical once-over.

'I feel it.'

'Good. Get some togs on. We'll go and grab a beer. We've got a fair bit to catch up on.'

He could say that again.

There was a piano bar in the hotel. We ended up there; a plate of mezes in front of us, a couple of fresh cold

Amstels at our elbow. The first ones hadn't touched the sides.

We were on our own. Apparently Ritter had an errand to run. I thought it more likely that Donovan wanted a quiet word.

I opened the batting.

'I thought you were dead, Harry,' I said.

'Funny,' Donovan replied, 'I thought the same about you. Should have bloody known better, though.'

'So, what did happen?'

'Christ!' Donovan muttered, shaking his head disbelievingly. 'D'you know how long ago that was?'

'To the day,' I said. 'I've still got the scars to remind me.' I had, too: a thin weal of fissured tissue on my left arm above the elbow, white now against my skin.

'How much do you recall?'

'Being shot, mostly,' I said. 'Then seeing that bastard Murad lose his face and you disappearing over the side. I came to on the patrol launch. I thought you'd been turned into shark bait.'

'I damned nearly was,' he admitted. 'You know, that lad was bloody fast. If I hadn't been moving myself he'd have finished me. Fact is, he almost did.' He pushed back the hair on his forehead and I stared at the thin ribbon of puckered flesh along his hairline. 'I went over the side all right, but I managed to grab one of the stern lines on the way down. When they towed the *boum* ashore, I wrapped the line around myself and hung on. I let go before they docked and got myself ashore. I've never been so banjaxed in all my life. And I was bleeding like a stuck pig.'

'Then what?'

'I found a local quack, who fixed me up, and lay low for a few days. Then I left town. It's a decision I've regretted ever since: leaving you to take the fall. If I'd known you were still alive, I . . .' His voice trailed off.

97

'Harry,' I said consolingly, 'there was bugger all else you could have done.'

He looked at me. There was a kind of sadness in his eyes. 'That's no excuse, Mike,' he said softly.

I took a long swallow at my beer. 'So, where'd you end up?'

'Dubai,' he said, still sounding subdued. 'I went back. There were a couple of things I'd decided to take care of. To make amends, you might say.'

I had a vague and uneasy premonition.

'I went to see Idrisi. Told him what had happened. I didn't want him to think we'd ripped him off. He was pretty damned good about it, to tell the truth, despite the loss of the shipment. I reckon he'd had his own suspicions about Malik for a while.'

'Jesus,' I said, 'it was a damned expensive way of proving it!'

Donovan shrugged philosophically.

'What was the other thing you had to clear up?'

'Malik.'

A cold feeling ran down my back. 'And did you?'

'Absolutely,' he murmured. 'Without the shadow of a doubt.'

The words carried a chilling ring, especially when he didn't elaborate. I decided it would be wiser not to press him about it. Maybe later.

'Then what?'

'Oh, I hung around for a while. Did a couple of odd jobs for Idrisi, then headed east.'

'East?'

'I'd put out a few feelers to some of my old contacts. A couple of jobs came up in Thailand. Personal protection stuff. Nothing very exciting.'

'You say.'

'Aye, well, some of the relief agencies were having a

98

spot of bother with one of the local warlords. Nothing too energetic. I was just sort of keeping my hand in. I spent quite a bit of time in that neck of the woods. Burma, Malaya, Hong Kong.'

'So, where's home now?'

'Spain. I invested in a patch of land on the coast. Near Puerto Banus; a couple of acres. I also have company there as well. A lady called Rosa. She keeps me sane.' At the mention of the woman's name, he smiled, his face reflecting fond memories.

I said, 'You know Idrisi got killed, don't you?'

'Yes, I heard.' Suddenly serious again, Donovan put his head on one side and squinted at me. 'You know he tried to buy you out of the nick?'

'He what?' My jaw fell open. Christ, I thought. But it sure could explain why I did not have to serve the full term. I relayed that possibility to Donovan. 'You think he might have crossed a few palms?'

'That's what I heard. I found out about it a long time later, mind you. After you'd been released.'

'I'll be damned.' I sank wearily back in my seat. All this was becoming too much to take in at once. My brain was reeling.

'All right,' I said eventually. 'So what's it all about?'

Donovan didn't reply immediately. He took another long pull at his drink. Then he said, 'We've been offered a contract, old son.'

'A contract?'

'A recovery job. Salvage work, if you like.'

'And for this you needed to break me out of jail?'

'That was part of the package. I wanted someone who knows these waters. Plus the job'll likely entail some diving, so I also wanted someone who's experienced in scuba work. You fitted the bill, Logan.'

'Well, you went through a deal of trouble to get me,' I

said. 'I think I'm flattered. But there must be other divers around, surely?'

'I didn't want other divers, Logan. I wanted you. Dammit, you're making this bloody difficult, you bastard.'

I looked at him.

He fidgeted uncomfortably, cupped his hands around the stem of his beer glass and stared into its tawny depths. 'Hell, the fact is, I felt I owed you.'

'Harry . . .' I began.

'Hey, give me a break, Logan. A man's got a right to suffer a little, y'know.'

I allowed him a moment of self-mortification, then said, 'So what about Ritter? Doesn't he dive?'

'He does but he's not in your class. In any case, I told our employer that unless I could have you, the contract was off.'

'And I'll bet that thrilled the pants off him. How did he react when he found out I'd been put away for drug-peddling'

'He knew you weren't involved in drugs, for God's sake!' Donovan spat back explosively.

'How could he be sure?'

'Because I bloody well told him so!'

There was a lengthy pause while I wondered what sort of job it was where the man pulling the purse strings evidently thought nothing of springing someone from jail in order for the contract to be carried out.

As if he could read my mind, Donovan said, 'The job's a bit delicate, Mike. He wants people he can trust and who trust each other.'

Now I was really intrigued. 'Okay, so who is this mysterious Magwitch?'

'You'll find out tomorrow,' he replied tantalizingly.

'Jesus, Harry!' I couldn't help my exasperation showing through. Then I had a sharp uncomfortable thought. 'This isn't illegal, is it?' I asked him suspiciously. 'Don't tell me I've swapped one prison cell for the likelihood of another?'

'Christ, no way. On my life, Michael. Everything is strictly above board. Believe me.'

I sat back and played with my glass. I wasn't any closer to obtaining answers. In fact, the whole enterprise seemed to be getting more complicated by the minute. I tried a different tack. 'Okay, who's Ritter?'

'Ritter's the fellow who helped me get you over here.'

'Come on, Harry! I didn't mean, Who's Ritter? I meant, Who the hell is Ritter? Where'd you find him?'

'I didn't. He was already on the payroll. A sort of general factotum, you might say.'

'German?'

'Aye, ex-Bundeswehr. A bit Aryan for my taste but a good bloke to have on your side. As you found out.'

'And that's it. That's all of us?'

'As near as dammit. Apart from the crew.'

'Crew? What crew?'

'The crew of the boat. Christ, Logan. I wish you'd keep up. I'll be asking questions later.'

'At the risk of appearing dim, Harry. What bloody boat?'

'The one that's going to meet us at Santorini tomorrow morning.'

'With the boss man on board?'

'Now you're cooking!'

'Ah,' I said wearily. 'I think I've got it. Just.' I looked at my watch then. As I did so a vision of Kasim, punctured and dying, floated in front of my eyes. I blinked and it was gone. I stood up.

Donovan's jaw sagged. 'Where are you going?'

'Out,' I said. 'There's somebody I have to see.'

'Who, for Chris'sakes?'

101

'It's personal,' I said. 'Unfinished business.'

He put a restraining hand on my arm. 'Michael?'

I finished my beer. 'I'll be gone a few hours.'

I could sense his brain working. He looked at me shrewdly, understanding. 'You want any backup?'

I shook my head. 'Not this time, Harry. But I could do with a sub until I can get back into my bank account.'

He mumbled something that I didn't catch and handed me a bundle of notes.

'Thanks, Harry. Give my apologies to Herr Ritter if he arrives.' I pushed my chair back and told him not to wait up.

8

It's a well-known fact that the appalling standard of Greek driving deteriorates with the light. Courtesy is non-existent, as is any form of allegiance to a highway code. But at least people stay on the correct side of the road. Well, usually.

It took about forty nerve-racking minutes in a dilapidated taxi to reach the harbour. It was a journey beset by a feeling of chronic claustrophobia on my part. I generally try to avoid cities at all costs. After the freedom I was used to on the *Kallisti*, my nerves begin to fray after about ten minutes on land.

Only the deaf find peace here. The noise really is indescribable. Day or night, it's a cacophony that thunders relentlessly along every avenue and across every square in search of an outlet that it never finds. Take the chorus of car horns, the clatter of exhausts, the squeal of brakes and the hoarse blare of motorcycle klaxons; mix this with the aroma of oily food perforating through the open doorways of a thousand tavernas and the pungent odours sifting through six miles of suburbia from the Piraeus, and you have Athens on a plate. It's a potent and deadly mixture, because the city is dying. Murder by pollution. Some would say suicide.

Zea marina isn't part of the Piraeus as such. It's a separate harbour around the coast to the south. The port isn't as industrialized, although it gets just as noisy and crowded, and a lot of yachts use the marina as a base during the winter months. There are the usual bars and open-air restaurants ranged along the waterfront, so it's a popular spot with the tourists; a fact occasionally reflected in the prices. A lot of the locals hang out there as well, however. I was looking for one of them.

There are some people who refer to Stavros as a pirate and there are those who consider him to be an entrepreneur. To me he's a combination of the two. He's the Greek equivalent to Henry Morgan. Morgan ended up as governor of Jamaica. Stavros, as far as I know, has never hankered after political office. It would undoubtedly mean a substantial drop in salary.

Some of his income comes from the half-dozen or so bars he owns on the quay, the rest from sundry investments. Not all of them strictly legal, admittedly, but he keeps people in employment and in this day and age that's no bad thing. The Greeks don't have a Mafia as such, but if they did, Stavros would probably be running it.

Tracking him down was relatively easy. He was holding court at his usual table in the Bacchus. It's a popular watering hole, quite small inside, but there's a covered terrace at the rear which overlooks the marina. One alcove is set a bit apart from the rest of the tables and it's from here that Stavros surveys his domain and grants audiences.

By the time I arrived the place was filling up. Non-Greek, for the most part. The locals tended to eat a lot later. Most of the diners looked like extras in a Martini advert: all-white cheesecloth shirts and baggy Armani trousers, the easier to show off their newly acquired tans. The wine was flowing well and there was a lot of laughter. Muted bouzouki music wafted from hidden speakers. There were a lot of Germans. Ritter would have been right at home. It was all a bit tourist-oriented for my taste, but Stavros is, if nothing else, a canny businessman. And business, it appeared, was booming.

Stavros had his back to the wall so that he could keep

an eye on all the toing and froing. He was eating. Rocco, his minder, was seated on his right. It was Rocco who spotted me first. I saw him stare then nudge his boss and nod in my direction.

Stavros is the only Greek I know who actually looks like Anthony Quinn. I'm not sure if he would regard that as a compliment or not. It would undoubtedly appeal to his sense of humour.

To my acute embarrassment, he leapt to his feet as I reached him, his plate of fresh *garides pilafi* temporarily forsaken, and smothered me in a bear hug. Rocco looked on stoically. He'd long got used to his boss's excessive ebullience. Stavros seems to greet every acquaintance or potential business partner as a long-lost member of his immediate family, a habit that must have given poor Rocco more than a few sleepless nights over the years.

I felt my ribs begin to buckle. I could have sworn there were tears in his eyes. To be honest, I have no idea how old he is. Sixtyish or thereabouts. He could easily have been older. One thing was sure, though. He was as tough as old boots.

He was a Cretan by birth and had come of age during the war, when his mother, father and both sets of grandparents were shot, along with all the other adult members of his village, by the German occupying forces in a brutal reprisal against the activities of the local resistance group. This action, far from dissuading Stavros from involving himself in the struggle to liberate his homeland, had the opposite effect. For no sooner had the echoes of the firing squad died away than he'd travelled alone to join the partisans in their enclave deep in the White Mountains. His hatred for the Germans had proved so acute and, in practical terms, so unequivocal, that a price had been placed on his head by the district commandant. Stavros had reacted to that particular threat with his accustomed aplomb. He'd placed a bomb under the commandant's bed. Stavros survived the occupation. The district commandant, on the other hand, did not.

After the war he'd taken to black marketeering as a duck takes to water. He'd been in charge of more fiddles than the conductor of the Royal Philharmonic. Cigarettes, petrol, booze, motor vehicles, ordnance. Name anything and he'd find you a buyer or a seller, never forgetting to subtract his percentage, of course. He'd started to invest in legitimate businesses in the fifties, consolidating assets here and there with a devotion that would have done justice to one of the monks on Mount Athos. If you didn't know otherwise, you'd have said that Midas was his middle name. Despite his undoubted wealth, however, he still managed to dress like an out-of-work fig picker.

Stavros and I go back to the first few months after I arrived in Greece, when I'd been on the lookout for charter work. As a newcomer to the area, I experienced more than a few problems getting any sort of business established. Officially, the Greeks didn't allow foreign yachts to charter out of Greek ports, but I knew it was only a matter of meeting the right people at the right time. So far, though, I hadn't met them and times were lean. Most of my money had gone on the purchase of the boat and the wolves were beginning to gather around my door. The local boys hadn't been hassling me exactly, but they hadn't been making it too easy for me either.

I'd been at a pretty low ebb at the time and seriously considering cashing in my chips and heading back to the Gulf, despite the unhappy memories. I'd begun to drink a bit, too, which hadn't helped matters. Looking back, I've often thought it funny how circumstances can be dictated by fate. Or should it be the other way round?

The date my fortunes changed doesn't spring immediately to mind, neither does the name of the bar, come to think of it. It was somewhere on the waterfront. The fact that I'd likely been in something of an alcoholic haze probably has much to do with my state of amnesia. I'd been feeling pretty sorry for myself; I do remember that.

I'd been in the bar for a couple of hours, fermenting away at one of the corner tables. Yet another week had drifted by and still no work, and I was growing maudlin. I'd thought that drink would help. I'd been wrong.

Over the centuries Greece has had more than its fair share of invaders. Depending on how far back in time you want to go, the roll would include Persians, Romans, Goths, Sicilians, Turks, Russians and Germans. Yet it's a sobering thought that none of these marauding armies had the ability to instil quite the same amount of fear and apprehension as did your average British football supporter.

Panathanaikos, the Greek champions, had been playing host to an English first division side during one of the early rounds of the European Cup. This was before FIFA had got their act together and banned English clubs from travelling abroad. I don't recall which English team it had been. It didn't really matter. What did matter, unfortunately, was that the visiting side had brought some of their supporters with them.

I knew they were British as soon as I clapped eyes on the four of them. Short haircuts, Union Jack tee shirts, Doc Martens boots. As if that wasn't sufficient, they had club scarves tied around their waists, the frayed ends hanging like sashes at their hips. Maybe they all thought they looked like Errol Flynn in *Captain Blood*. Even in my self-induced semi-trance, I thought they looked like potential trouble-makers. I wasn't wrong.

There weren't that many people in the bar, about half a dozen locals plus me. The place was a bit off the beaten track and I guessed the newcomers had stumbled on to the place by accident rather than design. Knowing the district, I reckoned they'd probably been on the lookout for a cheap rutting session with some of the local whores. Who very likely hadn't wanted to know. I suspected that most of the girls had boarded up their shutters with the alacrity of the townsfolk in a western movie when the cattle drive was over and the cowboys were heading their way. I could certainly tell that this wild bunch had had few tipples already, although they were quiet enough when they first came in.

Two rounds later, though, they were becoming rowdy and bothersome and something of an embarrassment. Some of the regular patrons had left. Those who remained were attempting to ignore them. There was a backgammon game going on at one of the tables and I could see that the four old boys who were playing were starting to throw the visitors a few baleful looks.

The patron was also casting anxious eyes their way, caught in the dilemma of whether to continue serving them or refuse their next order. Me? I'd decided I was going to leave them to it.

'Oi, Zorba!' The attempt at wit caused the four of them to dissolve into alcoholic paroxysms of mirth. 'Let's have another Fix!' More laughter.

Fix isn't an injection with a blunt needle. It's a brand of local brew. I'd lost count of the number of times I'd heard the same weak joke.

The barman served them warily. I admired his fortitude.

He finally lost his patience when they got up to dance. They'd no doubt seen it in the movies and thought it looked easy. They call it the hassapiko, the butcher's dance. A finger-snapping, slow-stepping, graceful set of intricate moves when performed by Greeks who understand exactly the emotion that the music conveys. As undertaken by a quartet of morons all worse the wear for drink, it was an unmitigated disaster. When they lurched drunkenly into the backgammon session, it was the last straw. The barman moved in close to remonstrate and one of the old men showed his displeasure by trying to push them away. That was the only excuse required. The old fellow's chair got taken from beneath him and he went over backwards.

By then I'd had my fill as well.

I sighed, and heard somebody say, 'All right, lads. That's enough.' And I realized it had been me. By this time I was on my feet.

They didn't hear me at first. I had to repeat myself.

One of the louts turned then. 'Piss off, you,' he said. His voice was slurred.

I said, 'You four are only visiting. I live here. You're becoming a nuisance. We'd all prefer it if you left quietly.'

I could see out of the corner of my eye that the locals had fallen silent and were watching my attempt at diplomacy.

His mate swung around, 'Who the fuck's this?'

'Some pissing drunk,' another one replied, and scythed an arm at my head.

I didn't hesitate. I went for him. Hard.

Some things you don't forget, they just come naturally. I'd gone in close and used my elbow. I felt and heard the crunch of bone, followed by a thin wail as he put his hands up to stem the flow of blood from his nose and counter the pain from his shattered cartilage.

By then I had their full attention.

And suddenly I was stone-cold sober.

It didn't take very long. We'd all had a few drinks. Unlike me, however, they'd had no training in taking hard knocks, unless you counted the devastating experience of having seen their team lose the match. Maybe, because of that they thought they had something to prove. I, on the other hand, hadn't. At least, I tried to convince myself of that afterwards. As a salve to my conscience.

Perhaps I was a bit hard on them. Maybe it was because by being British they were bringing me into disrepute by association – or perhaps it was because I was feeling really bloody and looking for an excuse to vent my frustrations at not making headway with the business – that I didn't pull any punches. Literally.

I left one out of the remaining three standing. I decided somebody had to be around in order to get the other ones home. I broke one arm and cracked at least three ribs that evening. None of them mine.

The bullyboys had limped out into the darkness, licking their wounds, and I was leaning against the wall, retching drily, when I felt an arm on my shoulder. I don't know who got the bigger fright, me or the patron. I turned fast and he made a rapid step backwards.

He didn't say anything. All he did was hand me a tumbler full of brandy and murmur, '*Efcharisto, kirie.*' He must have known who or what I was because he next addressed me in English. 'Sir, you are all right?' He'd likely recognized me as the mournful soul he'd seen hanging around the marina for the past few weeks, looking unemployed.

I nodded and took a few deep breaths. I couldn't recall the last time anyone had called me sir.

Everyone was staring at me wide-eyed. The old fellow who had been pushed down was back on his feet, dusting himself down with as much dignity as he could muster.

I was asked again if I was hurt.

I managed a weak smile and said No. 'What about everybody else? All okay?' My insides were churning. I hoped I wasn't going to be sick over somebody.

I received nervous nods.

110

The old man walked forward slowly and shook my hand solemnly. The barman said, 'Thank you for your help, sir. Tell me, you are English, no? Yet you try and stop them?'

'Let's say I didn't like the odds,' I wheezed.

I could tell that they weren't too sure what to do next. Should they call the police? In the end they didn't. We all tidied the place up and I nursed my insides. It took me about another ten to fifteen minutes to collect myself. By that time, the shakes had started again. Delayed shock. There was only one logical cure.

I had another drink.

And another one after that. I'd made friends. I didn't pay for another thing all evening.

The next day I received a summons to visit the terrace at the rear of the Bacchus, and I met Stavros for the first time. It had been one of his bars. Word had got around fast. From that moment on I was given the seal of approval. Stavros let it be known that I operated my business independently but under his patronage. He himself began to put a few interesting options my way. Nothing too spectacular, but sufficient to enable me to maintain something approaching a solvent business. A number of his deals were actually legal, too.

I'd never looked back.

Now, he released me and cupped my face in his calloused hands.

'Logan, my friend! I knew those Turkish bastards would not keep you for long!' he cried, grinning from ear to ear.

'Long enough,' I said, wishing he'd keep his voice down. I could sense that a few of the customers were beginning to tune in.

Unperturbed, he gestured to an empty seat at his table. 'Sit! Sit! Rocco! A drink for my friend!'

Anxious to assume a low profile, I sank into the space being offered. As if by magic, a glass appeared at my

111

elbow. Great service. It pays to be on good terms with the proprietor. Someone had decided I was drinking ouzo. I added water and watched the contents of the glass cloud and swirl.

Stavros clinked glasses. '*Gia sas!* Your health, Michael!'

I took a sip and felt the aniseed slide around my taste buds.

'So, Logan, you have come back from the dead. How is this possible? I read that you are to serve twenty years in prison. You must be one damned smart son of a bitch to escape after only three months, no?' He laughed wildly.

'Yeah, well,' I said. 'Let's say that they got a bit careless.'

'You mean they leave the key in the lock, yes?' His eyes flashed and I knew he was presuming, in his own inimitable style, that somehow, somewhere along the way, I'd managed to bribe somebody. Not so far from the truth, as it happened.

'Something like that,' I said, and winked conspiratorially.

He slapped his hands together with glee. 'So, tell me your adventures. What about your boat? Did you bring her back with you?'

I shook my head. 'No. They've still got her.'

The Turks had seized the *Kallisti* along with the cargo after they'd picked me up. She was in some marine pound, destined eventually, I suspected, to become the runabout for some enterprising Gumruk officer, may God rot his socks.

'I am truly sorry, my friend,' he said sadly. 'She was indeed a fine vessel.'

He wasn't wrong, although fine was perhaps putting it a bit strongly, unless by fine he meant rugged and seaworthy rather than beautiful.

She certainly hadn't been beautiful.

A Grand Banks 42 cruiser, four years old, blunt and robust. She wouldn't have won any competitions for the sleekest craft afloat. But inside she was roomy and comfortable, and the two big Volvo turbocharged engines residing in her specially strengthened hull were powerful enough to propel her along at twenty-three knots, if I'd felt so inclined. Perversely, because she had been no oil painting, I'd christened her *Kallisti*, the old name for Santorini. It means 'the most fair'.

I'd picked her up for a good price, too. Her previous owner, an Italian count of dubious extraction, had been forced to sell her to cover mounting debts. He'd needed a quick sale to keep the creditors at bay, so I'd been able to knock him down to some ten thousand pounds below market value.

I missed her immensely. She had been my companion as well as my home, not to mention my sole means of livelihood. I'd have sooner lost a limb than seen her reduced to her present circumstances: moored to some rusting pylon in a Turkish harbour. She deserved better.

In losing the boat I'd been immediately deprived of my chief asset. The bulk of my capital had been tied up in her. That was now lost for ever. I'd been maintaining funds in a local bank for a rainy day. I hadn't expected to strike stormy weather quite so soon.

'You have lost weight, Logan,' Stavros observed. His gravelled voice was weighted with concern. He frowned. 'This is not good. Here . . .' He pushed his plate towards me and passed me a fork. 'You should eat. Let my people prepare you something.'

He was about to raise his hand to summon one of the waiters when I stopped him. 'Later. It's not food I've come for. I need something else from you.'

'Anything, my friend.' He spread his hands.

'A favour.'

113

'Name it. It shall be yours.' He was a regent granting a boon. My wish was his command.

I told him what I wanted.

His immediate reaction was one of shock. 'Logan, you know very well I do not deal in such merchandise.'

'But you can get hold of it?' I pressed.

He pursed his lips and viewed me through dark, narrowed and calculating eyes. 'It is possible, yes,' Cautious and noncommittal. I hadn't expected anything less.

'Well, then.'

He clicked his tongue. 'It is for you? Surely . . .'

'If you mean is it for my personal use, the answer is no.'

'Then why . . . ?'

'To settle a score.' My choice of words had come automatically. I doubted he would cotton on to the irony.

Something of the anger I was feeling must have shown in my face. He regarded me speculatively. 'When would you require it?'

'Right away,' I said.

That shook him. His eyebrows took off. 'Now?'

I nodded. 'Can you do it?'

'Logan,' he rumbled, 'I think perhaps you are about to enter deep waters. It would grieve me very much to see you drown. You understand what I am saying?' A strong and mottled hand clamped itself over my wrist.

'I understand,' I said. 'And I appreciate your concern. Will you help me?'

He released my hand and leaned back in his seat. He wiped his lips carefully with his napkin. I could see his mind working, weighing up the pros and cons. There were an awful lot of cons, particularly for a man in his position. He was, after all, almost respectable in his old age. He sighed and said finally, 'Because I trust you, Logan, because I think you must have a very good reason for making this request, I will see to the arrangements.'

'Thank you,' I said. 'There is one thing.'

He waited expectantly.

'Regarding payment . . .'

He waved his hand dismissively. 'Consider it as a . . . gift.'

'I'll consider it as anything you want it to be,' I said.

'From me to you, Logan.' He rested both palms against his chest. 'No strings.'

He snapped his fingers then. A man appeared at his shoulder, of the same stamp as Rocco, but younger. He bent his ear low and, with a face that betrayed nothing, listened as Stavros gave him instructions. With a brief nod of understanding, he disappeared towards the rear of the restaurant.

'It is done,' Stavros said.

An hour later I had what I came for, in a shoulder bag that Stavros' man had brought back with him.

When I rose to leave he stood up and gripped my hand. 'Take great care, Logan,' he said. 'I will ask the gods to watch over you.'

'I hope they're listening,' I said.

I could feel his eyes on me as I made my exit.

Conceivably, the Plaka would be about the only part of the city that Byron, if he were resurrected, would still recognize. Nestling on the northern slopes of the Acropolis, it's a hotchpotch of narrow streets, winding alleyways and tiny magnolia-framed squares surrounding a disorganized arrangement of apartment blocks, high-walled villas, exquisite gardens and frescoed chapels, as well as tavernas, nightclubs, dimly lit cellars and rooftop restaurants.

The heartbeat of the city; the place pulsates. You can't

115

hear the traffic for the simple reason that there's too much other noise around. The primal throb of rock music competes with the strains of the bouzouki weeping like tormented souls from a hundred clustered doorways. Entering the area is like fighting your way into a rugby scrum made up of tourists who've come to sample the nightlife they've seen advertised in their holiday brochures and the locals who've come to sit and drink and exchange gossip.

Above the crowded pavements the dark crag of the Acropolis reared into the night. Floodlights, ranged along the crest of the great rock, illuminated the ruins in a fiery orange glow.

I made my way through the massed revellers and up the steps that would lead me eventually to Hammet's bolt hole, a compact residence hidden down one of the sinuous passageways.

Hammet was entertaining – verbally, that is; not adjectivally. And to say he was annoyed, not to say startled, at being disturbed would be something of an understatement. If I'd been in his position, I dare say I'd have been mightily browned off too.

He was in bed, and he wasn't alone. The youth keeping him company looked about fifteen. Pretty, I suppose, if you liked them that way. The boy was lying on his stomach, with Hammet's hand infiltrating the cleft of his slowly rotating buttocks.

'Hello, Hammet,' I said, as I stepped into the room. 'Sorry to bother you. Guess who?'

For a fat man, the Lebanese showed a remarkable turn of speed.

Rolls of flesh rippled like jelly as he jerked upright with the grace of a breaching manatee. Plump fingers drew the edges of the kimono together in a flustered attempt to

116

conceal his rapidly shrinking erection. A scarlet hem rode along hairless calf in a swirling fold of silk.

'Logan!' he exclaimed breathlessly. His eyes bulged. His voice was pitched high, like a eunuch's.

'Correct,' I said cheerfully. 'You win the thousand drachmas. And just when you thought it was safe to go back in the boudoir.'

His Buddha-like eyes roamed the room frantically.

'It's no use looking for the hired help,' I said. 'He's taking a nap. He'll be out for a while.'

The boy hadn't moved. He was still on his stomach, lips formed into a simpering Lolita pout. Beads of perspiration lacquered his forehead and shoulders. He seemed mesmerized by the gun I was holding.

As did Hammet. He licked his lips and blinked nervously.

The Star automatic had been donated by Stavros. I had other goodies about me. I was saving the best till last.

'Cat got your tongue, Hammet?' I asked him.

'How did you get in?' His bald dome and small eyes gave an almost oriental cast to his olive features.

'By the light of the moon. I walk only at night and my footsteps leave no trace.'

I'd come in over the roof, via balcony and open window. Hammet's minder, large and slow and clumsy, had been oblivious of my arrival. He'd wake up nursing a bruise over his carotid.

The Lebanese stared at the gun. 'But you were in prison!'

'You shouldn't believe all you read in the newspapers.'

'You escaped!'

'No, I'm just a figment of your fevered imagination. All this is just a nightmare. Or it soon will be,' I added pointedly. I moved in from the middle of the room. I didn't want my back exposed.

He blanched, his waxy skin taking on the texture of moist putty. A tremor seemed to run through him. Sweat had broken out along his upper brow.

'You conned me, Hammet.' I pointed the barrel of the gun at what passed for his midriff, and his face muscles tightened like an inflating balloon. I could smell the fear oozing from his pores. It was sour, like ripe cheese.

The boy shifted his position on the sheets, his slim body unblemished and peach smooth.

I tracked him with the Star. 'Tell your bum chum to stay where he is, otherwise he'll get something up his rear end that won't be your fat finger.'

The Lebanese gave an abrupt sibilant warning, and the languid youth lay back on the bed, long brown legs splayed like those of a courtesan.

'What is it that you want?' Hammet whispered.

'Your arse,' I said. 'If you'll pardon the circumstances.'

He jerked as if a current had passed through him. 'Logan, I . . .' The cringing denial began deep in his hull and emerged like a thin whine of flatulence.

'What's up, Hammet? You going to tell me it was all a big mistake and you didn't really send me over there to pick up twenty pounds of prime horse? Is that what you want me to believe?'

'I swear, Logan! I didn't know!' His chins shook.

'The hell you didn't, you bastard! You reckoned you couldn't lose. You'd take none of the risks and all the profit. All you had to do was hire good old Logan to bring out what he'd been told was a box of trinkets, when all you wanted was a mule to bring out enough snow to mainline half the junkies in the Med. Dammit! You know I don't touch drugs!'

Hammet lumbered across the bed like a broad-beamed ship turning turtle. Springs groaned alarmingly. He rolled to his feet, an ungainly, misshapen behemoth bedecked in crimson frippery. 'But I was as surprised as you, my friend. Was I not desolated when I found out that you had been arrested?'

'I wouldn't know,' I said. 'Were you?'

'But naturally! Logan, please, I implore you. I had nothing to do with the drugs!'

'You're lying.'

'How can you say that?' he replied blusteringly. 'Have we not always been honest with each other in the past? Surely there should be no disagreement between old friends.' Now he was really wheedling.

'You don't have friends, Hammet. Only victims.'

A smarmy smile broke across his lips. He was regaining his confidence. 'Ah, Logan! Always the joker!' Suddenly contrite, he went on, 'But seriously, let us say that this has been nothing more than an unfortunate misunderstanding, for which I am only too anxious to make amends. I shall see to it that you receive generous compensation. Please, allow me to make it up to you. Surely we can reach an amicable agreement. An arrangement of a financial nature, perhaps?' he added beguilingly, his porcine eyes glinting.

'What had you in mind, exactly?'

He perked visibly. 'Name your price! Ten thousand dollars? Twenty?'

I shook my head. 'I'll tell you what,' I said. 'I'll make it easy for you. I'll take one pound.'

'One pound?' He looked nonplussed. 'Of what?'

'Flesh,' I said.

The smile slid from his face. He seemed to shrink. I motioned him back to the bed. 'Sit down,' I said. 'And shut up.'

I reached into my shirt and hooked out the package that I'd received from Stavros, along with the gun. I

119

moved to the table and set it down. Transfixed, Hammet followed my every move.

There was a flask of iced water on the stand beside the bed. Next to it were a couple of tumblers. I carried one of them back to the table. I laid the pistol down within easy reach and picked up the brown paper package. I unwrapped the package and laid the contents in front of me. Three cellophane envelopes, each one about the size of a cold-remedy sachet. They all contained a fine white powder. As they came to light I heard Hammet give a start.

'What are you doing, Logan?'

'Making a delivery.'

'A delivery?'

'Don't look so worried. It's only what you asked for.'

I opened the envelopes and sprinkled their contents into the tumbler. I picked up the pistol, took the tumbler back to the bed and poured a little water into it. The powder began to dissolve. Minute bubbles floated to the surface of the solution. I swirled the glass around to hasten the process.

The first inklings of what I was about to do began to penetrate his brain. He began to tremble again. 'What is it?'

'Heroin,' I said. 'What did you think it was? Alka Seltzer?'

The two main types of heroin are known as Number 3 and Number 4, depending on the source of supply. Stavros had provided me with three envelopes of Number 4. It had probably originated in the Golden Crescent, in the foothills of the Hindu Kush. Number 4 is by far the more effective and thus the more expensive variety. Easily soluble and therefore highly suitable for injection, it is the type more widely used by western junkies. Number 4

120

heroin, manufactured in the Laotian highlands, had been the drug choice of the American servicemen in Vietnam.

Stavros had advised me that the stuff he had given me was virtually pure, about ninety per cent neat horse. I didn't ask him where he'd got it from. I suspected he'd had to use up a couple of favours.

The powder had dissolved. I held the glass towards him.

'Drink it,' I said.

For a moment I thought he was going to pass out. He clamped his lips together and shook his head violently.

'What's the matter? This is what you wanted, isn't it? This is what you conned me to bring out of Turkey for you.'

'My God, Logan! You're mad!' He tried to scramble away from me across the bed. His bedmate got in the way.

I leaned over him and pressed the muzzle of the gun against his ear. 'Drink it, Hammet. Or I'll blow your fucking head off.'

He tried to knock the glass out of my hand. I was quicker. I moved the glass out of his way. 'Nice try,' I said.

'Logan, I beg you! Please!'

I pulled back the hammer on the gun. The noise was like a dislocated shoulder sliding back into its socket. Hammet closed his eyes.

'I mean it. I'll shoot you dead, so help me.'

A tear trickled slowly down his cheek. His shaking hand reached out for the glass. I pushed the tumbler towards his mouth. His clammy fingers encircled my hand. He tipped the contents back into his maw, gagging slightly in the process as the bitter taste reacted against his tongue.

'There,' I said. 'It wasn't so bad, was it?' I set the empty glass back on the table.

Idly, I wondered which would go first, his heart or his brain. Once in the bloodstream, en route to his brain, the effect would be almost instantaneous. They say that Number 4 gives the imbiber a very particular degree of high, depending on how much it has been adulterated. A lot of different additives can be used: caffeine, lactose, even talcum powder and baking soda. The stuff I had forced upon Hammet hadn't been cut with anything. It wouldn't take long in his case, especially considering the size of the dosage, and him.

And he knew it.

A pungent smell had begun to permeate the room. Fear had caused the Lebanese to void his bladder. Shivers began to rack his body. Clutching his vast belly he began to shudder. It had started.

I left the empty sachets on the table, along with the wrapping. There was nothing about them that would identify their source. I gave Hammet a small wave.

'Don't worry,' I told him. 'I can see myself out.'

He had collapsed across the boy. His mouth had fallen open. He looked as if he was gasping for air.

I don't think he even heard me.

Neither did his bodyguard, who was still out cold. The boy I wasn't worried about either. By now he'd be pulling on his trousers so fast he'd likely be wearing them back to front. By the time Hammet's minder had surfaced, both the lad and I would be long gone.

And I felt no guilt at all.

I retraced my steps back to the noise and the crowds and the bright lights, and began to look for something that resembled a taxi.

That's when I saw Ritter.

He was seated at a table outside one of the cafés. He

didn't see me; I was hidden by the throng. There was a man with him: young, blond, square-cut jaw. They could have been clones. Presumably Ritter had finished his errand and decided to grab a drink. There were plenty of his countrymen around. It was hardly surprising that he should have struck up a conversation with one of them. I debated whether or not to impose myself upon them, and decided against it.

I had more pressing matters to occupy my time. Like returning the gun to Stavros. It had served its purpose and I had no further use for it.

I looked around for a taxi to take me back to Zea.

It was hard to believe that less than twelve hours ago I had been part of a prison work party. Following my speedy departure from the Citadel, I'd been on something of a high myself. I was only just starting to come down. Weariness was seeping into my bones. I needed to rest. Tomorrow I'd find out exactly why Donovan had sprung me from jail.

I could hardly wait.

9

Could be Plato was right. Could be this was all that was left of Atlantis.

Below us, in the centre of the caldera, the core of Nea Kaimeni smouldered like dragon's breath. Along what had been the eastern rim of the vast crater, a scimitar-shaped line of cliffs reared a thousand feet out of the sea like the jaws of a leviathan rising from the deep. It was a view I had seen many times before from the deck of the *Kallisti* but never from the air. The new angle didn't make the sight any less impressive.

Thirty-five centuries ago there had been a mountain here, until the explosion that geologists place around 1500 B.C. blew the top off the volcano and sent a tidal wave surging out across the Aegean with the speed of an express train. Some learned scholars believe that the wave was responsible for the destruction of the Minoan civilization on Crete, seventy miles away. I don't know if that's true or not. All I do know is that it must have gone up with one hell of a bang.

I've read that the force of the explosion that devastated Santorini was four times more powerful than that which obliterated Krakatoa, when the tsunami from that eruption swept around the globe to create high tides in the English Channel. In comparison, an atom bomb would have been about as effective as a damp squib. At the time it had probably seemed like the end of the world. For thousands of people it must have been.

The volcano is dormant. Over the intervening years there have been isolated rumblings, the last as recently as

1956. You only have to sail over the surface of the jade sea inside the crater, through the floating specks of pumice, and catch the whiff of brimstone to appreciate the nearness of hell. It's like being cupped in the Devil's palm.

The cliffs change colour depending on the time of day and the angle of the sun. This morning they were light brown, with veins of purple and red, as though streaked with blood.

Thera clings to the edge of the precipice in a white-washed straggle, giving the impression that at any minute the town will release its tenuous hold and plunge into the bay far below. There are three ways to scale the cliffs: by cable car, shanks's pony, or donkey. The cable car is by far the least stressful. Walking is for the fit or the foolhardy. The donkeys are for the masochists; they've been the accepted form of transport for God knows how many years but they still don't seem to have gotten used to the idea. It's said that they're possessed by the souls of the dead. Now, that could be true. The souls are probably the previous property of all those poor buggers who've had heart attacks thinking they'd be able to walk up.

There were a couple of small ferries tied to buoys opposite Skala, the tiny port tucked into the base of the rock.

'Fair takes your breath away, don't it?' Donovan said, looking down over my shoulder.

I could only nod in agreement.

The vessel we had come to join was anchored on the eastern side of the island, at Monolithos. We took a taxi from the airport.

I guessed it was our boat even before Donovan pointed her out as the taxi dropped us off at the jetty. She was moored a couple of hundred yards offshore, outside the breakwater, and my first impression was that she was expensive.

'There she is,' Donovan confirmed. 'The *Valkyrie*.'

A small launch was buzzing towards us. Donovan lifted a hand and waved. His signal was acknowledged by the man at the wheel.

'Let's go,' Donovan said.

Ritter and I trailed him to the water's edge.

'Hey, Marco!' Donovan hailed the launch as it swung in to the jetty. He tossed his bag aboard and dropped into the boat. Ritter and I followed suit. I'd managed to get to my bank before the flight and so I'd been able to reimburse Donovan and equip myself with a few essentials: a couple more shirts, jeans, trainers, swimming briefs, that kind of thing.

The young man grinned. 'Welcome back, Mr Donovan!'

'This is Logan,' Donovan said.

Marco shook my hand vigorously. He looked to be in his early twenties, very slim and tanned, with dark curly hair. He was casually dressed in a pair of stone-washed jeans and tee shirt. 'Hello, Mr Logan, sir!'

His good humour was catching. Well, with me, at any rate. Ritter didn't seem too bothered either way. He didn't speak, just took his seat and looked vaguely bored. Donovan shrugged and threw me a just-ignore-the-miserable-sod kind of look.

Once we were settled, Marco gunned the throttle and we headed out across the harbour.

As we drew closer to her I could see that the *Valkyrie* really was a beauty. Italian built, out of the Picchiotti stable. Not new – early seventies, perhaps – but she was seventy feet of gleaming luxury and at least a million dollars' worth of anybody's money. Very impressive.

Marco dropped us off at the ladder and zoomed back

to shore. He had further errands to run. Donovan led me through to the stateroom. That summed up the difference between this luxurious vessel and the *Kallisti*. The *Kallisti*, bless her, only rated a saloon. No one in his right mind would have had the temerity to call what I was standing in a saloon. It looked like the presidential suite in the Hyatt Regency.

And the man seated at the big desk over in the far corner looked as if he might have been the Hyatt's manager.

When we entered he stood up to greet us. Early fifties, I'd have said; medium height, slightly fleshy face, grey hair combed back and receding at the temples. His tan looked expensive: the sort that came with a villa and a permanent mooring off the Cap d'Antibes. He was dressed in an open-necked shirt and perfectly coordinated cream trousers. The shirt, I noticed, had the inevitable designer motif on the left breast. Lacoste. What else?

He was smiling. He was also holding out his hand. I presumed that meant he wanted to shake one of mine, so I gave him my right one to play with.

'Mr Logan, I am very pleased to meet you at last. My name is Gunther Prohl.'

Which, frankly, didn't mean a damned thing. But at least his name and his accent had narrowed things down. His English was good, but it wasn't difficult to detect the Teutonic inflection.

And then I thought, half a mo. Maybe you are kind of familiar, after all.

Prohl. Prohl the industrialist? As in Prohl AG? Electronics, Engineering and Pharmaceuticals? If so, I was in exalted company. Okay, maybe he wasn't quite as renowned as Thyssen, Krupp and Sachs, but he was still major league. His subsidiaries, as far as I recalled, dealt

127

in everything from drug development to the manufacture of computer components.

He was still smiling, as if he could sense the way my brain was ticking over. I guessed he was also engaged in some quick mental assessment of his own. Probably wondering if I'd been worth all the trouble it had taken to get me here.

'Would you care for a drink, Mr Logan?' he asked.

Donovan caught my eye and winked. Ritter had moved to one of the sofas and sat down. He was regarding me the way a boxer sizes up an opponent. I wondered why that should be.

'Thanks,' I said. 'Beer will be fine.'

'Excellent.' He turned to Ritter. 'Martin, would you be so kind?'

Ritter looked a bit peeved at having been relegated to barman but he wasn't prepared to argue the point. Donovan, never one to stand on ceremony, went and helped himself from the well-stocked fridge in the corner.

Prohl moved back to his desk. 'Sit, sit.' He gestured to a corner of Ritter's sofa.

I sat down and waited for someone to enlighten me.

Ritter handed me my drink.

Prohl said from behind his desk, 'Your friend Donovan has been most helpful in providing me with some facts concerning your background. You understand, I have to be somewhat circumspect about the kind of personnel I employ.'

I took a slow sip of beer. 'Oh, yes?' I said.

'I believe that you served in the British armed forces, as a Royal Marine commando. That is correct?'

Donovan had been busy. 'That's right,' I replied slowly.

'Later transferring to what is known as the Special Boat Squadron.'

There was an onyx-inlaid humidor on the desk in front

128

of him. As he spoke, Prohl lifted the lid and extracted a slim cigar. He clipped the end and set light to the leaf with a gold Dunhill.

Bloody hell, I thought. You have done your homework.

Recruitment to the SBS was by selection of volunteers serving in the Marines. The selection and training procedures were not unlike those of the SAS, with a few extras thrown in for good measure. As well as parachuting, survival techniques and advanced weapons handling, the course also involved seamanship, navigation, and diving. It had pretty much the same rate of dropout, about eighty-five per cent. Which, perversely, was one of the reasons I'd decided to try and make the grade. I'd wanted to prove something to myself.

Not that I hadn't had my share of scrapes with the cadre, of course. I'd done my time in Belize and Hong Kong as well as the Province. I'd participated in border recces in the Maya Mountains, winkled out illegal immigrants in Aberdeen harbour and back in seventy-eight, as part of 41 Commando, I'd patrolled the grey, rain-washed streets of West Belfast, searching people and houses and cars, and running the gauntlet of Provo Active Service Units on the loose in the dark alleyways of the New Lodge and the Falls Road. The Ulster tour had been a thankless task on all counts, owing as much to Westminster's lack of initiative as it had to the threat of a sniper with an Armalite.

I'd made the transfer three years later, just in time for the Squadron's involvement in the South Atlantic. Talk about from one extreme to another.

Precise details of SBS and SAS activities in the Falkland's campaign are still classified. Speculation, naturally, is rife. Suffice it to say that I'd spent more than a few interesting moments cooped up in everything from the hold of a C-130 to an inflatable Gemini in San Carlos

Water and the hatchway of HMS *Onyx* awaiting the go-ahead to infiltrate the mainland in search of Argentine Skyhawk nests.

It was during a beach recce to guide the paras in towards Teal Inlet that I'd received the acute and painful reminder of my own mortality.

Getting shot hurts, no question. We'd completed the recon mission and were pulling back westwards to meet up with 3 Para and 3 Commando Brigade when we ran into an Argentine patrol. They must have been part of a unit of their *Buzo Tactico*, their Special Forces, because they gave us quite a hard time. Not like most of their conscripts, who tended to raise their hands in the air at the mere sight of a British soldier. I took a bullet in the left shoulder and it was only the swift action of my oppo, Tim Gallagher, that saved me from pegging out there and then. He managed to feed me one of my morphine ampoules and slam a hunk of wadding into the mess, while the other pair in our four-man squad concentrated on returning fire. They stayed with me until the paras arrived. Not that I was in any condition to appreciate their efforts, mind you.

I surfaced in the main dressing station at Ajax Bay to find they'd removed the offending projectile and that my lowly part in the altercation was over. I travelled home luxury class on the *Canberra*. My return to the UK coincided with the expiration of my service contract. I chose not to renew it. In retrospect, that was probably a mistake. I was a fish out of water. I suffered from twinges of arthritis in cold weather and a surfeit of nefarious skills that no one in civvy street had the slightest interest in.

No one except Cameron, that is.

The late Iain Cameron had been a mercenary recruiter, operating out of an office in Sloane Street. Utilizing knowledge and contacts gleaned during his duty as a serving officer in the SAS, he specialized in providing ex-paras and SBS and SAS vets as security advisors to Third World countries, including the Gulf. It was he who'd provided me with the contract in Muscat. Which was where I'd eventually teamed up with Harry Donovan.

Talking of whom: during our previous times together I'd obviously revealed to the Irishman rather more about my background than I had thought. Prohl's recitation of my CV to date had convinced me of that. He had it all: my contract with Sheikh al Salh, the gold runs, my sojourn in the gaol in Bombay and, of course, my last triumphant run-in with the Turks.

Prohl tossed the contents of my résumé back at me like a fast bowler. 'Mr Donovan seems to have a high opinion of your capabilities,' he said. It was a statement, not a question seeking confirmation.

I maintained a silence and sipped my beer. I thought I detected the shadow of a smirk on Ritter's thin lips. I could have been wrong.

'Nevertheless,' Prohl went on, 'despite his inevitable bias, it would appear you do have a certain integrity. As well as a number of skills which may prove useful to our enterprise.'

'Thanks very much,' I said. 'It's a relief to know that all that expensive training hasn't proved a total waste of time.'

He frowned then. 'He also advised me to expect a certain amount of sarcasm and evidence of a tendency to defy authority.'

'In that case, unless you tell me what I'm here for, you're not likely to be disappointed, are you?'

I heard Donovan draw in his breath noisily.

To my surprise Prohl chuckled. He sucked on his Havana, then exhaled noisily. Misty blue tendrils drifted above his head. 'Ah,' he said, smiling. 'The British sense of humour. So refreshing. It served you well in the Citadel, no doubt?'

'If that's a hint that you want me to say thanks for pulling me out,' I said, 'thanks.'

He waved his hand dismissively. 'Thank your friend Donovan, Mr Logan. He was very persuasive. But your release was arranged for a purpose. It was not an act of charity. I'd like you to work for me.'

'So I understand. Doing what exactly?'

Prohl fell silent, as though reappraising the approach he was trying to make.

Finally he said, 'I wish you to assist us in the search for my father.'

I blinked. 'Your father?' I shook my head slowly. 'Herr Prohl, if it's a case of a missing person, you don't want me. I'd say you need a private detective.'

And then I thought, hang on, if Prohl was in his fifties, pater couldn't be far away from being an octogenarian, for God's sake. It seemed a strange age for a man to run off to join a circus, or whatever.

Prohl allowed himself another tight smile. 'An admirable suggestion. Alas, one that would not be practical. The circumstances of his disappearance were somewhat . . . unusual.'

I raised an eyebrow. 'Okay, when did he go missing?'

'Nineteen forty-five,' Prohl said, without a change of expression.

I stared at him. The glass tilted in my hand. I looked at Donovan. 'I take it he doesn't mean quarter to eight last night?'

There was the merest hint of controlled amusement in the Irishman's grey eyes as he pursed his lips and shook his head solemnly.

'Nineteen forty-five,' I repeated tonelessly. 'You're telling me your father's been missing for forty-five years

132

and you want me to help you try and find him? What the
hell makes you think I'd want to get involved in a lame-
brained scheme like that, for God's sake? Do me a
favour!'

'Er – Logan,' I heard Donovan say. 'I really do think
you ought to let him explain. I reckon you might change
your mind when you hear the rest.'

'Harry . . . !'

'Hey!' Donovan said sharply, pointing his finger. 'Ritter
and I got you out of that shithole primarily for you to
listen to what Herr Prohl has to say. You can at least do
him the courtesy of paying attention. You may just learn
something – to your advantage,' he added.

He was right, of course. I owed Prohl that much. If it
hadn't been for his timely involvement I'd still be lan-
guishing in a prison cell, with little to occupy my days
save for contemplating what the next fifth of a century
might be like without the luxury of a roll of soft toilet
paper.

I held up a hand to fend off his anger. 'Okay, you're
right, Harry. I'm sorry. That was out of line.' I favoured
Prohl with a conciliatory smile. 'Why don't you fill me
in?'

Prohl, to his credit, made no attempt to demean himself
by voicing a rejoinder. He took another thoughtful pull at
his cigar and got straight down to business.

'In 1945,' Prohl said, 'my father was an officer in the
Kriegsmarine. A U-boat captain, with the rank of lieutenant commander. He started his career in the merchant
marine, acquiring his master's ticket at the age of twenty-
four. He transferred to the navy in 1936 and graduated
from the U-boat school at Kiel in 1938. During the course
of the war he sank over two hundred thousand tons of
Allied shipping. He was one of the highest decorated aces
of the U-boat arm.' Prohl made no attempt to hide the
pride in his voice.

'Tell me, Mr Logan,' he said. 'Are you familiar with the events in Germany in the final weeks before the surrender?'

I shook my head and wondered where all this was leading. 'Not really. No more or less than anyone else. Other than the fact that things must have been in total chaos.'

He grunted. 'Chaos is right, my friend. That is exactly what it was.'

Unbidden, Prohl then proceeded to give me a potted history lesson. He started with the Fuehrer designating Doenitz as his successor and how Doenitz, from his HQ on the Danish border, had attempted to consolidate his forces by ordering his U-boat packs to Norway and the Baltic ports. By this time, of course, the Russians had crossed the Elbe, the British and Americans had forded the Rhine, Hitler had committed suicide and Berlin had fallen. Chaos indeed.

But there was more.

Not the facts, but the rumours.

'You know it is believed,' Prohl said, 'that not all of Hitler's council perished in the ruins of Berlin, don't you? And that a vast amount of treasure was smuggled out of Germany to South America to support these men in exile?'

'Of course,' I agreed. 'Bormann's been spotted down there more times than I've had hot dinners.'

'Therefore,' Prohl followed on, 'you are probably aware how the journey to South America was supposedly accomplished.'

I sighed. 'Don't tell me. By submarine, right?'

'So it is said,' Prohl replied.

'Are you trying to tell me that your father ferried Martin Bormann to Uruguay?'

I was beginning to think that Prohl was some sort of

certified lunatic. And Donovan wanted me to listen to this berk? Oh dear me.

'No, Mr Logan, I am not saying that at all. At least, not exactly. However, certain unusual events occurred at the end of the war which would lead me to suppose that such a plan could have been a distinct possibility.'

'In that case,' I said, 'your geography's way out. This is the Aegean not the Rio de la Plata.'

Prohl smiled patiently. 'Please, Mr Logan. Bear with me. There is more. Much more.'

I waited.

Prohl said, 'I was seven when I last saw my father. I will tell you now that for the past forty-five years I have believed that he was killed at sea during the last weeks of the war. It is only in the last few months that I have come to suspect otherwise.

'For that reason I have spent a great deal of time and effort in trying to establish my father's exact movements during the spring of 1945. What I have discovered has proved to be most enlightening.'

At this point in his narrative, I discovered that I'd finished my beer. Despite the air conditioning on board the *Valkyrie*, the stateroom was becoming unbearably warm as the hands of the chronometer on the wall crept towards midday. I could feel rivulets of perspiration trickling down under my arms.

Without waiting to be asked if I wanted topping up, I got to my feet and moved to the bar. I think that for a minute Prohl thought I was about to walk out. His jaw dropped momentarily and then sprang shut as I sifted through the racks for a refill.

'You don't mind, do you?' I asked him.

'Please, help yourself, Mr Logan.'

'Thanks,' I said. 'Harry?'

'Sure,' Donovan said.

135

I glanced at Ritter. He shook his head. Prohl also declined.

I tossed Donovan a can and went back to my seat. I took a swig and felt the chilled lager burn my throat. 'Go on,' I said. 'I'm still listening.'

Prohl continued. 'At the end of April 1945, following a patrol in the North Atlantic, my father's boat was one of a number of submarines ordered north by Doenitz to their bases at Trondheim. Before they reached Norwegian waters, however, my father received new orders to leave the pack and, instead, proceed to Bremerhaven. He arrived at the Bremerhaven yard on the afternoon of the first of May. That same night my father's U-boat left Bremerhaven for an unknown destination. Neither he nor his crew were ever seen again. All I have told you so far,' he added, 'is a matter of record. The German High Command, if not always entirely competent, were at least thorough in their documentation.' He smiled wryly.

Prohl had been so engrossed in his story he had failed to notice that his cigar had gone out. With a faint *tut* of annoyance, he flicked his lighter again, took a couple of quick puffs and once again launched himself into the breach.

'I managed to trace his last known whereabouts through naval records, up to the hour he departed from Bremerhaven. Officially, that was when Lieutenant Commander Dieter Prohl ceased to exist. On the seventh of May, Grand Admiral Doenitz sent a signal to all U-boats to surface, report their positions and surrender themselves to the Allies. As far as the official records are concerned, my father failed to respond to the directive. It was presumed, therefore, that sometime during the period of those seven days, my father's U-boat was sunk with all hands.'

'So what makes you think otherwise?' I asked.

'This,' Prohl said.

He opened a drawer in his desk and removed a small box which he placed on the blotter in front of him. He opened the box and lifted something out. He placed it in my hand.

I recognized it immediately. It was probably one of the most readily identifiable of all military medals.

An Iron Cross.

Still with a segment of faded ribbon attached. It was in pretty good condition, too. A bit scratched, admittedly, but not enough to obscure the swastika embossed in the centre of the design or the date etched on to the metal: 1939. The cross itself was edged in silver. Surmounting it was a silver brooch fashioned in the shape of an oak leaf. Below the oak leaf were two tiny crossed swords. Something else caught my eye and I took a closer look. Set into the silver leaf and the sword hilts were several tiny diamonds. There were no other markings on it. Nothing to identify the recipient. But that still didn't make it anything less than a beautifully wrought piece of decoration.

'You're going to tell me this was your father's?'

'I believe so.'

'How in God's name can you know that? There must have been hundreds of these medals given out.'

Christ, I thought, there'd probably been more German military personnel holding the Iron Cross than there were Frenchmen who'd boasted that they'd served in the resistance. And that was going some.

'Not like this one,' Prohl said. There was a distinct measure of pride in his voice.

'I don't get it. What makes this one so special?'

'It is not just an Iron Cross, Mr Logan. It is much more. It is a Knight's Cross with Oak Leaves, Swords and Diamonds.'

'So?'

'So, this was the Kriegsmarine's highest decoration. It was awarded to only three men. My father was one of them.'

I stared at the medal in my hand.

Prohl said, 'The only other U-boat captains to receive this medal were Wolfgang Lueth of the U-181 and Albrecht Brandi of the U-967.'

'Maybe this was one of theirs.'

'Impossible. Wolfgang Lueth was shot in 1945, ironically when he failed to respond to a password given by a German sentry. Brandi did survive the war. He became an architect. He died, however, in 1966. There is no way that this medal could have belonged to either of them.'

Now came the sixty-four-thousand-dollar question.

'All right,' I said. 'Where and when was it found?'

'Three months ago,' Prohl said. 'In the Sea of Crete. It was removed from the body of a dead fisherman.'

I went suddenly cold. It was as if a cloud had obscured the sun. The hum of the air conditioning seemed extraordinarily loud and intrusive. I handed the medal back to Prohl.

He didn't restore it to the box right away. He turned it over in his hands, like a medium attempting to contact someone through tactile manipulation of a personal memento.

I was aware of Donovan and Ritter studying my reaction.

'A *dead* fisherman?'

Prohl nodded. 'He was discovered drifting in an open boat. It was early morning. There had been a severe storm the night before. It was believed he'd had an accident, fallen and struck his head. There was also water in his lungs. He was found by another fishing crew. They

138

took him on board their own boat and found the medal clutched in his hand.'

'It strikes me,' I said, 'that something like this would have been in the local press.'

'It was,' Donovan said drily. 'But if you recall, you weren't in a position to read about it.'

Three months ago? He was right. That's when I'd been nabbed by the Turks. I'd been out of circulation. Unlike the newspapers.

'There is more,' Prohl said.

'Like what?'

'Mr Logan, it was by a stroke of luck that I happened to be in Athens on business when the story came to my notice. The *Athens News* carried a photograph and I recognized immediately the significance of their extraordinary find. I realized too that there was a danger that a collector might intervene, so I hurriedly made enquiries and met the family that had found the dead man. Fortunately they still had the medal, and it took little persuading for them to sell it to me. I made them a very generous offer. They were more than happy to accept it and relinquish their claim. It also enabled me to check the circumstances in which they had made their discovery.

'But what was more remarkable was the story they told me that had not been in the paper. I spoke to all three members of the family and they told me the same thing. All except the boy, Georgiou. He revealed that there had been something else in the boat besides the dead man. It fell overboard before he had a chance to save it and show it to the other two. He is not sure his father or grandfather believed him when he told them about it, so they did not tell the authorities or the reporters for fear of ridicule. Besides, only Georgiou had seen what it was. But he is sure.'

'Of what?' I asked.

139

'The boy said that there was a sack in the bottom of the boat. When he tried to lift it out, the bottom of the sack broke and the object that had been inside it fell into the sea and sank. He said it was very heavy, he could hardly lift it.'

For some reason my palms had gone suddenly clammy.

'The boy saw it for only a moment, but he is sure. He said it was gold, Mr Logan. A bar of gold.'

10

My throat went dry. From a thousand miles away I heard Donovan say, 'Told you it was a lulu, didn't I?'

I let my nerves settle down into some sort of normal working order before I found my voice. 'All right,' I said to Prohl. 'We've got a war medal and a nonexistent gold bar. You tell me what you think it means.'

'Ah,' he said smugly. 'I see I have caught your interest at last.'

He had to be joking!

'On the face of it, it means nothing, Mr Logan. Merely a remarkable story. Nevertheless, it prompted me to make further investigation into my father's role in the war. And my latest findings have led me to believe there was more to his disappearance than naval records would have us believe.'

Prohl was right. I was hooked. He was reeling me in like a fish on a line.

'I am a wealthy man, Mr Logan. As such, doors have been opened to me that would normally be closed. Some of those doors have opened up into twisting corridors of deception stretching back nearly fifty years in time. There were many transactions undertaken during the war, Mr Logan, the exact details of which have been kept hidden for reasons of both security and fear of reprisal. One of those transactions, I have since discovered, concerned my father's last voyage. By piecing together information from a number of unofficial sources I have been able to establish that during the late evening of 1 May 1945 a number of unusual activities took place on the dockside at Bremerhaven.

'One of which was that during the last few hours that the submarine was berthed it received new provisioning. Nothing strange in that, you may think, except for the fact that the submarine, although revictualled, was not rearmed. Normally a reprovisioning would include a fresh supply of torpedoes. On this occasion, however, none were loaded. What was also strange was that more than half the crew disembarked. They did not reboard.

'The next incident was also noteworthy. Following the restocking of the U-boat, a convoy of trucks arrived at the dockside escorted by a division of the SS. The contents of the convoy, several crates, were loaded on to the submarine. The dockworkers who witnessed this said that the crates appeared to be very heavy in proportion to their size. It is also said that a civilian boarded the submarine at about the same time. It is not known if he later disembarked or sailed with the crew. What is known for certain, however, is that the U-boat slipped her berth later that same night, and with very little fuss. One moment it was there, the next it was gone. Literally, in the span of a few hours. Naturally, this poses several questions. Why reduce the number of crew? Why was the boat not rearmed? And, more importantly, what was the cargo and the submarine's destination?'

'And what conclusion did you come to?'

'I believe the crew was depleted to provide storage space for the cargo. It is also reasonable to assume this was the reason why no fresh torpedoes were stowed. The cargo had to be placed somewhere. Even allowing for the extra room created by the reduction of the crew, the logical stowage area would undoubtedly be in the fore and aft torpedo compartments.'

'So what about the cargo?'

'I'm coming to that,' he said. 'My supposition is based solely on circumstantial evidence, you understand. However, taken in context, it has distinct possibilities. Initially it concerns two operations instigated by Emil Puhl, Deputy President of the Reichsbank, Oswald Pohl, Head of the Economic and Administrative Department of the SS, and Martin Bormann. These operations were known as *Aktion Rheinhardt* and *Aktion Feuerland*.'

'Which were?' Now I was really intrigued.

'*Aktion Rheinhardt* was primarily involved with the transfer of booty from German-occupied territory to the Reichsbank in Berlin. It was a vast undertaking involving considerable amounts of currency, gold coins, pearls and other jewellery taken from the victims in the concentration camps as well as substantial amounts of platinum, silver and gold bullion looted from the Czech national bank and the national banks of Hungary, Holland, Belgium and Albania. In modern terms it would run into millions and millions of pounds. The clearing house for these transactions was the Main Security Office, headed by Ernst Kaltenbrunner. *Aktion Feuerland* – Operation Land of Fire – was Bormann's brainchild. It was concerned with shipping the funds overseas to South America.'

I could see that Prohl was warming to his subject as he continued. 'By the spring of 1944 it is clear that Bormann knew that the war was lost. He began to supervise the removal of the funds from Berlin. Armoured convoys delivered consignments across France to Spanish ports, where they were taken on board a fleet of U-boats. From there the consignments were shipped to Argentina.

'However, following the Allied invasion of Normandy, the routes to Spain were blocked and it became impossible to move any more of the funds overland. For a short time the operation continued, using aircraft, but that soon halted. This still left the bulk of the reserves in Berlin.

'In February 1945 the Allies launched massive air strikes on the capital. During these raids the Reichsbank was severely damaged. To prevent the destruction of the remainder of the reserves it was decided to transfer them south for safekeeping, to the potassium mines in Thuringia.'

'This is beginning to sound familiar,' I cut in. 'But didn't I read somewhere that the stuff was then hijacked by the Americans at the end of the war?'

'Absolutely correct,' Prohl replied. 'It has been recorded as the world's greatest robbery. The gold alone would be worth more than one thousand million dollars at today's prices.'

'Jesus,' I breathed.

'However,' Prohl said, 'there is evidence that not all the reserves were removed from Berlin and taken south. Certainly, some gold did remain in the vaults. It is clearly a matter of timing. Again, I am referring to official documentation.

'The records show that as of 13 April 1945, a total of eight hundred and twenty gold bars were contained in the Reichsbank's vaults. On 14 April seven hundred and thirty gold bars left Berlin by road in half a dozen Opel trucks, bound for Munich. It was that consignment that eventually fell into the hands of the Americans. That left ninety gold bars still in Berlin.'

Prohl had now settled into his stride. 'By now, as you may recall, the Russian encirclement of the capital was almost complete. It was becoming obvious to all concerned that they would have to leave Berlin as soon as possible. Bormann was still there, trying desperately to persuade Hitler to fly south to Berchtesgaden. Hitler, however, refused to leave. On 22 April the Fuehrer had a terrible fit of temper and those around him realized that he was no longer fit to command. Bormann and the others began to make plans to save their own skins. That same afternoon, many of the Chancellery staff flew out of Berlin. Most went south. It is known, however, that one Junkers 352 flew north. It was suspected that the people on board were attempting to join up with Doenitz at his headquarters in Ploen.

'On that very same day, a detachment of SS, led by Brigadier General Josef Spacil acting under the direct orders of Ernst Kaltenbrunner, raided the vaults of the Reichsbank in Berlin and removed most of the remaining assets. Spacil was supposed to have loaded the haul on to an aircraft and flown to Salzburg, where he buried the proceeds of the robbery.

'Much of the rest is also known. By the twenty-fourth of the month Berlin was fully surrounded by the Russians. On 30 April Adolf Hitler committed suicide. On 2 May Berlin fell. On 15 May, Red Army Intelligence ordered the Reichsbank's vaults to be opened. Shortly afterwards the last remaining contents of the vaults disappeared.

'There are those who think the Russians took those ninety bars of gold, Mr Logan. I do not. I think they were taken by the SS back in April. But they were not delivered to Salzburg. It is my opinion that Bormann and Kaltenbrunner arranged for the gold to be flown north on that Junkers. To Bremerhaven. There to await Bormann's arrival. I think it was Bormann's intention to sail with the last of the gold to South America. You remember the civilian who was seen on the dockside on the evening of 1 May? His identity was never confirmed.' He stared at me, willing me to confront him with an argument.

I stared back at him, my senses reeling at the possibilities that unfolded. 'My God,' I said. 'It's crazy!'

'It's beautiful!' Donovan said behind me.

'All right,' I said. 'Let's hold it for a moment. Let's say, for the sake of argument, that the last of the gold was put on board your father's boat, along with this mysterious civilian. So how come we end up with what you say is your father's Knight's Cross here in the Aegean? Tell me that. What the hell was he doing in this neck of the woods? Dammit, you haven't even proved to me that he was here at all! All you've got is a small piece of metal attached to a strip of coloured ribbon. It's not much. It's hardly incontrovertible proof.'

'You'd better tell him the rest,' Donovan muttered.

'You mean there's still more?'

'Oh, you ain't heard nothing yet, old son.'

Prohl said, 'As you so rightly point out, Mr Logan, apart from the existence of the medal there is nothing to confirm Dieter Prohl's presence in the Aegean. Nothing, that is, until I turned my attention to British and American military records. What I had to do was try and establish a possible sighting of my father's U-boat in the Mediterranean at some time after 1 May 1945. The task was not as difficult as you might suppose. I calculated the time it would have taken for him to reach the Mediterranean area and then checked all signals after that date referring to naval engagements involving German vessels.'

'And?'

'I found two which were significant. The first concerned an incident in the Strait of Gibraltar on the night of 10 May. A British destroyer reported sighting a German submarine attempting to enter the strait on the surface. The submarine dived and the destroyer commenced an attack using depth charges. After a period of some fifty minutes, wreckage and oil was sighted and the U-boat was presumed to have been destroyed.

'The second incident occurred six days later in the

eastern Mediterranean, approximately one hundred and seventy miles east of Malta. A signal relayed to Naval C-in-C Malta from the crew of an American Liberator bomber on a flight from Benghazi describes what happened.'

Prohl looked down at some papers he had on his desk. He shuffled through them and brought one to the top of the pile.

'The crew of the Liberator reported that at grid reference 16 degrees 48 east, 35 degrees 57 north, they sighted a German submarine travelling on the surface on an easterly course. They had been descending through low cloud cover and came upon the vessel unexpectedly. From their report it appears that the crew of the submarine were just as surprised. From the actions of the men on the deck of the submarine it appeared that they were about to engage the deck gun. The Americans released bombs. The U-boat made an effort to submerge at speed. but in the opinion of the pilot the aircraft registered a hit. The submarine appeared to suffer damage and sank below them. The aircraft circled for several minutes before continuing to its destination.'

'That's it?' I said in the ensuing silence.

'No,' Prohl said. 'Not quite. I still required confirmation that both incidents involved the same U-boat and that it was my father's command.'

'And you got it?'

Prohl nodded. 'The final proof, Mr Logan, lay in the U-boat's insignia.'

From the look on my face he knew he had to explain.

'When a U-boat had completed its six-month trial period in the Baltic, it was declared "Frontreif", ready for action. The crew was then allowed the honour of painting an insignia on the tower. This was in addition to the flotilla emblem. Some insignias were rather famous.

Gunther Prien's, for example, was the drawing of a bull. Herbert Shultze's was a white witch. My father, too, had his own insignia.'

'Which was what?'

'It was the figure of a man with the tail of a fish, holding a fishing spear. *Ein Wassermann*. A . . .' Prohl searched for the word, his brow furrowing, 'a . . . merman, I think you would call him, yes? It was very distinctive. Both the destroyer captain and the crew of the Liberator reported seeing the insignia on the conning tower of the U-boat prior to it submerging. There is no doubt in my mind, Mr Logan, that my father sailed his submarine into the Mediterranean Sea.'

'But why? Why the Med? Why the Aegean?'

'Probably because my father operated here during the war. He was part of a flotilla that used to patrol the Malta convoy routes. He also provided protection during the landings in Crete. He knew these waters very well.'

'Makes a lot of sense,' I conceded. 'Where did he operate out of?'

'La Spezia.'

Northern Italy. Bloody miles away.

'Anywhere else?' I asked. 'What about a base further east?'

'I do not know. It is possible. If there was such a place he kept it secret. Many U-boat commanders were a law to themselves. They operated independently much of the time and remained out of contact for weeks.'

Well, it had been worth a try, I thought.

Prohl stubbed out the remnants of his cigar in the ashtray. I found that my beer was warm in the can.

'What do you think?' Donovan asked me excitedly.

'I think it's bloody fantastic.'

'But do you believe it?'

'Harry,' I said, 'how many stories have you heard about

148

buried treasure, for Chris'sakes? Friggin' hundreds, I should think. And they've all been variations of the same theme, especially where the Nazis were concerned. We've had everything from crates of jewels sunk in Lake Toplitz to Rommel's gold buried somewhere in the Libyan desert. If I had a pound for every one I'd come across I'd be rich enough not to have to listen to them any more. And Martin Bormann? Come on!'

Yet, despite my response, I couldn't help but ask myself the very same thing. Did I believe it? Correction: did I want to believe it? The answer was a resounding yes. Hell, I'm only human.

But if the loot was in the area, where was it likely to be?

'Where was the fisherman's body found?' I asked.

Prohl said, 'I have a chart. Come, let me show you.'

He had been anticipating my question. He had the chart rolled up behind his desk. He spread it out and weighted the corners with the humidor and a couple of ashtrays. I stood up and walked over to have a look.

'The boat was found drifting here, approximately.' Prohl's stubby finger prodded the chart and I stared down past his square-cut nail. Donovan was crowding over my shoulder. Ritter, presumably because he'd heard and seen it all before, opted to remain in his seat.

The dead man had been found some fifteen miles due south of Anafi, a small island about nineteen miles east of Santorini. Anafi was pretty isolated. A caique sailed there weekly from Skala. The only other link the place had with the outside world was the twice-weekly post boat from Piraeus.

'Did they find out where he was from?' I asked.

'Astypalea,' Prohl said. 'It is thought that his boat was wrecked in the storm and he took to the dinghy.'

149

Prohl had named an island to the northeast of Anafi, on the periphery of the Dodecanese archipelago.

'He was a fair distance from home,' I said. 'He must have drifted a hell of a long way south.'

Donovan stared at the chart. 'You know this area, Mike. What else is out there?'

'Stuff all, frankly. Nothing out of the ordinary, at any rate. You've got Anafi. There's Sofrana. And about halfway between the two you've got Mekos. Sofrana's just a bloody dot on the chart. Mekos is at least inhabited. It's generally classed as the most remote island in the Cyclades. Way off the tourist routes.'

'A good place to hide something, wouldn't you say?' Prohl murmured.

I looked at them both. 'Possibly,' I said. I showed them the point on the chart. 'You draw a straight line from Astypalea to where he was found and the line almost bisects the place.'

'It's a trifle bloody convenient,' Donovan muttered.

'It is a bit,' I admitted. 'But so far you haven't got a great deal else to go on, have you?'

'What do you know of this island?' Prohl posed the question this time.

I shrugged. 'Small. About three miles long by a mile and a half wide. As I said, it's off the normal sailing routes, so no amenities. By that I mean nothing to tempt your average tourist. No hotels, no restaurants, no shops. There's a small fishing village on the southern side. There are a couple of archaeological sites dotted around: the remains of a fifteenth-century fortress above the village, and some temple ruins on top of the cliffs on the western point. Just a couple of stone columns. A poor man's Cape Sounion, if you like. It's quite heavily wooded in the centre and there's a tiny beach on the north coast. Population around a hundred, I should say. Not exactly a bubbling metropolis.'

'Nowhere to park a sub then,' Donovan mused.

'You must be joking.'

'What about the locals?'

'What about them?'

'Would we be able to search the place in peace?'

'I don't see why not. They'll have seen a white man before. You do get the occasional yacht laying up for the night.'

'Anything else?'

I shook my head. 'Can't think of anything.' Then I thought, Christ, hang on just a sec. 'Er . . . yes,' I said slowly. 'Actually, there might well be.'

'Go on, Mr Logan.' Prohl waited expectantly.

'Probably nothing, but there are a couple of legends surrounding the place,' I said. Thinking, it couldn't be that obvious. It's too much of a damned coincidence. It had to be.

'Yes?'

'Well, the island's reputed to have been the lair of the sea monster who was summoned to devour Andromeda when she was chained to the rock, before she was rescued by Perseus using the head of the Gorgon.'

Prohl's eyes lit up. For sea monster read submarine. They'd made that connection. I could see that I had their full attention so I hit them with the rest.

'It's also,' I said, my throat constricting slightly, 'supposed to have been the birthplace of Triton, the son of Poseidon and Amphitrite, a real nasty piece of work by all accounts.'

There was a long pause during which I could hear the sound of brains ticking over. I could see they were in need of some assistance.

'Triton,' I said, 'was half man, half dolphin.'

There was a deathly silence. Broken eventually by Donovan.

'I'll be damned,' he murmured.

Prohl announced delightedly, 'You see, Mr Logan, already your assistance in our search has proved invaluable! I am beginning to think that our investment in you has paid off.' The corners of his mouth twitched with humour.

'Talking about investment,' I said. 'Let's say we locate the sub and your suspicions of the cargo prove to be accurate. Have you any idea how much the gold might be worth?'

'I was wondering when you would get around to that.' Prohl gave a knowing smile. 'However, I regret I can give you only a rough estimate. You understand? I base my calculations on the likelihood that each bar would weigh in the region of ten kilos. That being the case, the 1945 value of one ingot would be something like fifteen thousand dollars.'

'And now?'

'Perhaps eight times that amount.'

Dear God Almighty, I thought wildly. Times ninety. I could feel my brain cells going into overdrive.

Prohl sensed my dilemma. 'Approximately eleven million dollars, Mr Logan,' he said smoothly.

'Give or take,' Donovan added.

Bugger the give or take. Eleven million was good enough.

'Okay, let's get down to basics. What would be my cut?'

Prohl didn't bat an eyelid. 'Five per cent.'

Rapid mental calculation on my part. A cool half million. Steady, Logan, I thought. Steady.

Donovan grinned. 'Okay, Mike. You in or out?'

'You're in luck,' I said. 'It just so happens that my calendar's free at the moment.'

'Thought it might be,' he said.

11

'We'll be using sonar, Mr Logan,' Prohl said matter-of-factly.

I'd asked him, if the sub was there, how was he expecting to locate it?

He wasn't joking. The bridge of the *Valkyrie* was bristling with more electronic gear than it had taken to find the *Titanic*.

'All the equipment you see has been developed and manufactured by my own company,' he explained. 'I presume you are familiar with the concept of sonar?'

'The concept, yes, but don't ask me anything technical. I might disappoint you.'

It was certainly the only sensible way of carrying out a systematic search of the sea-bed. It would tell us if there was anything down there. The anything, of course, being one metal cylinder, two hundred feet long by eighteen feet wide. To wit: one German *Unterseeboot*. We were all of the opinion that if Dieter Prohl had ended his last voyage hereabouts it was likely that he had scuttled the sub and transferred the cargo to shore. We also based this premise on the fact that the medal which Prohl was convinced had belonged to his father was in such good condition. If the man in whose cold fingers it had been found had chanced upon it under the sea, it wouldn't have been in half such a good state. Not after forty-odd years. After nearly half a century immersed in salt water it would have had all the intrinsic appearance of a dead cuttlefish. In other words, it would have been totally unrecognizable.

When we were on the bridge, I'd also asked Prohl where the rest of the *Valkyrie*'s crew was.

'What rest?' Donovan said. 'Apart from Marco, Ritter and me, you're it.'

'Me?'

'You can sail a boat, can't you, Logan?'

'Yes, but . . .'

'Well, there you are then. What the hell did you think we'd asked you along for? Your looks?'

'No, it's because I know these waters and I can use scuba gear. At least, that's what you told me earlier.'

'So I did, and very handy that'll be too. But you might just as well make yourself useful in other ways. A boy scout should always be prepared.'

'Bollocks,' I said. I was also on the point of making a crass remark about never having been a member of a paramilitary organization. I bit my tongue instead. Bearing in mind my knowledge of Harry Donovan's shadowy background, I didn't think the remark would go down too well. And there was also the possibility – remote, I'll admit – that Gunther Prohl, knowing my luck, had been in the Hitler Youth.

'Okay,' I said. 'Just so long as I don't have to wear a blue and white striped jersey and a peaked cap with a dinky little anchor sewn on it.'

'Spoilsport,' Donovan muttered.

I asked Prohl when he wanted us to leave.

'As soon as we are all here,' he replied.

I remembered then that Marco was still ashore.

Prohl continued, 'We are less than forty miles from the island. I would like us to be there by nightfall. We can anchor and commence our sweep of the area at first light.'

Sounded fine, I said, and told Donovan that in that case, he'd better give me a guided tour, pronto.

At which point Prohl announced he had work to attend to. He would leave Donovan to show me to my quarters.

'Right,' Donovan said cheerfully. 'Let's go, Sinbad. Bring your gear.'

He started to move off. I grabbed his arm. 'Before we go, Harry, would you mind telling me how the hell you come to be involved in this fantasy?'

'Fantasy?' He stared at me askance. 'It's no fantasy, Logan my boy. This is the real *Treasure Island*. Yo-ho-ho, me hearties, and as many pieces of eight as you can wrap your hands around.'

God help us, I thought. It'll be Robert Newton impersonations next. All rolling eyes and Jim Lad shivering his timbers, or whatever.

'Seriously,' I said.

'Seriously?' he said. 'Not all that mysterious. I've been on Gunther's payroll a few times. Freelance work. Acting as minder for some of his senior executives. Not a bad number. First-class travel and hotels, all expenses paid. A very nice little earner, frankly. I imagine he liked my CV. Better the devil you know, and all that rot. Satisfied?'

'Oh, absolutely.'

'So, can we go now?'

'Lead on, Macduff.'

Talk about the lap of luxury. It's an old axiom and one that has been expressed many times before. A boat is merely a hole in the water into which you throw vast amounts of money. As far as the *Valkyrie* was concerned, I'd have said the hole must have been damned near bottomless. She made the *Kallisti* look about as prepossessing as the *African Queen*.

Donovan told me she'd been built in sixty-eight so I hadn't been that far out in my original estimation of her pedigree. Prohl had had her refitted in eighty-six, all the way from the mahogany planked hull and the installation

155

of the air conditioning through to her sophisticated radio and navaid systems. Beneath her teak decks were housed a couple of Baudoin 700 bhp diesels, giving her a cruising speed of fourteen knots. Her accommodation was superb. One master cabin forrard, three further guest cabins, as well as facilities for four crew. There was even an office, complete with telex machine and computer terminals. As Donovan pointed out, when you had a multimillion-pound business to run you couldn't afford to take too many days off. Just because Gunther Prohl was stuck on his floating gin palace didn't mean that there weren't deals to be made, contracts to ratify.

She was some craft, all right.

And the diving equipment that had been assembled would have done justice to a professional subaqua school. There were four complete scuba outfits, a dozen spare tanks and a compressor unit. Prohl certainly wasn't stinting in his determination, commitment or sponsorship.

I was on deck checking out the scuba gear with Donovan, the afternoon sun warming my back, when I heard the buzz of the outboard. Donovan didn't look up. 'That'll be Marco,' he said.

I looked out over the rail. It was indeed Marco. And he had somebody with him. I took a closer look. A girl.

Oh, wonderful, I thought. The silly bugger's picked up a bloody yacht groupie. Just dandy. Well, she was going to be disappointed. So was he, come to that.

The skiff swung out of view as Marco positioned it beneath the stern davits. Ritter was there. He turned the winches and I heard the skiff being hooked up.

The girl was stunning. My first reaction, as she appeared over the rail, was to think to myself, Marco, you lucky dog. The second was that it was a shame he'd have to throw her back. Only then did it occur to me that Marco must have had one hell of a rapport with his boss to be allowed to bring stray sun bunnies on board. Unless, I thought, Marco was pimping. Could be Prohl had asked him to procure a little extra provisioning along with the rest of the groceries.

I was still wondering what the score was, exactly, when she said, in a marked English accent, 'Thank you, Marco,' and smiled as he gave her a friendly salute of acknowledgement and tripped off towards the bridge.

I must have looked a comical sight with my jaw around my knee-caps, because I heard Donovan give a short chuckle in my ear.

I didn't have time to ask him what he found so funny because by that time the girl had arrived and was standing in front of me, summer bag slung over her shoulder. She cocked her head questioningly. 'You must be Harry's friend,' she said.

From a great distance I heard Donovan say, 'Michael Logan, meet Elizabeth Hammond.'

She held out her hand. 'Hello. Call me Liz, please.'

'Hello, yourself,' I said. She could call me anything she liked.

Her grip was cool and surprisingly firm. She was quite tall and comfortably clad in a dark green safari-style shirt tucked into a pair of white shorts, Scholl sandals on her feet. It was also abundantly evident that she had a terrific figure. Firm breasts nudged the olive material; shorts, not indecently brief but cut just low enough, revealed a pair of long brown legs the complexion of honey. Her hair was blonde. She had it drawn back from her forehead and tied in a thick corn-weave braid that reached to the top of her shoulder blades, the style serving to emphasize her high cheekbones. Her eyes were the colour of cornflowers but with a depth to them that was remarkable. The effect was totally arresting. Pert nose, too. Her lips, with the merest

157

hint of an overbite, were parted slightly as she waited for one of us to say something.

I felt it as soon as I took her hand. I think she did too. It was like a fusing. It wasn't anything you could explain. Nothing overtly sexual, more like a telepathic communion. It was something you read and hear about and never expect to experience in the course of a thousand lifetimes. It was so immediate it was unnerving.

I had the feeling that Ritter and Donovan picked it up on their antennae, too. Ritter's expression was the more interesting. His face had assumed the tincture of a thundercloud.

Donovan winked and said quietly but firmly, 'You can let go now, Logan.'

Our hands broke apart. The link between us was severed but not lost. She gave Donovan a mildly flustered glance and said, just a shade too hurriedly, 'Well, I think perhaps I'll go and take a quick shower.' I found myself staring into those eyes again and then she was gone. I was left with the lingering fragrance of sun-kissed skin.

Ritter turned away abruptly and busied himself with raising the davits.

Donovan stared at me with a kind of awe. 'Wow!' he said. 'If you could see your face.'

I stood against the rail and watched her departing figure.

Wow indeed, I thought. I didn't speak. I couldn't. My throat had dried completely.

'And now,' Donovan began, 'I suppose you're wondering—'

I held up a hand to cut him off, then found my voice. 'Not me, mate. What on earth gave you that idea? Seen one blonde, seen them all.'

'Yeah, I could tell that by the way your eyes were glazed,' he said.

'Who is she?' I managed to ask without any noticeable tremor.

'She's Gunther's secretary.'

'His secretary?'

Donovan grinned at my expression. 'Yes, that's what I thought, as well. But it's true. Mind you, they are close, that much is obvious. He treats her more like a daughter.'

I wondered idly if that meant hands off.

'You could've damned well warned me!' I said vexedly.

'And spoil all the fun? You're joking.'

'Okay.' I let out a long breath. 'Got any more surprises lined up, or was that it?'

Not another one like Miss Hammond, I hoped. There was a distinct possibility that my heart wouldn't be able to stand it.

Donovan showed his palms in mock surrender. 'On my life, Michael. So help me.'

'Young Martin didn't look too happy with the introductions,' I said in a lowered voice. 'If looks could kill he'd be dancing on my grave.'

'In that case,' Donovan replied, without missing a step, 'we'll have you buried at sea. Christ, just ignore him. He'll get over it.' He walked back across the sun deck to resume his check of the scuba tanks.

I joined him. 'Are he and she . . . ?'

He raised his eyebrows. 'Playing doctors and nurses behind the boss's back?' He shrugged. 'I would've thought she's got more taste, frankly. Seriously, though, I wouldn't know, old son, and I could care even less. But I can't say that I've noticed any furtive groping, if that's what you mean, so I doubt it. Not that it's any of our business,' he added, fixing me with a pointed stare. 'Is it?'

'All right,' I said. 'I only asked.'

He looked up. 'Yeah, well,' he murmured. He stared at me for a long moment and seemed on the verge of commenting further. In the end, however, he compromised by developing a sudden, convenient and all-consuming interest in checking the valve on the regulator he was holding. Subject closed.

Fair enough, I thought. In any case I was still on the slow descent to earth. The appearance of someone of Elizabeth Hammond's calibre had been an event I certainly hadn't expected. Neither, I reflected uneasily, had been the effect of our meeting. It was a long time since I'd felt a jolt like that. And it had absolutely nothing to do with the fact that I'd spent the last ninety-odd days in the sin bin, all of them celibate. No, it wasn't that which worried me. It was the realization that in less time than the blink of an eye, I had contracted what was commonly termed the hots for my new employer's most beautiful asset; a situation not especially conducive to the maintenance of team morale, especially if Ritter's expression was anything to go by.

Terrific.

All right, Logan, I censured myself. Don't be a berk. Just watch it, that's all.

We were under way thirty minutes later. With Marco at the wheel, the *Valkyrie* headed east. Santorini brooded astern as we slid through the darkening swell. Argonauts in search of a golden fleece.

I stood at the rail and stared out over the stern.

The island floated on an ink-blue sea beneath a silver moon. The *Valkyrie* rode at anchor two hundred yards from shore.

The run from Santorini had been smooth and unhurried, the hum from the big diesels almost imperceptible. For a vessel of her size, the *Valkyrie* had answered to the helm with a conspicuous lack of effort. If she had any quirks, Marco had long since learned how to counteract them. He'd shown a maturity beyond his years in the way he'd handled her.

I'd taken the wheel for a while, and as I steered her towards our destination Marco told me he'd been in Prohl's employ for five years, initially as mate, and then skipper after Prohl pensioned off the previous incumbent. Not bad for a twenty-six-year-old lad of Italian descent whose father had earned his living as a deckhand on the Brindisi–Corfu ferry.

The *Valkyrie* was usually berthed in Monte Carlo – where else? – stern-on to the esplanade with the rest of the fleet. Prohl only used her about half a dozen times a year, when the passenger list consisted of either himself plus a handful of executives from his various companies, or noted dignitaries of a political or commercial persuasion. Other than that, Marco and the other three regular crew had the boat to themselves. And very nice too.

Talking of whom: I'd asked him where the others were. Signore Prohl, he'd told me, had granted them an extended leave, all expenses paid. A very generous employer, Signore Prohl, I thought. Not to mention commendably circumspect, considering the nature of our quest. Where close to eleven million dollars' worth of treasure trove was concerned, the fewer people in the know, the better.

'And now I am fortune-hunter!' Marco had chortled as he retook charge of the helm. 'Just like Long Jack Silver, no?'

Yeah, well, whoever.

Scanning the southern coast of the island as we'd approached, I'd noted that the locals hadn't added to or improved on the architecture since my last visit, some eighteen months before. Not that there would have been much chance of that. There was no way that the island's economy, based precariously on its six-caique fishing fleet, would have been able to weather the expense.

The lack of change was no bad thing. Through the glasses, even allowing for the encroaching dusk, it had still seemed to be the same picturesque cluster of white houses, with only the stocky tower of the tiny chapel breaking above the crest of roof tiles, and above that the crumbled walls of the fortress showing through the bushes like grey decaying teeth. The village hugged the northern curve of the bay. A narrow crescent of dark sand ran westwards and fringed the shoreline, petering out after a hundred yards or so at the foot of a jumble of rocks. Then the land began to rise steadily to form the uplands and the high cliffs that fell sheer into the sea, out of sight round the point. Behind the beach a belt of scrub gave way to the woods that covered the centre of the island, a shallow valley that separated the high ground to the east and west.

Now, some three hours after our arrival, the view hadn't changed a whole lot. A couple of caiques were tied up to the wooden jetty, and down on the strand, drawn up from the edge of the sea, two upturned hulls awaited repair. There were people on the quay: a trio of fishermen hunched over a pile of nets and two elderly fellows seated outside the sleepy taverna. A peaceful view, quite medieval in a way, picture-postcard stuff; Greece-is-lovely-wish-you-were-here type of thing. As far as our presence was concerned, judging by the lack of activity on shore, the locals couldn't have given a toss.

That evening we had eaten al fresco under the stern awning, with Mekos outlined against the sky behind us, a dark and grainy shadow save for the lights of the village that twinkled like glow-worms.

It had been a pleasant and relaxing interlude. In the absence of the *Valkyrie*'s permanent crew, the girl had assumed the mantle of chef. And very adept she had proved, too. The mullet had been grilled to perfection, the tender flesh flaking away from the bone like liquefied butter. She served it with the crusty white bread, wine and fresh fruit she'd bought while she had been ashore at Monolithos. Clearly, not just a pretty face.

We'd drifted into the stateroom, where the talk had ebbed and flowed, initiated by Liz Hammond enthusing about the afternoon she'd spent among the excavations at Akrotiri.

The diggings form one of the most important archaeological sites in the Aegean, as significant as Knossos. They've been working there, on and off, since the late eighteen hundreds, but the last twenty years of systematic unearthing has revealed an area of human settlement that dates back more than three thousand years prior to the birth of Christ.

Walking the narrow ghostly streets between the old two- and three-storeyed pumice-grey buildings and wandering in and out of the low doorways in the sepulchral gloom was like travelling back through time. It wasn't hard to imagine what life must have been like before the colossal eruption had transformed the town into an undulating wasteland of volcanic ash, the closest thing to nuclear fallout that man had experienced pre-Hiroshima.

They found treasures buried under the lava. Magnificent frescoes, vivid representations of man and beast, vibrating with colours that dazzled the eye: greens, blues, orange and gold. Antelopes, monkeys, dolphins, child boxers frozen in time. Legacies of a bygone age, a civilization that had plumbing and flush toilets when we Brits were still daubing ourselves blue.

I wondered if our own treasure hunt would be as rewarding.

Fortified by a bottle of Prohl's Bisquit, our armchair

wanderings had ranged further afield, until the evening became a string of reminiscences that would have done justice to a meeting of Fogg's Reform Club.

I'd found myself relating my memories of the Mayan pyramids on the Yucatan Peninsula, an area I'd grown to know well during my tour in Belize. Donovan's contribution had been a highly embellished and totally unbelievable account of a covert expedition he'd been involved in to find a valuable stone idol supposedly concealed in the ruins of Angkor Wat, the old capital of the Khmer kings, in northern Cambodia. Marco had given us all an extremely candid description of the wall murals they'd found among the ruins of the brothels in Pompeii.

Even Ritter, coaxed into loquacity by the cognac, had entered into the spirit of the occasion. He'd given us a report of his visit to the Inca fortress of Machu Picchu in the Peruvian highlands.

But it was Gunther Prohl who'd held us all spellbound as he recounted the rumours surrounding Hitler's attempts to find the treasure of the Temple of Jerusalem looted by the Visigoths during their advance through Europe in the fifth century and supposedly concealed somewhere in the Languedoc region of southern France, among the foothills of the Pyrenees. The treasure was believed to have included the Ark of the Covenant, which simply went to prove that even Spielberg's vivid imagination had been based on an element of truth.

And, inevitably, with our own imaginations by then fully fuelled, our collective thoughts had been of the plans for the coming days. We had all been too fired up by the possibility of what lay ahead to even think of retiring early so it was close to midnight when the acrid aroma of Prohl's Romeo y Juliet, coupled with the brandy, had finally begun to have its heady effect on me. Leaving the rest of them to the fumes, I'd made my way back on to the deck to take in some fresh air.

I'd been there for a while when I heard the sound behind me. I turned. It was the girl. I was uneasily aware of the hollow feeling that had suddenly materialized in my stomach.

'Beautiful, isn't it?' she said softly, gazing out beyond me.

'I think so,' I agreed.

'The others were wondering where you'd got to,' she said. 'Harry and I thought you might have fallen overboard.'

I shook my head. 'You'd have heard the scream.'

She moved in close and rested her elbow on the stanchion. 'Are you all right?' She regarded me with concern.

'I'm fine. I just don't like to spend too long in enclosed spaces.'

'The wind in your hair and the spray in your face?'

'Something like that.'

She was still wearing the shorts but she had donned a sweater over her shirt. A stray hair had escaped and hung in a wisp down her smooth cheek. I resisted the urge to brush it out of the way.

'Was it very bad?' she asked gently.

'What?'

'Prison.'

'Bad enough.' I looked towards the lights of the village. Up until that moment the Citadel had seemed a million miles away, part of another lifetime. I wondered how much of my background she knew.

'Is that why you don't like being shut in?'

'Partly. Plus it depends a lot on who I happen to be shut in with. Present company excepted.'

165

She thought about that. 'You're among friends now, though.'

'I wouldn't know,' I said, thinking of Ritter's dark visage when I'd taken her hand during that first introduction.

Not the answer she had expected. Uncertainty clamped itself on to her face. She frowned, looked away quickly and fell silent.

I said, after a short while, 'Have you worked for Gunther long?'

She turned and gazed at me shrewdly. It was clear she was wondering whether there had indeed been another, none too subtle meaning hidden behind my enquiry.

She brushed the errant hair from her cheek and smoothed it off her brow. Eventually, she said, 'I've been with him for three years.'

I digested that. I said, 'I suppose what I really meant was how come you and not some strapping Bruennhilde.'

She laughed softly then; a nice sound. 'There's not much to tell. It's the old story. I was in the right place at the right time. I'd been on the move for a while after I left college; worked as an au pair in the States, stewardess for a private airline, holiday tours rep. I was back in Europe and working as a secretary for a bank in Zurich when I met Gunther. He was one of their main customers. He was there on business and he needed some translation work done.'

'His English sounds okay to me.'

'He wanted German into Italian. Things led on from there.'

'Things?'

'He asked me to go and work for him. I accepted.' She regarded me levelly and said quietly but firmly, 'I know what you're thinking and the answer's no.'

Her blue-eyed appraisal was overwhelming. We were

both considering the implications of her response to my unspoken question.

It was there. We both sensed it. The chemistry.

She stared out towards the curve of the beach, a shadowy crescent in the moonlight. There followed a silence that seemed to last for a very long time, until a voice broke the stillness.

'Evening all.'

'Hello, Harry,' I said, not without a little relief.

Good to see that his timing was as impeccable as usual.

An arm draped itself over my shoulder. He sighed. 'Romantic, isn't it?'

I thought, Very funny, Harry.

And Liz Hammond allowed herself a small noncommittal smile.

'Where are the others?' I asked him.

'Beddy byes,' he answered blearily. 'Which is where I'm off to. It's going to be a long day tomorrow.'

Liz Hammond laid a hand on Donovan's arm. 'Good idea,' she agreed, smiling up at him. 'Sleep well, Harry.' She held my gaze. 'You, too, Michael.' Then she was gone.

'Was it something I said?' Donovan removed his arm from my neck.

'Nope,' I told him. 'It was probably me.'

He raised one eyebrow.

''Night, Harry,' I said.

12

Mid-morning. First dive of the day.

We were lying some two hundred and fifty yards off the eastern point of the island. We had been trawling for a little over an hour.

Apart from us there hadn't been much activity in the area. An hour after dawn the island's tiny fishing fleet had returned to port, a gaggle of brightly painted caiques homeward bound in line astern, engines chugging throatily as they negotiated their way into the tiny bay after a long night at the fishing grounds. I had seen their stern lights the previous evening, a long way off, bobbing in the darkness like a circle of flickering Chinese lanterns.

We had decided on an anticlockwise sweep of the coastline. Marco had taken the helm; and with Prohl seated at the screen on the bridge, the *Valkyrie* had crept forward like a shark nosing its way into the deep ocean.

Prohl knew more about how the sonar worked than any of us so, leaving him to interpret the signals that were coming up on the electronic display, Donovan, Liz Hammond, Ritter and I made further checks on the diving equipment in the hope that it wouldn't be too long before we were putting it to good use.

In fact, it proved to be a lot sooner than any of us had expected.

I'd gone to join Marco and Prohl on the bridge, so I was there when we had our first bite.

Prohl announced suddenly, 'We have something!' He could barely keep the excitement out of his voice.

I felt my pulse quicken. I didn't need to tell Marco to

stop engines. As soon as the sound of the diesels died, of course, the others rushed to join us.

'There!' Prohl cried.

The object that we were all staring at was shaped roughly like one of Prohl's fat cigars.

Simply put, sonar is a means of detecting submerged objects by use of sound waves. Sound pulses are projected down into the water. By measuring the time it takes for the echoes to bounce back to the receiver on board the tracking vessel, it's possible to build up a picture of the sea-bed. Thus, if it takes x milliseconds for the signal to rebound off the bottom, it will take less than x milliseconds for the signal to rebound off a surface higher than the sea-bed, such as a rock shelf, a shoal of fish or a wreck. By transposing the signals into graph form, it's then possible to build up a three-dimensional outline of the area that is being swept. Which is what we had here.

Prohl's state-of-the-art equipment incorporated a computer screen on to which was projected an image of the area beneath our keel. What we had before us was, to all intents and purposes, a relief map of the bottom built up into a series of contour lines, not unlike an ordnance survey map. Thus, when the lines were wide apart we were looking at a flat expanse of sea-bed. When the lines began to converge it meant that we were looking at some rising obstruction. Rock formations or fish tended to form irregular patterns in the lines. Something that was a uniform shape, such as a wreck, actually showed up, if it was in one piece, as a keel-shaped mass, rather like looking up at the underside of a boat. Even if the wreck was lying on its side the general outline could be seen. It was too clearly discernible for it to be anything else.

The sonar equipment on board the *Valkyrie* had a range of about fifteen hundred yards. According to the readout, whatever it was that was engaging our rapt attention lay some thirty yards off the port side and some ten fathoms down. Not too deep; about sixty feet.

'How long do you reckon it is?' Donovan asked.

'Sixty metres, approximately,' Prohl said.

'By God!' Donovan cried, his face registering immediate joy. 'That's what we're looking for! That's got to be it!'

'Okay,' I said, feeling the adrenalin beginning to flow. 'Let's get to it.'

To abide by the first underwater rule – to wit: never dive alone – we had decided to operate two shifts. One pair would work for a set time, then be relieved by the other two, and so on. Just for something to do, we had drawn lots for partners, which was why I'd ended up being teamed with Ritter. Which just went to prove that you couldn't win all the time.

Typically, everyone wanted to go down at once, but as I'd been elected to supervise aspects of the scuba work, I vetoed that. Much better to see what we were up against first and then report back.

Our outfits consisted of the twin tanks, wet suits, fins, masks, watches, wrist-type gauges, weight belts, safety floats and knives.

Liz Hammond, it turned out, had quite a bit of subaqua experience. During her stint as a tours rep she had worked in the West Indies and had taken full advantage of all the local water sports on offer, scuba diving included.

From our partnership in earlier days, I already knew that Donovan was fully proficient. Ritter, I presumed, had learnt the technique during his military service.

I could tell that both Liz and Donovan were itching to go down with us. They could hardly contain their impatience as Ritter and I got ourselves ready. While I prepared my gear I wondered if Liz had told Prohl about our conversation the night before. There had been nothing in her manner to suggest she had. Or in his, for that matter.

Spitting into my mask to prevent the glass fogging, I clamped it to my face, adjusted the headstrap to ensure a snug fit, bit on the rubber mouthpiece and reached behind me to turn on the tank valve to check the airflow. The regulator was functioning perfectly. The scuba harness, supporting the twin tanks, each holding thirty-eight cubic feet of compressed air – enough for an hour's work – hung comfortably across my shoulders. I gave Ritter the thumbs up.

Ritter, having gone through the same ritual, returned the gesture to indicate that his own gear was operating. Holding our masks, we let go of the rail and tipped ourselves backwards into the emerald-green water.

I tumbled to establish my bearings, twisted again and struck away from the underside of the yacht floating above me like some strange hovering space-craft. To my right, eight or so feet away, Ritter was keeping pace with a casual flick of his fins, the bubbles from his breathing tube creaming behind him. Below the surface, sounds were amplified, and the rush of compressed air in my ears seemed like the pumping of an enormous pair of bellows. I banked and Ritter followed effortlessly as we glided down towards the bottom.

The water was very clear, and with sunlight filtering through from the surface, visibility was excellent; although, inevitably, the lower we went the darker it became.

We were not alone. Multicoloured fish jinked and darted away as we neared them only to re-form at a distance into glimmering shoals that chased the slowly wafting fronds of undersea growth at dazzling speed.

By consulting my depth gauge I could see that we had hit forty feet. We should have been able to spot the wreckage by now. Beneath us, the sea-bed appeared to be composed of sand dotted with weed-encrusted rocks and split with narrow fissures and canyons. I indicated to Ritter that we should widen the distance between us. He acknowledged my signal and slid away with a lazy thrust of his legs. Keeping each other in sight, we resumed our search.

It was Ritter who found it.

I had been keeping him just within the periphery of my field of vision. I saw him wave suddenly, then beckon, and then arrow his body down out of sight. I hauled up short and swam towards him.

Then I saw it.

Lying on its port side, the length of its keel half buried in the soft sand, hull plates rusted like the diseased scales of an enormous fish, it was a sad sight. A once proud vessel that had become a steel coffin.

Unfortunately, not the one we were after.

That much was patently obvious. It wasn't even a submarine. A freighter, as far as I could determine, judging by the shape that lurked under the layer of silt and algae. About the right length, sure enough, with the superstructure positioned amidships, just like the conning tower of a submarine, but definitely a surface vessel, no doubt about it. There was no way of telling how old it was or how long it had been down there. A lot of years, if the amount of decomposition was anything to go by.

Stifling my disappointment, I went in for a closer look.

There's something inordinately grim about a sea wreck. First, you wonder about the manner of the sinking and whether people lost their lives. And then you begin to wonder if, somewhere within that stricken hull, there aren't still concealed the stripped bones of long-dead crewmen. At which point cold fingers begin to caress your spine as you think of sightless sockets in fish-nibbled skulls and the remnants of what might be flesh clinging to slender fragments that sway to the slow rhythm of a dance that will endure until the end of time.

So we didn't enter her. We went in over her stern and swam along the length of her, around the shell-like remains of the bridge and wheelhouse and over the entrance to her holds that gaped beneath us like the openings to dark, forbidding grottoes.

Ritter, his expression enclosed and hidden by his face mask, pointed to the surface, and I shrugged and held up a thumb and prepared to follow him.

Then I saw the wound in her side.

It was situated in her bows, below where the line of her watermark would have run.

I looked for Ritter but he was already halfway back to the boat. I let him go.

It wasn't hard to see now what had been the cause of her demise. The damage didn't cover a particularly large area, but that didn't mean that once the plates had gone the water wouldn't have surged into the ship with the force of a high-pressure hose. I drew closer to the perforation and ran my hands along the scarred and buckled seams. As I peered into the bowels of the ship, something tugged at my senses. My probing fingers traced the jagged edges of metal and it hit me immediately.

The metal was bent inwards, meaning that the damage had not come from an explosion within. It had been caused by something striking the hull with great force from outside.

And she had been hit hard, no question. By some kind of projectile, a shell or a missile perhaps. At least, that's what I would have assumed had the hole been in her upper hull or in her superstructure. But the hole was lower, much lower. So it hadn't been a shell at all, or the result of a rocket attack. It had been something else that had slammed into her side and taken her to the bottom.

Something like a torpedo, for instance.

Ritter had shrugged himself out of his harness by the time I caught up with him. He gave me a quizzical look as I hoisted myself up the yacht's stern ladder and removed my mask.

'I was about to come back for you,' he said.

'I'm okay,' I reassured him, dropping my fins on to the deck. 'There was something I wanted to take a look at.'

Donovan took the weight of the air tanks on my back while I unclipped myself.

'No luck, then?' Liz said, judging our lack of enthusiasm as evidence that the dive had been unsuccessful.

'Maybe,' I said. 'Maybe not.'

'What the hell's that supposed to mean?' Donovan asked.

So I told them.

'It's a heck of a long shot,' Donovan murmured, laying the air tanks down.

'True, but then so is everything else about this enterprise.'

'Couldn't you tell how long the wreck's been down there?'

I unstrapped the knife from my calf. 'Not without a thorough survey of the area. I couldn't even make out her name because of the rust and crap on her, so she probably went down a fair while ago. If she was sunk by a torpedo, then she must have gone down in the war. Which at least tells us that there was a sub in the area. In which case, why not a German one? It could be we're on the right track.'

'Dammit!' Donovan pounded the rail in frustration. 'I really thought we'd struck it first time around.'

'Nobody could be that lucky,' I said. 'But at least it proves that the sonar works.'

Realistically, of course, I doubted whether any of us had fully expected our search to produce dividends within the first hour. That would have meant extending the boundaries of good fortune beyond all credible limits.

For a start, I told them, there was no guarantee that the U-boat, if it was down there, would even be in one piece. If Prohl had scuttled his vessel, it could be that he had done rather more than simply opened the tube doors and flooded her. He could have used explosives to send her to the bottom, in which case she could well be in little pieces sprinkled over the sea-bed, like so much metallic confetti. Which would make the read-out on the sonar screen look like the floor of a building site.

Alternatively, she could have been in one piece initially and broken up over the years by storm damage. That was a distinct possibility. We were also, it had to be remembered, only forty miles from Santorini, where they'd had that eruption back in fifty-six. The shock waves could have spread out in a ripple effect. Her hull could have ruptured and split apart. If she was anywhere in the vicinity, she had been there for nigh on half a century. Anything could have happened in that time.

And that wasn't taking into account the various permutations made possible by the discovery of the dead freighter.

Nothing else for it then, except to press on regardless.

Which we did.

It took us a little over five hours to complete our first circumnavigation of Mekos. In that time we had undertaken three more dives, none of them productive.

We had established one thing, however. The Aegean appeared to be littered with more bloody wrecks than the forecourt of a second-hand car dealer.

At various points around this one small island we had turned over, aside from the freighter, the remains of one motor cruiser and a brace of fishing smacks. The fishing craft were in pieces, possibly the victims of storms and heavy seas. The motor cruiser, on the other hand, carried the scars of fire damage. The hull was blackened and charred. It had been a stylish boat before it had been consigned to the deep. Some poor bugger's insurance premiums had no doubt taken off as a result.

We called a halt in the late afternoon, by which time we were back at our anchorage off the main jetty; two sets of dives each and somewhat tired after our efforts. And the only thing we had caught was sunburn. Still, tomorrow was another day. The next time we would be casting our nets a little further out from shore.

So, were the troops downhearted? Well, only moderately.

The next day was more of the same. At least we were improving our tans. And no wrecks at all this time, although we'd had a few false alarms. We'd made a couple of dives and discovered nothing save for several large oil drums, some bright spark's contribution to world pollution.

And we did have one visitor. Sort of.

It was late afternoon and we were making a sweep across the northwestern quarter when the helicopter flew over.

I was with Prohl and Ritter, watching the sonar screen. Liz and Donovan were sunning themselves on deck when we heard the clatter of the chopper's approach. It sounded low so I took a stroll to see what the noise was all about.

It was small; a Hughes 500. Bright red. It whirled overhead like a fat dragonfly, banked and came in on another run. I reckoned they'd probably caught sight of Liz Hammond reclining at the stern and decided to take a lecherous decko. I can't say I blamed them all that much. She was wearing a one-piece black costume that wasn't especially revealing, but it contrasted with her blonde hair and that, coupled with her skin tone, made her stand out on deck like the figurehead on a schooner. She looked terrific and didn't pay them a blind bit of attention.

One quick pass and the chopper flew off, heading west. Excitement over for another day.

We were pretty subdued by the time we had stowed the scuba gear, saddened that the day's labours hadn't turned up anything more rewarding than a ton and a half of scrap iron.

It was beginning to look as though Mekos was a dead end. The omens had not proved fortuitous after all. All that guff about Triton and mermen had been exactly that. Pure guff. No cryptic significance at all.

So, where did that leave us?

With our thumbs stuck up our rear ends, frankly. Because the only thing we had proved in the course of our two-day investigation was the unassailable fact that all our previous surmising had been a total waste of time.

All we needed was another clue.

All?

Over the meal that evening we held a council of war. Gunther Prohl remained convinced that the U-boat was in the area. We would make yet another sweep around the coastline, extending our net even further; by another mile.

I thought that was pushing it a bit. That put us almost two miles distant from the island. It didn't seem logical that Prohl, if he had scuttled his vessel, would have left himself such a long row back to shore. But, as Gunther Prohl said, what else did we have to gone on?

Not a whole hell of a lot, it seemed to me.

* * *

177

Which was probably why I was finding it difficult to sleep. My mind was just too active as it sought solutions to mysteries beyond my ken. I tried to imagine myself as the captain of a rogue submarine with a zillion dollars' worth of gold bullion on board. Where the hell would I have gone? Somewhere that I knew, was the only answer I could come up with. Brilliant reasoning, Logan. The fact was, I felt that I was missing something. I was certain that the solution was staring us full in the face, only we were too damned blind to see it. The wood for the trees, and so forth.

So, in the end I thought, Sod it, and got up for a stroll, hoping for inspiration.

The cabin I was using was part of the crew's quarters. Not as luxuriously furnished as the guest rooms, but comfortable none the less. My only gripe was that it was not as readily accessible as those occupied by Donovan and the others. My nearest neighbour was Marco, whose own accommodation was adjacent to mine.

I padded along the passage towards the companionway that led up on to the deck. It looked as if I was the only insomniac on board. What the hell time was it? I squinted at my wrist. One-thirty. Jesus! Maybe I'd grab a beer from the bar on my way up.

I was wrong, as it turned out. Someone else couldn't sleep either.

I heard voices as I passed the door to the cabin that Prohl used as his office. Correction: I heard one voice, male, speaking in German. It was pointless attempting to listen in, even if I'd wanted to. I don't speak the language. I could tell, though, that Prohl was speaking to someone who wasn't in the room with him. I guessed he was using a radiophone link. I recalled that Donovan had told me that the office was fully equipped with a telex and computer, so a simple implement such as a phone, on a boat this size, would have been a foregone conclusion.

It did seem a funny sort of time to be calling somebody though, but I supposed that as Prohl's interests were many and varied and distributed worldwide, there was no way that he could monitor his various commitments during his own daylight hours. Like most of the high-powered businessmen that I had met, his capacity for cramming thirty hours of work into a twenty-four-hour day was prodigious. It might be one-thirty where we were, but in Los Angeles it was still only four in the afternoon, while in Tokyo it would have already reached nine-thirty in the morning. Let's face it, Gunther Prohl hadn't made his first million by concentrating on his beauty sleep. He'd worked for it.

I left him to it and took myself off towards the stern awning, pausing on the way to help myself to a couple of cold cans from the bar.

The night was warm and sultry, the moon full, suspended like a pearl above a calm sea. Feet up on the rail, I tipped back on my chair and cogitated.

What were my options if our present search proved fruitless?

Good question. Well, I had a bit of money left in the bank. Not enough to compensate me for the loss of the *Kallisti* but enough for me to live on for a few months. There was always the chance that I could use my limited funds as the down payment on another boat and go back to chartering on my own. Failing that, I was pretty sure that Stavros would take me on, but I didn't want to presume on our friendship any more than was absolutely necessary.

The other option was for me to go back to my old trade as military advisor – a euphemism for mercenary. Iain Cameron was long gone, but both Donovan and I had established a number of strategic contacts over the years, particularly in the Gulf. And the pay was generally pretty good. Frankly, I viewed that alternative as a last resort. I'd enjoyed my soldiering, but enough was enough. I was after something a little more sedate in my old age.

I took a sip of beer, closed my eyes and thought about it.

Then heard a noise, opened my eyes, saw movement out of the corner of one of them and focused.

Liz Hammond had her back to me. She was wearing a long pale robe. Her hands were sunk into the pockets. She was staring out from the boat like Penelope awaiting the return of Ulysses.

'Don't do it,' I said. 'You'll frighten the fish.'

She jumped as if she'd been shot, and whirled quickly, revealing an intoxicating expanse of bare leg in the process. 'My God!' she gasped, eyes wide, right hand shooting up to her throat. 'You scared me to death!'

'We're going to have to stop meeting like this,' I said. 'People are beginning to suspect.'

Her hair tumbled loose, framing her exquisite bone structure. She lifted both hands then and ran her fingers through the blonde cascade. The movement was unconscious yet sensuous, fully accentuating the outline of her breasts. She wasn't wearing a whole lot underneath the thin material. I felt my breath catch.

'I couldn't sleep,' she said exasperatedly.

'Join the club.'

She put her head on one side. Her lovely face bore a troubled frown. 'Are you all right, Michael?'

'I'm depressed,' I said glumly. 'Comfort me.'

Her mouth split into an easy smile. 'Oh, Logan, I'll bet you say that to all the girls.'

Our eyes held then for what seemed a long, long

moment, and I felt it again. That tumbling in the pit of my stomach.

She came over to me and sat down in the next chair. The robe slipped momentarily from one smooth thigh before she caught the hem and drew it across her knee.

'Drink?' Half joking, I proffered her my second unopened can.

'Thanks,' she said, to my surprise. She popped the tab expertly and took a long sip, tipping her head back and closing her eyes as the chilled liquid tickled the back of her tongue. 'Mmn,' she murmured, 'that tastes good.'

We were silent for a moment or two, with our own thoughts; content in each other's company, yet aware that there was more to the silence than that. It was as if we were both waiting for the other to make the first move.

'What's next, Michael?' she said finally, holding the can in her slender hand.

I shrugged, and hung my head on my chest. 'Frankly, I haven't a clue.'

'No bright ideas?'

'Me? I haven't had a bright idea for yonks. I'm just going with the flow.'

'And where's that taking us?'

'Buggered if I know.'

'But you think we're close? You think the submarine's around here somewhere?'

'Gunther does, and he's paying the wages.'

'But do you?' She was leaning forward slightly. The neckline of the robe sagged. I could see the soft curve of her breasts.

Did I? As I considered my answer, I felt myself under intense scrutiny from those captivating blue eyes.

'Yes,' I said. 'It's here, all right. If we could only find the key.'

'Well,' she said, 'there's always tomorrow.' She sat back again. The shadow between her breasts lightened.

'You mean today,' I corrected her, and tapped my watch pointedly.

She took another pull at her drink. I watched her throat muscles contract. 'What if we do find it?' she asked. 'What then?'

'You mean me?'

She nodded.

'Buy another boat, I suppose. I haven't really thought about it.' The hell I hadn't. Half a million dollars? Who was I trying to kid?

'Ever thought about settling down?'

'You mean wife and kids?' I looked at her, aghast.

'Don't look at me like that,' she said, suddenly abashed.

So I stared out over the rail instead.

'Took the wind out of your sails, eh, Logan?' She chuckled. A sound not unlike delicate wind chimes tinkling faintly. Yet I felt the laughter had been used as a ploy to cover up another brief second of awkwardness.

'Kind of,' I replied, this time with complete sincerity.

'Scared about commitment?'

'Of course. Who wouldn't be?' I took a swig of my own drink to steady my nerves.

'Ever been close?'

I shook my head. 'Nope. Besides, who'd have me? The wrong side of forty, ex-gold smuggler, ex-gunrunner, and, this little jaunt notwithstanding, bugger all to show for it. Can't say I'd make much of a catch, frankly.'

'Oh, I don't know,' she responded softly. 'I've known women who've settled for less.' Her gaze was irrepressibly beguiling.

'Erm . . .' I began.

She grinned bewitchingly. 'If you could see your face!'

182

'Funny,' I said, attempting a recovery, 'that's the second time someone's said that to me.'

Her grin was transformed into a quiet satisfied smile as we slipped into another contemplative silence.

It was as if we were attempting to coax each other into uncharted waters; neither of us confident enough to let ourselves go, and yet both of us reluctant to resist the tide's inexorable pull.

'What about you?' I said, after a while.

No response. For a moment I thought that perhaps she hadn't heard me. Then she put her beer to one side and said quietly, 'There was someone.'

I tensed. There had been something in her voice.

'He died.'

Christ. I watched the cloud appear in her eyes and waited quietly for her to continue.

'He was French. A photo-journalist. Freelance. He did a lot of commission work for *Paris Match* and *Time* magazine. Officially, he was killed while reporting on a story in Afghanistan. I was told he was involved in a car-bomb explosion in Kabul. Appparently the rebels were attempting to assassinate a Russian general as a protest against the Soviet peace proposals, and Alain got in the way. He just happened to be in the wrong place at the wrong time.'

'You said officially? What was the other version?'

'Eight months ago I was in Geneva with Gunther. We attended a dinner and we were introduced to the leader of one of the main Afghan resistance parties who was shopping for funds. It was he who told me that Alain had been murdered by the Russians as part of a Soviet intelligence mission aimed at capturing one of the top rebel commanders. It all sounded very involved. I never got the full details. His sister died over there about the same time. She was a doctor working in one of the refugee camps in Pakistan. She was killed during a cross-border bombing raid by the Afghan air force.'

Her face was suddenly filled with the most immeasurable sadness.

Instinctively, I put my beer down and reached across to take her hand. God, but she was trembling like a bird. I was startled, too, at the force with which she returned my grip.

'It's okay, Liz,' I said. 'It's okay.'

A tear tracked down her cheek.

'Hold me, Michael . . .' she whispered softly, '. . . please.'

I got up quickly and moved to her. She came off her seat. I enclosed her, and her arms went around me. Soft hair caressed my face. Shivers racked her body.

'It's all right,' I murmured. 'It's all right.'

I held her for what seemed like several minutes, until her tremors subsided. We broke apart slowly. She traced the side of my face with her palm. 'I'm sorry,' she said. Her own face was still damp. 'It still gets to me sometimes. You'd have thought by now . . .' Her voice trailed off and she gave a helpless little shrug of defeat.

'Nothing to apologize for.' I wiped away a ribbon of moisture from below her left eye.

She gave a little grimace. 'Your shirt's all wet.'

'I'll send you the cleaning bill.'

She curled her right hand into a fist and punched me lightly on the chest. 'You're all right, Logan. Thanks.'

'For you,' I said, 'anything.'

She stiffened abruptly, her attention suddenly concentrated on something behind me. I turned.

Ritter.

Considering the hour, the promenade deck was becoming as congested as Piccadilly Circus during the rush hour.

He was standing as still and as silent as a rock. His face,

too, was rigid. Maybe it was due to the fact that he was encased in shadow that his eyes appeared to be devoid of light.

And then, just as silently, he was gone. He might never have been there. Except that I could still feel his eyes boring into the back of my neck, like an image etched on to a retina.

Liz Hammond shivered.

There was nothing between them. Of that Donovan had seemed reasonably sure. And nothing in their attitude towards each other over the past couple of days had led me to suspect otherwise. Pressed, I'd have said their relationship hadn't even been particularly sociable. More like polite toleration on both sides. Now, I was beginning to have my doubts.

'Want to tell me about it?' I asked.

She backed away from me, hugged herself, turned and stared out over the rail. She took a deep breath.

Somehow, I sensed what was coming.

'About a year ago,' she said, 'Martin made some rather obvious advances. He was most affronted when I told him I wasn't interested. Didn't like having his ego dented, I suppose.'

Poor old Ritter, I thought. We'd all been down that road.

'Did Gunther know about this?' I asked.

She shook her head. 'I didn't tell him. I knew it was something I had to resolve for myself. I thought I had.' She gave a helpless little shrug.

She'd thought wrong, I reflected.

It struck me, remembering the darkness in Ritter's eyes, that here was a man on whom rejection had not settled lightly. I told her so, adding that it couldn't have been easy for the two of them having to coexist in such close proximity.

185

She stuck her hands in the deep pockets of her robe and spent several seconds studying the honed teak deck beneath her feet.

'Not really. In the general run of things we'd hardly ever see each other. Anyway, it was a fact of life that Martin had to come to terms with. I knew we'd be together on this trip but I thought we'd both be able to handle it. We're supposed to be adults, after all.'

She gave a rueful little smile. 'At least that's what I thought before all this.' She swivelled back towards me. 'It's happening too fast, Michael. It's scary.'

'What is?'

'You and me,' she said.

My skin prickled.

'Liz . . .' I began, but she silenced me by placing the tip of her right forefinger gently over my lips.

'Sssh,' she murmured. 'Don't say anything.'

She slipped in closer then and placed both hands on my shoulders. Her breasts brushed against me as she lifted her face to mine. Her lips were warm and soft as she kissed the side of my jaw.

She pulled away quickly. Somehow, I had known that she would.

''Night, Logan,' she whispered.

'Honest,' I said, 'I *would* respect you in the morning.'

'I know,' she said gently. She hugged me again.

And left me.

Just when my toes were beginning to curl up, too.

Sod it.

13

Stuff all on the third day as well. The novelty of the search was beginning to wear off. Rapidly. Dreams of how I was going to invest my first half million were disappearing as fast as ice cubes in a heat wave. This was not good. Anybody struck by inspiration? No? Terrific.

Widening the search area hadn't served any useful purpose either. None whatsoever. Not even any oil drums this time.

We did see the helicopter again, though. It must have been the same one. There couldn't have been two identical models flitting around our neck of the woods. It came over for another quick look and zoomed off as before, sunlight glancing across its spinning blades. The odd thing was that I got the impression that the people in the chopper weren't the only ones paying us close attention. Strange that.

It was some time later, towards the end of the afternoon. We had completed our last run and were heading back to our usual anchorage, poodling along, not trying for any records. I was at the wheel, giving Marco a break. He was out on deck, bronzing his pectorals. Prohl was behind me, cigar clamped between his lips, eyes glued to the sonar. He had the screen switched on, probably in the forlorn hope that he'd suddenly pick up something that we had missed on an earlier sweep.

I was watching the approach to the bay, anxious to avoid carving up any of the local boats that might steer inadvertently into our path. We were about half a mile out when I saw it.

A brief flash, in the trees above the beach. Donovan came in through the hatchway and I said, 'We're being watched.'

He grinned. 'Get away!'

I suppose it hadn't been the brightest remark, considering we'd just spent the last seventy-two hours sailing rings around the bloody place. The people ashore were likely thinking that our damned rudder had got stuck. No wonder we were creating interest.

'All right,' I said. 'Amend that. We're under surveillance.'

He blinked. 'Say again?'

'About a hundred yards back from the beach. Field glasses.'

It was the sun reflecting off a lens that had caught my eye.

'Bird-watchers,' Donovan retorted glibly.

'Bollocks,' I said.

'That'll be them,' he chuckled. 'The lesser spotted variety. Come on, Logan! Surveillance? Who're you trying to fool?'

'Take a look,' I said. 'Eleven o'clock, to the left of those pine trees.'

Donovan peered out over the bow. 'Can't see a bloody thing,' he said. 'Are you sure? No, okay, sorry,' he corrected himself quickly, noting my expression. 'You wouldn't have said so otherwise. Wonder who it is.' He chewed his lip pensively.

Prohl had tuned in to our conversation. He reached for our own set of glasses and had a look-see for himself. He couldn't spot anyone either. 'One of the islanders?' he ventured.

Whoever it had been had gone. Maybe it had been the product of an overactive imagination. I shrugged. 'Probably,' I said.

Even to my own ears my reply hadn't sounded too convincing. But who else could it have been? There weren't any other visitors on Mekos, that we had seen. We were the only ones. I brought the *Valkyrie* to a stop and we dropped anchor. The chain went over the side with a harsh rattle and hit the water with a heavy splash.

I said to Prohl, 'I know this is probably a dumb question, but as a matter of interest, how many other people know about this little jaunt we're engaged on?'

He looked taken aback, alarmed that I'd even contemplated such a thing. 'No one.'

'No business associates? No chance the media could've got hold of it? It'd make a hell of a story.'

'Absolutely not!' he shot back vehemently. 'This undertaking has been carried out in the utmost secrecy. The only ones who know the full reason for our being here are the six of us.' Then he added tartly, 'I could ask you the same question.'

'And you'd get the same answer,' I said. 'If you recall, I hadn't a bloody clue where I was heading until I met you, and none of us have been out of each other's sight since.'

'Aren't we all getting just a bit paranoid here?' Donovan interjected quickly, in a bid to restore a bit of decorum.

He was right, of course. Both Prohl and I realized that.

Because it could just as easily have been the sun catching on a piece of broken bottle or a tin can or a pebble of quartz. Any one of a thousand things, right?

If it was paranoia setting in, then it was the inevitable result of our frustration at having drawn yet another huge blank in our search for the elusive U-boat. Our failure was beginning to have an unsettling effect on us all. And friction of one kind or another was bound to occur. We'd only been at it for three days, but it wouldn't be much longer before we'd be at each other's throats with a vengeance. And that wasn't taking into account the rift that was gradually developing between myself and Ritter. Ever since I'd met him, despite owing him my freedom, he'd remained taciturn and distant. And matters had not been aided by my blossoming relationship with Liz Hammond. If things came to a head, something told me that I might just have to watch my back. Along with other, more vulnerable, parts of my anatomy.

Donovan was still gazing thoughtfully over the bow towards the beach. He said quietly, 'You know what we really need, don't you?'

Prohl and I looked at him and then at each other and waited expectantly.

'Shore leave,' Donovan said.

Gunther Prohl said he had some business calls to take care of, Marco wanted to check over a glitch he'd discovered in one of the *Valkyrie*'s throttle controls, and Ritter came over all moody; so, in the end, there were just the three of us for the liberty boat.

But not before I had been collared by Gunther Prohl.

I was passing the door to the cabin he used as his office when he nabbed me. 'A word, Michael,' he said. 'If you please.'

Sounds a bit formal, I thought. He held the door open and I trailed him in. He closed the door behind us.

I'd paid little heed to Donovan's description of the facilities. I'd understood simply that it was the place where Prohl kept in daily contact with his worldwide group of companies, through use of telephone and telex. Having heard him at work the other evening, my expectations had been along the lines of a simple teletype and a radiophone. It was rather more sophisticated than that.

190

The place looked as if it had been lifted directly from a corner of Mission Control, Houston.

Like the sonar, radar and radio gear on the bridge, I presumed the equipment here had also been manufactured by Prohl Industries. On closer inspection, however, I noted that much of the hardware was either IBM or ITT. As well as the telex VDU there were three other CRT screens, a printer and three phone consoles. I couldn't make head or tail of any of the read-outs on the screens. Prohl took pity on me and explained that each screen was linked to a particular stock exchange: London, New York and Tokyo. The three consoles and squawk boxes were for conference calls. I was suitably impressed. But that wasn't why he had invited me into the inner sanctum.

'Now,' he said, gesturing me to a seat and removing a cigar from the humidor on the desk, 'I would like to talk to you about Elizabeth.'

He was standing over me and he had the words out before I'd had time to settle my backside. He could, as the saying goes, have knocked me the rest of the way down with the proverbial feather.

I know my jaw fell open.

He cut the end off the cigar and lit up. He inhaled. 'Michael, it is quite apparent that the two of you have formed an . . . attachment.' A wreath of blue smoke spiralled away from the end of his cigar and circled his head like a mystic halo.

My defences went up immediately. I wasn't sure whether the statement had been intended to elicit a response on my part or not, so I didn't answer. Frankly, I was too stunned to think of anything to say. My confusion must have shown.

He said, 'Please, do not misunderstand me. I am not

speaking as a jealous suitor, neither is this a lecture on morality.'

Thank God for that, I thought.

He looked at me with his head to one side, a hint of amusement on his face. 'I see by your expression that you are confused. I think perhaps I should explain something to you.'

I waited.

He took another long, meaningful puff on his cigar. No doubt it gave him time to collect his thoughts. Finally, he said, 'Michael, two years ago, my wife and daughter were killed in a car crash on the autobahn. You may have read of it in the newspapers.'

I hadn't but I didn't comment.

'As you can imagine, it was a time of great personal sadness for me.' He paused momentarily. 'Made a little less so due to Elizabeth's compassion and support. This despite the fact that she had only been working for me for a year when it happened. Her help during my time of grief was a source of great consolation. Consequently I grew remarkably fond of her. In truth, I came to regard her more as a friend than an employee. Eventually, she came to mean a great deal more than that.' Prohl's face softened perceptibly as he spoke. 'With the death of my daughter, Ingrid, Elizabeth became the closest thing to family.'

He faced me squarely. 'I do not know if you are also aware of the fact but she, too, has had more than her full measure of unhappiness . . .' His voice trailed off.

I waited.

'I know her very well, Michael. She suffered a great loss and she is still vulnerable.' He paused to let the meaning sink in.

I responded carefully. 'You're asking me if my intentions are honourable?'

His voice was pure steel. 'I do not want to see her hurt. You understand what I am saying?'

I stood up and confronted him. 'I'm aware of her loss,' I said. 'I know she's still grieving. And I give you my word that I will never knowingly cause her harm.'

His head lifted. He regarded me with renewed interest. 'I see that she has indeed told you everything. That could not have been easy for her.'

'It wasn't,' I said.

He nodded slowly, assessing the validity of my answer. Then he gave an appreciative nod. 'In truth, I expected nothing less. I believe I had already detected what it is she sees in you. Something your friend Donovan described to me when he recommended your services.'

'You mean my ability to laugh in the face of adversity?' I suggested.

He allowed himself another little smile. 'That also, perhaps. I was referring, however, to something we talked of when you first joined us. Your integrity.'

'God help us,' I said, mortified. 'Now you're embarrassing me.'

He chuckled softly then. 'I see there is no requirement for us to discuss the matter any further. We do indeed understand one another.' He extended his hand. 'As far as Elizabeth is concerned, I would prefer it if this conversation had never taken place.'

'What conversation?'

We clasped hands. 'Enjoy your trip ashore, Michael,' he said.

'Thanks,' I said. 'We will.'

And with that, he showed me out.

Talk about being nonplussed.

We landed on a tiny beach a few yards from one of the upturned caique hulls. Although it was still quite early, the day was already beginning to show signs of being another scorcher. The sky was blue and cloudless. The sand beneath our bare feet was warm and soft and oozed between our toes as we left the skiff and strolled up towards the village.

At the edge of the sand we slipped into our footwear, sandals for Liz, trainers for Donovan and myself. If we were to go gadding about the island, I wanted something on my feet. I had no intention of ending up with toes full of pine needles or soles smeared with goat droppings. Or worse.

As we hit the town, Liz went all gaga over the pretty whitewashed stone cottages and the riot of bougainvillaea that cascaded over the walls. A faint breeze from the sea ruffled the mass of scarlet flowers, and the heavy scent of geraniums lingered like a slowly departing guest.

The village consisted of about fifty or so houses that ranged up from the picturesque harbour in a fat crescent. Narrow, shaded alleyways separated the buildings. The place was plainly quite primitive inasmuch as there were none of the usual trappings common to the more readily accessible islands: eyesores such as TV aerials and the intrusion of pop music from somebody's transistor, for instance.

There were a few locals pottering about, middle-aged or elderly, most of them. This wasn't unusual. The young people all tend to scoot off to Athens as soon as they hit their teens, in the hope that they'll find work. Over the years, of course, the rest of the population dwindles away, until no one is left except the very old who've come back to die or those who never left in the first place.

It's a sad and not uncommon state of affairs because only remote island sanctuaries like Mekos and Anafi preserve the values and folk customs that are gradually disappearing everywhere else in Greece. In the big cities and towns the old ways are giving way to the ogres of commercialism: the lure of the Sony Walkman and the Big Mac.

There was a village shop of sorts, tacked on to the taverna, but its stocks were low. A sign that the island was due for an imminent visit from the supply boat from the Piraeus.

We bought a couple of bottles of cheap wine, a loaf of bread, some goat's cheese and a bunch of grapes. The proprietor was a roly-poly, smiling man, and as such was somewhat out of sorts with his rather run-down establishment.

'Check if there are any other strangers around,' Donovan suggested.

I posed the question.

The shopkeeper smiled and shook his head. No, we were the only visitors. He handed over the provisions in a string bag and counted out my change.

So much for that idea. I thanked him for the food and promised to drop off the bag on our return.

We went outside and Donovan said, 'Right. I'll leave you to it. Have fun. I'll see you later.'

Liz and I stared at him.

'Where the hell are you going?' I asked him.

He put his head on one side and sighed disbelievingly. 'Jesus, Logan. You can be bloody dense at times.'

'Sorry, Harry. You've lost me.'

'No,' he said. 'You've both lost me. Two's company, remember? Go on, bugger off, the pair of you.'

'Harry . . .' I started to say.

I could sense Liz breaking into a grin beside me.

'For crying out loud, girl,' Donovan pleaded. 'Do something.'

Liz tucked her arm through mine. 'Come on, you,' she

said, and tugged gently. Then she winked. 'Thanks, Harry.'

'My pleasure, love. Be gentle with him, won't you?'

He turned and began to stroll away, unconcerned, in the direction of the jetty.

I looked at Liz with suspicion. 'Did you put him up to this?'

She laughed. 'No, it was all his own work.'

'Sly bugger.'

'Yes, isn't he? Now, are you coming or not?' she added in mock severity.

'No,' I said. 'Just breathing rather heavily.'

'Oh, God.' She raised her eyes to heaven. 'Trust me to end up with someone who thinks he's a comedian.'

We left the village and followed the shore a short way, before cutting inland along a narrow goat track that led off the beach and wound its way through a frieze of tamarisk bushes and into the pine woods. Not surprisingly, there was no sign of our mysterious watcher. No one with a pair of Zeiss hanging around his neck. We might have been the only two people on the island. The resinous smell of the trees filled the air and our progress was accompanied by the chirp of cicadas and the shrill cries of hoopoes.

The ground continued to rise steadily and we followed the track as it meandered through shady oaken groves. On a small rocky promontory we took a breather. Looking down through gaps in the trees, it was possible to glimpse the beach and the town and the *Valkyrie* lying offshore, her white hull sparkling against the deep blue water. For one brief nostalgic moment I thought of the *Kallisti*. If only she had been down there instead.

Liz touched my arm. 'On your feet, lazybones. I want to see that temple you told me about.' She jumped up, eager to be off.

She was wearing a variation of the same outfit that I had first seen her in: shirt and shorts, her hair tied back as before. Like Prohl, she was probably able to maintain a tan most of the year round, although she was obviously careful not to allow her skin to get too dark. It was the colour of *café au lait* and had a sheen to it like the glaze on fine porcelain.

I watched the muscles in the back of her long legs tighten as she trod the rocky path ahead of me, and I tried manfully to concentrate on where to put my own feet rather than on the line of her bikini briefs, outlined through her cotton shorts. Not easy, believe me.

She stopped and waited for me to catch up. The wine bottles clinked in the bag that I had slung over my shoulder.

She brushed a stray hair away from her brow. 'How much further?'

'At the risk of sounding like James Stewart doing his wagon master impersonation, I'd say just over the next rise.' I was embarrassed at how much I was panting, though it could have been lust rather than exhaustion. More likely it was both.

'What happens if we get attacked by Indians before we get there?'

'We form a circle and fight 'em off.'

'You reckon?' She threw me an 'oh, yeah?' kind of look, one eyebrow arched critically.

'Well, all right, look at it this way: we might not stand much of a chance of fending them off, but think of the fun we'd have forming a circle.' I favoured her with my version of a wicked leer.

'I might have guessed!' She aimed a playful swipe at my ear.

We spotted the ruins through the trees.

Twenty-five centuries ago the temple perched atop the

197

western cliffs must have been an awe-inspiring sight. Visible from many miles away, it would have beckoned seafarers like a beacon. Now, it was little more than a forlorn rectangle of flattened slabs fronted by a crumbling façade of two weathered stone columns rearing towards the sky like broken fingers.

What was left of the façade overlooked the edge of the cliff. Originally there had been four columns. Now, only the two inner ones survived, the outer pair having collapsed during the long passage of time. They lay like two fallen tiers of draughts, one round stone resting upon another. The floor area extended back towards the trees. On either side of the main structure the remnants of smaller annexes lay scattered across the grass like outcrops of terminal moraine. Weeds sprouted in profusion.

Despite the island's connection with Poseidon, the edifice on the cliff top had been erected to another celestial being altogether.

Among the islands of the Cyclades there must be scores of temples dedicated to Apollo. Not surprising really, as during the so-called Archaic and Classical periods he was one of the most important deities around, his glory exceeded only by that of Zeus himself. Apollo, the sun god, was a bit of a hybrid: a cross between a patron of the arts, Daley Thompson and, for want of a better analogy, the Moderator of the Church of Scotland. He represented creativity in music, song and poetry, athletic prowess, respect for the law and moderation in all things. He probably gave great after-dinner speeches too. Delos was his birthplace but Mekos, Naxos and Anafi are just three of the other islands where there are the remains of monuments erected in his honour.

Interestingly enough, in some parts of Asia Minor he was also worshipped as Apollo Lykion, Apollo the Wolf;

another tantalizing yet false clue that we were close to the last survivor of Doenitz's wolf packs.

The temple wasn't the only spectacular thing about the site. The drop over the edge of the cliff was pretty breathtaking as well.

The lip of the rock had been worn away in many places. Small shrubs and unidentified flowers clung to the edge, defying the fall to the sea below. About a yard from the brink, I dropped to my stomach and eased forward gingerly. I was unprepared for the view.

Just below me, the face of the rock curved inwards before plummeting into the sea. There was literally nothing between the rim and the water one hundred and thirty-odd feet below, not even a jumble of rocks at the base of the cliff; just the sheer rock face cleaving like the blade of an axe into the emerald translucence. I reversed quickly and bumped into Liz, who was standing well back, trying to peer over at the same time.

'What's it like?' she asked.

'Terrifying,' I replied. I pointed to the ground. 'There's nothing underneath us. It's like standing on a diving board.'

She retreated hurriedly. I wasn't slow in following.

'Couldn't they have roped it off or something?' she said.

'Not much point. The locals know it's there and the place doesn't have that many visitors. It's hardly worth the effort.'

'That's probably what the architect said. I wonder how many people have gone over since.'

'And did they fall or were they pushed?'

She stared at me. 'You're not serious?'

I shook my head. 'As far as I know, they didn't go in for human sacrifice.'

'What did they go in for?'

199

'Prophecies, mostly. Probably catered for the passing trade. Like Pythia at Delphi.'

'What would that entail?'

'Pretty mundane stuff. Was the next harvest going to be bountiful? Who's going to win the three-thirty at Olympia? Things like that?'

'You're having me on.'

'Never.'

'How about calculating the chances of meeting tall, dark, handsome men?'

'Ah,' I said. 'In that case, you'd have needed to consult this.' I tapped the nearest pillar.

'What's that?'

'The personal column.'

She broke up. 'Oh, Logan, that's terrible!'

Anyhow, I told her, the place would have been riddled with tall, dark, handsome men.

'Really? How marvellous!'

'Probably not. Most of them were as bent as a leaf of wet lettuce.'

'What? They can't all have been queer!'

'The Greeks practically invented the word.' I was glad Stavros wasn't around to hear me say that.

'Oh, dear,' she said. 'What a let-down. You'd better peel me a grape.'

I peeled her several. We opened the wine as well.

We sat in the shade of one of the temple columns, our backs against the rough stone, and watched the choughs wheel and dive like Stukas across the top of the cliff.

My next recollection was of receiving a sharp elbow in the ribs and hearing Liz Hammond's voice. 'Hey, Logan!'

I opened my eyes quickly. Liz was kneeling in front of me.

'What?'

'You were asleep!' she said indignantly.

'Not me, miss.' I blinked rapidly. 'Must have been somebody else.'

She stared at me. 'I don't believe it! The man actually nodded off!'

'Must have been all those late nights.'

'I'll give you late nights! Talk about an insult! Is this how you treat all your dates?'

'Only the ones that nag,' I told her. And in the process earned myself another energetic dig.

She was very close to me. I found myself sinking into those deep blue eyes. I drew my legs in and she leaned forward and rested her arms across my knees. 'What does a girl have to do to get your attention, Logan?'

'Practically anything,' I said.

She lifted her arms, placed her hands on my shoulders and drew herself towards me. Her lips were as soft as they had been the first time. I brought my own hands down and cupped her waist. She trembled for a fleeting second and then eased her body away to allow me access to the buttons of her shirt.

Her breasts were full and warm. My thumbs traced taut nipples and she moaned gently. Our lips broke apart and she opened her eyes and looked at me. 'You ain't so tough,' she whispered.

I caressed the underside of her breasts and she gave a sharp intake of breath as her body responded to my touch.

'You won't forget though, will you?' I reminded her.

She ran sensitive fingers down my stomach. 'Forget what?'

'What Harry told you.'

Her eyes opened wider. 'What was that?'

'Be gentle with me.'

Her hands descended lower still. A slow and easy smile

spread across her face. 'Don't worry, Logan.' She chuckled softly. 'I will be.'

And she was too, very.

It was close to an hour later, while we were gathering the remains of the food and wine together, that I realized we were not the only ones on the cliff top. Not any more.

I heard a noise behind us; a soft footfall and the snap of a twig.

Two men. Young, lean, tanned. Twenty-five yards apart at the edge of the belt of cypress trees. Hadn't seen them before. The men, that is. Not the trees.

I wondered how long they had been there. I hadn't heard any applause. Maybe if Liz and I had known we'd had an audience we'd have been a touch more adventurous.

Then I saw the shotguns.

Nothing especially odd about that. A lot of men, particularly in isolated farming communities, carry guns. They are a means of keeping scavenging crows and suchlike from decimating the harvest. They also provide game for the cooking pot. But I wondered about that, because on Mekos there are no crops, not unless you count the half-dozen or so straggly olive trees on the terraces behind the village. As for game: forget it. There wasn't anything remotely edible as far as the fauna of this island was concerned. Not unless you're into hoopoe burgers or chough cutlets. And in any case, something told me they weren't even islanders. They were too young, for one thing. And, to cap it all, one of them had a pair of field glasses slung around his neck. Now, there was a coincidence.

Something else, too. The shotguns weren't broken open. They were closed. Liz came out from behind the pillar. 'What is it?' She was carrying the string bag

202

containing the leftovers from our picnic. She saw the two men.

'Don't move,' I said.

'Who are they?'

'I don't know. But I've got a feeling they're not here on behalf of the local residents' association. Keep behind me and don't say anything.'

The other funny thing was that I'd got the impression they weren't even Greek.

I faced them.

The one who stood slightly to my left stepped towards what had been the outer wall of the temple. His companion, shotgun cradled under his arm, strolled forward and stopped a yard from me. Mid-twenties or thereabouts. Hair cut very close to his scalp, small black moustache, blue-black five o'clock shadow. He was wearing jeans and a short leather jerkin over a grey tee shirt. His other half was about the same age, only he had a full head of hair and a beard. He was similarly dressed. They were very relaxed, both of them.

I felt Liz's hand on my arm. I half turned to her and said casually, 'I'll take the bag.'

She handed it over wordlessly, keeping her eyes on the nearest man. The bottles clinked musically. We'd only drunk one. The other was unopened and full. We still had half the bread and cheese and most of the grapes too.

The nearest man glanced down at the bag. His partner was regarding us speculatively.

'*Kalimera*,' I said. 'Can we help you?'

The stranger smiled. It was a nice smile, friendly and open. It transformed his features immediately. 'You are Logan?' he enquired, in a heavy accent.

The shock must have registered on my face. I heard Liz gasp.

'And you're the man from the Prudential,' I said.

203

Wrong. Not even close.

'No,' he said. 'I represent the organization which employed Hammet Rakim.'

I thought, oh, shit.

There wasn't time to dissect the whys and wherefores because he was starting to bring the barrel of the gun up. Liz sensed something violent was about to happen and jerked her hand away from my arm. Fast.

His big mistake was standing so close. My left hand was already sweeping round to push the muzzle away as the gun barrel started to rotate, his fingers whitening on the twin triggers. As my palm closed round the metal, he fired. Liz's scream was drowned by the roar from the gun. I felt a searing jolt along my wrist as the charge slammed through the length of my arm. My shoulder felt as though it had been wrenched from its socket. With my right hand I scythed the bag at his head.

The pellets went wide. The bag didn't. In the movies, bottles smash when people get hit over the head with them. In real life, it's not that spectacular. Usually. This occasion, however, proved to be the exception. There was a sickening crunch of bone as the bottles connected with the side of his skull. The glass shattered upon impact. Wine from the full bottle showered around us. The force of the blow sent him reeling across the ground. As he fell away I wrenched the shotgun from him, turned and pushed Liz down behind the nearest column.

With a shouted curse the second man fired. We were aided by the fact that his aim was obstructed by his companion, whose upper chest caught most of the blast. At less than twenty yards the result was terminal. The shots that hadn't shredded the first gunman's body splattered into the pillar above our heads. Small stones and strands of vegetation torn loose by the shot rained over us like hailstones.

The string bag, with its glutinous contents, was still wrapped around my hand. I tore it away, rolled off Liz and extracted the shotgun.

'You okay?' I asked her breathlessly.

She nodded her head dazedly. 'My God, Michael! He tried to kill us!'

'Not us, love. Me.' I snapped open the breech of the shotgun. It just wasn't our day. I hadn't really taken much notice of the force of the shot because I'd been too intent on deflecting the charge, so it was an unpleasant realization to discover that both barrels had been fired. As I opened up the gun I felt a twinge run through my left wrist. I'd definitely jarred something in there when I made my counterattack.

I peered cautiously around the curve of the pillar. The second gunman was crouched down over his buddy, confirming the extent of his handiwork. He didn't seem too keen on coming after us. He knew we had the gun. What he didn't know, of course, was that the bloody thing was useless. At least, I hoped he didn't.

'Michael, who are they?' Liz was wide-eyed with shock. She was pressing herself against the stone.

'You could say they're former business associates. Sort of.'

'But who—'

I interrupted her. 'It's a long story. Maybe later.'

If there was a later.

'What are you going to do?' she gasped urgently.

Good question. Couldn't think of a bloody thing.

I took another cautious squint around the stonework and nearly got my head blown off in the process. Moss and mortar ripped through the air like grapeshot. Chummy's period of mourning was obviously well over.

Come on, Logan. Think of something, for Chris'sakes!

We had nowhere to run to. We were cowering behind

what amounted to the only bit of shelter for yards. Matey with the gun could cover all the open ground with ease; and sooner or later he was going to twig that we didn't have the means to retaliate, and he'd come a-looking. I for one didn't want to be in the immediate vicinity when he did. Behind us was the edge of the cliff and then nothing but a long drop. It was a good hundred paces to the nearest tree. And neither Liz nor I were Olympic sprinters.

But it was me he was after, not Liz. Maybe he'd allow her to make an escape. No, on second thoughts, scrub that idea. Because if he killed me he sure as hell wouldn't want a witness running around loose. Liz was just as much a target as I was.

I rested the shotgun across my knees and stared at the cliff edge. Liz burrowed into my shoulder. She was still shaking like a leaf. I peeked round the pillar. There was another roar, and stones rained down upon my head. He was keen, I'll say that for him. Plus he had extra ammo. And about now he'd be wondering why I hadn't had a go with the gun. He couldn't be that stupid. He'd make his play soon.

I stared glumly at the precipice again. What the hell, I thought, you can only die once.

I said to Liz, 'I've got a plan.'

Her head came up fast. 'What is it?'

I took her hand. 'You're going to have to trust me. Okay?'

A grim little smile flitted across her face. She squeezed my hand and nodded.

'Whatever happens, don't let go of my hand until I tell you. Understand?'

'No,' she said.

'Don't worry about it. Just hold on. Got that?'

Another nod.

'Right,' I said. 'When I say Run, you run.'

She stared at me. 'That's it? That's your plan?' Disbelief accounted for the measure of hysteria in her voice.

'I haven't told you where we're going to run to yet.'

'Oh.' She looked at me dumbly.

'Ready?'

Another nod.

Keeping low, we crouched like runners on the blocks. I put the gun down. Where we were going, we wouldn't be needing it.

'Now!' I yelled.

I hauled her to her feet and pulled her with me.

It was clear that she hadn't guessed my intentions. And by the time the full impact of what we were about to do had penetrated her brain it was too late. Inevitably, as the realization dawned, her natural instincts told her to pull away from me, but I countered that by hanging tightly on to her hand and using brute force to drag her along.

It was only ten paces, but it seemed like ten miles. As we came out from behind the stone column, the man behind us bellowed in anger and I knew instinctively that he was going to fire. I pulled my neck in and the sound of the shot merged with Liz Hammond's desperate cry of terror as we went over the edge of the cliff.

14

Well, okay, I'd said it was a plan. I hadn't said it was a great plan.

And how long does it take to fall one hundred and thirty-odd feet? Answer: no time at all. It just seems like forever.

When Liz screamed, I let go of her hand because by then there was no going back. We were committed. Besides, I was too damned busy trying to manoeuvre myself into hitting feet first rather than head first, and the cliff was rushing past like the side of the QE2, and the sea was coming up to meet me, and maybe the man on the cliff top would award me marks out of ten for style, and maybe I'd break my back anyway.

I very nearly did. It was like slamming into steel plate. Painful.

By luck rather than judgement, I succeeded in entering the water somewhere approaching the vertical, which was just as well because if I had gone in horizontal I wouldn't have survived to reflect upon it. As it was, I could think of a thousand less traumatic ways of making a splash.

I went under with all the finesse of a drunken penguin. Blinded totally by the impact, I tried waving my arms and kicking my legs, but they went spastic on me and refused to cooperate. I descended through chartreuse-green layers into darkness. The thought entered my confused mind that maybe I'd never find my way up. Then, mercifully, I was slowing.

Suspended like a fly in aspic, I tried my arms again. This time they responded, albeit grudgingly. I clawed upwards. But which way was up? Where was the welcoming light that should have been filtering down around me? I hadn't gone that deep, surely?

Disoriented, I thought maybe I was heading down instead. I'd heard of that happening to divers suddenly deprived of guiding sunlight, unable to find their way to the surface before their precious air supply ran out.

Talking of which . . .

I knew I couldn't hold my breath any longer. I could feel my arms and legs growing heavier by the second, as if they were shackled to lead weights. Panic caused me to try and breathe in. Water surged into my nostrils. I began to drown.

And then my hand broke the surface.

I came out of the sea like a breaching porpoise. Spewed water and sucked in air, chest heaving with the exertion.

Blinded.

Strange. It hadn't been night when we jumped. Maybe someone had turned the sun off.

A dozen yards away there was a further commotion in the water; a sudden glittering eruption of phosphorescence. A dark form speared into view, sending out gleaming ripples. A hand and a pale oval face. A swirl of damp hair visible for a fleeting second, and she was gone without a sound.

Liz.

I went down fast, kicking frantically, stretching towards the spot where she disappeared. I couldn't see anything because it was too dark. Why wasn't there any light, for Christ's sake? Something brushed my hands but I wasn't quick enough to catch hold. I went deeper, lungs at bursting point, and my fingers clutched a segment of her shirt and then my hands were around her waist.

She clung to me as we trod water, spluttering and sobbing with relief, saying my name over and over.

209

Neither of us was hurt. Our would-be assailant's last shots had missed their target completely. Just holding her and knowing she was safe helped to calm my own nerves.

And still I wondered why it was so dark, and then I focused properly, and understood.

The undertow at the base of the rock must have been extraordinarily strong, hence the time it had taken me to establish my equilibrium and bearings. We had literally been sucked underneath the cliff. We were inside Mekos.

Daylight was filtering towards us along a passage separating the cave from the outside world. The roof, as far as I could see, wasn't much more than four feet above the water at the highest point, and the distance to the sea beyond was maybe three or four yards. There was no way of estimating the full width or depth of the entrance; most of it lay underwater. But at least we had found our way out.

My eyes were slowly becoming accustomed to the light, or rather the lack of it. I could tell that the place was vast, like the vaulted nave of some huge Gothic cathedral, with dark rock curving down into the water from the roof hidden high above our heads. Strange shadows cowered in the distant gloom as though afraid of our intrusion. A strip of sand, barely visible in the dimness at the far end of the cavern, indicated a tiny beach of sorts, and then my eyes followed the nooks and crannies along the uneven walls and, in the eerie half-light of this subterranean world, I saw the U-boat.

Cornered in its secret lair, the submarine loomed out of the darkness like some primeval sea monster, its plates rusted and stained like the decomposing scales of a thousand-year-old kraken.

Liz blinked the water out of her eyes. Involuntarily, her grip on my arm tightened. 'Michael!'

I shook water out of my eyes. 'I see it,' I said.

'It's fantastic!' Liz cried, the terrifying memory of our leap over the cliff temporarily forgotten in the excitement of this new discovery.

'Come on,' I said, nudging her towards the narrow scimitar of sand. 'Let's have a look.'

We swam in close.

The submarine appeared longer and thinner than I'd expected, like a knife set on edge. Only the swell of her ballast tanks detracted from the illusion. That and the conning tower that rose out of her deck like a funnel. There were huge uneven blotches on her hull: her camouflage scheme. I recalled Prohl telling us that the U-boat trims had been changed according to the season and the area of their patrols. In the Med, for example, the boat would have been painted in a combination of blue-grey on light grey. In the Atlantic during winter months it would have been an overall dark grey. Prohl's boat, at the time of his departure from Bremerhaven, had been cloaked in a combination of both light and dark grey, arranged in wide, near vertical stripes around her deck and superstructure. By now, of course, the drab colours had merged and faded and been attacked by salt-water corrosion. It was difficult to determine where one colour ended and another began.

Her rapier bow and the muzzle of her 8.8 cm forward deck gun pointed impotently towards the rear of the cave. The 2 cm flak gun was still in position on the platform directly aft of the tower, its slender barrel canted forlornly towards the cavern roof. My attention went back to the tower, and my heart leapt.

For there, drawn below the salt-encrusted rim, was the faint but discernible outline of a half-human figure holding a three-pronged spear. It was exactly as Prohl had described it. It was Dieter Prohl's personal insignia.

The sea god, Triton.

We paddled past the stern to the strip of beach. I helped Liz out of the water and we collapsed on to the sand. Taking stock of our surroundings, it was difficult to concentrate on anything other than the mass of the U-boat that lay only yards away, like a killer shark lying in wait. A fifty-year-old ghost that had haunted not only the high seas but also our imaginations.

Liz shivered suddenly. Whether it was from the cold and dampness of the cave or delayed shock after our dramatic scrape with death and subsequent escape, I did not know. I was feeling the cold myself. Out of the sun, the water had lost its colour and warmth.

Liz smoothed her hair back from her forehead. The shirt she was wearing clung to her like a second skin. The material had moulded itself to her breasts. Somewhere along the way she had lost both her sandals. She looked at me. 'That was some plan, Logan.'

'Well, short of "beam me up, Scotty" it was the best I could come up with.'

She continued to hold my gaze. 'Who were they, Michael?' she asked.

So I told her about Hammet.

'Dear God!' she breathed. Even in the bad light I could see that the colour had left her face. 'You mean you killed him?'

'No. Technically, he took his own life with an overdose. Though I suppose you could say I gave him a helping hand.'

'And that doesn't bother you?'

'Yes, it bothers me. But what bothers me even more is that the bastard set me up with twenty pounds of heroin for which I could have spent the next twenty years in a Turkish jail. I don't touch drugs. I never have and never will. The Lebanese knew that. As far as I'm concerned, what he got was justice. Poetic justice.'

'So where did you get the heroin from then?'

'That's privileged information. Sorry. Just because I don't deal in the stuff doesn't mean that I don't know people who do. And don't look at me like that. I never claimed to be Persil bright. I'm no saint. In my line of business there's no such animal.'

She was silent for several minutes. I could see that her mind was racing. Her perception of me had just been radically jolted. She was wondering how to cope with the realization that I was no knight in shining armour.

'Why come after you?' she asked finally.

'That's easy,' I told her. 'Revenge. The organization they work for doesn't take too kindly to having one of their major operatives retired early.'

'What organization? The Mafia?'

'Well, the men on the cliff didn't look like Mafia soldiers. They looked Middle Eastern, maybe Lebanese, like Hammet. The drug trade acknowledges no frontiers. It's an international network. It's possible that the stuff they caught me with was due to be refined in Mafia-run labs, but that's pure speculation on my part.'

'But how did they know it was you they were after, and how did they know where to look for you?'

'My guess is that they got hold of Hammet's boyfriend and he gave them a description. Hell, he even knew my name. It wouldn't have been difficult for them to trace my movements. The organization has a lot of people on its payroll. They'd have checked the airport and then found out that I'd boarded the *Valkyrie* at Santorini, and she isn't exactly a hard craft to miss. They were probably on board that helicopter we saw the other day, pinpointing our position. Then it was simply a case of choosing a time and a place to take me out. It was your bad luck you happened to be with me.'

'So what happens now?'

'I don't know. I reckon we might have been luckier than we think. There's no way that the second man could know we survived the jump. He'd have looked for us, no doubt about that. But as our bodies didn't show up he probably thinks we've drowned. With luck, he's retrieved his pal's body and called in the chopper to pick them up. I'd say he's gone back to report that the contract's been carried out. Let's hope his bosses believe him.'

'How are we going to get back to the boat?'

'We've no choice,' I said. 'We'll have to swim for it.'

Her face fell. 'But it's miles!'

'To the *Valkyrie*, yes, but it's not much more than half a mile or so to the place where the cliffs bottom out. We can make it there and walk the rest of the way.'

'Boy,' Liz said succinctly, 'you sure know how to give a girl a good time!' She stood up, leaving a damp patch on the sand, and stared at the cave mouth. 'Do you think it's safe out there?'

'We'll soon find out.' I stood with her. 'First, though, I want a closer look at that sub.'

Liz didn't appear too thrilled with the idea. I must admit that the hulk didn't look the most welcoming vessel I'd ever encountered. I also didn't want to leave it too long before we tried to make it back to the yacht. But we had begun the day early and there were still quite a few hours of daylight left. Paradoxically, because the cave entrance faced west, the lower the sun sank in the sky the further the daylight extended underneath the cliff. It was a pity to waste that advantage. There was certainly time enough to explore a little.

Liz took my hand without a word and we walked up the sand towards the sub. As we neared it I could see that in fact the U-boat was actually moored to a jetty that had been constructed along one wall of the cave. Mekos obviously hadn't been a last-minute refuge but something of a more permanent nature. It must have been Prohl's secret base during the time his boat operated in the eastern end of the Med and the Aegean.

Liz drew my attention to the lights. They were attached at intervals to the rock face and ran in a line along the length of the jetty. In a natural alcove I could see the fat, cylindrical shapes of oil drums, and at various stations the objects and equipment needed to keep the base operational: work benches, coils of rope and wire, tools of every description and a selection of hoists, pulleys and winches; all rust-coated and bearing the marks of years of disuse. A rectangular object covered by a heavy-duty tarpaulin invited further investigation. I dragged the oil-impregnated cover away to discover a portable generator of dubious origin. No doubt it had been used to run the lamps and some of the machinery on the jetty.

I noticed something else too. The jetty was littered with rocks. Some were small, about the size of a fist. Others were much larger, boulder size. I looked towards the sub. Debris lay scattered over the casing. Some of the deck plates had been buckled out of alignment. For the first time, I saw that the boat appeared to be listing slightly to starboard. Not by very much; a few degrees at the most, but off centre most definitely. I pointed it out to Liz.

'What do you think happened?' she asked.

'It's my guess it's a result of that last eruption on Santorini. The one in fifty-six. I reckon it sent out shock waves which dislodged part of the cliff structure. That might account for the lowness of the tunnel roof. It was probably a lot higher before the aftershocks. The sub couldn't have got in, otherwise. The tremors probably loosened the rocks above and caused the sub to tilt. Even if the boat was mobile, I doubt there'd be enough depth of water left beneath her keel to allow her to get back through to the sea. She's trapped here for eternity.'

The more I thought about it the more likely it seemed. We weren't that far from Santorini. Anafi was only ten miles away, and that island had had its fair share of misfortune caused by volcanic upheaval. The last couple of eruptions had forced the inhabitants to abandon it on both occasions. They'd returned eventually, of course, but they'd found their homes smothered in layers of ash. The same thing could have occurred here on Mekos.

A narrow and frail-looking metal catwalk linked the sub to the jetty. I tested it gingerly. It appeared safe enough. I crossed it and stood on the U-boat's slanted casing. The conning tower reared above me like the turret of a medieval castle.

I told Liz to stay where she was and made my way up the ladder to the flak platform and then on to the tower. As I did so, I saw that the U-boat had sustained a great deal of damage to her superstructure. Not just from the rockfalls. Chunks of metal had been gouged from her side. I recalled Prohl's mention of the attack made upon her by the American Liberator bomber. The aircrew's signal to Malta had been correct. They had scored a hit, but it had not been fatal. I wondered if she'd sustained damage below the waterline as well. Short of swimming down to take a look-see, there was no way of knowing.

The conning tower hatch was situated in the middle of the bridge, immediately forrard of a chest-high, cone-shaped pedestal which I presumed housed the retracted periscope. The hatch seemed very small and hardly wide enough to allow a man access, especially if he was wearing oilskins. It was closed. From what I could remember about the layout of boats like these, the control room lay directly beneath my feet.

It was eerie standing there on the bridge. Somehow I knew that I didn't belong. But curiosity got the better of me. I knelt down and gripped the handle on the hatch

216

cover. I half expected it to be rusted solid and immovable, but to my surprise all I had to do was lift the cover back.

I was unprepared for the smell.

It hit me like a blow in the face. It was the sickly-sweet odour of dampness and decay, and something . . . undefinable. I felt goose pimples rise along my arms.

Suddenly I wanted to be anywhere but where I was. I wanted to be out of the cave and in the light of day. I straightened quickly. Liz had seen my head disappear, and as I came up again I heard her call to me anxiously. I needed no second bidding. I left the hatch cover open and climbed back on to the flak platform and on down to the deck. My footsteps echoed around the cave as I renegotiated the catwalk and joined her on the jetty.

'Let's get out of here,' I said.

'What did you find?' she asked. She had sensed the unease in my voice.

'Nothing,' I replied. But I told her that I hadn't gone looking, either. To explore further we'd need lights. I wasn't about to go stumbling around that sub in the dark; not for all the tea in Lipton's.

We made our way down to the spit of sand and waded back into the dark water. Then we struck out towards the cave entrance and the blue sea shining beyond.

Fortunately, in contrast to the undertow, the surface currents were weak. Entering daylight again was a kind of rejuvenation. It was wonderful to feel the sun on my face. When we were clear and some fifty yards out, I trod water and looked back towards the land. I had been wrong in my assessment of the sheerness of the rock face. Directly above the cave entrance was a narrow overhang that had been undetectable from above. The overhang made the low mouth of the cave look like a long wedge of shadow and thus almost indistinguishable from the rest of the cliff. Even more so, I suspected, if viewed from a distance, especially from somewhere along the level of a ship's rail. Impossible to spot, that is, unless you knew it was there.

I also craned my neck and looked for signs of life along the top of the cliff, although it was virtually a foregone conclusion that our friend had long gone. Even if he hadn't, from such a range the shotgun would have been redundant. I was relieved, however, that I didn't have to put that theory to the test.

Thank God the sea was calm. Even so, it took a good thirty minutes for us to reach the first accessible part of the coastline where we were able to clamber ashore; on to a tiny stretch of rock-strewn terra firma, some three-quarters of a mile round the point from the sea cave. Not far, admittedly, but it had been a taxing swim. As I was stronger than Liz in the water, it was she who had dictated the pace. Nevertheless, if she hadn't been so fit we'd have taken a fair while longer.

We lifted ourselves out of the shallows and caught our breath.

'Nothing like a bit of exercise to get the old corpuscles flowing,' I said wearily.

'Don't tempt me,' Liz said, but she hugged me anyway.

Our next move was to start on the two-mile trudge back to the village. What had started out as a picnic had developed into something resembling an endurance course. Poor Liz was in bare feet, too, which wasn't helping matters, so stepping our way over the first barrier of rocks was hard going. I picked her up and carried her piggyback style over the last few yards.

The trek back to the beach where we had left the skiff turned out not to be as arduous as we'd both feared. Our main problem was jittery nerves, based on the outside possibility that still lurking somewhere on the island was the man who had tried to kill us. Definitely not someone

I was anxious to meet on a dark night. Or any other kind of night, come to that. Every tree, every bush and every rock began to take on a malevolence that was almost tangible. So it was with a great sense of relief that we finally emerged on the outskirts of the village to see the *Valkyrie* reposing at anchor before us, her white hull reflecting the warm glow of the afternoon sun.

There was a warm glow coming off Harry Donovan too. We found him on a seat outside the taverna, face upturned, eyes half closed, hands wrapped around a glass of ouzo.

'I can see you missed us,' I said.

His eyes opened slowly. 'Actually,' he said, 'I was just about to alert the troops.'

He focused then on my Levis. They were still damp after my enforced swim. Liz's shorts had dried quickly, as had her shirt, but he noticed she'd lost her footwear. He'd probably also twigged that somewhere along the way we'd mislaid the picnic bag. And was it his imagination or were we both looking a trifle ragged around the edges? He glanced at me quizzically, debating whether or not to come out with a smart-alec remark. Deciding against it, he murmured instead, 'Thought I heard that chopper buzzing around earlier.'

'Now there's a funny thing,' I said.

He took a slow sip of his drink and waited for me to elaborate. When I didn't, he said, 'Is there something I'm missing here?'

So we told him.

It seemed a shame not to.

By the time we'd finished, the rest of his drink lay forgotten. When his lower jaw was back in working order he had only one thing to say.

'I think we'd better go tell the boss man.' He shook his

219

head in mock exasperation, and sighed. 'Boy, is he going to love you!'

Back on the *Valkyrie*, in fact, Gunther Prohl couldn't decide whether to be overjoyed or furious. He tried furious first.

'Jeopardizing the expedition through reckless stupidity caused by a senseless personal vendetta' was one of the phrases he came up with, among others.

I reminded Prohl that at the time I had been dispensing my own particular brand of justice to the Lebanese I had not yet taken him up on his offer of employment. In any case, I told him, any vendetta I chose to embark upon, senseless or otherwise, was my affair, not his.

Then he started waving his cigar in my face and accusing me of insubordination. So I countered by telling him to stop acting like an *Obergruppenfuehrer* in the Wehrmacht. Which, not surprisingly, went down like the proverbial lead balloon.

And so it went on. At one point it grew so heated I suggested that he might like to have me taken outside and shot; it might make him feel better. Martin Ritter's eyes lit up momentarily at the thought. No doubt he'd have liked to have been put in charge of the firing-squad.

But I knew that Gunther Prohl's anger was, in truth, a direct response to the conversation the two of us had had earlier. For, despite my assurances to the contrary, I had succeeded in exposing Liz Hammond to considerable harm. So much for my integrity. It was apparent that Liz was not the only person having to make a reassessment of my previous sterling character.

I knew, without the shadow of a doubt, that Gunther Prohl viewed the incident on the cliff as a personal betrayal on my part. And I can't say I blamed him. He had every right to feel that way. Knowing that didn't help to assuage my feeling of guilt.

In the end it was Donovan, acting as self-appointed mediator, who argued succinctly that if it hadn't been for the vendetta we wouldn't have found the damned sub in the first place.

At which point we retired to our respective corners. After that a degree of common sense and practicality prevailed.

Albeit etched with concern.

Donovan raised the most pertinent question when he said to me, 'So, you reckon that they think you're dead?'

'Something like that, yes.'

'I hope you're right, old son,' he said with feeling. 'The last thing we need is attention from the Syndicate.'

'The Syndicate?' Liz Hammond enquired, puzzled.

He meant the drug network, I told her. He could just as easily have called it the Organization or the Firm. It amounted to the same thing: an outfit to be avoided at all costs.

Not that I expected any further trouble from that quarter, I assured them all. In the eyes of the men who ran the drug pipelines, I had been dealt with. End of story.

No one looked too convinced. But it wasn't anything anyone was prepared to dwell on. There were more pressing items to attend to.

Like the immediate matter of salvage, for instance.

I told Prohl, No, I hadn't ventured inside the sub. It had been too damned dark.

'But access is possible, yes?' he enquired earnestly, puffing at his cigar.

'I don't see why not,' I confirmed. 'I got one of the hatches open without much trouble. But we'll definitely need lights. It'll be impossible without them.'

'We've got flashlights,' Donovan reminded me.

'True, but it'd help if we had something a bit more substantial.' I turned to Marco. 'Would it be possible to rig up a cable from the *Valkyrie* to the sub and run lights off our batteries?'

He thought about that and nodded slowly. 'Sure, maybe. I will check when we get there.'

'You mentioned a generator,' Donovan said. 'Any chance we could get the thing cranked up?'

'It'd be a bloody miracle,' I told him. 'I didn't give it a full inspection, but after damned near fifty years in that place the innards have probably rusted away. There might be other equipment we can use though. We'll have to wait and see.'

'Right,' Donovan said. 'Let's go. There's still a couple of hours of daylight left. It'd be a pity to waste them.'

15

We used the skiff to ferry ourselves into the cave. All of us, that is, except Liz. As far as she was concerned, one visit had been more than enough. She'd elected to remain on board the yacht.

By keeping low, there was just enough room above our heads to enable us to paddle our way through the tunnel. As soon as we were in the main gallery we switched on our flashlights.

There was a collective drawing-in of breath as the broad white beams swept around the high, dripping walls and settled across the stained and calloused hull of the stranded submarine.

'Jesus!' Donovan exclaimed. 'No wonder we never picked her up on the sonar!'

'*Lieber Gott!*' Prohl whispered hoarsely. He was staring up at the sub's conning tower and the crudely drawn figure. '*Der Wassermann!*'

There was a strange fixed expression on his face. It was the look of a pilgrim come to pay homage. Reverence tinged with awe, and perhaps a degree of fear at what he might find inside that stained and battered hull.

I pointed to the bar of sand at the rear of the cave and we pushed our way towards it.

We climbed out of the skiff and pulled it up on to the sand behind us. I could make out the shape of footprints leading towards the jetty. A legacy of my previous visit.

I led the way.

The beams from our flashlights sprayed over the rock and the scattered debris. Marco pulled the tarp off the generator and I saw him shake his head sadly. So much for restarting the thing. Our footsteps echoed hollowly on the wooden slats.

The boat, Prohl told us, was a Type VIIC, used mostly in the Atlantic against the Murmansk convoys. In boats like this, a total of forty-one thousand men had fought the war at sea. Of that number, thirty thousand had lost their lives. A formidable statistic in anyone's language.

Ritter crossed the catwalk first. Prohl hesitated for only a fraction of a second before following.

With five of us on the bridge it was something of a squeeze. I asked Prohl what the pedestal was.

It did indeed contain the periscope. Technically, however, it was known as the UZO, the *Unterwasserzieloptik*, for want of a mouthful. It was, in fact, a surface torpedo-aiming device linked to what was euphemistically called the attack computer in the tower. You learnt something new every day.

We contemplated the open hatchway at the base of the cone. The smell was still quite appalling. Donovan and I probed the lower compartment with our lights. The interior of the sub didn't look any more welcoming than it had the first time.

'After you,' Donovan said, and grinned.

I gave him a thanks-a-lot look and put my foot on the first rung of the ladder. As I did so I had the distinct and chilling feeling that I was about to perform an act of desecration. Maybe Howard Carter had felt the same way the second before he entered King Tut's basement. The thought did little to hearten me.

I lowered myself into the U-boat. Donovan used the beam of his light to guide my feet. I tried, not too successfully, to quell my immediate sense of claustrophobia.

I touched bottom and backed away from the ladder to

allow the others access. I played my own flashlight around the control room. It looked like Dante's interpretation of a Chinese laundry. Every available section of bulkhead space appeared to be occupied by a bewildering array of circular gauges, pipes, switches, valves and electrical circuits. Two large metal wheels indicated the hydroplane positions. Many of the gauges were totally unreadable, stained as they were with streaks of rust and ancient gobbets of black mould. Half a century of condensation had taken its toll. The air was heavy with moisture. It was an unclean smell: the odour of human habitation long abandoned; a sourness, like rotten apples left out in the rain. I suppressed a shudder.

Donovan was the first to join me. He took in the view and grimaced. 'Christ! What a stench!' He moved aside for the others.

Gunther Prohl was next, then Marco. Ritter brought up the rear. It was even more cramped than the bridge. It was not hard to imagine what it must have been like in such a confined space during battle conditions, with destroyers and suchlike circling overhead like hungry buzzards. In my mind's eye I saw white-faced men hunched over their operating positions, teeth and fists clenched in equal measure, sweating with fear, as they waited for the succession of clicks that would herald the imminent arrival of the depth charges and their deadly loads.

Donovan tapped me on the shoulder and I jumped.

'You okay?' he asked, frowning.

'Fine,' I said, a little too quickly.

He threw me a curious look and turned to Prohl. 'You want to lead the way?'

Prohl flashed his light towards the forward bulkhead and the hatchway that led off into the bowels of the submarine. He swallowed and nodded, his round face pale and ghost-like in the unnatural light.

Directly beyond the hatchway lay two tiny compartments on either side of the passage. On the right was the combined radio shack and hydrophone booth. It was as cramped as a sentry box. Immediately opposite was the commander's cabin.

A once green curtain separated the interior of the cabin from the passageway. I call it a curtain; in fact, it wasn't much more than a half-rotted, faded piece of rag suspended from a narrow rail. Gunther Prohl jerked it aside to gain entrance and it virtually came apart in his hand. I heard him give a low moan, and as I looked over his shoulder I felt the short hairs rise along the back of my neck.

There was hardly enough room to swing a medium-sized kitten. There were a couple of lockers, a minuscule writing desk and a bunk. There were a few old sepia-tinted photographs tacked on to the locker doors. At the rear of the desk, racked against the bulkhead, were some mildewed paperbacks. A creased and much stained oilskin jacket hung on a hook by the locker. A small tobacco tin lay on the writing surface next to a cutthroat razor, some stubby pencils, a fountain pen and something wrapped in what looked like a waterproofed satchel.

And Lieutenant Commander Dieter Prohl was seated at his desk.

It was like looking at an exhibit in a chamber of horrors. In the semidarkness it appeared as if much of the once dark blue naval uniform had disintegrated, like the torn curtain. As had most of the flesh from the bones. The corpse was slumped slightly to one side, the way an elderly person might fall asleep in an armchair, head tipped back, mouth agape. In the skull, eyeless sockets gazed blankly at the ceiling. The open jaws revealed teeth set in a rictus. Strips of what looked like grey parchment clung to the ridges along the cheek bones and the front of the skull. It was as if the skeleton had developed some kind of creeping fungus.

One thin and withered arm lay across the knees. The other arm, the right one, hung down by the side of the chair. The remains of a hand protruded from the mucus-coloured sleeve. Caught in the bright beam from my flashlight, a slender finger of grey-white bone reached down towards the pistol that lay on the deck plates. A Luger automatic.

I moved my light up. My attention was riveted to the skull. On the right-hand side of the cranium was a small round hole. I moved closer and tilted the beam. The opposite side of the skull looked as if it had been struck by a large hammer, from the inside.

Gunther Prohl, his face waxen, staggered back into the control room. His place was taken by Marco, who, upon seeing the contents of the cabin, crossed himself hurriedly. Ritter, on the other hand, seemed unmoved.

'Not much doubt about how he did it, is there?' Donovan said.

I shook my head. 'Hardly.'

'But why, for Christ's sake?'

I had no answer.

Donovan frowned again. 'And why the hell was he all togged up in his Sunday best?'

'Beats me,' I said. I was also wondering about the rest of the crew. What had befallen them? I wasn't sure I wanted to continue our exploration of the darkened innards of the submarine in order to find out.

Gunther Prohl rejoined us. He'd told us at the outset that he wanted to find out exactly what had happened to his father. And now his question had been answered. But at what cost? It was difficult to tell in the dim light just

227

how much the discovery had affected him. That it had been a terrible shock had been evident to all of us. Although, in retrospect, as far as the crew of the U-boat was concerned, I'm not sure what any of·us had really expected to find. Rightly or wrongly, I think all of us had been a little too preoccupied with the possible existence of the sub's cargo rather than the fate of the men on board. Prohl's father included. But perhaps it was not the fact of death that had been such a jolt to the system as the manner in which Captain Dieter Prohl had met his demise. Suicide was something none of us would have considered.

Posing, as it did, more questions than answers.

Gunther Prohl, having composed himself as much as was humanly possible under the circumstances, took the lead once more as we moved further into the boat. None of us spoke. We were all too tense, speculating on what else we might find in this dark and dismal place.

The passage led on to another compartment, containing a couple of bunks, a stand of lockers and a small table. The area wasn't a whole lot bigger than the commander's cabin. Prohl told us that it was the wardroom. Only two of the officers could sleep at any one time. Shifts had been rotated accordingly. I couldn't get over how bloody cramped the boat was. God knows how the crew had been able to stand it for months on end. I'd have been climbing the walls, space permitting.

The next compartment was the CPOs' mess. Next was one of the two heads. Beyond this area lay the hatch to the fore-ends, the bow torpedo room and the ratings' quarters. Our lights cast strange shadows along the pipes and ducts above our heads. We were negotiating the low, narrow passage in single file. It was like walking through a catacomb. I was fully expecting to be confronted with the remains of other crewmen laid out in their bunks like

228

the bones of long-dead monks, but, to my intense relief, the sleeping platforms were empty.

Gunther Prohl ducked into the compartment and pulled up short. I heard him mutter something under his breath. There was a bit more room here and we were able to move more freely. With a full complement of forty-three men it must have been like living in a slave ship, with each man allotted a sliver of space that would have provided barely enough room for him to change his mind. Dieter Prohl, according to his son, had sailed from Bremerhaven with a much depleted crew. Even so, the living quarters seemed horribly confined.

A two-tiered system of bunks ran either side of the passage down towards the four circular hatches of the torpedo tubes in the bow of the sub. Although the bunks were mercifully unoccupied, they still held the detritus of human occupation: mould-ridden blankets; a few scattered items of soiled and ragged clothing; some books, the pages yellowed and faded; a couple of tin plates; a pack of cards; a draughts board. If it hadn't been for the lack of light and the cold and the fetid smell, I could have well believed that the U-boat was still inhabited.

I knew it wasn't, of course. At least, not by anything living. But there was a presence here, I could feel it. It wasn't just the memory of the dead captain that lingered, it was the sensation that there was an entity at work. There was an aura of something elusive, something unpleasant, something . . . evil?

Donovan was staring down towards the bow. 'Oh, my,' he said hoarsely.

We followed his gaze.

The crates were stowed at the far end of the compartment, up against the torpedo tube doors.

My throat ran dry.

We shuffled forward slowly. The boxes, isolated in the

229

glow from our torches, stood out in the gloom like a night bomber caught in the calibrated beams of five search-lights. There appeared to be about a dozen of them. Wooden. Two large ones at the bottom, I could see, with the other, smaller ones stacked on top.

The loud and rapid thumping I could hear was the sound of my heart, beating like a hammer on an anvil.

Donovan ducked down suddenly. He arose with a grunt of satisfaction, a dull gleam of metal in his hand. He was grasping a long metal rod with a flattened end; some kind of crowbar. He handed it to Gunther Prohl.

'You want to go first?'

Prohl stared at him, then nodded. Wordlessly he handed me his flashlight. We aimed the beams of our lights on the topmost crate. There was writing on it: *Geheime Reichssache*. Prohl slid the tapered end of the crowbar under one of the metal seals and twisted it. The thin band snapped, the two halves flying apart like the jaws of a trap. He severed the second seal. Jamming the point of the bar under one corner of the crate's lid, he levered again. There was a creak and the lid lifted half an inch. Prohl moved the point around all four sides, pulling upwards as he did so. When he had loosened the wood all the way around he gave the crowbar one final blow and prised up the lid.

No one said a word. I think we were all too stunned to speak. No one blinked for quite a while either. None of us wanted to risk reopening our eyes to find out it was only a dream.

The crate held four gold ingots. In the glow from our flashlights they gleamed like molten lava.

Prohl lifted one out. He had to use both hands to do so. As he held it up we were able to see the stamp of the eagle, the letters *RB*, and a date.

230

'Ten point four-seven-three kilos.' Prohl read off the weight etched into the metal.

One hundred and twenty thousand dollars.

Give or take.

Times four.

Per crate.

Donovan put down his own light, plunged his hands into the box, and withdrew another bar. 'We've done it!' he cried. 'We've bloody done it!'

His words broke the spell. We all succumbed to a kind of madness then, taking it in turns to lift the ingots out of the crate, laughing and grinning like idiots. Intoxicated by our newly acquired wealth.

Then, abruptly, Prohl went quiet and replaced the ingot he was holding in the crate. In a subdued voice, he said, 'We must check the stern compartment also.'

From his expression it was all too apparent that the discovery of the gold had reawakened a vision of his father, whose remains lay on grotesque display only a few yards away.

In swift and sombre realization, we returned the other bars to the box and followed him back through the boat to the control room. I couldn't help noticing that he did not break his stride as he passed by the commander's cabin.

We moved through the aft hatchway into what had been the PO's quarters. It wasn't a compartment as such; more like four bunks either side of the passageway. There was a tiny table in the middle with flaps that could be raised at meal times. It must have been like trying to eat in a tube train, with constant interruptions as crewmen moved through the boat.

The galley was next. I'd seen larger lottery kiosks. Beyond lay the engine room housing the two large diesels which lay side by side like a pair of ships in a bottle.

231

Christ, but the place was narrow! Barely enough room to allow two men to pass one another. We had to duck constantly to avoid removing the tops of our scalps on the overhead pipes.

And no sign of the rest of the crew. I was glad about that. But where were they?

Aft of the engine room lay the compartment containing the electric motors and the engine control panels.

Like an iceberg, the bulk of the motor casing was hidden from view, housed beneath the floor. When on patrol, the motors were powered by the boat's batteries, which were in turn charged by the diesels. The batteries themselves were also situated under the deck plates; in two recesses, one on either side of the control room.

In practice, however, the propulsion system was not as effective as it sounded.

While on the surface, the U-boat relied on diesel power to make headway. Submerged, the diesels had to be turned off as they consumed valuable oxygen; the only supply, once their air intakes sank below the surface, came from within the submarine itself. Hardly a viable proposition from the crew's point of view. Consequently, power was thereafter supplied by the battery-driven motors. When these ran flat, however, the sub had to resurface in order to rerun the diesels, which then recharged the batteries. And so on. Talk about laborious. Until one clever dick developed the *Schnorchel*.

What I hadn't known, and what Gunther Prohl informed me of, was the fact that the German Navy hadn't invented the device themselves. It was originally of Dutch origin. When the Germans overran the Low Countries they discovered the invention and adapted it for their own use. Once fitted with the air pipe, the boat was able to draw air down into the hull while it was still submerged. This air served both the diesels and the crew and, at the same time, the device expelled exhaust fumes. The other advantage of the *Schnorchel* was that it made the boat immune from air attack. In theory, anyway. It hadn't helped Dieter Prohl much. But then, according to Gunther, the Kriegsmarine hadn't begun to adapt their boats until 1942, and I for one hadn't even noticed if this sub was fitted with the *Schnorchel* or not. In any case, by now, the information was academic.

The rear section of the motor room also contained more crates. A further dozen, as near as I could make out. One large, the rest small. One of the small crates was lacking a lid. Shining our flashlights into it we saw that there were only three gold bars.

'Well, no need to ask where the missing ingot went,' I said to Prohl. 'It looks as if your young friend was right. That was gold he saw disappearing into the depths.' I made a rough calculation. 'Looks as if it could be all here. There must be twenty-odd of these smaller boxes. Four bars to each one. If you count the one that's missing, that's at least eighty of your ninety ingots.'

'Christ!' Donovan said. 'Who's counting?' Then he added, 'I wonder why he only took the one bar?'

'It was probably all he was able to carry,' I suggested. 'Besides, any more would be a bit of a risk. One bar wouldn't be too hard to conceal. Chances are he'd have wanted to see what he could get for it before he came back for the rest. The stuff wasn't going anywhere. It'd be like having your own security vault.'

'How'd he come by the medal?'

'Magpie syndrome. My guess is he found that first. It was small, silver, looked as though it might have been worth a few bob, so he helped himself. Then went over the rest of the sub and found the gold. I'd have liked to have seen his face. He must have thought it was Christmas. Like a forty-niner striking the mother lode.'

'I'll tell you something,' Donovan said. 'It took a lot of guts to come down here on his own.'

'You're right there,' I agreed. I turned to Prohl. 'What about the larger crates? What do you reckon is in them?'

Prohl shrugged. 'Currency. Jewels. Perhaps works of art. When the Americans blasted their way into the Thuringian mine vaults in April 1945 they found much more than gold. They discovered paintings: masterpieces by Rembrandt, Raphael, Titian, Renoir.' Prohl paused. 'They also found the Nefertiti.'

At the mention of the name it was hard to stop my mouth watering, because the Nefertiti was something I had heard and read about. An Egyptian statuette, three thousand years old, very small. It was one of the world's greatest treasures, with a value that was literally beyond price. Back in 1945 it would, undoubtedly, have been the single most precious art object in the whole of Germany.

The contents of those other boxes could prove to be really interesting, I thought eagerly.

But Prohl said, 'It is drawing late. I suggest we return to the yacht.'

'You don't want to look at the rest of the stuff?' Donovan asked, eyeing the large crate at the bottom speculatively.

'There will be time enough,' Prohl said. 'In any case, I do not think the cargo is going anywhere, do you?'

I had the feeling that Gunther Prohl's attempt at levity masked a sudden and strong desire to vacate the submarine. I can't say I disagreed entirely with the sentiment. The place was starting to get to me. It was all becoming a bit overwhelming, and the air inside the boat hadn't got any fresher since we'd entered it. If anything, the atmosphere was even more rank. Plus there wasn't a whole lot of room to start moving crates around, never mind opening them all up. We'd be better off checking the larger containers after we'd given ourselves a bit more space to work in.

'Makes sense,' I agreed. 'We can make an early start first thing. Should clear the stuff out of here in no time.'

No one came up with a better idea. Motion carried.

We retraced our steps to the control room, and fresh air. As we headed down to the place where we had beached the skiff, I noticed that Gunther Prohl was carrying something in his hand apart from his flashlight. It was the waterproofed package that had been on the desk in his father's cabin. I didn't challenge him. I reckoned he was entitled to some kind of memento other than the memory of finding the remains of his father's body laid out in gruesome array like a tableau in a travelling freak show.

In fact, it turned out to be a lot more than a memento.

A hell of a lot more. To all intents and purposes it was none other than Lieutenant Commander Dieter Prohl's last will and testament.

It was the U-boat's log book.

16

Had I made the discovery that my own father had committed murder, I admit, with all sincerity, that I have no idea how I would react. Undoubtedly, I'd be beset by a mixture of emotions: shock and horror certainly. Perhaps even a feeling of guilt as well. The sins of the father having being visited upon the son, and so forth. I simply do not know what my response to the news would be. All I am certain of is that when Gunther Prohl was confronted with that knowledge, he looked to be a man stricken in years.

The entries in Lieutenant Commander Dieter Prohl's log turned out to be a systematic account of his rapid descent into the abyss, resulting from his initial examination of the bullion crates and his subsequent decision to abandon the U-boat's designated course and choose his own heading.

They also provided an answer to one of our very first questions. One mystery had been solved, at least: the identity of the civilian last seen on the dockside in Bremerhaven. It hadn't been Martin Bormann. The man's name had been Moessinger. And whichever way you looked at it, his had been a terrible way to die.

Seated around the stateroom, we all listened in stunned silence as Gunther Prohl recited excerpts from his father's journal.

He began with the entries made during those nerve-racking minutes when the U-boat had been trapped beneath the Strait of Gibraltar while the flotilla of British warships circled above it like scavengers in a boneyard.

10 May 2015 hrs:
Oil jettisoned. Tubes fired. All motors stopped. Awaiting response from surface vessels.

10 May 2045 hrs:
Depth-charge attacks have ceased. Does this mean our decoys have been successful or are the British playing a waiting game of their own? Initial damage reports indicate that we have been remarkably lucky. Some seepage in forward crew compartment. Minor injuries only among the crew, mostly severe bruising, except for Seaman Beckert, who has sustained a broken arm.

10 May 2125 hrs:
Hydrophone operators confirm surface vessels have dispersed. Therefore I have given the order to restart motors and resume course.

10 May 2145 hrs:
Surfaced. Sea calm. No signs of pursuit. Further damage assessment indicates we have been losing oil. Fault traced and rectified. The most dangerous part of our journey is behind us.

The next significant log entry did not occur until nearly six days later, but it confirmed the information that Gunther Prohl had gleaned from Allied radio traffic.

16 May 1447 hrs:
Surfaced. Sea calm. Low cloud. Visibility poor. Position 170 sea miles east of Malta. Monitoring Allied radio broadcasts. Details surrounding the Fuehrer's death are finally emerging. It appears that he did not sacrifice himself as heroically as we were first led to believe. I have no reason to doubt the validity of the reports. The Eastern Front has finally collapsed. It is truly the end. The die has been cast. Now there can be no turning back.

16 May 1503 hrs:
Aircraft sighted. American Liberator bomber. Attempted crash dive. Aircraft opened fire. Bombs dropped.

16 May 1510 hrs:
Emergency. Boat submerged. We have suffered serious casualties. Five men were on deck at the time of the attack. Because of insufficient warning we were unable to save them. Upper hull and tower have sustained damage. Hydroplanes destabilized. Descended to fifty metres. Ejector valve to aft head ruptured, resulting in sea water entering the boat. Gas formed. In order to prevent further contamination we have been forced to secure aft watertight doors.

'Gas?' Liz queried, her brow furrowing.

'Chlorine,' I told her. 'Caused by seawater coming into contact with the acid in the sub's batteries.'

A real danger to the crew and a hideous way to die. As veterans of the Somme and Passchendaele would undoubtedly testify.

Gunther Prohl continued to read.

16 May 1627 hrs:
Reactivation of hydroplane operation completed. Surfaced. Ejector valve malfunction rectified. Gas dispersed but we are too late. Six men trapped and overcome by fumes. We buried our comrades at sea. They were brave men and deserved better. Lack of action dulled the senses. We grew complacent and it cost us dear. We are now down to seven. More than half my crew depleted in less than two hours. The responsibility for their loss weighs heavy. I have betrayed the men's loyalty and trust. What is to become of us?

That last sentence indicated that the first seeds of doubt had been sown. And then, two days further on, the boat's log recorded the following:

18 May 1837 hrs:
Landfall. Triton Base. No shipping in the vicinity.

18 May 1924 hrs:
Boat secured. We are home.

But for the weary U-boat crew the war was far from over.

Seven of them, Lieutenant Commander Prohl; his first officer, Schepke; Chief Engineer Bauer; Radio Operator Heller; Seamen Weber, Kessler and Schmidt. In the beginning it appeared, judging from successive entries in the log, that Commander Dieter Prohl had had a plan, of sorts. It had clearly been his intention to remain in the U-boat's secret base until events in Europe had achieved some semblance of normality. At which point he and the battered remnants of his crew would emerge into the sunlight, blinking and stretching like squirrels awaking from a winter of hibernation; the shock of their re-entry into the world being considerably softened by the fact that they would be taking with them approximately nine hundred kilos of gold bullion, former property of the Third Reich and worth at that time something in the region of one and a half million dollars, thus enabling them to live like emperors for the rest of their lives. Not a bad little nest egg, considering.

Not a bad little wheeze either. If it hadn't been for the fact that Lieutenant Commander Dieter Prohl had begun to develop serious uncertainties following his own particular course of action, as indicated in each subsequent log entry.

25 May 0945 hrs:

My conscience continues to trouble me. Bormann. Himmler. Kaltenbrunner. Those three arranged for the transfer of the gold; no doubt as a means of financing their planned escape from our country's inevitable defeat. They sold their birthright for plunder. But am I any better? By taking the gold am I any less guilty? By embarking upon this course of action I have betrayed the honour of the Kriegsmarine and the loyalty and memory of our dead comrades. Surely this makes me no better than a freebooter. A pirate. In voicing my doubts to Lieutenant Schepke, I have advised him not to divulge details of the consignment to the crew. He has agreed, though I suspect, to my regret, that he does not share my views.

31 May 1800 hrs:
It is now almost one month since the order to surrender was given. Unavoidably, the men's thoughts are turning to their homes and loved ones. What has become of our families? There is much concern that they have been taken by the Russians. The general feeling is that the Americans would not be so unsparing. Despite these fears and the wish of the men to return to our homeland, I believe that we should remain on the island for a while longer. Lieutenant Schepke, however, does not agree. I sense this is further indication that a confrontation is drawing near.

1 June 0930 hrs:
While the crew are searching the island for supplies of fresh water I plan to make a thorough check of the consignment.

Then came a most remarkable entry.

1 June 1035 hrs:
I have made a terrible discovery. The true nature of the cargo has been revealed. Moessinger was more than a courier. He was a guardian. To my horror, a phoenix has arisen from the ashes. I know there will be those who would look upon this as the heralding of a new dawn. In truth that prospect horrifies me. I am convinced it could result in the reawakening of dark forces and lead us on to still further carnage, despite the fact that the world has not yet emerged from the past six years of war. Is mankind's capacity for self-destruction so boundless? I must keep this information from the crew. What am I to do?

'What the hell,' Donovan asked, totally mystified, 'was all that about?'

'Christ knows,' I said.

'What did he mean by a phoenix?' Liz frowned, her expression mirroring her own bewilderment. 'I don't understand.'

I didn't either. Not fully, at any rate. Apart from the

clear indication that the sub had been transporting something else besides the bullion. Something that had infected the U-boat skipper with a severe case of the jitters. But what on earth could it have been? He'd written of the thing as though it was some kind of malevolent force. Very mysterious.

I cast my mind back to the things we had found during our examination of the U-boat. As well as the bullion containers there had been three larger crates on board. Whatever had put the fear of God into Lieutenant Commander Prohl had, presumably, been contained in one of those.

Based on the conversation I'd had previously with Gunther Prohl, my first guess would have been sculptures or perhaps paintings. His father, however, had hinted at something with a much darker potential. Something that, in his words, had the power to summon dark forces and herald a new dawn, whatever the dickens that meant. It all sounded highly fanciful.

Or did it mean something else entirely?

Put another way, it could plainly be interpreted to mean that Dieter Prohl had started to develop all the classic symptoms of rampant paranoia, the claustrophobic feeling that the rest of the crew, linked by some dark conspiracy and under the leadership of his first officer, had begun to side against him. Remorse and guilt affected an individual in a variety of strange ways.

And then my thoughts took me back to that moment when I'd first boarded the sub and that unaccountable sense of unease that I'd experienced when I opened the conning tower hatch for the first time. That feeling of impending dread had been very real to me.

Suddenly I was confronted with another memory: that of an evening on the *Valkyrie*, when we had been swapping travellers' tales. Remembering Gunther Prohl's contribution, I saw again the frightening images contained in the last few frames of Spielberg's epic when the Ark had been opened, releasing its occult contents into the world like the outpourings of some ghastly Pandora's box.

Christ! What was I thinking of? I collected myself hurriedly. Come on, Logan, get a grip. This is reality. Not the stuff of horror fiction, for God's sake!

'Strikes me,' Donovan said, interrupting my dark visions, 'that the fellow was on the verge of some kind of breakdown.' He looked at me as if seeking my agreement.

Despite the fact that his diagnosis went some way to echoing my own, I was filled with small comfort. I didn't comment. Instead I looked towards Gunther Prohl.

'Any ideas?'

He was silent for several moments, as if gathering his thoughts. Finally, he said dejectedly, 'I fear your friend may be correct. It does appear from the entries in this journal that my father underwent a profound change in his personality.' Prohl tapped the faded pages of the log. 'The officer who wrote these words is certainly not the same captain who led the wolf packs against the Atlantic convoys. These are not the admissions of a rational man.'

Sadly, none of us was prepared to contradict him. From the log entries, Lieutenant Commander Prohl's descent into the wells of self-recrimination, brought on by a massive sense of guilt following his purloining of the consignment, now seemed only too apparent.

As indicated by the next few lines.

3 June 0912 hrs:
My suspicions have been confirmed. Lieutenant Schepke has informed the rest of the crew about the gold and my once loyal officer has delivered an ultimatum. I am to turn the consignment over to him or suffer the consequences. In the light of my recent discovery, and with regard to Schepke's demands, I must consider my options carefully.

3 June 2047 hrs:
   I have reached a decision. It has not been easy. But circumstances have dictated that I should take drastic measures. In
doing so I will violate every creed that I have held dear. But I
do not believe there is any other way. I cannot risk the
knowledge of what is concealed here reaching the outside world.
The danger is too great to ignore. There is only one solution.
And I must be swift in my actions for I will not be permitted a
second chance.

The last entry in the U-boat's log was as follows:

4 June 0915 hrs:
   It is done. If any person should read this confession, let it be
known that my actions were governed solely by my loyalty to
the Fatherland as it was, not what it became. The phoenix has
arisen. But for the sake of future generations I could not allow
the bird to take flight. I have therefore clipped the wings of the
beast. By doing so, I accept that I have condemned my soul to
everlasting damnation. May God forgive me.

Dieter Prohl
Lieutenant Commander

It was Liz who eventually broke the spell of silence.
   'What did he do?' she asked, in a still, small voice.
   'He killed them,' Gunther Prohl said. His voice was
little more than a whisper.
   The final act had been both forthright and brutal.
   When the U-boat skipper had summoned his crew to
meet him on the jetty, the men could have had little
doubt that their captain was about to accede to their
demands. So it wasn't hard to imagine their shock and
horror as Dieter Prohl raised himself above the rim of the
conning tower and hosed them down with a burst from a
Schmeisser machine pistol. The carnage would probably
have been over within seconds, with the echoes of the
fusillade reverberating through the cave like thunder and

the cordite fumes and the stench of death lingering in the damp air like drifting pockets of poison gas.

He had disposed of the bodies by wrapping them in canvas sheets, rowing them out of the cave in one of the sub's life rafts and dropping them into deep water. We had probably passed over the bones during the course of one of the *Valkyrie*'s sonar runs.

Having thus accorded his former comrades all the tradition of a maritime burial as befitted officers and ratings who had died in action at sea, Dieter Prohl had returned to the submarine, retired behind the curtain of his cramped cabin and conscientiously completed the final entries in his log. That duty fulfilled to his satisfaction, he had then proceeded to dress himself in his dark blue naval uniform. Whereupon, retrieving his pistol, he had placed the muzzle of the weapon against his temple and blown his brains out through the side of his head.

In his madness he had taken the only honourable way out.

But I knew that we still didn't understand the full reasons why.

17

It was close to midnight when Liz made her way discreetly to my cabin. As we lay under the single sheet, her warm body nestling against mine, I listened to the waves lap gently against the *Valkyrie*'s hull.

Once again the sea was very calm, which made me reflect that we had been remarkably fortunate with the weather. Traditionally this was the season of the meltemi. The wind sweeps around from the northwest and can be immensely strong, sometimes gusting up to force seven or eight, although it doesn't blow as hard in the southern Cyclades as it does around some of the northern islands. Its duration can vary in length from a mere couple of days to a full fortnight, and at full spate the seas can be treacherous. Even hardy seafarers think twice before venturing abroad when the barometer indicates a sudden drop in pressure. I presumed that was what had befallen the fisherman in whose clenched hand the first clue in our search for Gunther Prohl's father had been found.

'Penny for them.' Liz nuzzled my throat gently.

I didn't reply immediately.

So she opened her eyes and eased herself up on one elbow, the sheet slipping from her smooth shoulder. 'Michael?'

'Just thinking.'

'About the future?'

'That too,' I said.

'What then?'

'Us,' I said.

She sighed and closed her eyes. 'That's nice,' she

whispered dreamily, drawing one long leg across my thigh.

'If I get myself another boat,' I ruminated, 'chances are I'll be on the lookout for a new deckhand.'

She opened one eye again and gazed at me speculatively. 'Is that an offer?'

'Kind of,' I admitted.

'Mmm,' she purred, lying down again. She lifted an arm and laid it over my chest. There followed several moments of mute contemplation. Finally she stirred. 'Make it first mate, Logan,' she murmured softly, 'and maybe you've got yourself a deal.'

Shortly after first light, with little expectation, we began our search for answers to the riddle.

There were four of us this time, Gunther Prohl, Ritter, Donovan and me. Marco had elected to remain on board the *Valkyrie* to try and rig up some way of providing us with a more durable light source utilizing, at my suggestion, the yacht's batteries. Liz had also chosen to stay behind. I can't say that I blamed her, frankly.

So, armed once again with our flashlights, we re-entered the sub.

We checked the stern first.

The crates were as we'd left them. Just one large one in this section, wooden, like the rest. Unopened.

No metal retaining bands, however. Obviously removed by Dieter Prohl prior to his own examination.

Donovan had retrieved our crowbar from the day before. I took his flashlight as he jabbed the flattened end of the bar under the lid of the crate and worked it round the rim. When he had loosened the lid sufficiently for it to be lifted, he paused. I was uncomfortably aware that my own palms were damp with sweat.

'Here goes,' he said, and slid the lid aside.

Lights trained, we all peered in.

It looked like an awful lot of money.

A real hotchpotch too: Portuguese, Swedish, English, Dutch and, God help us, Palestinian. Donovan ducked down and came up with one of the closely wrapped bundles. He held it up and examined it intently. 'Christ!' he exclaimed in disgust. 'Egyptian pounds! Bloody Monopoly Money!'

As we headed for the bow I couldn't help but feel secretly relieved that that was all it had turned out to be.

Donovan handed me the crowbar. 'Your turn,' he announced, and took my flashlight as compensation.

The first crate was a twin of the one in the stern. I applied myself to the task in hand, and levered with gusto. No surprises in this one either. Currency again. This was getting boring.

'It's got to be this one then,' Donovan said. We all looked at the crate lying at our feet.

It didn't have quite the same dimensions as the other two. It was longer but more shallow. No stencilling on it, either.

'Looks like a bloody coffin,' Donovan remarked.

At that precise moment I felt as if someone had walked over my grave. I shivered.

Unperceived by the rest of us, Ritter had already helped himself to the crowbar. Unprompted, he began to attack the lid.

Definitely not currency. Not this time.

It looked like a bundle of material.

Wine red, with the disjointed segments of some sort of emblazoned design discernible within the many folds: a pale full moon slashed with a crooked black cross. A swastika.

A banner of some kind, I realized, torn and tattered, stained darkly in many places.

Beside me, I could see, even in the dim light, that Gunther Prohl had turned as white as a sheet.

'*Mein Gott!*' he whispered hoarsely, taking a step back. '*Die Blutfahne!* The Flag of Blood!'

Across from me, his face cast in yellow ochre by the beam of his own flashlight, Ritter, his forehead glittering with perspiration, stiffened perceptibly. Though it may have been my imagination.

Donovan and I looked at each other. Donovan raised his eyebrows in exaggerated enquiry.

'All right,' I said. 'I give up. What the hell is it?'

Prohl stared fixedly at the contents of the crate, like a rabbit blinded by the headlights of an oncoming juggernaut. 'It was the battle standard of the Third Reich; the most sacred symbol of the Nazi party. There have been a thousand rumours concerning its whereabouts.'

There was a stillness, into which Donovan spoke.

'Never heard of it,' he stated flatly.

Prohl said, in a stunned monotone, 'It dates back to before the war. To 1923, when Adolf Hitler led a group of his supporters, including Hermann Goering, through the streets of Munich in an attempt to overthrow the government. His plan was to denounce the policies of Foreign Minister Stresemann and proclaim himself President of Germany.'

'I take it old Stresemann was none too thrilled about that,' Donovan said drily.

While I wondered where all this was leading us.

Prohl went on, 'Stresemann ordered troops to fire on the marchers. Sixteen of the protesters were killed. Goering was wounded, and Hitler suffered a dislocated shoulder. He was arrested and later imprisoned in Landsberg.'

'Pity he didn't break his fucking neck,' Donovan grated. 'Would've saved a heap of grief.' He flashed his light over the crate for another look.

Prohl ignored the comment. 'When the marchers fell dying, the flag behind which they had been marching, the swastika, fell with them. It became stained with their blood. It became *heilig* . . . consecrated. You understand?'

We all nodded dutifully. All of us except Ritter.

'Adolf Hitler rose to power in 1933. From that moment on, that same flag, still smeared with the blood of the martyrs, played an important part in all Nazi rituals. It was exhibited twice a year; in September to commemorate the march on the Feldherrnhalle, but most important of all at the annual party rally in Nuremberg. Whenever new flags were introduced they were placed in contact with the *Blutfahne*, in order that they might inherit the standard's power. They had a special name for the ceremony. They called it *die Fruchtbarmachung*. The . . .' Prohl's broad brow furrowed as he searched for the right word.

'The fertilization,' Ritter said softly from out of the darkness.

We all looked at him. He was standing as still as a statue.

'Yes,' Prohl said, almost cautiously. 'But there is another meaning.' He frowned again, unsure, hesitant. 'As with . . . animals?'

There was a silence.

Donovan said speculatively, 'You mean like . . . insemination?'

Prohl nodded vigorously, the light in his hand wobbling. '*Richtig!* That is so!'

The insemination. The word carried a frisson of unreality. For wasn't this the very core around which Nazi philosophy had been based? The systematic eradication of impurities in order to perpetuate the lineage of the blood order; the seeding of the master race.

I began to experience a strange sense of premonition. 'You think that's what your father was afraid of?' I said softly. 'The possibility that this flag would be used to recruit new blood?'

'I think that is possible, yes.' Prohl nodded.

'And that's it?' Donovan exclaimed, unable to contain his incredulity. 'That's what this has all been about? A flag? A bloody flag? Sweet Jesus!' He rolled his eyes in disbelief.

It sounded more than a bit far-fetched to me too.

Or did it?

Because the pages of history are littered with roll-calls of the dead: the names of the millions who flocked to their particular banners with the suicidal zeal of moths to a flame. The cross of the crusaders, the swastika, the Irish tricolour – it mattered not. Good or evil, they were all symbols of a kind, imbued with a power to exhort the warrior. Behind the flags of battle, men had forded the wildest river, scaled the steepest hill, laid siege to the stoutest keep.

And hadn't I taken an Argentinian bullet just so's the red, white and blue could be raised with pride above a windswept, godforsaken stretch of boggy pastureland way down there in the green-grey storm-tossed waters of the South Atlantic?

And, in 1939, hadn't this very banner, wielded by a maniac, served to whip an entire nation into a martial frenzy that, ultimately, had gone on to claim the lives of fifty-five million people?

Undoubtedly, I thought, if the Nazis had revered this flag as much as Prohl indicated, their number one priority would have been to remove it away from the risk of capture, particularly by the Soviets. Moessinger had, presumably, been chosen to carry the banner to a place of safe keeping.

Even if Harry Donovan remained unconvinced about the whole damned thing.

Yet, despite his scepticism, I would have thought that as an Irishman, he of all people might have understood only too well. Even before Gunther Prohl had put it into words, I for one had started to sense just what it was that his father had been so afraid of. He'd seen what the raising of the battle standard had done for his country once. He'd been appalled at the possibility of it happening again.

'Right,' Donovan grunted tartly, cutting into my thoughts, 'if we're all through with the history lesson, let's see what else we've got.'

He reached down, grabbed a corner of the banner and lifted it away.

And recoiled as if he'd been stung, the beam of his flashlight wavering in the darkness as he backed off hurriedly. 'Mother of God!' he breathed.

Skin prickling, I moved in to see for myself.

I heard Gunther Prohl groan like a man in pain as he saw what lay before us.

I looked down.

The Flag of Blood was more than a banner. It was a burial shroud.

Another body. Long dead.

Nestling in the folds of the Reich's faded and blood-soaked standard, like a jewel on a satin cushion, the skull, mouth half open in a travesty of a smile, stared out at us. At the time of interment the intention must surely have been for the body to attain a state of near preservation within its airtight container. In the years since Dieter Prohl's exhumation, however, dehydration had taken its toll of the cadaver. The flesh had tightened across the bones, metamorphosing into an almost mummified consistency, the colour reminiscent of burnt cork. Arms as thin as twigs protruded from the sleeves. A pair of hands, blackened and twisted like claws, clasped what looked

251

like a silver relay baton surmounted by the figure of an eagle.

But it wasn't the state of the body that had affected us so much as the clothes it had been dressed in.

Black trousers; grey jacket, double breasted with six silver buttons, the collar short and very wide, almost square. High on the left sleeve was the badge of an eagle. An Iron Cross was pinned to the left breast pocket. Above that the party badge. Below the Iron Cross was another medal which I didn't recognize.

'I don't believe it,' Donovan declared. 'It can't be.' He stared at me. 'Can it?'

'No,' I croaked, only too aware of the lack of saliva in my own throat and the violent thudding of my heart. 'He took poison, shot himself, and they burnt him.'

Prohl shrank back, his face still pale. '*Es ist unmoeglich!* he whispered. '*Unmoeglich!*'

For a split second I thought he was going to keel over. I put my arm around his shoulder, took his light off him and sat him down on a couple of the small bullion crates. His breathing was like a pair of old bellows.

I caught a glimpse of Ritter's face then. He was staring down at the contents of the crate. His expression shocked me. It seemed as if his eyes were aglow. It was a look I'd seen before, in flickering black and white newsreels showing massed rallies in torchlit stadiums. Then, in an instant, perhaps because he'd sensed he was being observed, the light died.

I stared at the remains.

It just wasn't possible, I thought wildly.

Every scrap of historical documentation available pointed unerringly to the fact that the man's ravaged body and that of his mistress had been consumed by fire in a shallow, rubble-strewn depression, only yards away from the rear entrance of the Fuehrerbunker, where, in the darkening shadows cast by the ruins of the shattered Chancellery building, within earshot of the Russian shelling, the final act of the *Goetterdaemmerung* had been played out.

With the Soviet Army less than a mile from the Chancellery, there could have been little doubt in the minds of the bunker's inhabitants that the end was exceedingly nigh. The entire cabal had been under no illusions about the fate they could all expect to meet if and when they were taken by the Russians. Their leader had been made well aware of the fate that had befallen his former ally, Benito. Il Duce's bloated body had been strung upside down from a lamppost for all the world to see. A similar fate was something the Fuehrer had not been prepared to contemplate. He had made it clear that he would not give Zhukov the satisfaction of displaying his body for public consumption. Hence the planned suicide pact and cremation.

At least, that had been the long-accepted theory.

But suppose there had been another pact? Suppose members of the inner circle had conspired to smuggle out of the smoking capital not only the Reich's sacred banner but the Fuehrer's body as well? In fact, not merely out of Berlin, but out of the country entirely. And by what better way than in one of Doenitz's U-boats?

If that was so, as the evidence before our eyes suggested, history would have to be rewritten.

For it appeared that Lieutenant Commander Prohl had inherited more than gold. As a consequence of his own actions he had become the unwitting beneficiary of a terrible legacy.

But was all this really feasible?

The U-boat skipper had certainly been in no doubt as to the identity of the corpse. From his entries in his journal, that much was evident.

Undoubtedly it had been his fear of that legacy and all that its discovery entailed that had finally upset the delicate balance of his already disturbed mind. His dread had been very real, founded not just upon the finding of the Reich's ancient banner but upon the existence of something of far greater worth, a relic which, to some people, would be considered as sacred as the Holy Grail or a splinter from the True Cross.

A relic which, if its existence became universally known, would have the power to reawaken dark forces, to inflame, to arouse and, finally, to resurrect the old order.

An old order but a new dawn.

A Fourth Reich.

Propelled by the wild imaginings of his already tortured mind, Lieutenant Commander Prohl had taken dramatic steps to ensure that such a thing could never happen. He had murdered the only other men who would have been able to bear witness to his discovery. And, to preserve it even further, he had killed himself.

And if all this was true, if our eyes were not deceiving us, it meant that we had stumbled upon an awesome secret.

Gunther Prohl stood up. He appeared to have regained some of his composure, if not his colour. It was difficult to tell in the darkness. I gave him his lamp back.

'Do you really believe this?' I asked him.

He shook his head distractedly, as if clearing it.

I shone my light on to the uniform jacket. 'What's the other medal?'

Prohl stared down. 'It was to denote that the wearer had been wounded in action.'

I remembered I'd read somewhere that Adolf Hitler had been wounded in the Great War. He'd been a

254

corporal then. All the evidence seemed to be sliding into place too easily, I thought bleakly.

'All right,' I said, trying to steady my own nerves. 'Let's not get too excited here. It's probably not even who we think it might be.'

Which sounded pretty bloody Irish, even as I said it. I played my light across the grisly remains once more. 'If it is him,' I said, 'why didn't Gunther's father destroy the body?'

I was rewarded with a look of scorn from Donovan. 'Christ, Logan! We're talking about a bloke who disobeyed the direct orders of his Commander in Chief, hijacked half a ton of gold bullion, shoved one poor sod out of a torpedo tube and killed half a dozen of his men in cold blood. We're hardly talking about a sane human being here, for God's sake! Maybe in all the excitement he simply forgot!'

Well, yes, there was that, of course.

'So,' I said. 'What do we do now?'

Donovan's eyebrows took off again. 'What d'you mean, what do we do? We put the lid back on, take the gold and bugger off. What did you think we were going to do? Give the bloody thing to the Imperial War Museum? C'mon, Michael!'

I looked at Prohl. 'Well?'

Gunther Prohl said wearily, 'Mr Donovan is right, Michael. The war has been over a long time. It would serve no useful purpose to open up old wounds. Let the dead rest in peace, whoever they may be.'

'Look, Mike,' Donovan cut in. 'We spill the beans on this and we are going to be knee-deep in media madness. I would have thought that you, more than any of us, wouldn't be too keen about that. I say we take the money and run. Maybe we'll give the newspapers an anonymous call while we're lazing on a beach somewhere. What do you say?'

I thought about that. About the attendant fuss and the publicity. Thought about photographs and recognition and the Turks reading about it and coming after me with even more of a vengeance. Thought about eleven million dollars' worth of gold bullion just sitting there, waiting to be claimed, no questions asked. Thought about all that. Came to a decision.

'Done,' I said.

'You're not serious?' Liz Hammond stared at me.

'Well, if it's not him,' I said, 'I'd like to know who the hell it is.'

'But . . . Adolf Hitler?' She had her head on one side and was regarding me with a bemused grin, not too sure just what to believe. 'Come on! You are having me on, aren't you?'

'Swear to God,' I said. 'Cross my heart. It's all true.'

'And he's just lying there?'

'Well he sure as buggery isn't performing cabaret. He's there, all right. Large as life. Well . . . death, at any rate.'

She was silent for several seconds. Then she said dubiously, 'Wasn't Churchill supposed to have had a double? Maybe Hitler had one too.'

'I'm tempted to say, "so what?" What'd be the point of going to all this trouble for a double? Wouldn't make sense.'

She had no answer to that.

'So, what now?' she asked.

I shrugged. 'We've been through that already,' I said. 'Gunther and Harry are of the opinion we do nothing.'

'Nothing? You're joking?'

I shrugged. 'Christ, Liz, who'd believe us anyway? I'm having enough trouble convincing you, for Pete's sake!'

256

'So you're going along with it?'

'That's about the size of it,' I said. 'Frankly, it's the safest option. We take the money and run.'

Marco had performed wonders. He had been able to run a cable from the *Valkyrie* through the cave entrance and into the sub. It was a bit of a jury-rigged affair, but the half-dozen lights we had managed to string together inside the U-boat's hull had done the trick. We dropped another anchor off the yacht's stern to prevent her swinging around and severing the cable.

We performed a tally and determined that there were twenty-two bullion crates all told, twelve in the stern, ten in the bow. Once we'd got the lighting system operational, we worked flat out, using the fore and aft torpedo-loading hatches as a means by which we could lift the crates on to the sub's deck. Just the bullion. We didn't bother with the cash. White fivers weren't much good for anything other than wallpapering the *Valkyrie*'s stateroom. The rest could go towards paying the lease on coffin space for the U-boat's two deceased occupants.

Once we'd got the crates on deck, we moved them down to the sub's stern in preparation for transfer.

Donovan stayed on the sub to offload. Marco and Ritter remained on the *Valkyrie* in order to receive the goods. I used the skiff to ferry the cargo between the two.

I limited the load to three crates at a time. By early afternoon we were almost there.

In fact, it was with something approaching relief that I cast off for the last time. I motored away from the *Valkyrie*'s hull, acknowledging Marco's cheery grin and wave, and headed across to the cave entrance.

Donovan was waiting for me patiently. He was sitting on the remaining crate. He stood up as I chugged in.

'All set?' I called.

257

He threw me a jaunty salute. 'Aye aye, skipper!'

Lifting the crate into the bottom of the skiff wasn't exactly easy but by now we had mastered the technique.

That part of the exercise completed, we spent the next ten minutes or so dismantling the last of the lamps that we'd strung up on the deck. We stowed them in the skiff with the crate.

'Looks as if that's it then,' I said.

Donovan nodded. 'Permission to disembark, cap'n?'

'Permission granted.'

He joined me in the skiff. I tugged on the starter line and the little engine rasped into life. I hauled away on the tiller and backed us away from the U-boat's hull.

As we headed towards daylight I felt as if a great weight had been lifted from my shoulders. On the submarine we had all been confronted by spectres from the past. Our memories of the encounter would never fade. Perhaps that was the price we would have to pay for having disturbed the ghosts in the first place.

Within seconds after we'd emerged into the welcoming afternoon sunshine both of us realized we had a visitor.

Donovan and I exchanged startled glances.

An Albatross.

But not the kind that had given the Ancient Mariner heartburn. This one had a much greater wingspan. A seaplane, manufactured by Grumman Aviation. The aircraft had been hidden by the *Valkyrie*'s bulk, so we didn't spot it until we began our swing towards the yacht's stern. It was squatting on the water like one of its plump namesakes, its plumage smoky white with dark blue trim.

'Shit!' Donovan cursed. 'Who the hell is this?'

Quite, I thought.

For this was hardly the most convenient time to be receiving guests. Not with twenty-one crates of appropriated gold bullion littering up our deck space.

Then I wondered vaguely if this was something that Gunther Prohl had arranged, as a more efficient means of transporting the bullion out of the country. Not a bad idea, come to think of it, even if he hadn't bothered to mention a thing to anyone else.

And then again maybe it was the authorities. Though it didn't look like anything the Greek police or customs would have used and there were no emblems of officialdom along the wings or fuselage, as far as I could make out.

My next spot of speculation didn't do a whole lot for my nerves either.

The Syndicate?

Couldn't be. They thought I was dead.

At least, that's what I thought they thought.

We were approaching the *Valkyrie*'s stern. I was vaguely conscious of Donovan sliding the bullion crate surreptitiously under the centre thwart with his heels.

'No point in advertising,' he murmured.

Amen to that.

I could see Marco, but no sign of anyone else. Maybe Liz and Gunther were entertaining the plane's crew down below.

We drew closer, and by this time I could make out Marco's expression. No welcoming wave. No happy grin either. He wasn't looking worried so much as scared stiff. And where the hell was Ritter? I began to get this very bad feeling.

Then I spotted Ritter. He had appeared behind Marco. He lifted an arm and waved us in. I relaxed slightly and steered the skiff towards them.

We were less than two yards from the *Valkyrie*'s hull when Marco sprang to the rail and opened his mouth to yell. His warning was eclipsed by a sharp staccato burst of sound.

It was one I recognized. Every weapon has its own particular sound, as individual as a set of fingerprints. I was still carrying the scar from my last encounter with this particular model. An Ingram.

I ducked and recoiled in horror as a spray of blood and bone erupted from the meat of Marco's right shoulder. Bright crimson flowers bloomed across his chest and his expression was one of shock and pain as he toppled over the rail towards us. His neck hit the gunnel and I heard the dry snap of bone the second before his body hit the water. The skiff rocked alarmingly as he went under.

We were too close to the *Valkyrie*'s hull to enable me to take evasive action. Before I had a chance to turn us away, Ritter was at the rail, machine pistol in hand.

'Cut the motor!' he yelled.

'Do it!' Donovan hissed behind me. 'He'll cut us in half if you don't.'

I did as instructed. The silence was absolute.

'On board,' Ritter said. 'Now. Bring the gold with you.'

We did as we were told and dumped the crate on the deck.

'What's going on, Martin?' I asked, eyeing the gun's muzzle.

He didn't answer.

A man appeared behind him. No one I knew.

Skeletal would have been the best way to describe him, with skin that was so pale it was almost translucent. His face was gaunt, hollowed by sunken cheeks. The hair on his skull was sparse and very white, and as wispy as dandelion spores. A pair of hooded eyes glared at us balefully. A beige suit hung upon his cadaverous frame, emphasizing his slightly stooped shoulders, although his thinness served to make him appear taller than he actually was. Under the suit, he wore a white shirt, the collar of which was unfastened, revealing a neck as mottled and wrinkled as that of a turtle. The sleeves of the shirt were too long. They extended below his cuffs and hung over his wrists, covering the balls of his thumbs. He had hands like talons, one of which was clasped round the neck of a wooden cane. He looked like something you'd see shuffling down the middle of a cancer ward.

And he was seventy years of age if he was a day.

Donovan looked sideways at me and raised his eyebrows questioningly. 'Friend of yours?'

'Nope.'

I didn't know anybody who looked that old, or that ill. I'd have remembered.

He moved forward awkwardly, favouring his right knee, and spoke rapidly to Ritter. The language was German. By his expression I presumed he was asking Ritter to confirm our identity.

Ritter answered tersely.

Satisfied with the reply, the old man blinked and regarded us speculatively. 'You are Logan and Donovan,' he said, in heavily accented English. As well as the inflection there was a distinct rasp in his voice.

It had been a statement rather than a question. There didn't seem to be anything worthwhile to say, so we waited.

He grunted dismissively. 'My name,' he announced stiffly, 'is Hans Josef Moessinger.'

Part Three

18

Donovan was the first to recover.

'Holy frigging hell . . .!'

I had been about to utter something along similar lines but the Irishman had beaten me to it. So I had to make do with trying to jack up my sunken jaw in a bid to restore it to full working order.

If the old man was in any way amused by our reactions, he didn't look it.

'You can't be,' I managed to say finally. 'He's dead.'

Which was pretty close to what Hammet had said to me when I'd appeared through his bedroom window, and just as banal. Not surprisingly, I was rewarded with the same sort of look that I'd given the Lebanese. As if I were something he'd found on the sole of his shoe.

He spoke sharply to Ritter, again in German, turned abruptly and limped towards the hatchway that led down to the stateroom. His progress was slow, his right knee stiff and unresponsive, bending hardly at all.

Ritter jerked the muzzle of his gun to indicate that we should follow.

Gunther Prohl and Liz were in the stateroom, seated on one of the sofas. Liz gasped with relief when she saw us. 'Thank God!' She began to get up but was pushed back down again.

The old man had brought reinforcements with him. Two of them. Young, about Ritter's age. One was blond, the other had grey hair. They both had blue eyes. I noticed. They were both armed as well. Ingrams again.

265

Very popular, very much in vogue. It had to happen sooner or later, I supposed idly. Designer ordnance.

The one with grey hair was the one who'd restrained Liz in her seat. But it was his companion who caught my eye. Something about him seemed familiar. And then I remembered. The evening I had made my house call on the Lebanese; he was the man I'd spotted with Ritter at that bar in the Plaka.

Small world, I reflected.

I asked Liz and Gunther Prohl if they were all right. They both nodded dully.

Liz said, 'We heard shooting. I . . .' Then she realized one of us was missing. 'Where's Marco . . .?'

Her expression told me that she had anticipated the worst.

'Dead,' I replied bluntly.

Her face crumpled. 'Oh, God! Why?'

'He tried to warn us. So Ritter shot him. Isn't that right, Martin?'

Gunther Prohl swore violently. Ritter just stood there with a half-smile on his face, letting the stream of invective wash over him, with an amusement bordering on insolence. The bastard.

'I take it introductions have already been made?' I said.

Two more brief nods.

The white-haired old man had made his way to Prohl's desk. With some awkwardness he sat down. I stared at him.

Moessinger?

Was it really him? The courier? The man that Dieter Prohl had supposedly murdered more than four decades ago?

But how . . .?

After the extraordinary events of the past few days, I

had begun to think that nothing would surprise me ever again. Turned out I was wrong.

Beside me, Donovan said, 'Okay. I give up. How'd you do it? How d'you come back from the dead?'

Moessinger said, 'Desire for revenge kept me alive.'

'Ah,' Donovan murmured with mock sagacity, folding his arms across his chest. 'The old desire for revenge trick. Works every time.' He bit into his beard, and passed me a brief wink.

Don't push it, Harry, I thought. For the love of God.

But to my surprise, Moessinger did not rise to the bait. Instead, he told his amazing story.

His quest for vengeance was born out of panic, hatred and rage during those moments after the torpedo tube hatch closed behind him, cutting off his frantic pleas for mercy as effectively as the blade of a guillotine slicing away the head of a victim.

During those first few terrifying seconds of incarceration, lying there in the cold blackness, encased in a stinking metal cylinder barely wider than a man's shoulders, overwhelmed with claustrophobia and the bowel-churning fear of what was to come, Moessinger's screams, in contrast with the noise of the sea booming around him, were silent ones.

In the bore with him were the other items intended as decoy material: a mattress, some clothing, magazines; all packed around his trembling body like wadding in a gun barrel. His fingers, bloodied by their impotent scratching of the metal, made tentative contact. Already the mattress was damp, from the water seeping in through the outer door of the tube.

It was at that point, curiously, that Moessinger, driven by the adrenalin coursing through his bloodstream, began to inch his way towards the fore end of the tube. Heart thumping, his slow movements finally hampered by the cloying folds of the sweat- and oil-stained mattress, Moessinger awaited death.

The worst part of his ordeal was the awful moment the tube flooded. The second the outer door had been opened to the sea, the water surged into the bore with the force of a high-pressure hose. In those brief freezing seconds, imprisoned by shock and the savage inrush, Moessinger felt himself drowning.

And then the tube was fired, so swiftly was the order given that there was scarcely sufficient time to flood the barrel. The rush of compressed air, as thunderously loud as the passage of an express train, was accompanied by a massive surge of pressure propelling him forward. In the roaring explosion, blinded and disoriented, he was conscious of only two things: the almost exquisite pain as his eardrums ruptured, followed immediately by the agony that engulfed him when his right shoulder and knee smashed against the rim of the tube door as he emerged into the broiling, inky darkness.

He hadn't been aware of making a conscious effort to save himself. Water was in his mouth and ears and nose and he was colder than he had ever been before in his life, and his body was numb with pain. He began to succumb to the sea's grip. Then his hand caught in something that was moving through the void with him. He caught hold, and felt himself drifting in a kind of limbo. He kicked lethargically with his sound leg, and the next second he broke surface. Coughing, spitting, spluttering, skin slick with oil, clutching the mattress that had saved him, he began to take shuddering gulps of air. The span of time between his ejection from the sub and his first lungful of air had been a little less than sixty seconds.

It had just seemed like a lifetime.

But that was behind him now.

Incredibly, he had survived.

The fact that Moessinger had lived through such an experience had indeed to be counted as some kind of miracle, whichever way you looked at it. I was aware that men had survived escapes from great depths before, without the aid of breathing apparatus. I seem to remember that the record was something over two hundred feet. But that had been exceptional. The U-boat had been down some sixty feet when the tubes were fired. Sixty feet was nothing. And had the pressure exerted by firing the tubes been any greater than in a controlled escape? Apparently not.

Moessinger was living proof.

'Who picked you up?' I asked. 'The British?'

As soon as I'd posed the question I knew that it hadn't been the British. Without doubt the signals that Prohl had traced concerning the identification of his father's sub would have mentioned the retrieval of a survivor. There had been nothing like that in any of the dispatches.

Moessinger shook his head scornfully. 'The British? They saw nothing. Only wreckage. I was in the water for two hours before I was found by the crew of a Spanish fishing boat.'

With the promise of a reward, the fishermen had delivered the half-dead Moessinger to the German consulate in Algeciras. From there, while undergoing medical treatment for his injuries, Moessinger had managed to contact the Abwehr's resident agent in Cadiz, Dietrich Niebuhr.

As Kaltenbrunner's man on the spot, Niebuhr had been responsible for transferring all the booty accumulated under the *Aktion Feuerland* operation on to German U-boats. The subs, operating out of secret bases on the Spanish coast, had transported the loot to South America.

'Then what?' I asked. 'A sea voyage to Buenos Aires?'

For the first time, Moessinger's pale eyes showed signs

269

of fire. 'How easily you mock, my young friend! No! Unlike others, I knew where my duty lay!'

It was as if he was willing me to challenge him. I said, 'So, Dieter Prohl was right then. It is him, isn't it?'

Moessinger's chin came up defiantly. 'I was charged with accompanying the body. It was a great honour. I vowed to guard it with my life!'

'Boy,' Donovan responded succinctly, 'did you fuck up!'

'I was betrayed!' The old man's tone of voice had risen sharply. It was the cry of a man who believed himself unjustly accused. 'By his father!' A bead of spittle exited from Moessinger's mouth and landed across a corner of the desk as he raised the point of his cane and jabbed it towards Gunther Prohl.

Prohl jerked back into his seat, stunned by the suddenness and the ferocity of the attack.

In a hasty attempt to defuse the situation, I said, 'Whose idea was it?'

Moessinger's hackles retracted slightly. His lizard-like head swivelled round to face me. I saw Prohl visibly relax as attention was diverted from him.

'Who planned it?' I asked again. 'Bormann?'

'There was a small group of us. A nucleus. Bormann, Rattenhuber, Axmann, Guensche, Linge, Stumpfegger and myself.'

Apart from Bormann, the names meant nothing to me. I asked Moessinger who they were.

A real motley crew, as it turned out.

Johann Rattenhuber had been commandant of the RSD, Hitler's bodyguard detachment. Axmann, the leader of the Hitler Youth. Guensche had been Hitler's adjutant. Linge, the Fuehrer's valet. Stumpfegger, a surgeon, had been one of the court physicians.

Moessinger said, 'We had known for over a week that

the Fuehrer intended to remain in Berlin until the end. Ever since the conference of the twenty-second. It was then that he promised us he would personally direct the defence of the city. Himmler, Goebbels, Bormann, everyone pleaded with him to leave before the Russian ring tightened, but he refused. Hanna Reitsch even volunteered to commandeer a plane from Gatow and fly him out. But he said No, he would not desert his country in its greatest hour of need. He would not betray the German people.'

Yeah, very laudable, I reflected.

'All that week the Reichsminister and Rattenhuber attempted to persuade the Fuehrer to accept Hanna Reitsch's offer to fly him to Berchtesgaden in the hope that he would be able to continue the fight from the Redoubt; but it was no use. The Fuehrer was convinced that General Wenck's Twelfth Army would arrive to relieve us at any time. The rest of us knew, of course, that that would never happen. Wenck's forces had already been routed.

'Many times Rattenhuber swore that he and his men would fight to the end to give the Fuehrer a chance to make his escape. The Fuehrer still refused to leave. Even up until the morning he dictated his will, Rattenhuber had felt sure the Fuehrer would see reason. Not until the will was witnessed by Bormann did everyone fully understand that the Fuehrer's mind had been made up.'

'And that's when your merry little band decided to step in?' Donovan said.

Moessinger nodded. 'When Bormann told Rattenhuber that the Fuehrer had stipulated in his will that his body was to be burnt, they decided to take the matter into their own hands. They made a pact, against the Fuehrer's own wishes, that they would attempt to smuggle his body out of Berlin. This was to avoid the risk of the remains falling

271

into the hands of the Russians. It was possible that if they were delivered to a place of safety they would become a rallying beacon.'

'Plus,' Donovan added, his voice heavy with sarcasm, 'it was probably a bit early in the year for a barbecue.'

Moessinger's eyes flashed once more but he managed to hold himself in check.

He went on, 'They knew they would have to keep it a secret from some of the others: Krebs and Burgdorf, and especially that posturing turkey cock Goebbels. He had become a liability. He was expendable. Like Himmler and Goering, who had shown their treachery by attempting to negotiate with the Allies. Our newly appointed Reich Chancellor had outlived his usefulness.'

'Pardon me for asking,' I put in, 'but what was your part in all this? How come you were around when all this was going on?'

'I was liaison officer between Kaltenbrunner and Bormann in the *Aktion Feuerland* operation. During this time Dr Kaltenbrunner was at his headquarters at Alt Aussee. We were aware that the Americans had found the bulk of the gold reserves at Merkers earlier in the previous month. That was why the three of us had arranged for the last shipment to be flown north instead of south. We had decided that the Fuehrer's remains should be taken north also, instead of to the Redoubt. To Bremerhaven, to meet up with the final consignment and accompany it to South America. We had many contacts there. Many sympathizers. With the Fuehrer's memory to inspire us and with the funds acquired through the *Aktion Rheinhardt* operation, we had the means to begin again.'

'So, how did you manage to save the body?'

'A substitution was made.'

'Substitution?'

'It was the only way. We had to arrange for another corpse to be burned.'

'Whose was it?'

'A man called Wengler, Otto Wengler. He was a medical orderly, one of Stumpfegger's assistants. He was the same build as the Fuehrer, or at least the closest we could get. He too had a moustache, but we had to trim it to make it look like the Fuehrer's. We had to cut his hair also. Stumpfegger took care of all that.'

'But how the hell did you make the switch?'

'It was when the Fuehrer and his wife left their suite to say goodbye to their staff. He shook hands and told us to make our own escape, to try and break through the Russian lines. He even dispensed a number of gifts to people. It was while this was going on that Linge and Stumpfegger made their move.

'Stumpfegger and Wengler were in Stumpfegger's rooms across the passage. The Reichsminister delayed the Fuehrer's progress in saying his farewells, and Linge called them into the Fuehrer's suite, where he told them the Fuehrer would be returning to thank them personally for their loyal support. While they waited, Linge offered them wine. Wengler's glass had been laced with poison. As soon as Wengler was dead, Linge and Stumpfegger concealed his body in Eva Braun's dressing room. Stumpfegger then left, leaving Linge with the body.'

'Then what?'

'The Fuehrer and his wife returned to their suite and closed the door. Everyone else waited in the passageway outside. About fifteen minutes later we heard the sound of a shot. That was our signal to enter the room.'

'Signal?'

'That Linge had made the switch. Once the Fuehrer and the woman had taken the cyanide, Linge removed Wengler's body from the dressing room and placed it on the sofa. He and Stumpfegger had already dressed Wengler's corpse in one of the Fuehrer's spare uniforms. The Fuehrer's body was placed in the dressing room. Using the Fuehrer's gun, Linge then put a bullet through Wengler's head. That way the damage to the skull and the blood would help to mask the substitute's features. That was our signal.

'Axmann was the first into the room. Then Guensche. They came out and confirmed that the Fuehrer was dead. Goebbels and Bormann went in next, but Axmann and the Reichsminister prevented Goebbels from examining the corpse too closely. That wasn't hard. Goebbels was very squeamish. I do not know how the man ever plucked up the courage to kill himself or his family,' Moessinger sneered, then went on. 'He saw only what he had been meant to see. He never noticed that a switch had been made. With all the activity, no one realized that Linge was already in the room. Then Rattenhuber turned up. Linge covered Wengler's corpse with a blanket to conceal the head and shoulders, and he and Guensche carried it out. Bormann dealt with the woman. The bodies were taken into the garden and burned. Rattenhuber and Guensche performed the cremation.'

'What about Hitler's corpse?'

'It remained where it was while the cremation was taking place. Linge kept everyone out of the suite. That wasn't hard either. With the Fuehrer dead, people were too busy planning their own escape. Goebbels was arranging his family's suicide. We left him to it. While Bormann ordered people to clear the area, Linge and Rattenhuber wrapped the Fuehrer's corpse in the standard and transferred it to a more secure container.'

'The Flag of Blood,' Donovan interpolated.

'Yes. It was our intention that his remains should be buried in it.'

'I can't believe that no one knew what you were doing,' I said. 'Goebbels, the rest of them.'

'As I told you, there was a great deal of confusion. You must also remember that the bunker was not just a few rooms off a single corridor. It was a large complex with offices, living quarters, store rooms, guard posts, canteen, and tunnels linking various command centres. There were a lot of people about, also. All in various stages of panic, all intent on their own safety and survival. Many of the bunker's occupants were not even aware that the Fuehrer was dead. No, it was quite easy.'

'How did you get out of the city?'

'By air.'

'Air!'

'By seaplane, arranged by Doenitz and flown by a Luftwaffe colonel named Manfred Gratz. Gratz had been standing by at Doenitz's headquarters in Ploen for a week, awaiting the order to fly in. At that time it was still hoped that the Fuehrer would see sense and flee the capital.'

'Where the hell was he going to land a seaplane, for Christ's sake?' Donovan enquired.

'On the Havel Lake,' Moessinger replied, 'southwest of the city. Landing and taking off within the city limits was impossible. Von Griem and Hanna Reitsch were the last people to fly in and out using that route, the day before the Fuehrer's death. Von Griem had flown in on the Fuehrer's orders. Reitsch was his copilot. The Fuehrer had summoned the field marshal to advise him that he was to replace Goering as Commander in Chief of the Luftwaffe. Goering was being deposed because the Fuehrer discovered he had made secret contact with the Allies in the hope of negotiating a peace settlement. The Fuehrer also hoped that von Griem would be able to rally the

Luftwaffe into attacking the Russian positions around the capital and so assist Wenck in forcing his way to us.

'We used Reitsch and von Griem to deliver a message to Doenitz telling him to stand by with a plane. We had already discussed that possibility with the grand admiral during his last visit to the Fuehrerbunker on the twenty-first. At that time there had been two alternatives planned: fly the Fuehrer south to the Redoubt to continue the fight or fly him north to the Baltic for transfer to a U-boat. By the time the Fuehrer was dead, there was only one alternative left.'

'What about getting the body out of the bunker in the first place?' I asked.

'It was decided that I would accompany it. If Linge or Guensche or any of the others were found to be missing, Krebs and Burgdorf and the rest might have suspected something. I, on the other hand, would be judged to be involved in Reich security business.'

'Okay, so you went where?'

'Rattenhuber assigned a small unit of the Fuehrer's SS bodyguards to escort me. We commandeered the Reichs-minister's scout car for the first part of the journey, as far as the Charlottenburger Chaussee. Then we used some of the old abandoned tunnels in the subway system to cross the city. The Russians had infiltrated many of them but some of the deeper ones were still accessible. And it was night time. We were able to move quite freely. We made it to the headquarters of the Hitler Youth at Pichelsdorf. I was carrying a pass, issued by Axmann, directing the battalion commander to provide us with a guide to take us the rest of the way. He found us a boat. From Pichelsdorf we sailed down to Pfaueninsel, an island at the southern end of the lake.'

'Didn't the escort know what they were guarding?'

'They obeyed orders. General Rattenhuber told them

we were transporting top-secret documents that on no account were to fall into Soviet hands. That was enough.'

'Once you reached the island, what then?'

'We concealed ourselves. We had dispatched one of the Hitler Youth Brigade back to the bunker to advise Bormann and Rattenhuber that we were safe. Bormann sent a message to Doenitz telling him to send Gratz to pick us up. The message was the agreed code that would inform the grand admiral that we would be flying north and he should prepare a U-boat for immediate departure.'

'So the plane arrived and you got away?'

'That is so. But at great risk. The Russians bombed the island many times. The plane did not get to us until the next evening. The Russians fired on us and two of our escort were wounded. We had to leave them behind. Doenitz met us in Bremerhaven. The Fuehrer's body was placed in the casket that had been prepared and we were transferred to the U-boat that same night.'

'What about the others left behind in the bunker?'

'It had been planned that the Reichsminister and the rest should wait a few hours before following us. It would have been suspicious if we had all left at once, in such large numbers. It had been decided that once I had relayed the message that I and the body were safe, the rest should leave along the same route. Unfortunately, they had left it too late. That did not happen.'

'Did they get out?' I asked.

'Rattenhuber, Linge and Guensche were captured by the Russians. They spent ten years in labour camps. Stumpfegger was shot and killed during his escape attempt. Only Axmann made it out of Berlin. But he was captured by the Americans in Bavaria about six months later.'

'And Bormann?'

277

'Bormann escaped. He sheltered for a while in Eich-mann's bunker under the Kurfurstendamm. And then he tried to join Doenitz in the north. It took him over a month to reach the admiral's HQ at Ploen, but by that time, of course, it was too late. Doenitz had already been arrested by the British. Bormann crossed into Denmark. Then, later, he retraced his steps south to Bavaria and moved into Italy, where he was provided with a fresh identity by Vatican officials. He didn't arrive in Argentina until May 1948.'

'So he did survive the war, after all.' I said.

'Indeed,' Moessinger said. 'He survived. As did many others: Mengele, Cukurs, Barbie, Schwend, Rauff.'

'Is he still around?'

'Bormann?' Moessinger shook his head. 'He died in 1978 in La Paz.'

'And all those rumours about him moving around South America in the sixties and seventies were true?'

'Of course. But he was not as active as the reports would have had the world believe. He suffered a major stroke in 1966 that left him partly paralysed, and he later developed what is now known to be Alzheimer's Disease. He was quite senile towards the end and was under constant supervision. The rumours kept the Jewish snatch squads busy, however, which caused us some inconveni-ence.' A flicker of irritation scarred Moessinger's pale face.

There followed a long period of silence as the import of Moessinger's testimony sank in.

I said finally, 'But what about the Russians?'

'The Russians?' Moessinger's eyes narrowed.

'I was under the impression that they were able to confirm that the teeth and bones found in the Chancellery garden were Hitler's. If you're telling us that you'd already made the substitution, how could that be?'

278

Moessinger waved his mottled hand airily, as if the question was of no consequence. 'You are forgetting that the Fuehrer's personal physician was also involved in the deception. The Fuehrer's dental records were stored in the Chancellery laboratory. Stumpfegger switched the Fueher's dental charts with those of Wengler.' A further shrug served to emphasize that he thought the solution should have been obvious.

'That still leaves the identification of the bones,' I pointed out.

Moessinger smiled thinly. 'That was the simplest ruse of all. The Russians based most of their evidence on the words of one man, a member of the Fuehrer's bodyguard, Harry Mengerhausen. It was Mengerhausen who confirmed that the bone fragments were the Fuehrer's remains.'

'He lied?'

'Mengerhausen was one of many officers who were captured by the Russians. Rattenhuber and the rest were confined in the same camp. It was during his imprisonment that he was presented with a box containing various bone fragments. It was from those that he made the final identification.'

'You mean he was got at?'

Moessinger didn't answer my question. Instead he said, 'The Russians later arranged for Rattenhuber, Guensche, Linge and Axmann to be flown to Berlin. They wanted them to describe the events that took place during the final hours. They were taken into the bunker and the gardens, and made to show where the bodies had been burned. It was more than we could have wished for. It was so easy. The Soviets never realized that they were playing a major part in the subterfuge.'

'You're saying it was easier for them to accept the

evidence as presented to them rather than to admit that they'd let the body slip through their hands?'

Moessinger nodded smugly. 'Precisely. They had already boasted to the world that Adolf Hitler was dead and that they were in possession of his remains. Do you think they would have been prepared to admit later that they were wrong? Never. They would never have recovered from the embarrassment.'

Moessinger had a point there. The Russians had been paranoid about capturing Hitler before the Americans and the British could get to him. I'd even heard stories that at one point they'd accused the British of spiriting Hitler and Eva Braun out of Berlin and over to England. Presumably that had been before the bodies were discovered and Mengerhausen made his timely contribution.

And that had been it. As far as the world was concerned, provenance had been well and truly established.

Until now.

'So what happened to you after you arrived in Spain?' I asked him.

'I remained in Madrid. There was still much work to be done. For the *Kamaradenwerk*.' Moessinger's frail chest appeared to swell as he spoke.

The *Kamaradenwerk*: the secret underground rescue group formed at the end of the war to assist Nazi fugitives to escape from Europe. It had been financed by German financiers and industrialists.

'Just goes to prove,' Donovan said drily, 'that you can't keep a bad man down.'

'Skorzeny and I ran the European end of the organization.'

'Skorzeny?' Donovan perked up visibly at the mention of the name. 'Otto Skorzeny? The fellow who rescued Mussolini?'

280

'A great soldier,' Moessinger said, his chin lifting. 'A true hero of the Reich.'

'Weren't they all,' I said sarcastically.

But, admittedly, the Mussolini operation had been rather special. Skorzeny, an SS colonel, was another of Kaltenbrunner's mob, the RSHA. His brief had been to conduct sabotage and assassination strikes behind enemy lines, often wearing Allied uniforms. His greatest coup was leading a band of parachute troops in a glider-borne raid to free Mussolini from imprisonment in a mountain stronghold in 1943.

Anyone who'd spent any time in a Special Forces' environment, as I had, inevitably harboured a sneaking regard for the man's ability.

Interned at the end of the war by the Americans, he had been acquitted of war crimes and escaped from custody through the intervention of *Die Spinne*, the SS escape apparatus. He'd disappeared for a couple of years, eventually resurfacing in Spain. Which tied in nicely with Moessinger's account.

'But Skorzeny's dead now,' I said.

Moessinger nodded. 'I was elected to take over the running of the organization.'

'You mean to say the thing still exists?' Donovan's eyes were wide with amazement.

I could see Donovan's point. If Moessinger's age was anything to go by, the *Kamaradenwerk*'s AGM, if it was ever convened, probably had all the ambience of a branch meeting of the Darby and Joan Club, with its membership list declining with every passing year.

'The organization has undergone many transformations,' Moessinger said. 'The *Kamaradenwerk* was merely the seed. From that seed sprang the *Movimiento Sagrado para el Tercer Mundo*, the Sacred Movement for the Third World—'

'Sounds more like a dago dancing academy,' Donovan broke in. 'What do you do on open days, Hans Josef? Dress up in your little leather tutus and practise the bossa nova?'

It was the moment that Ritter had been waiting for. He moved in and jabbed the squat barrel of the Ingram into Donovan's belly. The Irishman went down like a felled ox, nursing his stomach, wheezing in pain.

'Bright, Harry,' I told him. 'Very bright. You've got to remember not everyone has your sense of humour.'

'I know,' he groaned through gritted teeth, 'I keep forgetting.'

'For God's sake, Moessinger,' I said, 'can't you people just admit that it's over? No one's interested. No one cares any more. You're just a bunch of feeble old men with stars in your eyes. Why don't you just crawl back into the woodwork and retire gracefully with the rest of your festering buddies?'

Moessinger stood up then. He supported himself with his cane and glowered into the room. 'You are mistaken, my young friend.' His voice was a sibilant hiss. 'Since its inception, the movement's strength has grown day by day. Its influence has spread all over the world: through Europe, the United States, Latin America, South Africa, even Japan. Our numbers can be measured in tens of thousands!' His voice rose higher. 'But always we must be vigilant! Wiesenthal may be an old dog, but the pups he has spawned are tenacious and have a savage bite. The Legion must be able to defend itself against its enemies!'

The Legion?

So that was what they were calling themselves now. I recalled the quotation. Biblical, spoken to Christ by a man with an unclean spirit.

'My name is Legion, for we are many.'

282

Moessinger had given a virtual paraphrase. My skin crawled.

But how many, exactly? Moessinger had said tens of thousands. Could be worse, I thought abstractedly. Could be hundreds of thousands. Could still be. Maybe he was being modest.

But just how far did the Legion's tentacles extend?

I considered some of the extreme right-wing factions that I'd heard about. Most of them generally kept a low profile. In Europe, at any rate. There'd been some resurgence in West Germany. With the NPD back in the sixties and, more recently, with the Republican party, but by and large the old wounds were still too deeply felt for there to be much chance of a complete revival of Nazism. Or so I had thought.

Austria was a different kettle of fish, however. After allegations that its president had been implicated in Nazi atrocities in the Balkans, something like half the population voted 'so what'; which says a lot about that country's political bent. But at least they were open about it. It was the underground movements you had to watch out for, the fanatics. And there, presumably, was where the Legion secured most of its support.

Italy had the NAR. That organization had emerged from under its stone just long enough to massacre eighty-four people in the Bologna railway station. In France, Le Pen's National Front party had always managed to secure a goodly percentage of votes at election time. Belgium had its Flemish Militant Order. Spain had the New Force. Britain had the British Movement and Column 88.

Were they all independent entities or were they linked by some vast covert web woven by Moessinger and his followers?

I wondered about the rest. The United States? The only organization I could think of was the Klan. And what

283

about the reference to South Africa? Did it mean that the Legion was the power base upon which the AWB was founded? Were Terre 'Blanche and his supporters merely puppets of a greater, hidden force? And what of the BBB? That was even more extreme.

South America came as no surprise. According to Moessinger, that was where the Legion had taken root, nourished by the regimes that had provided sanctuaries for the old guard: Bormann, Eichmann, Freddie Schwend, and the rest. They were the countries where the heads of state had been paid blood money. Perón and Alfredo Stroessner, among them. Many of them had come and gone, but the support had always been available. Bought with the funds accumulated by the leaders of the Third Reich.

And Japan? Ultranationalist movements in that part of the world were certainly nothing new, but I could only hazard a guess at the degree of influence the Legion could command in such a society. Unless Moessinger had been referring to the Kuromaku. They were linkmen. They acted as brokers between the rightist underworld, the Yakuza, and the legitimate business world of high finance and politics. If the Legion had men like those in its power, then Moessinger's boast had been, if anything, something of an understatement.

I looked at Ritter and the other two goons.

And these, presumably, were examples of the organization's new blood.

I said, 'So what are you, Martin? The sorcerer's chief apprentice?'

In other words, centurion or foot soldier?

'Martin is one of my most trusted agents, Mr Logan,' Moessinger said. 'We have many such men and women working on our behalf; every one of them committed to our cause. Though not all are active. A great number are dormant, and have remained so for many years, biding their time until the moment of their reawakening and the opportunity to serve the movement. They are our eyes and ears, watching, waiting, reporting back to us. We have a great number of representatives within commerce and industry. I could list many more institutions, apart from Prohl AG – I. G. Farben and Krupps to name but two – in which we have a vested interest. In Martin's case, we were very fortunate to have had someone placed inside the company at such a high level.'

I said to Ritter, 'I suppose that was you in the telex room the other night, relaying info back to the Obergruppenfuehrer here?'

Just his cat-that-ate-the-cream look was sufficient.

'Who's been a clever boy, then?' I said.

So Ritter had been the Legion's fifth columnist. Skorzeny would have been proud of his successor's protégé.

Moessinger said, 'Even with the full resources of the *Kamaradenwerk* at my disposal, I was unable to discover what had happened to Commander Prohl and his crew. It was as if he and his U-boat had vanished off the face of the earth. I assumed, therefore, not unnaturally, that the vessel had been sunk; along with the crew and the consignment.

'Over the years, of course, I had always hoped that one day I would chance upon a clue that would lead me to the solution of the mystery surrounding Commander Prohl's disappearance. Our agents within the company had always been given specific instructions to report back to the movement if any information relating to Dieter Prohl ever came to light. It was a few months ago that I received a report from Martin that Gunther Prohl had begun his own investigations into his father's disappearance.

'And now, finally, my patience has been rewarded! A long time to wait, you may think, but a mere blink of an

285

eye when compared to the span of a thousand-year Reich! The Legion's destiny is about to be fulfilled! At last we can lay claim to our rightful inheritance!'

Through thin bloodless lips Moessinger bared his teeth. He crabbed his way around the desk, a frail, white-haired old man, crippled in mind as well as in body.

'We were betrayed once. We shall not fail again! This time the Fuehrer will be restored to his rightful place. He shall be enshrined in glory and his name and memory will live on through the movement!'

God save us, I thought. He really means it. He's convinced the spirit of Adolf Hitler is going to lead the forces of the Legion into battle, a god-like mechanized version of El Cid.

From somewhere near my feet, I heard Donovan croak, 'Moessinger, have you ever considered psychiatric treatment?'

Moessinger was that fired up, I don't think he even heard him. A blue vein throbbed across his temple and a bright light shone in his eyes. As it had done in Ritter's that time on the U-boat, when we made our discovery of the crate's contents.

What was it with these people?

It was like watching a couple of converts at a Billy Graham crusade. I knew that modern scholars had long considered Nazism to be not so much a political doctrine, more of a religion. And from that gleam in Moessinger's eyes, I could see why. Without doubt, the supporters of National Socialism had displayed something approaching religious zeal in the way they followed the whims and crazed oratory of their dotty leader, looking upon him as a prophet rather than as a politician.

The night-time rallies that I had seen on the TV and newsreels, with their dark overtones of Valhalla, had certainly been as hypnotic in content as any American

286

evangelical meeting. Only instead of 'Praise the Lord' the exaltation had been 'Sieg Heil'. In Moessinger's ravaged face and Ritter's clean-cut features the signs had been clearly visible: that glazed, adoring look of the true believer.

To them, it was the Second Coming. The return of the Messiah.

A dark Messiah.

It was as Dieter Prohl had predicted. This was the new dawn.

'We will restore order out of chaos!' Moessinger cried. 'Chaos initiated by the Zionists and the godless forces of Communism!'

'Oh, for crying out loud,' I said. 'Not the Jews again. Haven't they had enough?'

'The Jews! The blacks! All the inferior breeds! They are mongrels! They are cancerous! They are corruption!'

He was well away now. There was no stopping him. Interesting that he'd brought colour into it. It'd be the Yellow Peril next. At this rate, there weren't going to be too many of us left. I stared at him in disbelief, anger mounting upon anger.

'You are out of your tiny fucking mind, Moessinger! You're certifiable! The godless forces of Communism?' I gazed at Ritter in wonderment. 'And you're going along with all this crap? Come on, Martin! This is like something out of an Erich von Stroheim film, f'r Chris'sake!'

Donovan grunted. 'You tell 'em, Logan.'

'Who asked you?' I said.

Ritter's expression was hard and unyielding. I saw in his mask-like expression a younger, more virile clone of Hans Moessinger.

Moessinger declared stridently, 'You will now assist us.'

I jerked round. 'To do what?'

287

'You will bring the casket to me.'

'Casket? You're getting a bit carried away, aren't you? The thing's not much more than a reinforced orange box.'

'About all the mad bugger's worth,' Donovan muttered.

I was glad to hear that the Irishman's humour was being slowly restored. Which was more than could be said for Moessinger's sanity.

This was like some horrible dream. This was not happening. Any minute now I was going to wake up. Please let that be so.

'All right, Moessinger,' I said. 'Tell you what, I'll do you a favour. You can have him, lock, stock and barrel. I'll even throw in his winding sheet as a bonus. Then you can have him stuffed and mounted on a horse, if you like. How's that?'

His eyes glittered. 'Your blasphemy will be punished,' he grated, his voice dripping with venom.

'I can hardly wait,' I said, adding, 'I suppose asking you to leave the gold behind is out of the question?'

His expression was all the answer I needed.

'What's up, Hans?' Donovan was back on his feet at last. His breathing was close to regular. 'The old coffers running a bit low, are they? Or have we mislaid the keys to all those Swiss safety deposit boxes?'

'We will take what is ours by right!' Moessinger railed. 'The gold is the property of the Reich. It was stolen by this man's father!'

Well, that was one man's opinion. Personally, I could think of at least six million reasons why it wasn't the Reich's property at all. I didn't say anything, though. I wasn't the one holding the gun.

'What d'you reckon?' I looked at Donovan.

He shrugged. 'Don't reckon we got much of a choice, do you?'

Not much, now that he came to mention it.

'Martin and Joachim will help you to retrieve the container,' Moessinger said. He indicated the blond gunman. 'Erich will look after Prohl and the woman. In case,' he added, 'you are thinking of attempting something foolish.'

'Not as daft as he looks,' Donovan said. 'Is he?'

'He couldn't be,' I replied.

Only Harry got the joke.

Lugging the bullion boxes on to the deck of the sub had been bad enough. Manoeuvring one coffin-sized crate out on to the uneven casing was something else. Hernia-inducing, for a start. How they ever got the bloody torpedoes loaded, I'll never know. Must have taken them ages.

Being supervised by an armed and looming Ritter wasn't that much of a joy either. Added to which, he'd delegated his oppo, Joachim, to give us a hand. Which, judging by the latter's expression, hadn't been a piece of legislation too well received.

They used to load the eels, as they'd called them, via a combination of winches, hoists, blocks, tackles and a fair amount of brute strength. The three of us, supervised by Ritter, had to make do with just the brute strength. By the time we'd got the bloody thing up through the hatch and on to the deck, I felt as if I'd just completed the practical in a midwifery exam.

We were using two dinghies for the retrieval. Ours plus the Gemini inflatable from the Albatross. We used the inflatable to transport the crate, with Joachim babysitting. Ritter, Donovan and I took the skiff. Not that Donovan or I would have tried anything. Not with Liz and Gunther still on the *Valkyrie*, chaperoned by the gun-toting Erich.

By the time we got back to the yacht, it was quite late

in the afternoon and, with the sun making its gradual descent towards the horizon, the sky had begun to turn a hazy shade of orange. The cliff face was streaked with purple; the sea was topaz green. In the fading afterglow we hitched the crate to the *Valkyrie*'s stern davits and hoisted it aboard.

Moessinger was on deck to witness the crate's arrival. He could hardly contain his impatience. Almost as soon as it had been released from the winch, he ordered Ritter to open it up.

The lid was prised back, and Moessinger hobbled forward. With a shaking hand he reached out and drew the flag away from the body beneath. As I watched him, his expression changed. At first he had looked full of trepidation; as though he could not quite believe that his long search was finally over. That gave way to something approaching a silent act of communion as his gaze took in the sight before him. Then, incredibly, he was weeping. His head was tilted to one side, and tears trickled down his emaciated cheeks as he gazed with a kind of pious longing upon the dark and shrunken features of his former leader. It was a strange, haunting and deeply disquieting moment.

Broken by Donovan, who said, 'Gets you right here, don't it?'

Slowly, Moessinger raised his head and stared at the Irishman with total and undisguised malevolence. At that moment, more than at any other, I realized the true depth of the old man's madness. Hate radiated from him like a force field. I felt the chill of winter run down my backbone.

Curtly, Moessinger ordered the crate resealed. Then he rapped out an order to Joachim, who disappeared down into the stateroom. A minute later he reappeared with Erich, Gunther Prohl and Liz. Gunther had lost quite a

290

bit of his tan by this time. Liz looked scared stiff. She started towards me but Erich restrained her. He seemed to enjoy the experience. Liz's blue eyes were puppy-dog wide with fear.

'So, what now, Moessinger?' I enquired.

Ritter looked at me as if he couldn't believe that I could be that stupid. Then he gave me what could only be described as an apologetic little smile.

And Moessinger said, 'What do you think, Logan?'

And I thought, Oh, Christ.

There then followed a conversation between Ritter and his boss, in German. I couldn't understand what they were talking about but Liz obviously could, because she went even paler than before and said something to Ritter. She looked and sounded as if she was pleading with him.

And that was when Gunther Prohl's pent-up anger and frustration finally erupted. With a desperate cry he hurled himself at Moessinger.

I'll say one thing for him: he certainly had guts. But that didn't mean that he'd stood a chance. Not in a thousand years. Liz Hammond screamed as Erich swung round, his fingers biting into her arm.

And Ritter brought up the barrel of the Ingram.

'No!' I yelled, and started to move.

And Ritter fired.

The range at which Ritter let fly was so close that Prohl's body appeared, literally, to run into a glass wall. The burst from the Ingram was little more than a second in duration, but the result was no less savage than it would have been from a prolonged fusillade. Under the shocking impact of the bullets, Prohl's body jerked violently and hung in the air like a suspended marionette for what seemed an age, before finally slamming backwards against the edge of the aft hatchway in a tangle of twisted limbs. Blood began pumping out of the wounds in his chest, staining the varnished deck.

Liz let out a dreadful groan of terror and fell to her knees. Ritter rapped out a command to Erich and the latter, with a nod of acknowledgement, pulled Liz roughly to her feet and dragged her back through the hatchway.

Moessinger looked down at Prohl's corpse with the sort of contempt usually reserved for an inebriate sprawled in a gutter. He gestured, almost perfunctorily, towards the body with his cane and murmured something to Ritter; presumably a directive to have the place tidied up.

Ritter replied with what sounded like a question. He had nodded in our direction at the same time, so it wasn't hard to work out what he was asking.

Moessinger shrugged dismissively. '*Erschiessen Sie ihnen*,' he said.

The one thought that flashed through my mind like a rocket was, Logan, you are about to die.

And Donovan pulled me overboard.

19

Donovan had been standing close beside me at the stern. He, too, started forward as Gunther Prohl made his suicidal move, only to stop dead as Ritter made his counterattack. I could sense the Irishman strumming with rage at the callousness of the act. Not only that: he was seething at our own inadequacies, at our total inability to prevent the slaughter. But with three guns trained on us there was bugger all else we could do.

I knew that when Erich took Liz down below, the odds shifted slightly in our favour. But not by enough. It was now down to two against two – I wasn't counting Moessinger – but the other duo were still armed. Donovan had also been weighing the odds all the time.

We were standing by the stern davits, next to the gap in the rail where the stern ladder hung down into the water. By the time Moessinger gave Ritter the order to shoot us, Donovan had already worked out what he was going to do.

As Ritter turned to face us, I felt Donovan's hand at my back. The next thing I knew was when he hooked his fingers into my belt and yanked me backwards through the gap in the rail. I don't know who was more surprised, me or Ritter.

Fortunately, I recovered my wits faster than Ritter did. But he was still bloody quick.

I sensed the wind of passing bullets as Ritter hosed off what sounded like half a magazine; heard the *spang* of metal on metal as a slug richocheted off one of the stanchions; and felt the scorching pain as something white-hot seared its way across the muscles of my back.

Donovan and I hit the water simultaneously, just missing the skiff.

It wasn't as spectacular as my headlong dash over the edge of the cliff. For one thing, it wasn't that much of a drop. And the other thing was that this jump had been unexpected. So I'd hardly had a chance to catch my breath, literally, before I went under.

But fear can be a miraculous spur.

I went deep, instinct pushing me away from the hovering shadow of the *Valkyrie*'s keel, towards the only refuge available to us: the entrance to the sea cave.

If someone had told me that I'd have been able to cover damned near thirty yards underwater without coming up for air, I'd have laughed in his face and laid money down.

I'd have won my bet, too.

I made about five-sixths of that distance before conceding defeat. And the only thing that saved me from getting my head blown off when it broke the surface was the fact that Ritter hadn't expected me to make it even that far.

All the same he came pretty damned close to finishing me off. It was, apart from the moment that Donovan had swept me off the yacht, the fastest drawing-in of breath that I have ever taken. I heard someone yell loudly as I inhaled, and bullets peppered the sea around me as I went down again, striking for the shelter of the tunnel entrance with all the inherent grace of a turtle on methanol.

Undoubtedly, it was the undertow that saved me. I surrendered to its pull and allowed myself to be carried under the rock for the second time. I came up halfway along the tunnel, wheezing like a grampus. And then I nearly passed out from fright when Donovan's head and shoulders burst into view no more than six yards away.

Ritter would have to have been exceedingly dim not to

realize where we'd ended up. And I knew he wasn't that. So I pressed myself up against the rock, my nose barely above the water line, and waited for the chug of the outboard to signal that he was coming in to finish us off.

Only he wasn't.

What I heard instead, after what seemed an interminable period of expectation, was the stuttering cough of the Albatross's engines being fired up, followed almost immediately by a rather more subdued murmur as the *Valkyrie*'s diesels were coaxed into life.

With her hull outlined against the fiery glow of the dying sun, the yacht began to inch forward. As her stern swung around, the seaplane became fully visible, twin props a blur as she turned onto her takeoff path.

Throttles open, the aircraft began to gather momentum, skimming over the water like a pebble, its wake creaming as it fought for height. The run was very short. After what amounted to not much more than a hop, skip and a jump, the Albatross was airborne and turning away, its stumpy wings catching fire as it banked towards the sunset.

The *Valkyrie*'s progress was more serene. She cut through the water with all the effortless grace of a model on a catwalk, her aerodynamic lines as beautiful as a sculpture by Michelangelo.

I watched helplessly as the yacht's bow slid around, aiming for the open sea. There was a presence at my shoulder. Donovan, treading water, followed my impotent gaze. He said, 'We had no choice, Michael. You know that. Ritter would have killed us.'

'And Liz?' I shot back at him, as the *Valkyrie* headed away, picking up speed. 'What about her?'

'If Ritter wanted to kill her he'd have done so.'

'So what the hell . . .?' I yelled, swallowing a mouthful of water in the process.

'I don't know. Christ, she's blonde and beautiful. So's he. Maybe he plans for them to make beautiful babies together. Create a new master race.'

'Fuck you too, Harry,' I said, coughing.

'Dammit, Mike,' he replied heavily. 'She's alive. Just like us. Alive, we can go after them. Dead, we're no bloody use.'

Something small and white was bobbing and jinking in the yacht's wake. The skiff. They hadn't even taken the time to hoist it aboard. It was attached by a line to the stern rail and looked like an abandoned duckling trying to catch up with its mother.

'Why didn't Martin come in to get us?'

Donovan spat out a gobbet of saliva and salt water. 'Would you have done?'

Against us? I thought, No, probably not.

The *Valkyrie* was moving fast now, following the track of the seaplane.

As I watched her go, I knew in my heart of hearts that Donovan was right. Two armed men against two unarmed men? Automatic weapons on one side, no means of defence on the other? No question, no contest. This way, at least we'd get another chance.

Maybe.

Dusk had turned quickly into evening as we left the shelter of the cave. The yacht had disappeared and the sky was as dark as my sorrow. The only sound was the slap of waves against the underside of the cliff.

It was another tiring swim. Tiring because the wound over my right shoulder blade, although no more serious than a line of broken skin, was smarting like the very devil from its contact with the salt water. Added to which, my back muscles had begun to stiffen up. The discomfort acted as a stimulant: a reason for making landfall as quickly as possible.

We beached almost at the point where Liz and I had swum ashore.

My thoughts were only of her.

Out there, somewhere. Alone. Afraid. And beyond my reach. I stared out over the water, hoping for some kind of telepathic link.

But it was Donovan who read my mind. 'We'll get her back,' he said. 'Don't you worry.'

I rounded on him. 'And how the fuck are we going to do that? We don't even know where she is.'

A strange look came over his face. 'Who says?'

I stopped dead in my tracks.

'What?'

'I said—'

'I heard what you said, for Christ's sake! You're telling me you know where they've taken her?'

'Maybe.' He was already striding away.

I ran after him and grabbed his arm. 'How . . .?' I began.

He stopped. 'Because towards the end, when Erich asked Ritter if he was going to deal with Liz as well, Ritter told him no, she was going with them. That was when Erich took her back down below. Remember?' He grinned at my expression. 'Sometimes it pays not to advertise the fact that you can speak the lingo, old son.'

I was dumbstruck. 'You sly bastard,' I said eventually.

He chuckled. 'Ain't I just. Your Uncle Harry, Logan, is not just a pretty face.'

'So where?'

His brow furrowed. 'Some place called Kereka? Kirika? At least, that's what it sounded like. An island, I think Ritter said.'

A cold hand gripped my heart and began to squeeze. 'How about Kyriki?'

'By God, that's it.' His face lit up. 'That's the place. Mean anything?'

'The monastery.'

'Monastery?'

'Ayios Stratiyos. Saint Michael's. Kyriki's the name of the island it's built on.'

'Where is it?'

'Close. About ten miles northeast of Anafi. It's even smaller than Mekos.'

'Inhabited?'

'Sort of.'

He frowned again, puzzled. 'Which means what, exactly?'

'Well, there haven't been any monks on the rock for nigh on thirty years. The order practically died out. The last few survivors moved across to the mainland; to Dekoulou and Porto Kayio.'

'So . . .?'

'The place fell pretty much into disrepair until it was bought in the early seventies by one of those pseudo-religious groups. You know the type: purple anoraks and Hush Puppies.'

'The old enlightenment trip.'

'Trip being the operative word. They used to say that even on a clear day you couldn't see the island for hash fumes. Didn't last too long, mind. The sect disbanded after they did the Grand Panjandrum for tax evasion. He was jailed in the US for a couple of years before he disappeared to a commune in Tibet or somewhere.'

'And the island?'

'Snapped up by one of the big shipping magnates as a private retreat. Niarchos or Papadopoulos – I forget who, exactly – but I do recall he was well in with the colonels before they were ousted by Karamanlis. Used to entertain them on his floating gin palace. Greased a few palms, kept them sweet. That was just before he lost his shirt during the oil crisis when he had to sell up. Rumour has it that the place has been bought by some commercial consortium that plans to use it as an international conference centre. They're still renovating the place.'

Donovan pursed his lips. 'No need to ask who's likely to be behind the consortium.'

No need at all, I thought. Moessinger must have been somewhere close in order to receive details of our progress in the search for the sub. Kyriki was certainly close enough.

But how did we get there?

Only one way. By boat. That meant hiring or stealing one. And the nearest place to do that was Mekos village.

The sooner the better.

Stumbling along the rocky paths in the grey gloom of twilight was an interesting experience, neither of us being too keen on twisting an ankle in the dark. We finally made it to the beach in something like forty minutes. Once there, we crouched in the lee of one of the upturned hulls and watched the village. For all we knew, Ritter or one of the others had been dropped off to wait for us.

Moonlight danced across the water and small waves lapped the shore. In such a location our situation seemed unreal. Tranquillity and sudden death were strange bedfellows.

While Donovan scanned the shadows for signs of a threat, I looked for a boat.

The island's caique fishing fleet hadn't yet departed on their nightly foray. I could see their slim mastheads above the harbour wall.

Although I had thought about stealing a boat, our best bet was to pay somebody to take us where we wanted to go. They'd earn more from us than they would trawling for mackerel, and my conscience would rest a lot easier.

And then I spotted something else.

A motor yacht. A fifty-footer. Quite sleek, but with old lines. One of those service launches that the RAF used at the end of the war. It had a long, uncluttered foredeck with the bulk of the superstructure extending over her aft quarters. A real workhorse.

She was a late addition to the fleet, because she certainly hadn't been around during the time the *Valkyrie* was moored offshore.

Donovan had set his sights on her too. 'That'll do nicely,' he whispered.

Across the strand the lights in the taverna were brightly lit. I could hear music, from a radio or a very old gramophone. It was a love song. Above the singer's voice I could hear the strains of a bouzouki. On Mykonos or Naxos it would have been classed as tourist fodder, but not here. Here it was just the locals socializing.

By the light of the moon and with the aid of one of the hurricane lanterns suspended from the masts of the fishing caiques, I was able to get a better view of the motor yacht. I stared at her and pulled up with a jolt, my heart beating fast. Then I read her name, *Circe*.

Donovan, taken by surprise, collided with me. 'What the hell?'

I silenced him with a touch. Maybe God was on our side, after all. I looked up towards the taverna, turned and grinned at him. 'Fancy a drink?'

His jaw dropped. 'What?'

As I set off in the direction of the inn, I heard him curse colourfully, but he followed me anyway.

The outside tables were empty. All the action, what there was of it, was inside. Donovan caught up with me as I walked across the veranda and stepped through the open doorway.

The place was half empty, or half full, depending on

300

your point of view. Half a dozen white-haired old men, faces like weathered teak, occupied the table nearest the door. Four other men were seated round the table in the far corner of the bar. Sensing new arrivals, everyone looked up. The proprietor, recognizing us from the day before, favoured us with a brief nod of greeting. Their curiosity temporarily slaked, the old men resumed their game of dominoes. The reaction of the four men seated round the corner table was a little different. With Donovan at my shoulder, I headed towards them. We were about halfway there when one of them lurched to his feet. He was big and broad, with hands like oaken clubs. A savage grin split his seamed face.

'Hello, Stavros,' I said wearily. 'I could murder a beer.'

I'd thought the motor yacht looked familiar. I'd been on her enough times. And one thing was certain: she wasn't half as decrepit as her design would have you believe. I knew for a fact that Stavros had had her completely refitted only a couple of years before. Under her deck were housed three six-cylinder turbocharged Thornycroft diesels. They'd give him twenty knots at a pinch. He actually employed an ex-Royal Navy man to look after them, a dour Scotsman by the name of McBain. McBain was one of the men at the table. The third man was Rocco. The fourth was the younger version of Rocco whom I'd met at the Bacchus, the one who had supplied me with the pistol and the dope.

I tried to avoid Stavros's customary mode of greeting. And failed. He clasped me in his usual bear hug and I managed to suppress a yell as pain flared across my back when his brawny arms raked the wound in my shoulder.

Poor old Rocco looked on resignedly. I got a friendly grin from his young partner, whose name I remembered was Ari, and McBain regarded me stoically over the rim of his glass.

'Hello, Mac,' I said.

'How are you, Logan?' he grunted. Grizzled, he looked every inch a hard case. Which he was, even in his mid-fifties.

'I've known better,' I said. 'How's yourself?'

'Oh, bearing up, laddie. Bearing up.' A damp, home-rolled cigarette adhered limply to his lower lip.

I extricated myself from Stavros's embrace, to find him staring speculatively across at Donovan, who was himself looking decidedly intrigued.

I said, 'Stavros, this is Harry Donovan.'

Whereupon, to my total amazement, Stavros said, 'But of course, my friend. How are you?'

I gaped at them both, the significance of the words only too clear.

I addressed Donovan, '*You know each other?*'

Stavros, looking surprised that I'd even asked the question, exclaimed, 'But of course!'

Donovan had the grace to look sheepish as he said, 'Where d'you think I got the hardware to bust you out of the nick?'

I was thunderstruck.

I found my voice finally. 'I don't believe this!' Then I rounded on Stavros. 'Did you know what he was planning to use the stuff for?'

Stavros took a step back, looked pained and spread his hands.

'Of course he bloody didn't!' Donovan said.

Stavros chuckled then. 'If I had known you were friend of Logan I would have given you big discount!'

'Now he tells me,' Donovan muttered under his breath.

McBain, acutely vigilant, interrupted. 'You look like a man who could use a wee dram.' He gave me a sly wink.

302

'Thought you'd never offer, Mac,' I responded gratefully.

McBain raised his finger to gain the attention of the hovering proprietor and rapped out an order in fluent Greek. He'd been with Stavros for fifteen years and, despite speaking English with a distinct Clydeside accent, he could speak Greek like a native.

Stavros chastised the table with the flat of his hand. 'But naturally! I am being forgetful! A seat for my two friends! Quickly!' He cuffed Ari, who got to his feet good-naturedly, purloined a couple of chairs from an adjoining empty table and dragged them over. 'Now, Logan!' Stavros enquired, frowning, 'what the hell are you doing here?'

Then, for the first time, he noticed the blood on his hands and the stains on my still damp shirt. 'What is this?' he cried, the concern in his tone fully evident. He turned me round and grunted as he saw the broken skin. He recognized what had caused it. He sucked in breath. 'Logan! I think you are in big trouble! You want to tell me what is happening?'

I slumped into the provided chair and sighed, wondering where to begin. Oh, what the hell, I thought.

I said cautiously, 'Er, Stavros . . . how'd you like to do me another favour?'

McBain came out of the wheelhouse, wiping his hands on an oil-stained rag. This was a fact of life that never ceased to amaze me. Because where the grime came from I had no idea. I'd seen the launch's diesel compartment. The place was spotless. Cleaner than McBain usually looked, at any rate. You could have eaten food off every surface.

He performed a feat of manual dexterity which resulted in the reappearance of another Rizla special, popped it into his mouth and lit up.

'Well, now,' he said, fastening me with a penetrating stare. 'A fine night, is it not?'

Donovan was down below with Stavros and Rocco. Ari was at the wheel.

We were some four miles east of Anafi, pushing eighteen knots through a calm sea.

Heading for Kyriki.

When I'd asked Stavros if he'd take Donovan and me to the island, he'd put his head on one side and asked me, shrewdly, if my request had anything to do with the other favour he'd done for me four days earlier. And I'd told him no, nothing.

I wasn't sure he believed me.

But he'd agreed to deliver us anyway. At this rate, my favour account was in danger of becoming severely overdrawn.

Up on deck, I asked McBain what their business had been on Mekos.

He wiped his hands with the rag, drew on his cigarette and regarded me levelly. 'Och, a wee bit a this, a wee bit a that. Nothing for you to trouble y'rself about.' Then he gave a broad wink. Maybe he was right. Maybe it was best if I didn't know. Stavros had more fingers in more pies than I could begin to count. I knew that, like me, he had an aversion to drugs. Which still left a thousand other interesting and lucrative sidelines for him to be engaged in. Cigarettes and booze, to name but two. I wouldn't have put it past him to be carrying items of an archaeological nature, either. There was big money to be made by smuggling artefacts out of the country, for distribution among private collectors. As I knew full well; I'd been involved with the Turkish end of the market. Until my little run-in with the Gumruk, of course.

I looked at my watch.

'Won't be long now, son,' McBain said.

I knew that. It would put our arrival at sometime around two-thirty, when it was still nice and dark.

McBain threw the butt of his cigarette over the side and returned to his engines. I went below to join the others. There was a bottle of Metaxa to hand. Stavros poured me a slug. It hit the back of my throat like a stream of liquid fire. There was also food: some bread, cheese and olives.

I hadn't realized how hungry I was. Or how tired. I had no recollection of falling asleep – who does? – but the next thing I registered was the sound of Ari's voice calling down to us from the wheelhouse.

Kyriki was in sight.

The island rose sullenly out of the blue-black water half a mile over the starboard gunnel. Above it a crescent moon hung like a bright jewelled pendant.

Ari cut the engines back until their beat was no louder than a dull hum and we drew closer. Donovan had joined me in the bow. Stavros had provided us both with dry clothes. We were dressed in black trousers and heavy navy sweaters which smelled of engine oil. I wondered vaguely if McBain had used them to wipe down his beloved diesels.

Stavros passed me a pair of night glasses. I put them to my eyes and scanned the darkness. Couldn't see a thing at first. Just an indistinct line where sea and sky met.

And then the black crag of the island slid abruptly into view and I adjusted the focus.

Still nothing.

I followed the run of the shoreline, trying to pierce the curtain of night. Then moved on slowly, paused a moment as the message filtered through to my brain, and swung the glasses back.

A landing stage and a string of lights. And, trapped in their wan glow, a distinct wedge-shaped apparition. The sleek hull of a motor yacht.

Unmistakable. A lump rose in my throat.

The *Valkyrie*.

And a vague bird shape squatting beside her. The Albatross.

With barely suppressed excitement, I passed the glasses to Donovan, and saw him stiffen as he trapped an image in the lens.

'Bingo,' he muttered softly. His grip on the glasses tightened.

I wondered what plans Moessinger had for the sub's cargo. I presumed that he'd returned to the island in order to prepare the consignment for transportation. But to where? Perhaps he was intending to ship the coffin and remains to the Legion's centre of operations in South America. If that was so, he wouldn't be using the Albatross. It didn't have the range. But that didn't mean he wasn't planning to deliver the crate to Rome or Lisbon and transfer it to a regular cargo carrier – Aerolineas or Alitalia, perhaps – listing the casket as freight. As for the bullion: there was nothing to prevent them using the *Valkyrie* to sail it to the gold markets in Tangier or Alexandria.

'See anyone?' I asked.

He shook his head. 'We're too far out.'

I looked at Stavros and, without my vocal prompt, he raised a hand towards Ari at the helm and motioned him to take us further in. The deck lifted beneath our feet as the bow rose.

Half a mile out, I asked Stavros to douse the lights. Quickly, he complied. Ari cut the engines. The momentum carried the launch forward in silence. I took the glasses again and trained them on the shore.

Kyriki was shaped like a reverse comma, with the jetty-cum-breakwater extending at a ninety-degree angle from

306

the comma's tail, thus forming a lagoon between it and the bulk of the island.

In the old days, when the monks were in residence, the jetty hadn't existed. Boats had been used, of course, to transport the monks and their provisions, but there had been no shelter for them at all. So they'd used wooden cranes built into the rocks to hoist the boats out of the water and moor them in midair. It had been an ingenious system. Over the years, however, following the construction of the landing stage, it had fallen into disuse, although many of the ancient beams, blocks and pulleys were still in place along the edge of the cliff in some of the more protected inlets around the coastline. From a distance they looked like the birdcages you see hanging in an oriental bazaar. Some of them, consisting of little more than a weathered crossbeam trailing a length of tattered rope, looked more like gibbets.

In the early days, during the times of religious persecution, because of its relatively isolated position the monastery had been something of a political as well as a religious sanctuary. Like the churches perched high on the crags of Meteora, over on the mainland, where the only way in and out had been by baskets lowered on ropes, the way the monks of Ayios Stratiyos had once moored their boats.

There were also supposed to be tunnels under the rock, according to Stavros.

'So that during the old days the monks could conceal themselves in times of trouble,' he explained, adding, 'There are those who say that some of them were lost in the darkness and they are still down there searching for a way out. At least that is the legend.' He rolled his eyes melodramatically.

I asked him then if he knew anything about the layout of the property.

307

He shook his head apologetically. 'Alas no, my friend. I know little of the island except that in the past visitors have not been made welcome. A cousin of mine told me that one night he was turned away by men with guns when he tried to shelter from a storm. Not many people go there, unless they are invited.'

And I couldn't see Moessinger giving us an engraved invitation, somehow.

Through the glasses I could pick out details.

The lights I had seen from further out seemed to be the mercury-vapour type. They were suspended from a number of tall metal stanchions set at intervals along the jetty, and bathed the *Valkyrie*'s hull and the Albatross's stubby fuselage in a harsh sulphurous glow.

Behind the lagoon, at the top of the steps leading up from the jetty, and well outside the immediate circle of illumination, the land appeared to rise darkly in a series of terraces up beyond an encircling wall, above the crest of which I could make out the parapets and roof of the main building, and two pepper-pot towers. The island seemed quite densely wooded in parts, with the bulk of the monastery nestling behind a clump of cypress trees. Their slender columns were vaguely discernible against the slope of the rock.

It all looked remarkably quiet.

And then, as I lowered my sights. I saw a thin grey shadow detach itself from the shelter of the *Valkyrie*'s rail. Illuminated in the soft glow from the lights on the yacht's after deck was the figure of a man. A guard on the move.

I'd expected that. But how many more were there, besides this one?

'It's your show,' Donovan murmured in my ear. 'How do you want to play it?'

The launch lifted on a moving swell. I lowered the glasses and considered the possibilities.

I said, 'It's too much for us to take it on alone. We don't know how many we're up against. We're going to need help.'

Donovan nodded slowly, 'Thought you might say that.'

We looked at each other.

'We'll have to tell them the whole thing,' I said. 'It'll mean giving them a cut.'

'You trust him that much?' Donovan asked.

I thought about it. 'Yes,' I said.

'What the hell then.' He shrugged. 'There's plenty to go round. Are you going to give them the pitch, or am I?'

'I'll do it,' I said.

'Okay.'

The big Cretan was standing behind me, legs braced against the rolling of the boat, itching to know what was happening.

I grinned at him. All mates together.

'Stavros, old friend,' I said cheerily. 'Have I got a deal for you.'

20

I'll give Stavros and McBain their due. They didn't interrupt me once. When I'd finished it was McBain who spoke first. His eyes were half closed as protection against the evil fumes that were coming off the end of his cigarette.

'Is he serious?' he said to Donovan.

Donovan nodded. 'Swear to God, Mac. No word of a lie.'

McBain shook his head, depositing ash on the deck. 'If I didna know ye better, Logan, I'd have said that spell in the nick addled your brain.'

Which was as much as I'd been prepared to expect, frankly.

Stavros was still thinking about it. I could tell that his brain was working overtime, aided by the occasional slug of brandy to hasten the thought processes.

He regarded me seriously. 'This woman, Michael. She is very important to you?'

'Yes.'

He smiled. 'And she is beautiful, yes?'

'Yes,' I said. 'Very.'

There followed a considerable period of silence. Finally, he looked up, gave a knowing grin and slapped me on the shoulder. The pain was marginal. 'My heart is glad!' He turned to Donovan. 'You know how many times I tell him he needs a woman?' He patted my knee. 'You have been too long alone, Michael Logan! That is not good for a man.' He jutted his chin at Donovan. 'Is this not so, my friend?'

'Oh, absolutely,' Donovan agreed, with a sly glance in my direction.

Stavros spread his arms expansively. 'Of course we help you!'

McBain looked as if he'd lost a fiver and found ten bob.

'Down the middle,' I told them. 'Fifty-fifty.'

As McBain immediately rediscovered his faith in human nature I sensed Donovan wince. But I didn't need to remind him that without their help we'd likely end up with bugger all.

Stavros put Rocco and Ari in the picture. It was the nearest I'd come to seeing Rocco break into a smile. Whether it was the scent of money or blood that had perked up his interest, I couldn't be sure.

'We're going to need some hardware,' Donovan said. He turned to Stavros. 'Got anything we can use?'

Stavros gave a lupine grin. 'Come,' he said. 'I show you.'

With a nod from his boss, Rocco slid away the false panelling from under the starboard settle and he and McBain started to unclip the weapons from the fixtures behind.

I wasn't surprised.

I'd had a similar hideaway aboard the *Kallisti*. Which had been yet another nail in my coffin, as far as the Turks were concerned. The drugs had been bad enough. One Star automatic, a Beretta 128 and an Ithaca 37 twelve-gauge had been well out of order. That small array of concealed artillery had probably accounted for at least five years of my imposed sentence.

What they'd have done to Stavros and his crew if they'd been confronted by the arsenal currently being unearthed was anyone's guess.

McBain laid the guns on the table. They were Mini-Uzis, 9 mm sub-machine pistols with retractable stocks

311

and twenty-round mags. Israeli made. Very compact. Donovan picked one up, checked the slide and firing mechanism and nodded with satisfaction. Rocco passed out the magazines.

'How about handguns?' McBain asked.

'What've you got?'

'Astras. Fifteen-round mags.'

'Sold,' Donovan said.

McBain snapped a finger and Rocco handed them over. The pistols were secured in professional rigs: leather shoulder harnesses comprising underarm holsters and attached magazine pouches. It meant we wouldn't have to stuff the bloody things into our belts and pockets and thus suffer the risk of blowing our private parts to kingdom come, or anywhere else for that matter.

I calculated we had enough ordnance to start a small revolution.

But Stavros hadn't finished.

The crates were concealed in a recess under the deck in the engine compartment. Four of them. McBain and Rocco hauled one out and carried it up to the saloon, where Stavros opened it up with a flourish.

'Holy Mother of God!' Donovan said, when the contents were displayed before our astonished gaze.

We were staring at what appeared to be the component parts of an RPG-7 grenade launcher.

'What in God's name do you expect us to do with one of those?' I yelped. 'Start World War Three?' I stared at McBain. 'And you had the nerve to ask if *I* was serious? Jesus!'

Meanwhile, Donovan was looking as if he was in seventh heaven. He lifted one of the grease-proofed packages out of the crate. 'By God,' he whispered. 'What we could have done with a few of these in the old days.'

312

Then he caught me watching him. He smiled an apologetic little smile. 'Another place, another time, Michael. When I was young and foolish.'

I said nothing. But I had a pretty good idea about the time and the place to which he was referring. I'd been there.

To McBain, I said, 'A little bit of this, a little bit of that, eh?'

'Aye, well . . .' he said shiftily, and looked towards Stavros for guidance.

And I thought, Cyprus. It had to be.

The rumours had abounded for a long time about surreptitious arming of the Greek Cypriot forces on the island. Stavros's name had surfaced a few times as a man who had the necessary contacts. There'd been talk of midnight rendezvous with Cyprus-bound freighters and the clandestine transfer of illicit cargoes. The island was less than three hundred and fifty miles away: not even two days' sailing in a sound vessel.

Which meant that Stavros and co had been on Mekos on their way to or from a pick-up point.

I held up my hands. 'I don't want to know,' I said. 'Just put the bloody thing back where you found it.'

Somewhat chastened by my marked lack of enthusiasm, Stavros retrieved the launcher from Donovan. McBain and Rocco pushed the crate underneath the chart table. Inwardly, I breathed a sigh of relief.

'We're going to have to take out the men on the perimeter as quietly as possible,' I said, slipping on my gun harness. 'I don't suppose you've got any suppressors?'

Stavros looked blank.

'That's a fancy word for silencers,' McBain said.

Using them, we'd have to be pretty damned close. They had a tendency to cut down range as well as velocity.

In the event, Stavros shook his head.

313

I shrugged. 'Never mind. Can't win 'em all.'

'But perhaps I have something else,' he said. There was a sly grin on his leathery face.

Did he ever.

A crossbow, with wooden stock, aluminium barrel and steel bow. It was quite small, about the length of a sawn-off shotgun. A beautifully designed and formidable weapon, with, at a guess, a breaking strain of around two thousand pounds. At fifty yards that was enough to send a steel bolt through an oaken door and the man standing behind it.

'How in God's name did you come by this?' I enquired, cranking back the Dacron twine cord and feeling the responding pressure.

'It belonged to my cousin Demetrius. He used it to hunt jackals and foxes, sometimes ibex.'

I turned the weapon over in my hands. Anyone who hunted jackals, foxes or 'sometimes ibex' with this thing had to be either the world's greatest optimist or the best shot this side of the black stump. Although I had heard that the ibex population, which still existed in the high mountains of Crete, was fast diminishing. Which, presumably, meant that the animal hadn't been such a difficult target to hit.

Donovan looked at the bow in awe, and then at me with interest. 'Have you ever fired one of these things?'

'How hard can it be?' I said, and added to Stavros, 'I'll take it.'

Donovan shook his head in wonderment. 'God save us,' he murmured. 'Thinks he's fucking William Tell!'

'I heard that,' I said.

Stavros passed me the quiver containing six bolts. Each one was about nine inches long, with a hard wooden shaft and a broad metal tip. They seemed very light, considering the amount of damage they were capable of inflicting. I slotted the quiver on to my belt.

314

'You want grenades?' Stavros enquired earnestly.

I blinked. 'Grenades?' Good God! What the hell else have you got down there?'

He chuckled. It wouldn't have come as a total surprise to discover that he had a couple of howitzers stashed away, as well. In the end we compromised and made do with a gutting knife each.

'Just like old times,' Donovan said, as he rammed a clip into the grip of his Uzi.

His words echoed my own thoughts. 'You know there's only one way to go on this,' I said. 'Don't you?'

He grinned. 'Wouldn't have it any other way, old son.'

'Right,' I said. 'In that case, all we need now is a plan.'

I passed McBain the Uzi and the crossbow and followed him over the side. Donovan and Stavros were already seated in the dinghy – one of the launch's black rubber inflatables. They waited in silence as we joined them. McBain laid the equipment in the bottom of the boat, settled himself and passed me one of the short paddles.

'Here ye are, lad. Might as well make yourself useful,' he grunted.

At the rail, Ari and Rocco raised their hands in silent farewell, their hangdog expressions a clear indication of how they felt at being left behind. I dug the paddle in and we began to pull away. The launch, still with lights extinguished, began to merge back into the gloom.

It took a little over ten minutes of sustained and concentrated effort from all four of us before we reached the shore, beaching at a point some four hundred yards or so west of the jetty.

Donovan was the first to touch land. We followed him swiftly, dragged the inflatable out of the water and concealed it among a jumble of wave-dampened rocks. Weapons were distributed.

315

Then we went hunting.

For a man built like a bear, Stavros moved with feline stealth. McBain was more like a terrier itching to be let off the leash. Like Donovan and me, the two of them were dressed in dark clothing: navy sweaters and jeans, woollen caps which, when rolled down, became balaclavas, rope-soled deck shoes on their feet.

We were all similarly armed. Not counting my possession of the crossbow, we each carried an Uzi machine pistol, an Astra automatic in a shoulder harness, and a gutting knife. Frankly, I was beginning to suspect we were rather overdoing it. But then, not knowing what or who we were up against, we couldn't really afford to take any chances. It was the old maxim: better safe than sorry.

From somewhere up on the high ground the plaintive call of a night bird intruded, like a child in torment.

Beside me, McBain tensed, frozen into immobility by the woeful sound. In the ensuing quiet, I felt something nudge my foot and heard it retreat and skitter away into the darkness, pebbles sliding, mandibles clicking in annoyance. A marauding crab, disturbed in its search for fresh prey.

I let out a long breath. McBain threw me a leering grin, his eyes unnaturally bright. My immediate thought was that we were fortunate he was on our side and not theirs.

We covered the final yards in a running crouch. Concealing ourselves among the boulders at the point where the jetty merged with the land, we considered the prospects.

Which, quite candidly, didn't appear too encouraging.

Fifty yards away, inside the lagoon, the *Valkyrie* was berthed stern-on to the jetty, with the Albatross moored on her starboard beam, broad snout nudging the landing stage like a duck awaiting a handful of breadcrumbs. On

316

board the *Valkyrie* lights were showing. The aircraft, however, save for the illumination cast upon it by the arc lamps, floated in darkness.

A hand alighted on my shoulder. Donovan, with a silent warning.

I couldn't tell if he was the man I had seen earlier. Then, he had been little more than a distant, anonymous figure. Now, as he stood in the patch of light at the *Valkyrie*'s stern rail, his features were clearly visible. He was someone I did not recognize, although it was evident he had been cast from the same mould as Erich and Joachim. He was of a similar age and build: late twenties or thereabouts. Slim, with short fair hair. Dressed in jeans and a dark leather blouson. Around his shoulder was slung a machine pistol. A Scorpion or maybe a Steyr. It was hard to tell at that range.

And there was no way we could cross the jetty without him seeing us.

In holding our council of war, our main concern had been estimating how many picquets there were likely to be. This was taking into consideration the nature of the cargo, weighed against our belief that Moessinger would not be anticipating a counterattack. The number we'd come up with, by popular consensus, was not less than three and not more than six. Either way, manageable odds, or so we felt.

Bearing that in mind, I didn't like the idea of using the crossbow to take the guard out where he was. I wanted him away from the boat, isolated, where the chances of a silent kill would be greatly improved.

Stavros, finger on his lips, was pressing my arm. 'You wait,' he said softly, handing me his machine pistol and Astra.

Then he was gone.

I realized suddenly that he was in the water, feeling his

317

way along the base of the jetty. A gleam of ripples betrayed his passing. He made no sound.

In anticipation, I squatted with my back to the pilings and used the loader to cock the bow. I took a bolt out of the quiver at my waist and slotted it into the prod, lifted the stock to my shoulder, and waited.

The splash, when it came, was sharp, like the rising of a fish. At night sound is magnified tenfold. Over water even more so. The man on the boat turned and peered into the darkness.

A second splash, lighter than the first. Followed by what sounded like an asthmatic clearing his throat.

I couldn't help grinning.

Stavros was doing animal impersonations.

Dolphins and porpoises are plentiful in the Aegean. At night they betray their presence by their harsh and raspy breathing. It's very distinctive, the bottle-nosed dolphin in particular. Though I wasn't sure the fellow on the yacht would appreciate the difference. In any case, that wasn't the point of the exercise. All Stavros was aiming for was his undivided attention.

The man on the boat straightened. I held my breath. Stavros widened his nocturnal repertoire to include a series of asdic-like clicks. Dolphin talk, presumably, for 'hello, sailor'.

The guard moved round to the gangway. There was no urgency in his stride.

'Come on, sunshine,' Donovan breathed. 'Move your arse.'

It was as if the man had heard him. Casually, machine pistol still slung over his shoulder, he sauntered down the gangway on to the jetty with the nonchalance of a man stretching his legs.

The sound of his measured tread was like the steady

318

ticking of a carriage clock. He crossed the jetty diagonally, paused at the edge and gazed out over the water; seventy paces away, side on to me. Trapping his profile in the crosshairs, I waited for a bigger target.

He began his slow amble back, allowing Stavros to come up for air.

He was some fifteen paces from the *Valkyrie*'s stern, directly under one of the lights, when he halted and began to tap his pockets. Pulling the pack of cigarettes from the inside of his jacket, he slipped one into his mouth. I sensed Donovan and McBain growing impatient beside me.

I waited until he bowed his head towards his cupped lighter before I took him. I didn't want his fingers anywhere near the trigger of his gun.

I fired as he inhaled.

There was a deep thrum of sound as I loosed the bolt, followed a split second later by what sounded like someone thumping a hammer into a cabbage. The guard tottered back drunkenly for several paces, sagged on to his heels and collapsed as if he'd fainted. There was a dramatic, reverberating thud as his body hit the jetty.

By which time, Donovan, McBain, and I were up and running.

Donovan reached the gangway a second before I did, with McBain finishing in third place. Which meant that Donovan got there at the precise moment that the second guard arrived on deck to investigate the absence of his partner.

Donovan's speed of reaction was phenomenal. He hit the after deck like Nemesis, and didn't hesitate. Gripping his gun by the magazine housing, he swung it against the side of the man's jaw.

'*Was macht*—' was all the poor bastard had time to utter before my ears caught the brittle crack of breaking bone and he went down as if he'd been pole-axed. I doubt he'd even been aware of who or what had hit him.

I gave the crumpled body a cursory glance. Didn't recognize this one either. Yet another Aryan replica. I wondered vaguely if Moessinger had a hatchery somewhere that was churning out these *Wunderkinder* like mannequins on a conveyer belt.

Donovan picked up the second guard's gun, a Scorpion, and dropped it over the rail into the lagoon.

A noise behind us on the gangway.

The three of us turned together, gun muzzles sweeping around, lifting . . .

Stavros, dripping like a sheepdog on a mat, squelched on to the deck, and I passed him his weapons. He looked down at the felled guard without sympathy.

'Don't tell me there were only two of them,' Donovan grunted. 'I don't believe it.'

No one replied. No one had a chance to. Because that was when the third man put in an appearance. He must have been on the bridge. He came round the corner of the deck at a run, machine pistol in his hand, not knowing what to expect but prepared for trouble.

'*Rudi? Was ist hier los?*'

Then he saw us at the last moment and his jaw dropped in shock and recognition.

Grey hair, cut short. Joachim.

He screeched to a halt, then started to backpedal.

McBain attacked.

With stunning ferocity, whirling like a top, his right arm a dark blur as it scythed around. A bright flash of a blade, a gurgling sigh, and a viscous crimson spray erupted from Joachim's torn throat. Neck agape, the legionnaire's corpse toppled to the deck like a steer in a slaughterhouse. It had been as sweet an execution of the

320

Glasgow kiss as I was ever likely to see this side of Sauchiehall Street.

Ignoring his victim, McBain wiped the blade of the cutthroat razor on his sleeve and, with a dexterous flick of his wrist, snapped the wafer-thin sliver of steel into its tortoiseshell handle and restored the weapon to his pocket.

'Stupid bastard,' was all he said, his voice holding nothing but contempt.

We split into two pairs then, and checked the rest of the yacht. No one else was on board. The whole exercise had taken less than two minutes. And we had managed it without having to resort to the use of firearms and thus without alerting the rest of Moessinger's retainers in the main keep.

The boat was ours.

So was the cargo.

The bullion crates had been moved down below and were stacked in the main stateroom. The crate containing the flag and remains still sat on the after deck, covered with a canvas sheet. Which meant that Moessinger intended to use the yacht to transport it to its final destination, unless he simply hadn't got round to transferring it to the seaplane. Either way, it didn't matter. We had achieved what we had set out to do.

Secure a bargaining tool.

Donovan and McBain lowered the bodies of Joachim and the other guard into the still dark waters of the lagoon. No doubt the same fate had befallen Gunther Prohl. They'd likely dropped his corpse over the side too, probably sometime during the run from Mekos. The only evidence that anything untoward had taken place was the group of dried bloodstains on the deck where he had fallen.

I went back down the gangway to the man I had felled.

The bolt had penetrated the left side of his chest and, judging from the amount of blood that covered him, the heavy tip had ruptured his heart. There was no sign of the bolt itself. Curious, I turned him over. There was blood all over his back, too. The missile had gone straight through his body. The power I had unleashed had been truly awesome.

I rolled the corpse to the edge of the jetty and tipped it over the side. I dropped the Scorpion machine pistol into the water after it. The body did not sink. It rolled like a log, coming to rest face down, and bumped slowly against the jetty pilings.

I turned and ran back to join the others.

'All set?' I asked them.

They nodded silently.

'You going to need any help?' Donovan enquired.

I shook my head. 'They won't try anything.'

'You hope,' Donovan said grimly.

'If I'm wrong,' I said, 'you all know what to do?'

'Don't you worry, laddie,' McBain said. 'Leave it tae us.'

Satisfied, I slipped off the shoulder harness and laid it on the chart table. Unarmed, I left them and made my way back to the jetty. McBain pulled the gangway on to the stern behind me. I untied the line securing the yacht to the mooring ring and threw it up to him. He caught it deftly, and held up a fist in salute.

I turned and walked towards the bottom of the steps that led up to the main gate.

From behind me, there came a low rumble, like the sound of a train in the distance. Stavros, firing up the yacht's diesels. At first, it appeared that she wasn't moving, then with infinite slowness she began to creep away from the jetty. With her engines barely ticking over she glided through the smooth water like a grey wraith, searching for the entrance to the lagoon and the dark sea beyond. Her wake was a ripple of gleaming phosphorescence, like a string of diamonds cascading on to black velvet.

On the other side of the wall, the first lights began to bloom.

There were shouts then, and sharp cries of alarm. I heard a dog bark, and the rush of pounding feet.

I waited.

The main gate swung back. I stepped out to where they could see me and raised my arms above my head.

They stopped dead.

The one leading them looked as if he'd seen a ghost.

'Hello, Martin,' I said, smiling breezily. 'Take me to your leader.'

21

'That's the deal, Moessinger,' I said. 'No catch. A straight swap. The casket for the girl.'

I was the fly in the spider's web.

And the spider was Moessinger. Pale. Deformed. Twisted. Like Gollum, a creature who preferred darkness to the light of day. Like Sméagol, Moessinger, too, had lost his most precious possession. And he'd do anything to ensure its safe return; I was banking on that.

'I should have made sure of you earlier.' His voice was a sibilant hiss. His eyes were the colour of stone, and just as hard. 'The other man, Donovan. He is here also?'

'Close by,' I said.

He digested the answer, his knuckles whitening like chalk. The obsidian stare intensified. 'I confess I am most curious to know how you discovered our whereabouts.' He leant on his cane, claws gripping tightly. A vulture contemplating a fresh carcass.

It seemed a pity not to tell him, so I relayed what Donovan had told me. Moessinger absorbed the information. Finally, his neck creaked round and he fixed Ritter with a basilisk glare. 'How very careless of you, Martin,' he murmured, still in English, in a voice that was glacier cold.

Despite the chill in the accusation, Ritter's face burned.

Ignoring his lieutenant's flush of discomfort, Moessinger added, his head tilted like a bird's, 'One wonders, also, how you managed to follow us here so soon.' A cryptic pause. Then, with a glimmer of understanding, he

324

said, 'You had assistance.' A flat statement, not a question.

When I didn't reply, he shrugged, almost dismissively. 'I suppose it matters not.' His gaze became even more reptilian and penetrating. 'The bargain to which you refer does not appear to include the bullion.'

'Correct. The gold stays with us. Call it our commission.'

'But it is ours by right!' Ritter flared. He raised the muzzle of his machine pistol.

'No it's not,' I said.

Moessinger intervened. 'And if I refuse your offer?' he enquired, with a calculating look.

'Oh, come on,' I replied. 'Be serious.' '

Moessinger's head seemed to sink back into his neck, like a tortoise retracting into its shell. I could see he was turning over his options. Not that he had been given that many.

I said, 'The casket will be destroyed, along with its contents. This time there really will be a funeral pyre. In other words' – I favoured him with another grin – 'you can kiss your Adolf goodbye.'

'You really believe you can threaten us, Logan?' Ritter snarled. 'I will tell you what will happen if you do not return the casket intact. The girl will die!'

I shook my head and managed to keep my voice calm. 'Wrong, Martin. It doesn't work like that. And by the same token, if anything happens to me, Donovan will destroy the remains.' I looked at Moessinger. 'Go on, tell him.'

Moessinger said, in a low voice that implied some degree of internal pain, 'Very well. I agree to your terms.'

Ritter turned on him quickly. '*Aber—*'

'*Das ist genug!*' The old man's voice was high and reedy

325

but the sheer force of the put-down rocked his subordinate back on his heels. Ritter blanched.

'And I want to see her,' I said. 'Now.'

Moessinger considered my demand, before nodding tiredly. 'Bring her,' he said to Ritter.

Ritter looked at us, one to the other. Then he stormed out of the room.

'I hope you can keep him under control,' I said. 'I'd hate to think that he'd try something stupid.'

Moessinger's bloodless lips parted fractionally. I realized it was his interpretation of a smile. 'Have no fear, Logan. Martin will obey orders.' He grunted and added, 'Bringing the girl here was a mistake. That, I will admit. An indulgence for which I am not prepared to sacrifice all that I have strived for during these past years. Clearly, you and I both realize that neither side has anything to gain by issuing veiled threats. Especially as a result of such a trifling . . . misjudgement. As each of us has something the other desires, it would be very foolish, therefore, to jeopardize the one logical solution to our dilemma. Let us complete the . . . transaction . . . with as little rancour as the circumstances will allow. Agreed?'

'Agreed,' I said.

He nodded, satisfied.

And Ritter pushed Liz Hammond into the room. It took me but a second to realize that Ritter had given her no warning of what to expect.

Her face went slack and drained of all colour. For a moment I thought she was going to fall, but Ritter's grip on her elbow prevented her from doing so. She stared at me; her expression ran the gamut of emotions – shock, relief, joy and fear. As I gazed back at her, I saw a tiny, pearl-shaped tear appear in the corner of her eye and trickle slowly down her cheek.

Before Ritter could stop her she had broken away.

Crossing the room at a run, she threw herself into my arms. 'Oh, God, Michael! I thought you were dead!' Gripping me fiercely, she began to tremble.

'No chance, love,' I said. 'Harry and me are the good guys, remember? They can't get us. We're immortal.'

She lifted her head. Her eyes glistened. Confusion masked her face. 'But when they killed Gunther and I heard the shots, I—' Choking on a sob, she buried her face in my shoulder.

'It's all right,' I said gently. 'You're safe now.'

From behind her back Moessinger said, 'So, as you can see, she is . . . unharmed. Do we now have an agreement? Your word, that if we deliver her to you, you will return the casket to us?'

'Yes,' I said. To Liz, I added, 'Don't worry. They won't harm you. We'll see each other in a little while. It'll be all over soon. Think you can hang in there?'

Liz lifted her chin, and with the heel of her hand wiped the moisture from her cheek. Her lips formed a determined smile. 'I can now,' she said.

Before I could respond, Moessinger said, 'What will be the arrangements?'

I gave Liz a reassuring squeeze. 'The yacht will be anchored outside the lagoon. Ritter brings Miss Hammond out to us in a dinghy. I'll have the casket with me. We do the exchange. Miss Hammond returns to the yacht with me. Ritter takes the casket. Then you can load up the plane and get the hell out of here.'

'When?'

'One hour,' I said. 'Sunrise.'

First light.

And a subtle transformation was taking place.

A raw, golden glow was spreading fast across the eastern horizon, driving a burnished wedge between sea and sky, bringing with it a light breeze that plucked at our backs like an infant vying for attention. Along the *Valkyrie*'s waterline, the sea was changing colour from jet to turquoise.

It was almost time.

Beside me, still clad in a dark sweater and wearing his shoulder rig, Donovan raised the binoculars to his face and surveyed the shore. The jetty and the lagoon were in full view. Beyond them, touched by the morning sun, the slopes of the island and the crenellated battlements of Ayios Stratiyos sat perched atop the outcrop like a marzipan crown.

Donovan stiffened. 'Here we go.'

I raised my own glasses and followed his gaze. A small group of people was making its way in procession down the stone stairway towards the landing stage. Moessinger, tapping the ground with his cane like Blind Pew; Erich; three other men whom I didn't recognize; Ritter; and, at arm's length from him, Liz Hammond.

I heard a gun being cocked behind me. McBain, drawing back the slide on his Uzi.

From his position on the bridge, I knew that Stavros, also armed and waiting, would have them in his sights as well.

I watched as Liz lowered herself into the dinghy, followed by Ritter. With a few last-minute words to the party on the jetty, Ritter lifted his paddle and began to dig his way towards us, slowly.

'My God,' Donovan breathed. 'It's going to work.'

I glanced down at the two small craft lying motionless alongside the *Valkyrie*'s hull: the skiff and, behind it, attached by a line, the inflatable containing the makeshift casket.

'Of course it's going to work,' I said. 'I made him an offer he couldn't refuse. Mind you,' I added, 'keep your eyes peeled, just in case.' I climbed over the rail into the skiff, cast off and pushed myself away from the side of the boat. Connected by its nylon umbilical cord, the inflatable trailed heavily in my wake.

At a point one hundred yards from the yacht, we made the transfer.

I handed Ritter the line as Liz joined me in the skiff. 'Go ahead, if you want to check it, Martin. I don't mind waiting. He's all there. Right down to his fossilized toenails.'

Ritter hauled the inflatable towards him. I watched as he pulled it alongside. Gingerly, he manoeuvred the casket lid aside and lifted the rolls of the shroud away from the remains. He stared at them for several seconds, then, satisfied, he rearranged the disturbed folds of the banner and closed the lid. The inflatable bobbed as he transferred his weight.

'There,' I said. 'That wasn't so hard, was it?'

Ritter's ice-blue eyes glinted as he faced me. If looks could kill, I'd have been ten fathoms deep. Over my shoulder he could see Donovan, McBain and Stavros lining the yacht's rail. My insurance policy. And round the point, out of line of the jetty, the *Circe*, with Ari and Rocco holding station in case they were needed.

'I underestimated you, Logan,' Ritter grated.

'Don't let it worry you. So have a few others. You're in good company.'

'And now you are willing to simply let us fly away?' His scepticism was only too apparent.

'Why not?' I said. 'You and Moessinger and the rest of the Legion are living in dream time. You seriously think the appearance of a few old bones will change the world? Your movement's a joke, Martin. You and your kind have about as much chance of establishing a new order as

329

a pack of Brownies. A Fourth Reich? Don't make me laugh. Your lot couldn't organize a piss-up in a brewery.'

I began to pull away from him, back to the yacht.

He called after me, 'Guard yourself well, Logan. The Legion has a long memory.'

I grinned.

''Bye, Martin,' I said.

Donovan was waiting to greet us. He helped Liz aboard.

'Hello, Harry,' she said, giving him an affectionate hug. 'Am I glad to see you!'

He grinned at her. 'Welcome back.'

I saw her looking puzzled then.

So I could see it was time for further introductions.

'Liz,' I said. 'Meet Alexander McBain. Last of the Gorbals Diehards.'

To my amazement, the usually taciturn Scot gave her a smile that would have charmed Medusa. 'I see what ye mean, laddie,' he said, giving me a broad wink. To Liz he said, 'Pleased to meet you, lassie.' If he'd still been wearing his cap, he'd have taken it off, twisted it between his hands and scuffed one foot in the dirt. He looked totally smitten.

Liz smiled hesitantly, still unsure.

A booming voice announced, 'And I am Stavros, dear lady! At your service!' The big Cretan shouldered his gun, lumbered forward, took Liz's right hand and lifted it to his lips.

Liz regarded him with astonishment. Then she turned to me and raised her eyebrows.

'He's harmless,' I said.

Stavros chuckled. 'My God, Logan! For this one I would enter the gates of hell!'

'Talking of which . . .' Donovan said, almost absently.

He was standing at the rail, eyes glued to the shore. We joined him. Liz slipped her arm through mine.

Ritter had reached the jetty and they were loading the casket into the seaplane. One of the men I had not recognized must have been the pilot, I reasoned. The other two strangers would have been more of Moessinger's gunsels. Legionnaires.

I could see someone on the jetty untying the aircraft from its mooring. I raised the glasses for a better look. It was Ritter. Seconds later, he had closed the fuselage door behind him. There followed a throaty growl as the pilot turned over the engines. The blades began to revolve, becoming an irridescent shimmer as they were lanced by the sun's rays. Slowly the seaplane eased away from the jetty and turned its nose towards the entrance to the lagoon. As soon as it had negotiated the entrance, the pilot applied more throttle, the engine pitch changed sharply and the aircraft began its takeoff run.

We watched in silence.

Gradually, a bow wave began to build up under her nose as she gathered speed. The wings flashed silver as the aircraft hurtled across the emerald surface, throwing up spray. The nose began to lift: like an overweight chick attempting to launch itself into the air for the first time, almost with reluctance, as though it did not want to lose its tenuous hold on the earth.

Then, abruptly, it was airborne and climbing away, engines droning like a swarm of bees.

Liz watched it and shivered. 'I can't believe they're going to get away with it,' she said bleakly. 'They murdered Gunther and Marco and we're just standing here, letting them go.'

Donovan said quietly, 'Oh, I wouldn't say that.' He was staring at the aircraft, now half a mile away and executing a banking turn. He put his hand in his pocket and fixed me with a neutral gaze. 'Do you want to do the honours?' he asked.

'It's all yours,' I told him.

Donovan took the small rectangular object from his pocket. Wordlessly, he took hold of the nub attached to one end and extended the aerial. There were two controls on the box. A two-way switch and a circular red button. Donovan flicked the switch with his thumb.

The Albatross had completed its turn and was heading northwest.

Without taking his eyes off the aircraft, Donovan pressed the button.

The explosion was like a muffled thunderclap. It was accompanied by a bright fireball that expanded outwards as the fuel on board the aircraft ignited. Small gouts of flame rained down towards the water, like extinguishing distress flares, as echoes of the detonation rippled across the sky, like widening eddies on the surface of a pond.

I said softly, 'You really should have checked more thoroughly, Martin.'

Liz Hammond gasped and gripped my arm. Her fingers dug in tightly and a shudder moved through her.

'Call it a little going-away present,' I said.

We had placed it inside the coffin, beneath the body. It was similar to the device that Stavros had provided Harry Donovan with for breaking me out of the Citadel – the one that had reduced the patrol launch to matchwood and rendered the Turks incapable of pursuit. Radio-controlled. Very small, very powerful, very lethal.

She turned to face me then. Behind her, a display of smoking trails marked the descent of debris. Distant eruptions in the water indicated the entry points of the Albatross's remains.

I said, 'You didn't imagine, for one minute, that we were going to let them get away with it, did you?'

There was a light splash as Donovan dropped the transmitter over the side of the boat. A grim smile of satisfaction flitted across his bearded face.

Stavros crossed himself and returned to the bridge to radio the *Circe*. While McBain, unperturbed by the pyrotechnics, began to construct one of his foul-smelling cigarettes.

'It won't bring Gunther back,' I said. 'Or Marco. But maybe it'll go some way towards evening the score.'

Wordlessly, Liz Hammond disengaged herself. I made no attempt to restrain her. She left my side and made her way slowly across to the opposite rail and stood there, her back to me, gazing out across the water in slim, silent vigil.

Beyond her, the sun hung low in the sky, suspended like a huge molten shield, radiating warmth and energy, and the promise of another glorious day. It heralded something else, too. Something all of us would have to face in our own particular way.

Dieter Prohl had both predicted and feared it. Hans Josef Moessinger had been prepared to sacrifice his soul for it. For one of them, it had been the threat of a nightmare; for the other, the promise of a dream. One had killed to prevent it; the other had murdered to preserve it. How ironic that neither of them had lived to see it.

A new dawn.

And not only that . . .

At first I thought I'd imagined it, but then, with a sinking heart, I realized that it was no illusion. What had begun as a tiny dot, a small, insignificant speck tracking along the line of the distant horizon, was now rapidly starting to take shape.

There was a bright flash as sunlight danced off the canopy, and for the first time, as it turned towards us, my

333

ears picked up the uneven beat of rotors and I knew beyond any shadow of a doubt.

Donovan had caught the sound and the look on my face. He turned quickly.

And I thought, Oh, wonderful.

The clatter of spinning blades was growing stronger, more insistent. Reaching out towards us. It was coming in very low, very fast, skimming the waves, fuselage glinting like the plumage of a bright, beautiful hummingbird, its identity unmistakable.

A helicopter.

A Hughes 500.

A red one . . .